Tom Blackburn

Morgan's Eddy

A Novel

Morgan's Eddy is a work of fiction. Any resemblance to actual persons, places, or events is coincidental. Gabbro County and the towns of Gabbro, Greenly, and Bozlee cannot be found in North Carolina, though the state itself is real enough. Actual North Carolina towns (Asheville, Boone, Greensboro, Laurinburg et al.) are used fictitiously.

Cover design: A. Acorn

Books by Tom Blackburn:

Fiction:

The Cello Francesca, or, Balderdash

Hap Maryland Adventures:
   Surviving Mozart
   Thanks to Mister Merrydown
   Roots of Evil
   On Honeyman Bald
   Dancing With Granny
   Assisted Living

The biography of Faye Bynum:
   Time and Chance
   Morgan's Eddy

Nonfiction:
   Equilibrium: A Chemistry of Solutions
   Getting Science Grants

MORGAN'S EDDY

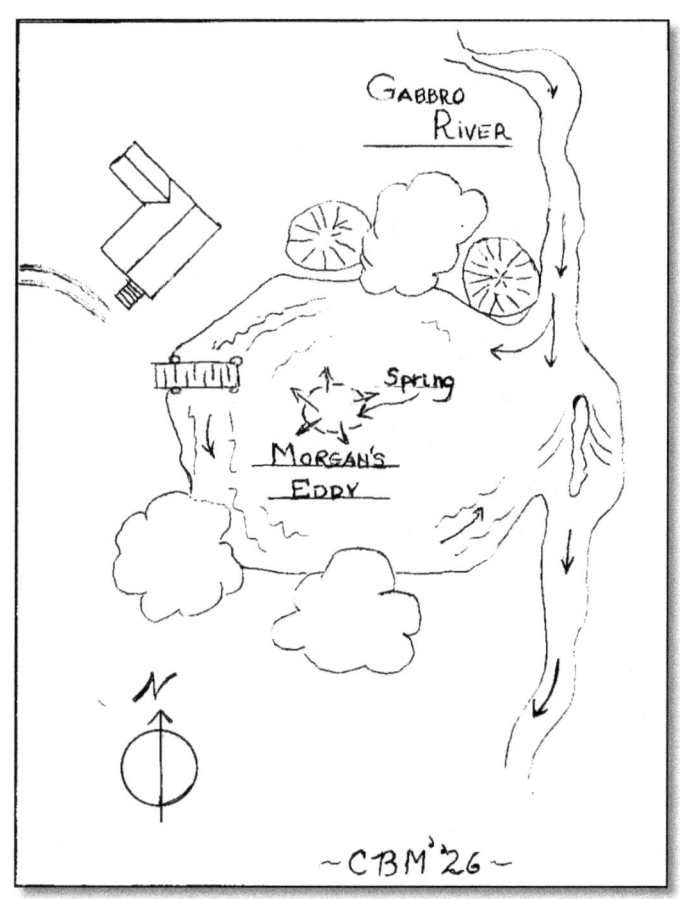

Morgan's Eddy (Sketch by Custis Morgan, 1926)

Plaisir d'amour ne dure q'un moment;
Chagrin d'amour dure toute la vie.
- Jean-Pierre Claris de Florian

O wad some Power the giftie gie us
To see oursels as ithers see us!
It wad frae mony a blunder free us,
An' foolish notion.
                    -Robert Burns

Prologue

T HE FIRST TIME he saw her naked, he fainted.

"I did not," he said a year later. "It was the laudanum."

"Uh huh," she said, and chose to say no more.

"Plus, you give me a bloody nose in there somewhere. Could we just say, I lost consciousness?"

"Why don't we just not say anything? C'mere. Anyway, it's nice and soft, just in case."

"Um," he said. "Jesus, you are just *so* beautiful. It would be a darn callous fella that wouldn't pass out."

He looked into her eyes, and she could see a pulse jumping at the base of his throat. She held up a delaying finger, and reached into her pack for a very small bottle of very clear blue liquid. Holding it between them, she spoke a series of alien syllables and held it to Forde's mouth. He drank.

"How'd you …?"

"Our sister Annie. I'll teach you, but for now …" And she spoke the charm again and took a swig in her turn.

He kissed her eyes and her mouth, awkwardly, tasting the liquid on her tongue; and murmured, "So. How is this supposed to go, again?"

1.

F ROM THE GABBRO *INTELLIGENCER*, a thrice-weekly newspaper published in Gabbro, NC, for Friday, October 24, 1947:

Schools Bond Passes By 427 - 93
Supt. Mack promises "Across -the-board upgrade" of all schools in County...

Quarrymen Open Season With Tie
 A last-minute goal-line fumble foiled coach
 Lester Lorain's charges...

Intelligencer to Welcome New City Editor Bynum.
Intelligencer Managing Editor Forde Morgan is pleased to announce the creation of the new position of City Editor, to be responsible for repotrage and commentary on matters affecting the growing and vital city and county of Gabbro. The new post will be filled by Miss M. Faye Bynum, an experienced journalist and prize-winning writer from St. Louis ...

*   *

The bus was a prewar holdover with an old-style protruding hood - complete with external radiator cap - enclosing a clattering diesel that would haul it through a sultry Carolina October. Negro passengers handed brown tickets to a Negro porter and entered the rear of the bus through a door half-way back, resigned to arrival at their destination as much as two seconds behind the white passengers who handed their white tickets to the white driver and found plush seats near the front. A white line just forward of the rear door, not captioned but perfectly understood, delineated a boundary that was anyhow obvious because the seats behind it were rattan, some of them broken through and unusable.

City Editor-elect Faye Bynum slumped irritably into a smoky-smelling plush seat forward of the line of demarcation. Eying the unreliable-looking lot of fellow passengers, she slipped her mother's garnet ring from her right ring finger onto the left, and turned the stone inwards so it would resemble a wedding ring. She began to page through the rest of a set of *Intelligencers* that Forde Morgan's daddy Custis had mailed her. Setting off with good intentions, she'd been too sleepy to finish them on the overnight train from St. Louis to Raleigh. Not that there was a lot to plow through: "Jaycees Set Jelly Sales Drive;" "Ferguson Tractor Dealership to Close;" "School Bond Issue Vote Today," with a matching editorial urging a Yes vote, "for our children's brighter future." Faye thought she detected Forde's idealistic touch in that one.

No international, and almost no national news beyond whether Governor Sanford might be persuaded to run to replace controversial Harry Truman, who'd had the unconstitutional gall to racially integrate the Army in defiance of "cultural norms of decades' standing." Probably Custis at the typewriter for that one. No wonder the thing only published on Monday, Wednesday, and Friday, a detail Forde had omitted when he urged her to take this job. On evidence, no more than three days worth of anything happened in a Gabbro week.

There were very few other editorial comments on anything more urgent than good wishes to the Gabbro High Quarrymen football team, and an occasional syndicated-conservative column. A good sprinkling of typos and awkward phrasing, sentence constructions that would have drawn the disdain of Sister Rose

Penitentia, who frog-marched Faye and any number of other Mount Saint Anne High School rookies through the coarser and finer points of English composition. The story about her hiring seemed to have more than its share - she had to wonder what "repotrage" was , and whether she could provide it - but otherwise did not violate the truth more than every other paragraph; and there were only two. It had not occurred to her to look up who, where, or what the town was named for, or what a "gabbro" might be, and here she was hurling herself southeast to live and work in a town named for gibberish. *Orlando Gabbro, North Carolina senator and orator.*

She saw suddenly that she had made a terrible mistake in agreeing to come to this barren corner of the South, to accept Forde's challenge to bring some kind of civic sophistication to a population of realtors, farmers, and dropouts from inferior schools. True that she very much needed this job; but also annoyingly true that Forde, a fellow intern on the Charlotte *Star-Dispatch* last summer, had created it for her so that he could take up his pursuit of her where it had been broken off by her parents' death in August.

She had lived in two medium-big cities, St. Louis and Charlotte. Her impressions of small-town life were that they lacked decent libraries and the public transportation to take her there. Now, she thought, add to that the fact that the grandpappies of these particular hicks had died in a losing cause to defend slavery and subjugation, and their descendants had been sore and mean about it for eighty years. Who was she to bring enlightenment to this twilit corner of America?

Faye was not ready to be there, not ready for this new phase of a life upended by bereavement and orphanhood - though at twenty, this was hardly as poignant as it might have been a few years ago - and by the untimely death of a rotten bastard who had in two months made of himself a parachuting corporal, a fiancé, a hotly longed-for partner, the father of a miscarried child, a hated two-timer, and a corpse. She had gone through it all with spirit; now that it was over, she felt that she had somehow survived an

6

earthquake. To the world, she appeared calm with a potential for perkiness, with glinting dark eyes and pixie-cut black hair. In spirit, she was sitting disheveled among the rubble, the track of tears shining in the dust of disaster. She was unready to stumble alone into what was coming before the past had been properly hosed down.

There was a creak and a thump from the door, and a grinding of gears. The bus lurched out of its bay, on its way south to Chapel Hill, Fayetteville, and points beyond, including Gabbro, North Carolina. Too late to flee. Faye slipped last week's *Intelligencer* into the seat pocket and opened the last of them. "Daughters of Confederacy Present Tableaus of Antebellum Social Life;" "Quarrymen Outscored in 4th Quarter;" "Sheriff Burns Takes Oath, Promises 'Peaceful Streets'." Ads for Christmas sales, a cotton gin, and the Gabbro Salonnette, Salon de Beauty Pour Madame.

Lord. "Quarrymen?" I thought there was nothing but sand there. Do they quarry sand? Why bother? The paper slipped from her fingers, and she dozed.

At Fayetteville, a half-dozen Fort Bragg soldiers entered and surveyed the ridership for good-looking women. Mostly, their eyes slid right over Faye, who was at that stage of her life skinny with mourning, work and poverty, and sported a hairdo so short that you had to wonder about a recent de-lousing; and was not only unconscious, but wearing that gold band. One corporal saw that her face, slack with sleep but kind of cute under the very short haircut, might prove more lively when awake. Anyhow, she very much resembled a longed-for girl back in Syracuse. He slipped into the seat next to her and adjusted his olive-drab tie.

A contingent of five co-eds from Fayetteville State emerged chattering from the depot and lined up at the front door with their white tickets showing. The quick thinkers among the soldiers plunked themselves into the aisle seats of empty doubles and repulsed any squad-mate who made a move toward the window seat. The girls stumbled blushing past the knees of corporals and sergeants and folded into window-seat captivity, busying themselves with pursed lips over books and sandwiches. The engine clattered, the gears crunched, and the bus took up its progress. After a half-mile of polite silence, the soldiers turned as one man to their seat-mates and asked, "Where you from, Honey?"

Faye opened an eye six inches from the new stripes and yawned. "I'm from Hell, by way of St. Louis. I used to date a corporal, but I murdered him."

*   *

The driver's polite jostle woke her to late sunshine and a whiff of exhaust. Outside her window, a sign proclaimed "**Terminal Café**/*Coffee - Sandwiches - News.*"

"Gabbro, Ma'am. Your grip is on the sidewalk."

"Oh. Already? But - "

"Faye! Over here." And here was Forde Morgan, grinning and pleased as could be that she had materialized, though he had been counting the days for a month. She thought he might have lost some weight, gotten a little more solid looking than the pink-cheeked boy of last June. He had the look of one who was growing up faster than he had counted on. He was thinner, his face had tiny creases of sternness, where it had been mild and a little vague as recently as June. Maybe managing a newspaper had done that.

As if in the opening chorus of an operetta, a mule-drawn wagon passed behind him, loaded with watermelons. The mule took the spotlight of her attention as a cue to deposit some fertilizer on the graveled street. *The South for real this time. Where's Porgy and Li'l Abner?* "Forde, hi. You didn't have to come meet the bus, goodness." Her voice was dusty, enervated.

"Not a bit of trouble. Lemme take that," plucking her single suitcase from Faye's hand. "Didn't want you to get overwhelmed by the hustle an' bustle. I still got that coupe of Uncle Harold's. The sheriff told him if he caught him driving again at his age he'd confiscate it, and I bought it off him for twenty bucks, bless his heart."

Faye laughed and let herself fall into the operetta, too exhausted and disoriented to do otherwise. *Long as I don't have to sing.*

After a journey of at most four blocks, the grey DeSoto pulled to a stop in front of a storefront with familiar gold lettering:

F. W. Woolworth 5¢ - 10¢ - $1.00

"Here we are."

"Wait. You publish a newspaper out of a dime store?" Faye looked behind to see if the bus was still in sight.

"Course not. But they's a real cute apartment upstairs, empty just now, that I thought you might be comfortable in. If you don't like it, we can look at some others, but I gotta say, it's not a lot of choice."

"Well, let's see it. But Forde, you didn't have to - "

"Couldn't leave you to manage on your own, hardly. Big city like this, some slicker'd leave you broke and lost in five minutes."

They entered a door next to Woolworth's show window (dusty papier-maché crèche; pencil cases and a pair of roller skates done up in curly ribbons) and climbed a long flight of wooden stairs, Forde still swinging her jammed suitcase. Evidently, the dime store below had a generously high ceiling for these stairs to rise above. At the top, a stifling hallway high under the roof, lit by a window at each end and a forty-watt bulb half-way along. "Not so cute here," Forde admitted. "They give me a key an' told me, behave myself. Heh."

"Heh. I never knew you to do anything else, Forde." *A garret. Maybe I can take in sewing, like Mimi.*

Forde unlocked a door near the light, and stood aside. Faye walked into a large room with a white tin ceiling and scarred floors that creaked under her step. To her left, a window showed a tree with wide, pale leaves over a back yard with a bench, a couple of lawn chairs, a trash can and cigarette butts. Evidently the staff break room for the Woolworth's downstairs. The apartment was an "efficiency," furnished with a plush rocker with a brand-new antimacassar, a couch of the maple-and-plaid tribe, and a bookcase. Near the window at the left, a dining table and two straight chairs. The area next to the window was dedicated to kitchen purposes - a porcelain sink, a stove, and a refrigerator with exposed coils on top. Three or four cabinet doors stood open as if for inspection. On the wall by the stove hung a calendar with the same "Autumn Splendour" print that her Charlotte landlady had owned. The calendar was open to the present month of November, 1947.

"Huh," Faye said. "Did the old tenant just move out?"

"Place has been vacant since June," Forde said. "Me an' Pop come up and sort of spiffed it up a little."

"Land, Forde, you didn't have to do any such thing. Guess I won't be looking anywhere else, you went to that much trouble."

"The next one down the list is over McLaurin Hardware, next to the Gabbro Southern crossing. It's cleaned up too, but freights come through pretty regular, and some of 'em still got steam engines."

"Well, I think you did just fine, Forde. Let's see the rest of it."

"Uh huh, well, the rest is just the bathroom and a, um, a bedroom off behind it." Forde inclined his head to where two doors punctuated an otherwise featureless wall. The door on the left was a closet, and the other a pass-through bathroom that opened into a bedroom that ran lengthwise to a window overlooking the street from which they had climbed. The bathroom had a tub with a hand-held shower plugged into the faucet. The bedroom had a dresser, a chair that looked like the ones in the Woolworth back yard, and a maple child's bed wider than a cot, but smaller than a twin. Faye vowed to replace it as soon as decently possible. The available floor space was not much more than necessary to walk from the dresser to the bed. *Have to do my exercises in the living room.*

"Nice view of the courthouse, out the front," Forde said.

Faye peered out the window to see across the street a leafy park and the top floors of a handsome limestone building with a clock tower that seemed to be functioning. "Goodness," she said, nearly meaning it. "I can wake up in the morning and know what time it is right away."

Forde looked out, and checked his watch. "You know that saying, how a stopped clock is right twice a day? Well this is one of those times. It's always five o'clock in Gabbro."

2.

F ROM THE GABBRO *INTELLIGENCER* for Monday, November 8, 1947:

THIS TOWN'S TIMES
by Faye Bynum, City Editor

Good morning and warmest greetings to my new neighbors in Gabbro, North Carolina, from your new City Editor. *That's me, ha.* I almost can't tell you how thrilled I am to become a new citizen of this charming, bustling town, and of Gabbro County. I have only begun to explore the town, and the hills, farms, and forests of beautiful Gabbro County. I am already in love with them, and so very grateful for the friendly welcome I have enjoyed with so many of you. I can see that Gabbro will be a warm and nurturing place, and that I will find a home among you. *Pray Jesus it won't be upstairs over the Five and Dime for too long.* I want to add here a most grateful thank-you to your Managing Editor Mr. Forde Morgan, for believing in me and helping to make my arrival in Gabbro as easy as possible, and most affectionately and respectfully to Mr. Custis Morgan, your retiring Editor in Chief, who has been a caring and welcoming mentor to me during my first days on this job.

The Managing Editor has asked me to be responsible for news of general interest to Gabbro city and county, so I ask your help in meeting this pleasant duty. When you find yourself curious, or proud or perhaps upset, about any issue of interest to all of Gabbro, I do most sincerely invite you to drop me a line about it, and you can expect me to take your questions seriously, and to follow up. Of course, all of the regular professional staff of the Intelligencer will be on the job, so sports news will continue to go through Rob Stoker, and deaths, obituaries, and social news to Jenny McCall, and so forth. My desk will be specially concerned with news and issues that touch the lives of every Gabbro resident. If you want to thank a City employee for "going the extra mile," let me know. If you want to know what all that digging out on West Church Street is supposed to fix, I'll find out. If you want everyone to know about a problem that affects us all, I'm your ~~woman~~ resource.

Finally, both Mr. Morgan's have asked me in particular to feel free to cast an eye on Gabbro ways and habits, both to better understand my new home, and to bring a newcomer's perspective.

Conversely, not a Southerner myself - yet! - I look forward to learning the ways of the modern South. As a new citizen of Gabbro, I cannot but wish that we may all learn from each other and walk together into this new and exciting post-War America that we share.

In deepest respect and gratitude for your welcome -

M. Faye Bynum
City Editor

That ought to butter up the yokels … What about that apostrophe in Morgan's?

3.

C OME IN, PLEASE, AND TAKE A SEAT." Gabbro County Superintendent of Schools Minor Mack beckoned Faye into his office.

"Thank you, sir. I appreciate your making this time available. I expect you must be pretty pleased about the bond issue passing."

"Oh, of course." Mack beamed, and checked out Faye's ass as she smoothed a skirt under it and dropped it into a straight chair. She held a little steno notepad on her lap, wishing it was the size of an art portfolio.

"You told the *Intelligencer* you expected an across-the-board upgrade for every school in the system, I think?"

"That's right, Miss, uh … " He squinted at the card Faye had sent ahead.

The Gabbro Intelligencer
M. Faye Bynum, City Editor
Gabbro 1, N.C.
SAndhills 3573

"Faye Bynum, sir. I'm passing on a question from a reader who was curious about the school bond issue. Am I right that there are four grade schools, two junior high schools and two high schools in the Gabbro system?"

"No, miss. You might have overlooked the Indian schools. A grade and a junior high."

"Oh, of course. No high school?"

"By and large, our Indian folks drop out to work farming or trades after Fifth, and certainly by the end of junior high. Th'Indian junior high takes up a couple rooms in the basement of the grade school building. Once in a while a Indian youngster finishes junior high, and he can apply to go to high school, where he's tolerated like a white boy. But it's rare enough, you could hold a Indian <u>high</u> school in your bathtub."

"I see." Faye resisted entertaining the image; and jotted notes, stalling for time. "Well, what I was going to ask, the whole bond issue amounted to $50,000, isn't that correct?"

"Yes?" *Rising tone. Defensive?*

Faye took time to get in strokes. "I bet every one of those schools and all the teachers and principals are as pleased as can be about it."

Mack leaned back, head tipped to one side with residual wariness. "You just bet, little lady. It's been over ten years since Gabbro schools have had a chance to do any serious upgrades, what with the War Effort an' all. Lot of our schools, they're running on equipment and textbooks that haven't been replaced since before the Depression. I did a visit with Carver Elementary, over East Gabbro th'other day, they was just grinning ear from ear, thinking about the upgrades they'll be seeing."

Faye smiled warmly and brushed her new bangs to the side of her forehead. "What I - what our reader wanted to ask about was, you mentioned, let's see…" Faye consulted her notebook and pretended to count up. "… Nine, ten schools just now. How much of an upgrade can you realize for what would average out to just $5000 per school?"

Minor Mack snorted gently. "Realize. Why, Miss Bynum, you'd just be astounded. First off, don't forget, you're in the South now, and dollars are still right big here, not like your Northern markets, prices through the roof since controls went off. That fifty thousand would look like a hundred, where you come from."

Faye doubted it, but kept a sunny face while she scribbled a note to make some phone calls.

"Second, you're right about the averages a course, but remember, grade schools are smaller and cheaper, what with no shops or labs, no team sports. Them four grade schools will only take up maybe fifteen - twenty percent of the whole Issue. And, of course, we still got the regular tax appropriation for this year, plus some state money, so the whole fifty will be going just for upgrades, and not regular operations. Plus, don't forget the educational discount. A pencil that'd run you a nickel at Woolworth's don't run us but about three cent."

"Mm <u>hm</u>." Faye wondered if the reference to Woolworth's was some kind of dig or threat - *I know where you live, little lady* - but chided herself for paranoia. "Can you give our readers an idea of the kinds of upgrades you'll be prioritizing?"

Mack leaned back and looked at a ceiling fan that rotated gently, not making much of a difference that Faye could feel, sitting across from him. Even in December, Gabbro weather could be pretty balmy, and she expected that the damp circles under Minor Mack's arms were probably matched on her own blouse, under the crisp jacket that covered it.

"Quite a lot of that yet to be decided," Mack said at last. "School Board will be meeting, setting up a committee to make allocations."

"Sir? You didn't have a spending plan before you put together the bond proposition?"

"Course we done, Miss Bynum. But broad-brush, conceptual, see? Not pencil by pencil. Getting bids on lab equipment for the biology programs, architect's drawings for remodeling. We have standing bids on textbooks, a course, but a lot of the nuts an' bolts details are all yet to be worked out. I expect all the schools will be seeing new textbooks after Christmas."

Faye scribbled in her notebook. "And all the schools, black, white, and Indian, will be sharing equally in the upgrade?"

"Every single school will be replacing their old worn-out books, that's right. That's what they was so hipped about down at Carver."

Faye nodded, having long since passed the limit of what she could dream up to ask the guy. "Thank you, sir. I do appreciate your time to follow up on a question from one of our readers. I expect they'll be right pleased. And how do you like our chances against Bozlee this Saturday?"

Minor Mack had acted like someone expecting to be asked an embarrassing question, though Faye couldn't think what that might be. Still, she thought a little more looking around might be in order before she went public with a gush about the exciting future of across-the-board prosperity. Returning to the *Intelligencer*, she smiled a busy-boss greeting to Sharon the receptionist, and entered her space - almost an office of her own, really an alcove created by two and a half walls and a bank of file cabinets. In any case, a huge upgrade from the folding card table she'd occupied in Charlotte.

She paged through the slender phone book, and under "Gabbro," found the listings for all of Gabbro's public schools. Planning to visit a white school and a colored one, she figured that the two high schools would be the best bet. The phone book was silent on racial matters, but one of the high schools was named Frederick Douglass, leaving Gabbro High School - home of the Quarrymen - as the clear choice for "white."

The Douglass phone rang and rang while Faye kicked off her shoes and put her feet up on a desk drawer like Sam Spade, *Should I have a flask of rye in that drawer?* and looked around her modest domain: a desk with a functional typewriter, an alarming but fairly safe swivel chair, a visitor's chair that looked like the straight chairs in Minor Mack's office - clearly meant for sitting, but not to encourage lingering in comfort - and, on the wall, her own personal touch: a framed Bible verse that advised her,

"Whatsoever thy hand findeth to do
Do it with thy Might"
..Ecclesiastes 9:10.

This verse had also graced the wall of Sister Rose Penitentia's classroom, back at Mount St. Anne High School. Sister Penitentiary had strong notions about hard work, and saw to it that her charges internalized them. Faye's copy of the advice had been the austere reward for an essay on the relationship between Christian sanctity and American values, and had to a small extent salved the sting of Sister's years-long discipline.

The distant ringing stayed un-answered. Faye looked up from her doodling, and saw Forde Morgan hovering at the edge of her alcove. "Hey, F - Mr. Morgan," she said, and stashed her stockinged legs under the desk.

"Hey yourself, Miss Bynum. You got any plans for lunch?"

"Well, I was hoping to ask the Douglass High School principal to lunch, but they aren't answering. Funny thing, wouldn't you think? Eleven on a Tuesday morning?"

"Colored schools are shut down for Christmas."

"Really? Why ever? It isn't but the ninth."

Forde frowned, whether in thought or because he sensed trouble coming. "Gives 'em a little jump on Christmas work, see. Lot of these families, they wouldn't have much of a Christmas if the kids that could, didn't pitch in and earn some extra."

"Huh. Doesn't that get them in trouble with the state? Number of days in the school year, that kind of thing?"

"They make it up with a shorter Easter break and getting out later in the summer. Also, I'm not sure if state requirements are the same for colored schools in the first place."

Faye rolled her eyes. "Probably not. So anyways, less competitive for summer jobs and - oh, silly me, they aren't allowed to go to the beach in April anyhow, are they?"

"There's a colored beach along north of Myrtle. Lunch?"

Over chicken salad sandwiches and sweet tea at the Terminal Café, Faye remembered to ask Forde about "Quarrymen."

"That's easy. You didn't visit the quarry yet?"

"Didn't know there was one. What do they quarry, sand?"

"Why, gabbro. It's a kind of black rock, they use it for gravestones and landscaping. Once in a while a bank that wants to look serious uses it for facing stone. I think, last I heard, it's about played out, as a quarry, but you can still get in. Want to go see it?"

"Heck, I live in Gabbro, how could I not? Do you all grow up using that cute little 'wont' when you mean 'want'? Or is it something you get from each other, like the flu?"

Forde snorted. "We get it by eating grits. We get it at our Mammy's knee. No, I'm being defensively Southern, I think you called it one time. But it be's right contagious awright, and I bet you <u>won't</u> get ta no dang Easta-time 'fo' you doin it yo'se'f."

"Bet not."

"Bet so. You already done said 'You all,' not two minutes ago. Also, your greeting this morning was 'Hey,' and not 'Hi.' C'mon, though, we got a quarry to get to, and I got to talk to Pop about his retirement money this afternoon yet."

*   *

"Well, now," Faye marveled. "Now I'm a real Gabbro-ite. A Gabbrovian. Got my own piece of gabbro, anyway."

They stood together on the lip of a quarry, into which Forde had slithered to retrieve this sample, while Faye wondered how she was going to explain his foolish and untimely death to Custis and the rest of the town, when Forde's rumpled hair disappeared behind a sheer-looking edge, twenty feet down. *He's going to fall and kill himself. I am a fatal woman. I should go into a convent.* She looked over a scene of all but abandoned enterprise, a front loader and a truck pushing around dirt and rocks sixty feet below, cliff-like walls opposite showing streaks of black rock fingering into something pale and un-commercial looking. Nothing down there looked like an ambulance, or a hook and ladder to pluck Forde from a crumbling ledge.

But Forde returned safely, dusting off a torn knee in his seersucker trousers, panting, and rubbing the sample on his haunch to remove excess dirt.

Faye bounced the square-cut chunk of black rock in her hand to cover her surprise at this athletic feat by one she had considered pretty much a marshmallow. "And I owe my new status to your apparent willingness to risk everything - neck, honor, reputation as the level-headed young fella Minor Mack called you last week - to fetch me this representative paperweight. I will take it home and clean it up good, and put it on my desk. But you know, I could just kill you for the lamebrain idiot you have just proved yourself. Do you realize I was standing up here making up excuses to give your father about losing you?"

"You don't have to lose me. We could say, like people do about engagement rings, 'He gave her a big rock, so I guess they must be an Item.' You know, a Thing."

"No, let's not. I dread the day people start to say, you gave me this job because you and I were a Thing."

"Capital T? Well, could we be?"

"Well. I suppose we might be a very incipient, tentative, lower-case thing, Forde. Frankly, I would probably welcome sharing some form of thingness with you, some day. But right now, I'm still wrecked about Gordon, and being pregnant, and then not, all that stuff. I feel guilty about all of it, like everyone I touch comes to grief. And look here: I can't base a writing career, I can't let people think, that you gave me ... well, like I'm some kind of project. Or some loose ... I don't know. Floozy, that you installed in the newsroom for your own purposes. We are going to need to be, well, conservative." Sister Penitentia was forever denunciatory of loose women, and women - like half her charges - with loose tendencies.

"Faye, you have got to be the farthest thing from a floozy anybody could ever invent, and still stay a girl. A lady. But I do see the point. Let's agree to think this over. I wouldn't want to settle into some status that would keep me from ever, for example, getting the kiss you know darn well you owe me for risking life an' honor to give you this chunk a gabbro."

"Well, it's a handsome rock, all right. So <u>that</u> kiss you can have right now. Here."

She grabbed his head and gave him a good, swift kiss on the cheek. He breathed in a delicate scent that he realized he had been breathing all afternoon, and that must be coming from her.

But when Forde tried to expand the kiss beyond what the merits of a medium sized black rock would reasonably support, Faye gently pushed him away. "See, that's what I'm talking about. I bet every window in that whatever-it-is, that hotel over there, is crammed with people taking pictures and getting ready to gossip."

"Bet not. That's the San, used to be a spa and a TB sanatorium. Now, it's where they run Gabbro Baptist Academy; I think they got maybe a hundred, hunnerd'n fifty students and a dozen professors. All the classrooms, offices, and dorm rooms for the students are in that one building, and they're all busy with their Bible verses."

"Yeah, Second Samuel, where David spied on Bathsheba."

"You had that? I thought the nuns skipped over all the hot stuff."

Faye turned, and began to walk back to the DeSoto. "Doesn't mean we didn't read it after school. Anyhow, the point is, we're in public, even out here by a quarry. So please don't - "

"Yeah, I get it." He sighed. "Sorry. I didn't mean to get testy. That's a right pretty perfume, by the way."

"It's called 'Silken Rain.' Makes no sense, if you think about it. But me too, Forde. I don't mean to tease you, either. Listen, though, things will maybe, you know. People will get used to me, and stop paying so much attention. Then maybe we could see what's possible, without a lot of social pressure."

"Maybe. As for you, you need to know that you're getting awful damn pretty, and I don't care who hears me say it, they'd all agree. I guess your hair growing in, and it's just real cute, with the little dark bangs, and just your ears … " Forde threw up a hand at the impossibility of justice to Faye's ears. "Not to mention, well … Aw, hell," he concluded. "You decide what you're wearing to the Christmas party?

Faye's charm notwithstanding, her current outlook was if anything too optimistic. Approaching Christmas a year ago, she had been a parochial schoolgirl, buying schoolgirl presents for her

Mama and Pop, playing mistletoe games with a footballer from Northside High, and thinking nothing of what might come next; half-expecting to end up as Mrs. Footballer. Now her family and the footballer were all dead, Faye the bereaved mother of a lost defective fetus, child of the footballer.

She knew her guilt and sorrow were making her brittle and touchy, but her depression had left her skeptical of the reality of the world around her, unsure of her place in it, and unable to imagine a future that did not frighten her. What she knew for certain was that without this job as City Editor of a marginal newspaper in a hick town in Dixie, invented by Forde Morgan to rescue her from wage slavery in a St. Louis dime store - and to bring her within wooing range - she would starve to death trying to earn money by writing what no one cared to read.

*   *

The Christmas party took over the ballroom of the old Gabbro Sanatorium, now the chapel of Gabbro Baptist Academy. For the occasion, the galvanized dunking tub was filled with cotton wool and paper snowflakes, and the spa's Gilded Age crystal chandelier, still in place to mock the Baptists, held mistletoe above the heads of the small crowd. The *Intelligencer's* workforce of a dozen would have been lost in the chilly, frugally heated space - Gabbro Baptist Academy being a frugal operation - but the WGAB ("All Country, All the Time") staff were invited to make it a media party, and everyone was invited to bring a spouse ("Wives Invited," the invitation read). So the place was comfortably occupied when Faye walked in, to the strains of "White Christmas" from an elderly piano-accordion duo. She wore a sober charcoal sweater-and-skirt set she'd picked up with her second paycheck, and rendered the overall effect festive by pinning a band of white angora across her head. She added a drop of Silken Rain to a pulse point or two, hoping it would please Forde without encouraging awkward behavior. The angora contrasted handsomely with her Black-Irish hair, and she decorated it with a sprig of plastic holly from Woolworth's. She felt that she could risk a little of her City-Editor dignity in this way, and still stay well short of floozyhood, which was good in view of her thorough looking-over from the invited wives. Forde, dressed in three-piece blue serge relieved by a Santa tie, greeted her with a glass of Ohio champagne.

"My, you look just, um - "

"Un-floozy? I sure hope so, I'm getting the twice-over from everybody's wife."

"Aw, don't pay them no attention. You're the cutest thing here by a mile."

"Even if that were so, that's just it, isn't it? You best step a little back, or there goes our discreet incipient 'thing'-ness."

Forde stepped back. "Huh. I wasn't sure we had one, after that discussion out by the quarry. I did like the way you cleaned up your chunk of gabbro, though."

"Handsome, isn't it? 'Gleaming dark as the depths of Sheol.' "

"Huh?"

"Oh, just something that stuck with me from a supposedly naughty romance that a lot of girls read at Mount St. Anne's. I believe it was the heroine's eyes that did that. Or maybe the fireman's that she fell in love with. It never explained about Sheol's dark gleaming."

"Well, maybe down at the deep end. The nuns let you read that sort of stuff?"

"That's the second crack you've made about nuns. I was taught by religious sisters, yes. I have a lot of respect for a bunch of women who gave up everything to live that life and teach a bunch of restless brats. Does that spoil anything for you? I understand Southerners have a thing about it. But don't worry, I'm not practicing."

"Oh, golly. Faye, you could be Hindu, and - "

"Back, Simba. I'm sorry if I sounded touchy just now. Sometimes, for no reason, I feel like I'm about to break into tears. Or just break. Why don't we drift over and chat with your Pop, and let him twirl me around the floor before one of those geriatric cases gives out and we've got no more music."

Custis Morgan was more than happy to have a dance with Faye. It had been quite a few years since he'd had a legitimate opportunity to handle a female fanny, Mrs. Morgan having preceded him to Glory by that long. Faye put up with it for a minute or two that felt much longer, and then, improvising, cleared her throat. When that only caused a shift to a more intimate location, Faye fitted herself against him, put a gentle hand behind his head, ruffled his hair until she felt a subterranean response, and murmured in his ear, "Mr. Morgan. I so <u>much</u> appreciate all you and Forde have done to welcome me into a new community. But with all respect, sir, if you don't get your hand off my butt, I'm going to have to scream."

Custis sighed, and Faye smelled the bourbon with which he'd fortified his champagne. "Little lady, don't be cruel. You owe me some innocent fun for how I went along with hiring you, and besides - the hand went back to pat the area, and lingered - You got about the handsomest little butt it's been my very great privilege ta - "

"Eek," Faye said, in a conversational tone. "That's Level One. I go up to Level Fifty, and not by ones, either. Want to hear Level Thirty?"

Custis sighed again and raised his hand to waist level, without losing contact. "Thank you," Faye said, pulling down the rumples in her skirt. "You are evidently a gentleman after all. Why do you think the Baptists let you all serve alcohol in their chapel? Isn't that a deep sin for them?"

"They need the money, bad. As you surely know, money will buy a world of sin. We pretend we doin' a dry party, and they pretend not to notice that we ain't. Nobody gets all huffy. Or screams about it, far as that."

"Huh. How - " Faye was about to say, "How Southern," but censored herself.

"Now, take your own sweet little self, honey," Custis went on. "You got a high school education and three months' experience, but my son thinks he's in love with you, so you got a good-payin' job on a well-established newspaper. I don't deny you can write pretty good, specially for a wet-behind-the-ears school girl. But still, right now you're playin' some above your league, and I'd bet you'd be just like the Baptists. F'r example, if I was to say somethin' like, 'I will grab your ass all I like, and if you yell at me, you pack your bags and take the next bus out of town.' And don't think I can't make that stick, little girl." And he grabbed Faye's left buttock and squeezed hard enough to make tears jump to her eyes.

"**EEE**gh! Jesus, you old -" Faye jumped back and stamped her foot. A hand on her shoulder steadied her, and a voice from behind said, "Ho ho *ho!* Got him good, din'cha?"

Faye spun and saw a lean and plausible-looking lad with taffy-colored curls and pale grey eyes, in a Santa hat and a red vest. The guy winked at her, and turned to the staring dancers behind him. "One a them thousand-legger bugs crawled right up over this little lady's foot, like ta make her jump onta the chandelier. But you stomped him flat, huh, Miss?"

Faye recovered herself and looked at the bottom of her shoe, a brand new black pump with a perfectly clean sole. "I believe it was an ol' cockroach. Used to be." She turned her back on Custis. "Thank you so much for your assistance. My name is Faye Bynum."

"How do, Miss Bynum. I'm Travis Wayland, WGAB radio, the Voice of the Sandhills. Care to dance?"

4.

M OMENT TO MOMENT improvisation was all the script Faye had to navigate the ghastly comic operetta through which she moved. She navigated by reflex to avoid major crashes.

The dance floor scene at the Christmas party, and his witty, dismissive chit-chat about Faye's embarrassment while they danced, and his slender way of dancing, led to an improvised grateful friendship with Travis Wayland. He confessed, over a thank-you lunch Faye gave him at the Terminal Café, that he'd met Forde Morgan entering the Gents' as Travis was leaving, and reasoned that he might get a chance to check out the new City Editor while Forde was otherwise occupied. He had been approaching to cut in on Custis Morgan when the butt-squeezing scene erupted, and he recognized a perfect opening for an introduction.

"Hope you wouldn't think I'm some kind of opportunist."

Faye set down her glass of tea. "Well, of course you are, or you wouldn't have exploited the opportunity so gracefully. I guess that doesn't signify one way or the other. I am a little lonesome and disoriented here, and on the lookout for uncomplicated friendships, if that is what you have in mind. But keep your hand off my butt, if I ever happen to dance with you. If it wasn't so completely improper, I could show you some bruises that would knock your socks off."

"Very well, that's a promise. If you will do your part by not referring to things, the very visualization of which would place me under the kind of strain that modern thinkers call a double bind. Ma'am."

"Land, you're a talker, aren't you? I notice the local accent drops away pretty fast when you're talking to me. I suppose it's part of your professional tool kit."

"My tool kit … you naughty girl. You talk pretty slick yourself; want to think about coming on the show some time? We got a segment, 'Gabbro Voices,' that we ran dry of decent material about three years ago."

"Well, of course, it's a flattering offer. Who were your last three guests?"

Wayland grinned. "OK, that's a challenge, remember those folks six weeks back. Let's see. Working back from last week, Betty Floyd McFee, children's librarian, Christmas books for kiddies. Custis Morgan, occasion of his retirement. Uh, gosh, wait… Oh, yeah. Minor Mack, about the bond issue."

"What a group. A groping ruffian and one who would have been if he'd dared. I don't know about Betty Floyd, but doesn't sound like it."

"Not hardly. Fell asleep in the middle of the interview. I thought she was dead, and cued up organ music."

Faye laughed, and felt a little of the tension leave her. "Really. Did she eventually wake up?"

"She did, but she looked a little bewildered. Think maybe she was looking around for St. Peter."

"What did you think of Minor Mack? Sounds like a character in a play. Or maybe in a phone book, backwards."

Travis Wayland didn't smile. "Our sainted Superintendent. He talked around in circles about bringing the best possible education to our boys and girls, which he considered to be 'Gabbro County's most valuable crop,' is the way I think he put it. You could about see a John Deere pulling a combine machine through a field full of the little blisters. Why?"

"Oh … maybe nothing. I did an interview with him last week, and I kept feeling like he was expecting some embarrassing question that I never asked him. I swear he was relieved when we ended up, like he was avoiding something that I missed. Maybe it's just a feeling."

"Learn to trust your feelings, that's what they always told me in Radio School."

"Yes?" Faye felt the scenery shifting, all the characters moving to their spots for the next scene, she alone standing on stage ignorant while the spot came sweeping toward her and the pit orchestra started vamping. She broke into a cold sweat, and put a hand to her head. "There is such a thing?"

"Sure, I guess, but I never went to one; I was just blathering. You OK? You look a little pale, just now."

"I'm fine. I'm always pale."

"Hm. Well, what I was going to say, I had no training at all. I just applied for an opening, and started making it up as I went along. That's what I'm still doing."

"You too? Making it up as I go along would count as sober professional planning on my part. I have a parochial high school diploma and three months' experience as an intern on the Charlotte *Star-Dispatch*."

Travis smiled. "So I understand. I admire a lady who doesn't put on an act. But as a matter of fact that's more - "

"So you understand? What, you went and looked me up?"

Serene smile, charming. "Well, of course I did. A new woman moves into a tiny town, apparently with a brain and some spunk to her, and then it turns out she's right good-looking? Hell, what kind of journalist wouldn't do a little research? Turns out the Britannica I looked you up in never heard of you, but I managed to get a little off-the-record information from ol' Custis, preppin' him up for his 'Gabbro Voices' interview."

In spite of past experience and her brief pregnancy, and of how she would have resisted being called a "girl," Faye had somehow never thought of herself as a "woman," or being discussed as such in her absence. As that level of factor, a "new woman" in the social network, for one thing. Or as "womanly," which would involve marriage, sex, babies. She might have said that she was neither girl nor woman, but something else entirely. It was further disorienting.

"I see. How bracing to think that one is the subject of analysis prior to one's arrival on the scene." She drew a dizzy sigh, and waited for a cue from the wings. "I hope Forde's obvious crush on me was not put forth as a reason for my hiring."

"Not in so many words, no. Again, a good journalist is sometimes able to gain inklings from what is not said, as much as what is. Like you, with ol' Minor Mack."

"Our sainted Superintendent, you called him. Or was it "tainted?""

"Where'd you get that?"

"I suppose I gained an inkling from something you didn't say."

Travis gave that the laugh it deserved, Faye thought. He had an appealing laugh that invited collaboration, and she collaborated. "Very good for you, Miss Bynum. You are fun to talk to, and I certainly look forward to doing so on the air."

As they walked out of the Terminal to part ways on the sidewalk, Travis turned to her. The December calendar had managed at last to put a chill into the air. Faye shrugged herself a little deeper into her jacket, and Travis Wayland's breath could be seen.

It smelled of tea and Chiclets as he said, "I would be interested in an uncomplicated friendship, if that means nobody puts any pressure on anybody to go anywhere they aren't ready to go. Nobody has to spend a half-second thinking, '*What did she mean by that?*' or '*Should I tell him about this?*' In all things, what you see is what you get. I find Gabbro County a little disorienting too, so maybe we could uncomplicatedly help each other out with it. Orientation, I mean. On your part, you never said anything about reciprocating any crushes. What could a good journalist inkle from that?"

Faye shrugged and smiled, feeling just the least bit as if she might know at last when and how this scene was going to end, and where her exit cue would come. "Sometimes a silence is just a silence. I like Forde quite a bit; I enjoy his company. Beyond that, neither he nor I have the least inkling what more there may be to say. We have no 'understandings' or commitments beyond my contract with the *Intelligencer*. I have barely spoken to him since the unfortunate incident on the dance floor."

Faye waited a beat or two, wavering, and then plunged. "I am open to all the, the aspects of uncomplicatedness that you listed. In fact, I practically insist on them, and maybe a few more in the same vein, I guess that would depend. But on that basis, I'd be happy to be your uncomplicated friend. Maybe we can plan some uncomplicated wholesome activities, like sledding and cocoa this winter yet. Merry Christmas, Travis."

"It never snows here, but we'll see what we can do. Merry Christmas, Faye."

*   *

Back at the *Intelligencer*, Faye slid into her alcove and sat down to take stock. Charming guy, apparently interested in her, God help us. Thank you, St. Anne, for not letting me blather to him about my unhappy past, my guilt about Gordon, or my short pregnancy. It could certainly have happened, and shut down his interest even in friendship. I said nothing about any of that, which by his rules, of course means I blurted out the whole thing, somehow. What does the script say I should feel about that?

Faye drew a sigh, and remembered that she had not, in fact, sought or found any resolution with Forde about his father's boorish behavior and her "cockroach" crack. It would have to be done, or it would just sit there, a bad incident that would spoil the barrel. Plus, she would have to see what had not been said by or about Superintendent Minor Mack. *Wow, three problems. I'll have to make a list.*

*   *

"Principal Evans, I very much appreciate your taking the time to see me, with the Christmas break coming right on."

"It is my pleasure, Miss Bynum. I was quite struck by the tone of your initial editorial, and I said to my self, Anson, there's a lady that might reward a good talk about Gabbro High School with some good notice in the paper. Good press is important to the schools, you know, Miss Bynum."

"Well, of course the High School is a big factor in the life of the town, so I will need to know all about it, as time goes by." *Cliché.* "Right now, I'm very curious, and I represent reader curiosity here too, about what you see as the impact of the new bond issue funding."

"Sure thing, Honey. You want to take a little walk?"

After a pretty thorough tour of Gabbro High - classrooms, gym, a science lab still, on December 20, filled with buzzing activities and the reliable school smell of sweat, books, and pencil sharpeners - Faye had a notebook full of 'upgrades.' Three new microscopes promised for the science lab; replenishment of two floors worth of supply closets; two dozen basketballs and a re-varnish of the basketball floor; new curtains for the Little Theater; even a new coffee pot in the teachers' lounge, all promised to be in place by the end of Easter vacation at the latest, except for the floor varnishing, which was scheduled for next summer.

"My," Faye allowed, when they had returned to Principal Evans' office. Evans was opening his mouth to confirm, when his secretary put her head through the door and said, "They're here, Mr. Evans."

"Ah," Evans said. "You're here for the first big moment. All brand-new textbooks. Thank you, Miss Squire."

Faye expressed polite enthusiasm, and a Negro janitor came through the door pushing a box-laden dolly. Seeing Faye, the janitor started, and began backing out the door, but Evans beckoned him in. "Come in, come on in, Theodore. Maybe you could open a box for Miss Bynum."

"Yes, sir. Yes, ma'am." Theodore drew a pocket knife and cut the tape on a box that read, "Southern Schoolbook Corporation." He folded back the flaps and took out a dull olive volume printed *WORLD HISTORY* front and spine, and handed it to Anson Evans, who passed it on to Faye. "Maybe Miss Bynum should have the honor of taking the first look."

Faye opened the stiffly bound book toward the end, and found a discussion of World War II, illustrated by a halftone photo of a mushroom cloud. The paste-and-paper smell of the book was familiar to Faye from a hundred such that had fallen under her hands as a library assistant in St. Louis. "Very nice," she said, riffling pages. (George Washington, Christopher Columbus, Jesus.) "I'm sure all the schools in the system will be as pleased as can be, if they have even half of the exciting new things you're anticipating here. I'm looking forward to sharing what I've seen with our readers." She rose, drawing a last breath of new-book air. "I'm sure you and your staff have a thousand things to do before you break for Christmas, so I guess just one last question, if I might?"

"By all means, if I can answer it in the next two minutes. Ha ha."

Faye chuckled *like a sycophantic idiot.* "I understood from Superintendent Mack that there were quite a few decisions yet to be made about spending, and that the kind of detailed plans you have showed me were yet to be worked out. You seem to have your share of the bond issue money already figured out."

Evans raised an eyebrow. "No, all these lines were spelled out in the original proposal for the bond issue, right down to the chalk and erasers for the supply closets, and down to the new coffee pot. We couldn't hardly get the Council and the banks to underwrite some vague, gimme-the-money kind of proposition. Minor must have misunderstood your question, don't you think? Or possibly you misunderstood his answer."

Faye, having learned from hard experience, shrugged. "Possibly so. It wouldn't be the first time. Well, thank you so much for your time, sir. I do congratulate you on this wonderful advancement for Gabbro High. I expect I can find my way out."

Not a chance I misheard him, pal. Walking the three blocks back to the *Intelligencer* building, Faye flipped back through her notebook, and found "Conceptual/~~pencil by pencil~~/bids

/nutsbolts," and reconstructed from that exactly what Minor Mack had in fact said.

5.

O N CHRISTMAS EVE, Faye and Forde had what Sharon the receptionist called a screaming row. It came about in this wise:

Forde stopped by Faye's alcove at 11:30 AM on Wednesday the 24th. Because it was Christmas Eve, there would be no regular edition of the *Intelligencer* that day, or the day after Christmas either, and things were pretty relaxed around the newsroom, with a little desultory work toward Monday's paper. Otherwise everyone was scheduled to leave at noon. There had been little or no chatter between Faye and Forde since the Christmas Party, and every passing day made chatter - which was going to have to start with someone apologizing - that much harder to initiate. Nevertheless, Forde knocked on one of Faye's alcove walls.

"Miss Bynum, could you join me in my office, please?

"Yes, Mr. Morgan. Shall I bring a notebook?"

"I don't think that will be necessary."

Almost inaudibly, the sound of a muffled snare drum came from Rob Stoker, at the Sports desk, to accompany their otherwise silent march to Forde's office: *Ffthfth-dum, ta-da-dum, ta-da fthfthfthfth-dum.*

"That will do, Stoker." Forde stood aside for Faye to enter, and shut the door after himself; and closed the old-fashioned Venetian blind on it.

"Uh oh," said Stoker.

Forde turned to Faye, who stood with her back to his desk. "Faye," Forde said, drawing himself up. "I wish to apologize on behalf of my father for his behavior at the Christmas party."

"Really. He can't apologize for himself? Or won't?"

Forde grimaced and scratched the back of his head. "I'm afraid he feels that it is up to you to apologize first. I don't necessarily - "

"Incredible! For what? For screaming when he assaulted me? I'm still black and blue. What on Earth can the old lecher imagine that *I* have to apologize for?"

"Please, Faye, I understand that you're sore, and you have every right to be. But - "

"It's not a matter of my right to be sore, Forde. I just am. I'm sore where it hurts to be sore."

"Yes, I understand. I want you to please remember that he is my father, he is an old man who was raised in a different time, and furthermore that we both owe our jobs to him."

"He can have the damn job, if he thinks it gives him the right to maul me in public."

"In fact, he thinks no such thing, Faye. He admits that he got out of hand with that. What it is, he says you insulted him in public."

"Huh? By screaming?"

"No. Apparently you called him an old cockroach. By the way, I hope you understand how extremely painful this discussion is to me."

"Poor you. You want to see painful? Have a look." Faye faced right, ran down the zipper at the side of her skirt, and began to peel down her slip and panties on the bruised side. Forde jumped to cover any possible slit of visibility in the Venetian blind and snapped, "Stop that, right now!"

Faye paused long enough to make her point, and reassembled. She considered briefly whether she ought to say what she in fact said: "Like father, like son, I see. If you think our working relationship will encompass your yelling at me like that, well … think again, that's all." She began to shake, and tears made an appearance.

"Aw, Faye." He stepped toward her, arms outstretched.

"Stop! Get away! Do not think that you can comfort and jolly me out of this situation." Faye took a hankie out of her pocket

36

and blew her nose. "Your father so far forgot himself that he brutally and humiliatingly assaulted me in front of all my co-workers, their wives, and a bunch of strangers. I couldn't sit down comfortably for a week. An apology straight from him, in person, is the, the *sine qua non* for any getting beyond this mess."

Forde sniffed. "Huh. *Sine qua non.* You seemed to be sitting down pretty comfortably at the Terminal with that Travis Wayland this week, what I hear." A terrible mistake, and Forde knew it as soon as he began saying it.

Faye's lip curled, and she spoke at first with a velvet clarity that anchored and maintained a continuous crescendo until it reached somewhere into the low forties on the vocal scale she described to Custis.

"Really? Oh my, Fordie, do you really want to get into that? Travis is just a nice guy who is, like me, a stranger to this town and who is looking for a nice, uncomplicated friendship. That suits me right down to the ground, and if you are half as smart as you think you are, you will not butt in. (*Voice Level 20 exceeded here.*) Believe it or not, I'm quite aware that I am, as your father kindly put it, 'playing some above my league,' and that I owe the chance to do that both to your and to his good will, and to your kind offer of the opportunity. All right, then, at any time whatsoever that my work does not please you, you can *fire* me, and I will not say a peep about it. But until that time, please, *(30)* please do not imagine that my dependence on your good opinion gives you the teeniest right to offer judgments or comment on my activities outside the office, or on my choice of friends. Is that *perfectly* **goddamn CLEAR**?"

The last three words of that long crescendo were perfectly clear to Sharon, Rob Stoker, Jenny McCall on obits, Ellen the copy girl, and two press mechanics who were doing routine maintenance half the building away. Faye's exit from Forde's office did not involve slammed doors or walloping Venetian blinds; only the deadly gentleness with which she allowed the latch to click behind her.

*   *

On the next day, Christmas, Forde knocked at Faye's apartment door with a present, over which he had taken much trouble, thought, and expense that he didn't want to have wasted. There was no answer, because Faye was two hundred miles away in Asheville, sledding with Travis Wayland. There was a note in her handwriting and bearing Forde's name, Scotch-taped to the door frame:

Dear Forde:

I more than half expect to find this note still here when I return to Gabbro this weekend. However, I am leaving it here on the off chance that you might drop by while I am away seeking rest and relaxation.

I most sincerely wish to apologize for shouting at you yesterday. It was the female version of male physical brutality, and I much regret that I allowed myself to be so rude to someone who could not honorably defend himself. I have been, you might have noticed, rather brittle lately. I suppose it comes of all the trauma of this past summer, which in fact I never could have survived without your unfailing kindness, generosity, and good humor. I am eternally grateful to you for that, and I still believe that it will figure into our eventual relationship, or even "Thing," if such a thing is ever to be. So please do not take my behavior of yesterday as anything more than an expression of my very deep ... what? Of the way in which the events of the past six months have made my life difficult to lead in the healthy and loving way that I hope some day to show you.

Your special friend,
Faye Bynum
Christmas, 1947

*   *

In Asheville, Faye and Travis Wayland rented a toboggan, slogged up hillsides that were at this date innocent of lifts; plummeted down whooping and delirious with Faye tucked

38

between Travis's legs and arms, and took spills that left her red-faced and charming. Stray snow crystals made a star chart of her cap of deep black hair, in which Travis claimed to find a new Zodiac that included Inkarius the Printer, The Quarryman, and Custis the Cockroach.

Faye clutched her head in horror. "No, no! Make 'em go away!" and Travis did, by breathing warm Chiclet air on them. Having arrived in Asheville in late morning, they played and cavorted all afternoon until the westering sun turned the snow to sensuous dunescapes of rose and blue, and then sat panting for a time on the edge of a forest, enchanted at the play of color across a meadow of unbroken snow while their pulse rates came back to normal, and then increased a little with consciousness of their bliss and the linkage of elbows across neighboring knees; and while the sweat of their sport slowly dried. The daylight abandoned them, the blues and pinks became grey, and they rose reluctant to break the hush of the moment.

They returned to town to drink tea-with-rum in an Alpine-themed grille and, thawed, walked hand in hand window-shopping and laughing the eight blocks to their hotel to rest and change into dry and comfortable clothing. They had reserved separate rooms, and over a dinner of lamb chops, yams, and salad, Faye took Travis's hand and broached the topic.

"Travis," she said. "I don't know when I have had such a wonderful and hilarious time with anyone. Well, yes I do: Exactly never. I have <u>never</u> in my entire life up to now had such fun with a boy. A guy. I have never in my life, after the age of maybe four, had such a wonderful Christmas. Thank you, thank you for this Christmas present. If this is what uncomplicated friendship involves, you can sign me up for good."

She sighed, and traced patterns on his hand. "Now. The next question of course is sleeping arrangements. Right now, I am so happy and relaxed that you could suggest about anything, and I'd probably just say yes and let it happen. But the whole premise of this friendship is uncomplicatedness, and I can't think of anything that complicates life more than sex does. We could sleep together tonight, and I expect I would love it for as long as it lasted, which could be all night, as far as I'm concerned. But - as, famously, for *Romeo and Juliet* - morning will come, the lark will sing, and the complications will start, don't you agree? So."

Travis smiled and closed his hand on her pattern-tracing fingers. "So. Why don't I walk you up and see you safely into your room and wish you sweet dreams? Maybe a day will come when sex will be the <u>least</u> complicated thing for us, and then, well, Yay for us. But as it happens, I agree with you completely. Sex with you, first time out of the box, we're not married or even very familiar with each other, would certainly complicate my life too. Ready to go up?"

"Yes. Yes, I am. I am woozy with fatigue and happiness. And relief, frankly. You want to come up and tuck me in? No, wait. Strike that from the record, it would surely lead to complications. Come up with me and give me a nice uncomplicated Christmas kiss, and shove me through my door."

"Good to go."

They rose next morning to grey skies and snowfall, and recognized that there could be no matching the previous day's hilarity in snow play, so they sat in the hotel lounge and drank coffee, stretched their sore muscles over adjoining lounge chairs and talked, and talked. They talked about the snow, and about Gabbro, and about their work; about North Carolina, which in those days was beginning to pride itself on being <u>in</u> the South, but not as "Southern" as, for example, South Carolina, let alone the Deep South. They debated which Gabbro politician was most hilariously untruthful. They talked about being young in their professions, and where they wanted to be when they should be, unbelievably, middle-aged; and about writing *vs.* talking for a living. In mid-morning, they went out on the hotel terrace and had a snowball fight. When they came back in, laughing and snow-powdered, they ordered more coffee and talked about books they loved (no real overlap), then about movies, about their childhoods, and finally about what time it was getting to be, and when they would need to leave to get back to Gabbro at a reasonable hour.

Summing it up: everything they did was what a healthy young man and woman would do, who are in the process of falling in love. Faye was uneasily aware of it, and of the danger of falling into the script of some cheesy musical comedy; but at each moment, the charm of proceeding so outweighed the danger, that there was no thought of not proceeding. *I'll think about all this when I'm back in Gabbro.*

"Oh, I hate the thought of going back," Faye said as they walked toward the elevators. "I had such a horrible row with Forde on Wednesday, and now I have to … oh, damn." *Your special friend, Faye Bynum.*

"It's only Friday. If you like, I can talk to the desk about extending our rooms for another day. I don't have to be back at the station until Saturday night."

"Oh, gosh. Travis, that is so tempting, but I truly don't think we could get through another bedtime without complications. Do you? Yesterday, we were … well, still more new to each other than we are now. The whole virtuous renunciation thing might have just been a one-time business, something we were trying on to see how it felt. And it felt good, I'm happy to tell you - well, obviously, I'm speaking for myself here. But we're behaving like supporting cast in a Bing Crosby movie." She sighed. "Or an operetta. Something where you know they're going to get together in the end."

"Um… and what would be wrong with that?"

"Oh, maybe nothing. There's sure nothing wrong-feeling about it. But things are going kind of fast, and if we sign on for that, then we're buying into the whole script, except that maybe something awful will happen, and we'll break up, and there we are in a complicated mess. I'm already in one complicated mess, and I can't take on another one, that's all." She sighed, and held his arm. "I guess."

"Hm. Well, I don't see the 'script' thing. But it's pushing noon, so let's check out and get something to take with us for lunch."

At the desk, Travis wondered about Faye's ability to afford the tab ($20 each for the night, meals, and toboggan, plus $2 extra for the coffees) and what might be inferred if he offered to pay her share. But Faye, smiling, pulled a wad of bills out of her wallet. "I got the proceeds from selling my folks' house last week. I'm as rich as ... who's that guy? Midas?"

Travis smiled. "Croesus, I think. Don't ask me who he was, though, some very rich guy apparently. I don't mix in those circles. But I'm impressed, anyhow."

Packed, checked out, fed, and mingled with eastbound traffic, Faye fell asleep in the front seat of Travis's Studebaker as it droned east from the mountains toward the Sandhills. Sitting at a traffic light in Hickory, Travis looked at her sleeping, felt stirrings of a mix of emotions, and turned on the radio at super-low volume. But starting up again and a burst of static made Faye stir, sit up, and rub her eyes.

"Where are we?"

"Hickory. Another couple of hours, yet. Sorry about the radio; you want to tell me about the complicated mess you're already in?"

Faye sat silent, considering. "If I do, am I going to hear all about it on WGAB?"

He snorted. "Really, Faye? Of course not. This is exploration of another possible facet of the uncomplicated friendship. The non-judging, sympathetic ear."

"I see." She knew that she would be giving him something that she had not asked from him. Still, maybe the "sympathetic ear" business had something to it. "OK, well, non-judging it is. Though if you had any sense ... OK, here goes. Less than a year ago ... "

*   *

In Gabbro, Forde Morgan had been greatly cheered by the tone and content of Faye's note, folding it into a breast pocket on the way back home, and re-reading it several times during the course of Christmas Day. "*...our eventual relationship ... healthy and loving ... Your special friend ...*" All these and other words plucked out of context, and the simple fact that she had troubled to write and stage the note for his possible dropping-by, warmed Forde to confront his father more firmly than before, and to extract a grudging promise of a face-to-face apology, to be rendered at first opportunity and regardless of whether she had previously apologized for the 'cockroach' remark.

But back in his office on Saturday, slumped in the chair that once was Custis's, and with Faye's note again open before him, it occurred to Forde to wonder where Faye had gone seeking the rest and relaxation the note spoke of. As far as Forde knew, Faye had no relatives closer than Missouri, nor means to purchase a resort stay, though there he was wrong. He picked up the phone and called WGAB.

"Travis Wayland, please. Gabbro *Intelligencer* calling."

"I am sorry, Mr. Wayland is away from the station at this time."

"Oh, shoot. Know where he went?"

"Mr. Wayland is vacationing in Asheville, sir. Can I have him call you upon his return?"

Finding the WGAB receptionist clear and firm on Wayland's absence from the station, but vague on when Forde might expect a return call, Forde hung up, frowning.

Asheville.

*   *

In the little apartment above the five and dime, Faye folded and tucked away a load of laundry she'd carried up from Sudsies across the street, and wondered what Travis had thought about her long debrief about Gordon and pregnancy and death.

She had pretty much opened herself to him, and was not sure whether she felt any better for it. Different, though. He had sounded, well, non-judgmental. Sympathetic, but reserving comment. Also reserving any reciprocal confessions about himself, if there were any there to confess. Lying in the small bed an hour later, she tried not to think about the nonjudgmental sympathetic ear, or about rose-and-blue sunset snow meadows, and coffee, laughter, snowballs, romantic boy-girl duets sung to off-screen string sections, and uncomplications. There was no not remembering them of course, but they wavered and rushed like a plunging toboggan into unrelated and noncommittal dreams.

6.

PRINCIPAL ABRAHAM L. COUSINS of Frederick Douglass High School welcomed Faye with about the same degree of ceremony as had Anson Evans of Gabbro High or, "real Gabbro High," Sharon the receptionist had called it. Cousins was a tall Negro with a sad countenance that Faye thought might have been achieved either by interviewing all the naughty kids sent to his office, or by trying to make a run-down shambles into a "real" high school for his 200 or so charges.

"Mr. Cousins, thank you for taking the time to see me this morning," Faye said. "I'm here because I'm working on an editorial and a feature story about the impact of the bond issue on all the schools in the system. I suppose you're as excited as Mr. Evans, I interviewed last month, about getting new equipment and textbooks?" Faye looked around Cousins's office; tidy but not spiffy, as had been Evans's. A world globe, scuffed, with a concentration of finger-smudges on eastern North Carolina. A single bookcase with biology titles showing, evidently Mr. Cousins's area of study before he became a school principal. The flags of the US and North Carolina. "Would you be willing to show me around, to see where you are planning to upgrade?"

Cousins gave that a melancholy smile. "Upgrade. Well, let's see. We held back a little money from summer school, took a run down to Waccamaw in time for Christmas sales, and come up with a gross of brand-new plates, cups, an' saucers for the cafeteria, threw out ol' scratched-up stuff kids have been eating off for about thirty year."

"Yes, well good, but I meant your use of bond issue money. Superintendent Mack told me that there would be across-the-board upgrades for every school in the County. New equipment, new textbooks, upgrades to facilities, I don't know what all. Mr. Evans showed me, I don't know, a dozen places where they were either replacing old books or upgrading equipment. Revarnishing the gym floor."

Cousins looked at Faye unreadably for a moment, and then rose. "Our gymnasium is outdoors, with a dirt floor, so varnish would be kind of a waste. But come along, Ma'am, I will show you our new textbooks."

Faye felt a pang of unease; Cousins was so immovably phlegmatic. She followed him out of the office just as a bell rang for classes to end, and the hall filled with Negro adolescents. As they encountered Cousins plowing upstream, the girls sketched walking curtsies, and the boys stepped back, nodding their heads. "How do, Mr. Cousins," they said. "How do, Principal." Cousins greeted each by name: "How do, Mr. Wilson. Good morning, Miss Archer." Faye got curious looks, cut short as soon as she met the curious eyes. The freshet of kids receded, and classroom doors slammed shut. Principal Cousins turned left at the end of the hall and entered a utility room.

"Here they are. Just came yesterday, so we didn't get a chance to unpack 'em yet."

Faye frowned. The boxes were all sizes, and bore the logos of Ball Mason jars, Procter and Gamble, Campbell Soup, Necco Wafers. God, was Jim Crow so bad that Negro schools had to buy their new texts from colored-only publishers who couldn't afford their own boxes? Or was it that the same publishers the white schools used, refused to waste new boxes on books for Negro schools? Faye felt her breath shortening. By God, somebody was going to hear about this. She composed an opening sentence for her next editorial. Still and all, new books …

Principal Cousins, with a gesture, invited Faye to have a look. She opened the top box, scribbled "9th Grade Bio" on a taped-on piece of 3-ring paper, and pulled out the first book. Her mouth opened to object, and nothing coherent would come.

"But … "

"Yes, Ma'am. There's your upgrade. Gabbro High gets brand new, we get what they don't need any more. Still, big improvement on our old books. Look here, this book is hardly written in at all. Part of that across-the-board upgrade you mentioned just now." He reached into a box next to the furnace and pulled out a book called <u>New Practical Biology</u>. It was tattered, and some pages appeared to be missing out of the middle. "This is one of our old books, that we will be thankfully replacing. Let's see, yes, the front matter is still in place. This book was published in 1917, and spent its first, mm, fifteen years at Gabbro High. Transferred to Douglass in 1933, been used here up till last Friday."

Faye took the book and paged through it. Some of the pages were torn and repaired with Scotch tape. One of them showed a grinning rustic atop a tractor from about 1916 with steel wheels, plowing corn. The caption read **A MODERN MECHANICAL TRACTOR MAKES THIS FARMER'S WORK GO FASTER.**

"Oh," Faye said. She took the replacement book and read its publication date: Chicago,1932. "Oh, no, oh, my God … " She flittered through the pages. Several had marginal notes about homework assignments, or other matters: *"Bobby likes you. Can he call?" "Bio SUCKS"* A photo showed a white-jacketed white man peering through a microscope: **A SCIENTIST ON THE TRACK OF KILLER MICROBES.** The scientist sported a long beard, done in blue ball-point.

"Oh, this is just … this is …" Faye kept her face into the book, reluctant to reveal her full reaction. "I suppose there's no point in asking you about new microscopes, new sports equipment, all that, is there?"

"That replacement book has a picture of a microscope, I see. That's a step up from iron-wheel tractors, but it's the only microscope our kids will see in this school."

Faye turned to look at Principal Cousins. He offered her a tissue from the box he kept handy for transgressors, and she blotted her eyes and cheeks, then pounded her knees with furious fists. "Those mean, bloody liars … Oh! Let me assure you, sir, I am going to write an editorial about this that will make that smarmy Minor Mack fall over backwards in his chair."

"Yes? Well, good for you and good luck to you, Ma'am. It is good to meet with an outspoken Christian response from a white person. However, I infer from your voice that you were not raised hereabouts, so I suppose some of our ways may seem strange to you. From a certain point of view, with which I have never lost touch and which I encourage our students not to lose touch, a textbook that is only fifteen years old instead of thirty is a significant upgrade, and a huge improvement on a burning cross. I understand that I have no right to ask this, but could you possibly be so good as to let me review your draft before you publish it? It is not out of the question that one or more of your readers might think of retaliation upon myself or this school, for allowing you to see these upgrades."

*   *

Having filled her new Mont Blanc pen without getting ink all over her desk and hands, Faye sat down to write a note:

Wednesday, January 7

Dear Forde -

As you can see, I am using my new Christmas pen, and I am completely <u>thrilled</u> with it. You were very generous to think of it, my heavens. It makes me feel that everything I write with it is massively true and significant.

However, this note is to request an urgent meeting with you, and possibly with your father, on a matter that I have discovered in the process of interviewing school personnel about the bond issue. I am of course reluctant to meet with Mr.

A knock on her wall interrupted, and rendered moot what she had been about to write, that she hated the thought of meeting Custis without the apology that she felt she had coming before she could countenance exchanging a word with him.

It was Custis.

"Yes? Good morning."

"Morning. If you had a moment, Miss Faye."

"Please come in. I'm sorry I don't have a comfortable chair for visitors … "

"Don't, eh? Well, we can do something about that. Not that you want to make 'em too comfy, mind. Get more news out of somebody ain't too much at ease, I always found."

"Yes?"

"Uh huh. Whyn't you take yourself a walk over to Wegeman's, pick out a nice-looking, oh, one of them dinner chairs, some padding, not too much, see what I mean. Charge it to the paper."

"I will do that, thank you … is that what was on your mind?"

"No, course not. Don't crowd me, now." Custis stood up straighter and took a breath. "Miss Bynum, you have been living up in every way to the expectations Forde led me to believe I could … well, expect. From you."

"Thank you."

"Uh huh. Folks get old, if they're a little lucky, not too much, mind. Anyways, one consequence of that is, drink goes to their heads quicker. Must have to do with stiff arteries, something like that."

Faye had a window at the end of the bank of file cabinets, and Custis walked to it and looked out. Faye, across the room from him, knew that his view was confined to the alley that ran next to the *Intelligencer* building, carrying a chill January rain to the street.

"And so it done with mine," Custis muttered. "Mind, when I was growing up, most men felt pretty free to put their hands on a good-looking woman, and either the women didn't mind, or they at least knew better than to make a fuss. And, of course, no lady would have deliberately stirred a man up like you done, whisperin' in my ear like that, when she knew he'd been drinking. Still, the other night, I done things I wouldn't have tolerated another man doing to my daughter, which I somewhat think of you. As."

"That's very kind of you."

"Yes. So I … " Custis drew himself up again. "I apologize to you for my unseemly behavior at the Christmas party. There."

Faye rose from behind her desk. "Well, that is very handsome of you, sir." *A little late, but hell, the bruise is about gone.* "For my part, I apologize for deliberately inciting you. And for saying what I did, afterwards."

Rueful grin. "I had something like it coming, Honey. I do admire a quick mind."

"Well, then," Faye said. "I suppose we can consider the past to be past, and all apologies accepted. With thanks. May I - or maybe I should say, <u>dare</u> I offer you an apology-accepting hug?"

"You dare. Don't worry, I'm stone sober."

"Well, that wasn't what I meant, but anyway, good. Here." They leaned together gingerly, and his hands went no farther south than her shoulders, so she threw in a polite kiss on his bristly cheek.

"Sir, - "

"Would you for God's sake call me Custis?"

"I'll try. Custis, I'm glad you've come in today. I have something to discuss that I think you should be aware of. A matter of policy."

"Well, fine, but you know, I gave complete authority to Forde. I'm not going to be one of these old geezers that has a problem letting go of his alleged power. Whatever Forde says on any subject, goes for me too, even if I think he's crazy."

"I think Forde is in this morning, so let's go down to his office. I need to feel that I have his backing on something I'm about to write, and it would help to have your thoughts as well."

Custis shrugged, and they repaired to Forde's office. Forde looked alarmed for an instant to see them together, and rose warily.

"Miss Faye here has something she wants us both to hear."

Forde, thinking Faye was resigning to marry Travis Wayland, or just resigning about her damn bruised butt, paled, and sat down suddenly.

"First," Faye said, "I'd like you to know that your father and I have exchanged apologies, and consider that whole business at the Christmas party to be past history. Right, sir? Custis?"

"That's right. Can we have a seat? How's come neither of you got anything comfortable for visitors to set on?"

"Sit down, Pop, it's the same chairs you had. What is it, Faye?"

Faye shut the office door and drew a breath. "First of all, I guess I'd like to check. What do you two understand when somebody says, 'Separate but equal?' Schools, for example."

Custis raised an eyebrow. "It's the law of the land. Keeps the races apart. We don't mix 'em down here, whatever you're used to."

"Matter of fact, Missouri schools are segregated too, so that's not what I'm asking about. It's the 'equal' part."

"They got their schools, we got ours. What's not equal about that?"

"I see." Faye turned toward the seat of power. "Forde?"

Forde put his chin on his fist. "The schools aren't very equal, for one thing. Is that it, Faye?"

"I guess that's part of it. No, but here's the infuriating part. Well, for me, but I need to check and see if this is the way you've always done it. It would affect the way I comment on it, provided Forde agrees to let me do so."

Forde glanced at Custis, *See what I got to deal with?* "Go ahead."

"Would you call it an across-the-board upgrade, when the white schools get all new textbooks, new supplies, goodies galore, and the Negro schools get the hand-me-down textbooks from the white schools and no goodies at all? That's separate, OK, law of the land and all that. What about equal?"

Forde and Custis scowled separately and about equally, but Forde's scowl was more troubled. Custis spoke first.

"Everybody gets an equal upgrade."

"From the standpoint of textbooks, I guess you could argue that. The one example I saw, the white school advanced from 1932 books to 1946. The Negro school went from 1917 to 1932, which is actually a year more of an upgrade. Lucky Negroes, huh? Next thing you know, white folks will be agitating to send their children to the school that got a year more of upgrade than the other one they'd been using. But what about equipment? New microscopes for the white school, a picture of a microscope in a 15-year-old textbook for the colored school. New varnish on the gym floor for the white school, don't need it for the colored school, 'cause their gym has a dirt floor. Again, lucky darkies."

"Easy does it, Faye. We don't use that word anyhow." Forde was scowling harder than ever, but Custis had lost his scowl in favor of a heaven-help-us grin.

"Well, it ain't news that the colored schools are not as top-class as the white ones. But they are just as perfectly adequate to the need they serve, so they are equal in that way."

Faye looked at Forde to clarify. Forde sighed. "What that means is, by that way of thinking, at least, fancy schools would be wasted on colored folks. I'm not sure everyone would agree with that any more, Pop."

"Wasted because … " Faye wanted to see if Forde would say it. Forde did.

"Because they wouldn't be up to taking advantage of … of, well, the advantages."

"Microscopes," Custis shrugged. "Would you give a horse a microscope? What for?"

"Well," Faye said, getting huffy. "A Negro is not a horse. Or any kind of animal. A Negro is a person. I have known smart Negroes and dumb ones, kind ones and worthless ones, just like white people. My land, Custis!"

"Well, good for you, little lady. You're gettin' up the line a little bit here, by the way. What was that, about a 25, 30? We're right here in the same room."

"Excuse me. I didn't go into this intending to shout, and I apologize, which it seems like this is the day for it. So, Forde, is that what I should take as the policy of this newspaper? That Negroes are not people, but inferior animals? Because if it is - "

"Stop. Wait. Don't say whatever it was, you were about to. It is the policy of this paper that … well, that … "

Custis broke in. "Nobody said inferior. I don't think horses are inferior to human beings, which I bet would get me a argument most places in this town. They are God's noble creatures, and way better than people in a mess of ways. I just don't think they belong at Gabbro High School."

Faye stared at Custis for a long half-minute, and then sank back into her chair and spoke carefully. "I think we've fallen into a pretty fundamental argument here that I doubt the three of us are capable of resolving. I'm not going to beat you two, and I don't particularly want to, yet. One of my nun teachers" - here a glance at Forde - "Sister Penitentia used to tell us, 'A man convinced against his will, has the same opinion still.' Is that what we're up against here? Because if so, we have a paper to put out, and it's supposed to have a City Editor's piece in it, and I'm not going to convince you two against your will before tomorrow, which is the deadline for my piece."

"Your nun sounds like a smart lady. On the other hand, it's possible that this fella that has the same opinion is still just as wrong as he was to start with. Let me talk to Forde a little."

"Fine. Maybe I'll write something about the new goodies at Gabbro High without saying anything about the textbook shuffle. For now."

That sounded fine to Forde, but Custis held up a hand. "Careful, though. Nigras read the paper too, and you don't want them gettin' ideas about … well. They might have something, you know. Comin to them."

Faye grinned at him. "Imagine, horses that can read. How do you guess they manage that, in their perfectly adequate schools?

7.

F ROM THE GABBRO *INTELLIGENCER* for Monday, January 12, 1948:

OUR TOWN'S TIMES
By M. Faye Bynum,
City Editor

One of the most charming and pleasing things I have encountered, in becoming a new citizen of Gabbro County, has been the warmth and generosity of my new neighbors. The old saying about "Southern Hospitality" *A mile wide and an inch deep, I mean* has certainly proved true in my experience. You have stopped me on the street to tell me how much you liked - or sometimes, didn't like, but with the kindest intent - something that I have written. People have brought casseroles and pies to me here at the *Intelligencer*, telling me they know how difficult it can be to find home cooking in a new town.

But above all, I have been deeply impressed by the young people I have met in the course of visiting your schools. They are clean, well-dressed, friendly, and polite to a nosy stranger. They account well for themselves whether in the classroom, in the halls, or on the athletic fields. I would like to tell you about two in particular who impressed me with their maturity and the breadth of their hopes to make contributions when they grow to become adults. They are both named Chris, and that is not a coincidence; I have changed their names to spare them unnecessary embarrassment.

'Christine' is a 3rd-grade girl who wants to become a nurse. She showed me a little hospital that she made out of shoe boxes and popsicle sticks. At the time of my visit, a small stuffed bear was having his appendix removed in a beautifully equipped operating room, complete with an operating table, overhead light, and a surgeon who began life as a stuffed rabbit. The long ears hung out of a realistic surgeon's cap. In an adjoining shoe box, a young mother cat cradled a newborn kitten, attended by a stuffed-cat nurse. Again, all the appointments of a maternity recovery room are carefully drawn on the walls of the shoe box in red crayon. Christine confided to me that the nurse was herself, because of all the things about being a nurse, she thought that welcoming new children into the world must be the "most happiest part."

'Christopher' is a high school senior. He has maintained straight-A report cards for the last three years. He serves as an altar boy in his church, and is president of his youth group. He brings communion and

Bible readings to home-bound members of the congregation. He sings tenor in the school choir (he sang a verse of "How Can I Keep From Singing" for me, without accompaniment, that brought tears to not only my eyes, but those of his Principal, who was passing by). He is an obvious natural for a career as a Christian minister, but his ambition is to become a test pilot for the Air Force. "Man," he said to me when I spoke with him after school one day. "Those guys are going twice as fast as sound itself. Can you picture that?" No, but I could easily picture Christopher going that fast, and singing like an angel the whole time.

Both Christine and Christopher are modest, bright, well-brought-up young people with wonderful ambitions for how they want to contribute to the world of tomorrow. *But I am sorry to tell you that as things now stand in Gabbro County, neither of them has the slightest chance of realizing those ambitions.* I will tell you why, in next week's column. Meanwhile, if you think you know what the problem is, drop me a note here at the *Intelligencer*.

*   *

From Our Town's Times, Monday, January 19, 1948:

.... and Jaycee president Beachum Prothroe informs the Intelligencer that proceeds from this year's light bulb sale will go "110 percent" to the renovation fund for Gabbro Memorial Hospital. So brighten up those dark corners as we head into the darkest weeks of winter, and support the Jaycees with a purchase and a gift to this entirely worthy cause.

Last week's column about the ambitions of two Gabbro youngsters brought a small but perceptive and, in some cases, strikingly generous return of mail and comment. Six Gabbro folks thought that the reason the two Chrises might never realize their ambitions was a lack of funds to finish the necessary education - flight school and nurse training, respectively for "Christopher" and "Christine." Of those, *every last one* offered monetary help, ranging from modest to substantial. See, that's just the kind of people we have here in Gabbro! Three correspondents just wanted to offer opinions - which you can read on our Letters page - about what a shame it was that such nice kids should be thwarted in their ambitions, and I can only agree whole-heartedly. One writer thought that the problem was prejudice against Southern youngsters. And one guessed the real reason for such a waste of talent, but unfortunately, used language that we at the *Intelligencer* will not countenance in connection with these matters.

But, yes, the problem is that both "Christopher" and "Christine" are Negroes. Not that there are no Negro pilots, now that the armed forces are racially integrated, and there are plenty of Negro nurses, most of them of course serving in segregated hospitals, but serving all the same. It's just that Gabbro County's colored schools are entirely inadequate to provide the basic schooling its colored children will need to have a chance at professional training, from Officer Training Corps to nursing schools. The problem is that simple, and that shameful.

The law of our land states that education through the 12th grade will be offered to all its children in *Separate* but *Equal* schools. Well, we fulfill the first part of that law just fine. Our schools are so separate, you can hardly squeeze them into the same paragraph on a page of newsprint. It is on the second half that we fail totally. There is an unbridgeable gulf between the education we provide our white children - a quality education that opens every conceivable profession to them - and that which we offer our colored children, that leaves them unable to compete for places in respectable professions. Is that how we - a County chock-full of generous, warm-hearted Christian people - want to be known to the rest of our State and to our democratic United States, a country built on the

assertion that All Men are Created
<u>Equal</u>, and that so many of our boys
gave their lives to defend in the war
just ended? The Gabbro *Intelligencer*
thinks not.

*   *

(Marching music, fading)

<u>Wayland</u>: "We've got a very special guest on this edition of 'Gabbro Voices,' the City Editor of the Gabbro *Intelligencer,* Miss Faye Bynum. Welcome, Faye."

<u>Bynum</u>: "Thank you, Travis. It's a pleasure to join you this morning."

<u>Wayland</u>: "Faye, just a couple of background questions, and then I know you're eager to discuss some of the controversy there's been about your schools editorial. How did you happen to take your job at the *Intelligencer*?"

<u>Bynum</u>: "I'm not sure "eager" is the word I'd choose, but I am anxious to clear up any misunderstandings that may have arisen around what I said. But to answer the question you actually asked me: Forde Morgan, whom I knew when we worked together on the staff of the Charlotte *Star-Dispatch,* wrote to offer me the position, and it seemed like a good chance to come and work in a fine little community. Plus, to be honest, I had no other job prospects at the time."

<u>Wayland</u>: "I think you mentioned that you were on your way to the University of Missouri"

<u>Bynum</u>: "Yes, in a way. I had a good relationship with some of the journalism faculty there, in that they liked an essay I'd written about school segregation in St. Louis. But I had some family crises just then, that made it impossible. My mother and father were killed in an auto accident."

<u>Wayland</u>: "Well, you certainly have our sympathy on that score. You mention school segregation, so let's just get right into

what has upset a few folks here in Gabbro. First of all, are you in favor of integrating the races in the schools?"

Bynum: "Travis, I believe that every boy and girl deserves a quality education as good as we can afford to give them, so they can realize their God-given potential to become a contributing member of society. Whatever a person might think about school integration, I do believe that we should work toward the ideal of quality education for all kids, whether the schools are separate or integrated."

Travis twinkled at Faye, from which Faye concluded that he thought she'd managed that one pretty well. She relaxed a little, and tried to picture Custis Morgan with his ear to a table radio, grumping, taking notes, grinning Lord Help Us. In fact, Travis was twinkling because he couldn't help hearing the throaty purr in Faye's voice when she pronounced his name, and because she looked so damn cute in the headset.

Wayland: "The ideal, you mean, of quality education for all races of students. In other words, Faye, you weren't talking about "separate," but about "equal.""

Bynum: "That's exactly it, Travis. Our colored schools are just flat not equal to the white schools, and all anyone has to do that doubts it, is pay a visit to one of each."

Wayland: "Wouldn't bringing the colored schools up to the level of the white ones be awfully expensive? Who's supposed to pay for that?"

Bynum: "Well… that's an argument I haven't heard much, *and thank you so much for springing it on me live on the air*, Travis, and of course it's a serious consideration. I truly doubt that the colored schools could be brought to the level of the white schools with much less of a per-pupil budget. And therefore, of course, at a considerable increase in costs. The alternative, short of integration, would be the transfer of assets from white schools to colored ones, and I don't mean worn-out textbooks. I mean things like new, useable lab equipment, sports equipment, library books, teachers' supplies. That would reduce the quality of the white schools, so if the white schools wanted to replace what they gave up, somebody would have to ante up to pay for it. I doubt that white parents would stand still for that. Does that mean we shouldn't pay to bring all schools up to the level of the white schools? I guess we could put the question to the voters, who were generous enough earlier this year to support a bond issue that will be going *one hundred percent* to the white schools."

Wayland: "What? No, but the Superintendent promised an across-the-board upgrade."

Bynum: "From what I have been able to learn by visiting the schools, that "across the board upgrade" that was promised consists of all new equipment and books for white schools, followed by the passing-down of the no longer needed, used books - and no equipment - to the colored schools. So in a sense, all of the schools are benefited because every school gets newer books than they had before; although colored schools are still left with inferior and outdated materials. To look at it another way, though, the entire proceeds of the bond issue, the cost of which is shared to some extent by the Negro community, will go to expenditures for the white schools only."

Faye saw Travis's hand twisting a knob, and background music began to swell in her headphones. "We're going to take a little break here, and come back after these announcements, when we'll be opening the phone lines and inviting your comments and questions."

A plug for Wegeman's Furniture and Undertaking came on, and Travis muted it. "Jesus, Faye."

Faye took off her headset and brushed the hair back from her damp temples. "Yes, I know. But I absolutely can't lie about what I've seen, and I won't cooperate in a lie about "across-the-board upgrades.""

"Uh huh. Well, let's see if anybody's listening, and if so, whether any of them can do elementary reasoning. Just, be ready for some abuse. Headset on, here we go."

Wayland: "Yes, good morning, and we're talking to Gail here, calling from Gabbro. And you are on the air, Ma'am."

Caller: "Where did this person grow up, New York somewhere? We don't mix whites and Nigras here, and that is just the way it is."

Wayland: "Thanks for your call, Ma'am. Faye?"

Bynum: "Yes. If you were listening, Ma'am, you will recall that I said nothing about mixing - "

Caller: "Oh, pooh. You know perfectly well that the only way we can afford to give the coloreds a white education would be to bring them into the white schools. We can't be buying new books and equipment for every school in the County, there isn't that much money in all the banks in Gabbro."

Bynum: "Ma'am, I'm not sure what you mean by a 'white education.' It seems to me there's good education and there's - "

Wayland: "I believe that caller has gone off the line, Faye. But seems to me she had an argument to make. Isn't the logical consequence of what you're talking about integration of all the schools from Kindergarten up?"

Bynum: "No, it is not, Travis. It would not be impossible to offer the very same education to all the children of Gabbro County, in separate locations. Of course, doing so would be more expensive than what we do now, and probably more expensive than full integration. But that's a separate argument. My point is simply that we ought to either pay for full equality of education, or admit that our colored schools are inferior because that's the way we want it. I don't see a third way."

Wayland: "We're talking to Gary, calling from Bozlee. Welcome, Gary, and what's on your mind?"

Caller: "Your little Commie bitch is looking for - "

Wayland: "Oh, I'm afraid we've lost Gary's call. But maybe that's OK, because it reminds me to give a reminder about our ground rules, for you potential callers out there. We want to hear from everybody, regardless of their point of view, but we do not allow profanity or insulting language. Here's Annette, from

Morgan's Eddy

Bozlee. Lots of interest over there, looks like. You are on the air, Annette."

Caller: "Well, I just wonted to say, pay no mind to the previous caller. I know who he is, and - "

Wayland: "Yes, Ma'am, thanks, but we also don't encourage callers to get into arguments with each other. Did you have a point or a question you wanted to ask?"

Caller: "A question, I guess. Miz Bynum, isn't it so, that your Nigra child has only a certain capacity to learn, and will just become frustrated and confused if you try to lead them to the higher concepts that are part of the white education? So that's why our colored folks seem to be perfectly content with the schools they have, which are not the equal of the white schools, because the students are not the equal of white students."

*   *

Faye gently tapped her lip with the massive and significant Mont Blanc and considered what to say.

OUR TOWN'S TIMES, Monday, January 26, 1948:

Well, my land. You'd think I had run naked into the street yelling for the Dictatorship of the Proletariat. All I said was that ...

> ... I had met some Negro students of great promise in the course of visiting Gabbro County Schools - when, by the way, I also met white students of great promise, in their own well-equipped and professionally staffed schools - and that it appeared to me that the shortcomings of the colored

63

schools, through no fault of either the students or their teachers and principals, were likely to prevent that promise from being fulfilled. It is difficult for me to see how that idea is anything but the true-blue patriotic promise of America, Land of Opportunity. Life, liberty, and the pursuit of happiness, is what they talked to me about when I took Civics, and I bet exactly the same thing is taught here, at least in the white schools, where it would not be considered dangerously radical to tell a student that he or she is entitled to an education that assists in the pursuit of happiness.

Now. Many kind, well-meaning, and Christian folks in our town have told me that the proper "pursuit of happiness" for a Negro would not involve higher education but rather a stunted life of contentment with menial jobs, poverty, and the dismal prospect of watching his children grow up condemned to the same limited life. "They don't mind," I've been told. "Just look at them, you can see they are happy with their lot." "Your Negro (or a ruder slang term that won't be found in this newspaper) is not capable of higher thinking, and will only be confused and frustrated by any attempt to lead him to it."

I am not a scholar of human psychology or sociology, so I cannot offer scientific comment on this kindly, paternalistic line of thought. I have heard of the likes of George Washington Carver, Frederick Douglass, Benjamin Banneker, Franklin Frazier, Samuel Coleridge-Taylor, Scott Joplin and, yes, Jackie Robinson, and I can't imagine how they could have attained their prominence in their fields, if they had started with inferior mental endowment. I was educated by teachers who claimed that every human life is infinitely valuable. I know of and have visited schools elsewhere in America where Negro children study alongside whites and graduate to go on to higher education. And finally, I can imagine that a happy-faced mask of simple-mindedness might be a useful disguise to turn away the wrath of a white boss who is capable of beating or killing me. I suspect that a Negro is a human being, no more or less, and I'd suggest that none of us really knows the answer to the claim that the Negro is incapable of profiting from a first-class education, until we try offering him one.

-M. Faye Bynum, City Editor

*   *

From a statement signed, "The Editorial Staff," and published in the Gabbro *Intelligencer;* Friday, January 30, 1948:

"The Management of the *Intelligencer* considers carefully before publication, and upon publication stands entirely behind, what its writers have to say, even when it touches on sensitive matters."

8.

THE FIRE-BOMBING of the Gabbro *Intelligencer* offices took place some time between 1:30 AM and dawn on Saturday, February 15, 1948. The previous evening, Faye attended a poetry reading in Chapel Hill with Travis Wayland that ran late, when you include stopping off for sundaes at a Velvet Freeze afterward, exchanging cleverly uncomplicated Valentines, and talking until they flashed the lights at 11:30. The drive back to Gabbro was accomplished in dozing silence on Faye's part, and was followed by Travis's insistence on walking her up the Woolworth stairs to her door ("You don't know who might be lurking up there, controversial celebrity like you."), a chocolatey and gently sticky good-night kiss, and glumly shared re-avowals of un-complication that nevertheless brought forth the off-screen strings, to Faye's chagrin.

She entered the apartment, listened to Travis clumping down the long stairs, and turned on the exhaust fan she'd bought for the kitchen window. She figured later that she was probably pajama'd and brushing her teeth when the bottle of kerosene broke blazing through the alley window, rolled across the floor of Faye's alcove, and came to rest under her desk. The sprinkler system kept the damage to a minimum, except for two material victims.

"My block of gabbro split in two in the heat, and, Forde, darn it, my beautiful Christmas pen is ruined, and I loved it so!" Faye held up the blackened and misshapen remains of the Mont Blanc, burned beyond recognition except for the star logo at one end.

"Aw, damn, Faye. Well, the main thing is, nobody got hurt. We'll get you a new pen out of the insurance money. What else?"

"Well, my notes from interviews. One of the new visitor chairs is pretty scorched. My typewriter was down in the press room, one of the fellas was fixing the ribbon feed, so that was lucky. They knew which window to throw their bomb through, though, didn't they?"

Forde scratched his head. "All the other windows face onto a street, and they're made of tempered glass. Yours is the only one that's just window-glass, and the only one that's out of the public eye. Such as it might be, at that hour. So chances are, the thing wasn't aimed at your office, specifically."

"Still, look at it another way," Custis harrumphed, "we were not in any particular danger of being fire-bombed before we started on this rampage about school integration."

"It's not integration," Faye sighed. "I thought I made that completely clear in my last editorial. But you're right anyhow, Custis, even being wrong about that. I stirred this up, so it's poetic justice that it was my office was wrecked the worst." She took her framed Ecclesiastical verse from the wall, and wiped soot from the glass. The paper that bore the verse was artfully scorched around the edges, but the message was untouched. **Do it with thy Might.**

"Poetic horse crap," Custis fumed. "Look there, what the Bible's telling us. 'Whatever you're fixin' to do, goddam <u>do</u> it and don't footsy around.' You gonna mess with school politics, do it all the way. You gonna get the good folk of Gabbro stirred up, stir 'em all the way up." He looked thoughtful. "Still, that still don't give them the right to throw Molotov cocktails in our windas. I'm going down to County Chambers and get a fire lit under somebody's ass. 'Scuse me, Missy. Sore subject, I guess ... oh, shit. Should I just shut up, here?"

Faye smiled at him gratefully. "Probably. But I suppose I better pull back on the equal-schools thing for a while. Maybe people need time to think about it, get used to the idea."

Forde nodded. "Let's see if there wouldn't be some more kind of slantways approach, we could keep the subject alive, but wait and see if anybody else wants to take up the push."

Custis shook his head. "We opened up this can a worms, we can't let nobody think the *Intelligencer* can be pushed around. We pull in our horns, that's a white flag. My advice, which of course Forde is free to ignore and I won't fuss about it, would be, confront the community along the lines of, 'Is this the way we're gonna discuss things in this town?' How about a signed joint editorial?"

"OK, maybe. Faye, I'm giving you the assignment for a first draft. We need to see it by ten this morning, I'll get the press boys to hold off on Monday's edition, and save - oh, maybe ten-fifteen inches across the Front? You can work in my office, I gotta go down and see Sheriff Burns about this. Coming, Dad?"

Faye nodded. "Wish I had my good pen. It writes better than I do."

OUR TOWN'S TIMES
Monday, February17, 1948

The Intelligencer received a message this weekend, in the small hours of Saturday morning. It was a message of hate and cowardice: a fire-bomb thrown through a window that burned a desk, some staff personal effects, and notes from interviews. Well thrown, someone. If you think this act of cowardice will in any way affect how the Intelligencer *goes about its job of reporting and commenting on the news in our community - well, think again. We have a duty to serve the God-fearing people of this town and this county with the news and information that they need to live their civic and personal lives. And we will continue to carry out that duty to the best of our ability, without intending to offend anyone, but without regard to the prejudices of anyone to whom the facts and the truth may be distasteful. We are not here to pander to the closed-minded, but to serve Gabbro citizens with the news that they need and that other newspapers ignore.*

We call upon all our friends and critics alike to support us in meeting that duty.

> *Custis Morgan, Editor in Chief Emeritus*
> *Forde Morgan, Managing Editor*
> *M. Faye Bynum, City Editor*
> *Rob Stoker, Sports Editor*
> *Jenny McCall, Society Editor*
> *Peter Maribel, Photographer*
> *Fred Winslow, Pressroom Supervisor*
> *Clay Abbott, Chief Press Operator*

Such was the worked-over text of the *Intelligencer's* defiant response to fire bombs. It was toned down from the draft that Faye placed in Forde's desk that Saturday morning, but not too cravenly, she felt. It was Custis' idea to recruit some of what he called "the lower orders that make the thing actually run," meaning that it would help to look a little more democratic than a statement from just the elite management types. Winslow and Abbott shrugged and cooperated, but Stoker dragged his feet, claiming that the bombing had nothing to do with sports, and that opposition to integration *("For the thousandth time, it's not about integration.")* was particularly strong among his athletic sources, and thus that his name on it could shut him out of locker rooms.

"Well, golly. If that's what happens," Forde mused, "Looks like we'd have to find a new sports editor."

*   *

With the receipt of her February second-half paycheck, Faye found that she had accumulated a small surplus of $300 through frugal living, even as regular eating of Gabbro cuisine had cushioned her lanky frame to something that, while far from what Harry Golden would ever have called *zaftig*, was relatively sleek. Her cheek- and collarbones receded a little into the background, and she had to make some minor underwear adjustments.

On Saturday morning she took her new look and most of her $300 to Gabbro's strip of car dealerships on the north side of town, to see if she could afford to own her own transportation instead of walking or begging rides from Forde. Her strategy was to look as juicy and helpless as a fat earthworm, and then to reverse-slam the gathered robins with what she hoped would be guile. A neglected top button on a blouse that once had fit a little more loosely, was part of the worm disguise.

Stan Hubbard, at Hubbard Chev, greeted her eagerly, striding onto his lot through the early spring sunshine. "Hey there, little lady. You looking for something to get you around town today?"

"Wah, yes, sir. You got a good used Chivvy in stock?"

"Got dozens of 'em, Honey. Now, help me out here. What was you thinkin' to pay up front?"

"Reckon I could come up with a hunnerd, hunnerd fifty, caish. What could a person (*hand to chest*) buy into for that?"

"Mmm. That cuts it down some. Lotta demand for cars these days, folks wanting to get rid of their old flivvers and get something postwar. Wait list for a postwar car anywhere in this part of the state would be no less than three ta six months. Used, prewar, I got a sweet '36 coupe right over here, low miles, runs like a clock. C'mere, take a look. Open it up, set behind the wheel for a minute, see how it fits. Trouble is, that would be $200 down, low monthly payments for 24 months. I suppose we could cut the down to $175, up the payments a little. You got a regular job, or would Pop be paying for this?"

Reference to "Pop" brought a tear to Faye's eye, which she used to get Ed down to a final offer of $150 down, 3 years of financing; Faye loved the humpbacked little coupe, which had a rumble seat and what had been in 1936 the "Master Deluxe" packet of amenities, including a radio that still worked.

"That is very kindly of y'all," Faye allowed, blowing her nose. She ran a hand over the steering wheel and wiggled the gearshift. "What if Ah was to take it to a fella Ah know, have him give me a little backup own this large investmint?"

Ed pondered that while he started the engine and raised the hood for Faye's admiration. "Don't ordinarily allow stock off the lot without some security," he mused. "What you got, you could leave with me, make me confident you weren't on your way ta California, somewhere? Driver's license?"

"How'm I supposed to drive into town, right past Sheriff Burns, with no license? But, well … What <u>would</u> you wont?"

Inta that fancy bazziere you're pointing at me, Honey. "Oh … I bet you're holding out on me just a little. How much caish you got on you?"

"Not har'ly no more than the hunnerd fifty I already told you. But … " Faye squinted into the sun. "Oh, <u>do</u> I hate to do this. I could let you hold this garnet ring that belonged to my own mother, that got killed when Pop done too, which is why Ah teared up a little back there. The setting is solid gold."

"Really. Give us a little peek at your finger, then … well, 'tain't brass, anyways. Aw right, that an' fifty will get you an hour with it. Buy the car, I'll keep the fifty and credit you sixty. I'll see you back here with your friend at … oh, noon, say."

"One. A girl's gotta eat lunch, after all."

"Quarter to. You drive a mean bargain, little lady."

Long's I can drive your ol' flivver, Mista Hubbard. "You won't be sorry. I'll see you at a quarter ta one, hear?"

An hour later, Faye, who had been prepared to spend all day looking and bargaining, tooled the faded maroon coupe back onto the Hubbard lot with Travis Wayland sitting next to her, looking knowledgeable and skeptical. Ed Hubbard emerged from his showroom, wiping his chin.

"Afternoon, Honey. What's your friend - why, hey there, Travis! You this sharp thing's advisor? You be careful she don't advisee you right outa your shoes. How'd you like this little honey?"

Travis grinned and nodded. "She's about the prettiest - oh, the car. Why, it's a nice enough piece of antique cast-iron, for maybe a hundred off the price she tells me you're asking."

Ed made scoffing noises. "You ain't fooling me, you're buckin' to impress this little darlin' by gettin' me down ta where I'd starve if I sold ever car I got, that low. Come over here."

"Nuh uh," Travis said. "Faye is part of the haggle, or it's no deal. Gonna be her car, after all."

"Thank you, Travis," Faye said. "Mr. Hubbard, do you take me for the kind of dumb female you can pull some kind of shady deal in front of while I stand around with my thumb in my mouth? I asked Travis to advise me on the soundness of this car, not to bargain on my behalf."

"Behalf. Notice you done lost that dumb-female way of talk you were peddling this morning. All right, all grownups here. The car sells for $399.99, cash, or $175 down and 24 payments of $11.50 per month over two years. I could cut ten bucks off the top line and still put food on the table That would add up to $441.00, or $41.01 carrying charge over the course of two years, which averages out to just over five percent a year on the financed amount, not compounded or amortized. Do we have a deal?"

"Possibly. Travis - and I - noticed a whiney noise in the motor that Travis believes is the water pump, whatever that is, about to go. Put in a new water pump, and we're done."

Ed shook his head, smiling, and addressed the neighborhood of Faye's neglected button. "Good gracious, li'l ladeh, you gon' have me in the po'house fo' sho'. But yes, for such a charming vision as you have vouchsafed me this day, I will replace the water pump with a sound, operating, used water pump from out back - " he tossed his head at the auto graveyard behind the lot - "And I will take care to pick out a good one. At that, you get the part and the labor to install it for nothing, so that's my final position. Are we done?"

"Soon as you give me back my Mama's ring. It has been a sincere pleasure doing business with you, Mr. Hubbard."

Ed Hubbard nodded without enthusiasm. "Take Gus fifteen minutes ta put in the water pump. Make yourselves at home."

On the way back to town, Faye jammed on the brakes. "Wait a minute. He promised to give me $60 off the price in exchange for the $50 earnest money I gave him to drive into town and bring you out. He owes me ten dollars."

Travis sat back and smiled at her. "That would be the ten he knocked off the price. But even a used water pump would run you ten-fifteen bucks retail, and you got him to throw it in for free. I think you got a good bargain, Faye."

Faye put the Chevy in gear and drove on. "Cost him nothing, and I just hate to be tricked like that. Well, all right. I just love this little car, and guess what, it's all mine. Or almost half of it, and more every month. Thank you so much for helping, Travis."

Travis sat crosswise in the seat and shook his head. "Thank you for thinking of me. What say we celebrate and drive up to Greensboro tonight? There's a concert of cello music going on at the Women's College, I want to catch."

"Well, that sounds fine, Travis. Sure, I'd love to."

"Oh. Jesus, Faye. You know, sometimes you do this funny little growl when you say, 'Travis.' It gives me the shivers."

"What, like I'm going to bite your head off?"

"No, it's friendlier, and I guess more complicated than that. Intimate, almost."

"Well, there's that bug, where the female bites off the male's head, while they're being intimate. And he just keeps on. That's a complicated friendship for you."

"Your little growl is not in the least like some kind of bug sex. It is entirely human in its tone and effect. Also, it makes you pucker up your mouth. However you do it, I love it. I swear, I hear it in dreams some times."

"Uh oh."

"Yep, uh oh. Complicated and friendly, I just said."

"Yep."

At five that afternoon, after she'd dropped Travis at the WGAB transmitter shack and driven the Chevy on a round of the grade schools in Gabbro County, including all the way out to West Primary, Faye parked in front of Woolworth's. She climbed the stairs through hotter and hotter zones, entered the airy, baking apartment, and took a glass of sherry into the bathtub to slick herself up for the evening. The hand shower, running only cold, was still body temperature.

Clean, already sweating again, she finished off the sherry and stood before her bathroom mirror in the front-to-back breeze that transected the apartment, holding a toothbrush and reluctant to take on the suffocating burden of clothing. "Travis," she said, watching her mouth. "Trravis …Travis … Forde … Forrde … Forde …

"Huh. Well, … Huh."

9.

TRAVIS! HEY, Travis!"

"Oh. Geez. Brace yourself, Faye. Hey, Claude."

Faye, elegant in a knock-off New Look skirt and diaphanous blouse, braced herself, and turned to see a short, dapper fellow making his way through the departing crowd. The dapper fellow, in fact, who had conducted, while playing in, a double cello quartet rendition of "Liebesleid." The silken, broken-heart beauty of the melody, and the husky harmony of eight cellos had gone straight to Faye's heart, along with the program's explanation of the title. It sounded like Love's Sorrow to Faye, all right, but the Pain part was there too.

"Faye Bynum, Claude Reynard. Claude's a Gabbro product, believe it or not. Apparently, they called him "Clodey" back then. His folks moved to Gabbro from Montreal, so he was pretty darn exotic."

"How do you do, Clode," Faye said, trying for authentic pronunciation. "I did very much enjoy the concert. I loved that last piece. It was so …" She sighed. "So plangent."

Travis raised an eyebrow at that, but Claude nodded. "Plangent as all hell. The Pain of Love, ah, how it smarts, hey, Travis?"

"I'm not sure I would know. Miss Bynum and I are uncomplicated friends. Wouldn't you agree, Faye?"

"Absolutely. We are exploring a new type of male-female relationship, the thoroughly uncomplicated friendship. We have high hopes for it." She took Travis' arm in as uncomplicated a way as she could manage.

"How fascinatingly fragile. Well, do you think it would complicate matters too much for you to join me for a drink?"

Travis looked reluctant, but Faye beamed at Claude. The notion of a drink with a real French-Canadian-Gabbrovian with lacquered hair, a little pencil mustache, and a Boulevard air was too far from the *Intelligencer* newsroom to miss. "Come on, Travis. We'll have one drink and then head back to dear old Gabbro." She put her best full growl into "Travis," and he capitulated. Faye rewarded him by rubbing the diaphanous blouse against his arm, just a little, not enough to complicate his thinking. Trouble was, of course, that in this year of 1948, nothing diaphanous was meant to be worn without a decent slip underneath; a rule that Faye decided could not possibly apply in walk-up apartments above 90° F.

At the Sober Quaker Grille, Travis ordered a highball, at which he intended to sip gently, and probably leave half full. Claude, seeing Faye undecided, said, "Dear, you simply must try this new wine out of Portugal. Mateus. It's just divine, and so gentle, you hardly know you're getting hammered. Two Mateuses, waiter. Matei."

Faye, still a little relaxed from her bath-time sherry, giggled. "You've had the advantages of a classical education, then, Claude?"

"Bits and scraps. Mostly classical music." And a solid quarter-hour later, he said, "But enough about me. I know all about boring old Travis; but you, you're something new under the sun. Whence came you to our whereabouts?"

"Oh, from St. Louis." She drained maybe her second Mateus, having found it all that Claude had promised. "Yummy. I'm the so-called City Ed'tor of the Gabbro *Intelligencer*. Which would be more impressive if there was more of a city. To edit." She snapped her fingers. "I come a long way from St Louie, but baby ..." Faye was aware suddenly of being out of control.

"We still got a long way to go," Travis said, standing. "Great to see you again, Claude. We must get together some time and relive those thrilling days of yesteryear."

"God, must we? However, I count any evening golden, in which I am privileged to make the acquaintance of such a charming, and so forth, et cetera, you can fill it in for yourself. Good night."

"G'night, Clode." Faye tottered against Travis and stayed there out to the parking lot, fell into the passenger seat of the Studebaker, and, in its familiar embrace, passed out.

"Holy smokes," Faye muttered, hours later, as they mounted the endless Woolworth stairway. "Cou'n' we stop an' rest a while? I could make you up a li'l pallet here on the landing."

"Buck up, Faye. Here, give me your key, I'll get you in the door."

"Better do more than that. Ver' complicated, hallways, room after roo', getting back to the bedroom. Gotta go through the bathtub. Bath. Room. OK, come on then."

Travis walked her in the hall door, looked about for the bedroom - the bathroom door had blown shut in Faye's absence - and following her limp gestures, got her through the bathroom and sitting on the childish bed.

"Goo'job, Travs. Travis. Wanna come to bed?"

"Lord, yes. But it's been a long day, it's almost two in the morning, and we'd be full of chagrin tomorrow morning. When I'm on the air at six, anyhow."

"Chagrin *d'amour*," Faye nodded. "Funny, tha's the same thing as *Lible's* ... you know. *Liebesleid*." Faye triumphant at this blurt of trilingual cogency.

"What that bug gets when his mate bites his head off, I guess. No, my dear Faye. We're avoiding that complication for now, but I can inkle from what's not being said, that it might be in the cards. Probably best if we're not drunk, though, don't you think?"

"Surely. Don't know how two glasses of that Matoos stuff got me so darn relaxed. You'll think I'm a loose ..." It seemed to Faye that to call herself a 'woman' would be irreparably loose, and she stopped in time.

"Well, I think it was maybe three glasses, though. Or so. Claude can talk you unconscious. No, for now, just call me 'Travis' one more time, and I'll see myself out."

Faye fell back and kicked off her shoes. "Thank you, Travis. You are a perf' gentleman. Trrr ... I s'spect unner the surf's chatter, I ... I ... But her eyes closed, and what it was that Faye suspected, was lost in the gentle breath of sleep. Travis got her out of the New Look skirt and the gauzy blouse. He put them on the dresser and returned to gaze at her for a solid minute, pensive, tracing the still slender opulence. Kneeling, he bent his sweaty forehead and laid it on her hip between garter and panties. The cool touch on her skin made her stir and smile from the depths. He stood then, wiped his eyes, and covered her with a bath towel, rather than trying to maneuver her under the sheet.

*   *

Sunday, Faye put on a pair of jeans and a Mount Saint Anne sweatshirt, and let herself in to the *Intelligencer* building to comb through the wreckage of her office and see what else might be salvaged, now that the Gabbro VFD had gone over it and verified what no one doubted, that the fire was deliberately set, and that the accelerant had been kerosene - also unquestioned from the beginning. The glass bottle that held it had shattered in the heat, and no particular hope was held out for fingerprints, or for telltale clues in the alley outside the broken window.

Faye wandered queasily through the abandoned stink of ashes, and found that her office-alcove had been barricaded with sheets of plywood. She sat down in one of Forde's visitor chairs, unwilling to usurp his desk, and pressed her hands to her eyes. Last night's overdo with Mateus had her head still throbbing and dizzy. What had she been thinking?

"Not thinking. Not a damn think. Thing."

And what had she said to Travis? She remembered climbing the Woolworth stairs, longer and higher (and hotter, even at 2 AM) than Jacob's ladder, and wanting so desperately to stop climbing. She remembered, Oh God, asking Travis if he wanted to sleep with her. She did not remember what he'd said, but she thought she remembered his taking off her skirt, and definitely waking at a grey hour wearing a bra, panties, stockings, and a bath towel. What the hell? She frowned and concentrated, but she simply could not account in any detail for the time between the stairs and the grey waking.

The queasiness grew until she had to trot to the Ladies' that she shared with Sharon and Jenny McCall, and upchuck the coffee she'd forced down at ten, thinking that she would need to be alert today, having lost track of the day of the week. She wandered back toward Forde's office feeling wretched, and the memory of Mateus sent her back, gagging and retching *(Wonder if that's the same word as wretched. Sure feels like it.)* to the cramped Ladies' again. When she got back to the newsroom this time, Forde was sitting at his desk.

"Hi, Faye."

"Hey, Forde. Done with Sunday School?" Forde was the only adult she'd ever met who still attended something called Sunday School, but that's what men did down here. Faye wiped her mouth and belched.

"You look a little peaked, I have to say. Late night last night?"

Faye started to roll her eyes, found it too painful, and returned them to the forward position. "Yuh."

"I tried to call, about six, see if you wonted to get some dinner." Forde tried, without much success, not to sound accusatory.

"I went to a concert in Greensboro with a friend." Faye couldn't tell if she sounded defensive. "It was very pleasant."

"Hn."

"Cello music."

"N-hn."

"There was a very lovely piece called 'Liebesleid,' that I particularly enjoyed. Eight cellos."

"Pains of Love. I heard of it." Forde had taken a couple of semesters of German before busting out of pre-med at Chapel Hill. "You went with Wayland?"

"Yes." Rallying her strength to sound steely. "Forde, you do not need to feel jealous about him. Nor do you exactly even have a claim to the standing to feel jealous. I have told you, Travis (at pains here to suppress the growl) is a friend. An uncomplicated friend." *That I might have slept with last night.*

"OK, OK, fine. How lovely for you both. Am I so complicated?"

"You ... have a number of aspects, yes. In addition to being a friend of pretty long standing, you are now my supervisor as well as the beloved son of my sometimes abusive employer, so that's two complications right there. You have also expressed interest in being part of a "Thing," with me, which if it happened would compromise my standing with my fellow journalists, who number in the ... well, the severals. Compared to my relationship with Travis, ours has as many moving parts as a ... a '36 Chevy, which I bought one yesterday, how do you like that? No more begging rides, taking you out of your way."

Forde was not distracted. "Congratulations. You have a 'relationship' with Wayland, do you?"

Chagrin. What was it about chagrin? "Oh, come on, Forde, give it a rest. Travis ... " But the set of jaw needed to keep Travis' name out of growl territory triggered another wave of nausea, and Faye had to trot offstage, where Forde could not help hearing her as she knelt over the Ladies' commode.

"You seem to be coming down with something. Take the day off tomorrow, we'll push the column off to Wednesday."

Faye sagged against the door frame, wiping her mouth with a paper towel. "Thank you, Forde. I expect this is just a 24-hour thing. I should be OK by tomorrow."

"N hn. Give it a day so you don't spread it around, OK?"

Faye retreated, suspecting that Forde knew it was a hangover, and was having a little fun punishing her for it. She spent the rest of Sunday sleeping it off and pretending that she had a 24-hour bug; and almost convincing herself. The Sunday funnies from Raleigh, pajamas, aspirin, a last trip to the bathroom to retch unproductively; soft-boiling an egg that tasted good until her fork pulled up a string of underdone white and she had to sprint to the bathroom. Mateus. Jesus, never again.

Travis phoned around four, checking up, and besides wailing about the hangover, she tried delicately to learn if he had slept with her, and if so, what else might have happened. Asking about "chagrin" was probably a little too delicate, because he didn't figure out what she was getting at, until she blurted, "Travis, for God's sake, I'm sorry, but I can't remember. Did you sleep with me?"

"Oh. Heavens, no."

"Well ... good. You don't have to sound so horrified."

"You don't have to bite my head off, either."

"Grr."

They laughed, and made plans for next weekend, when Travis should return from following the basketball Quarrymen to the state tournament in Charlotte.

"I should be done with this hangover by then."

"Can I bring you anything?"

"Please don't. You'd spend an hour climbing my stairs, and for what? I'd probably throw up on your shoes."

*   *

Monday, her quarantine day, brought greater clarity, and Faye spent it visiting the two each colored and white grade schools, and learning nothing new, except that the injustice was smaller in scale, amounting to no more than a few hundred dollars worth of new readers for the white schools, and no-cost hand-me-downs for the colored ones, which allowed them to replace their ancient McGuffey's. Faye took notes, uttered compliments that were received as due by the white principals, and with veiled irony by the black ones. Black and white, the children themselves seemed happy enough and adorable, and Faye drove away from G. W. Carver Elementary fuming. The whole operation felt like an improvised literacy mission run by earnest Presbyterians, and its teachers made no effort to conceal their distaste at her faked cheerfulness and the dismay she could not hide. No ear-to-ear grins that she could see.

She wrote an anodyne editorial about the adorable elementary kids for the Wednesday paper and, that pressing business done, walked in to the Gabbro Salonnette to see what might be done about her erstwhile pixie cut, which had by now grown out of pixie range into a shaggy mess, if she was not careful to keep it slicked and pinned back behind her ears.

"G'morning, dear. He'p you today?

Faye explained the problem, and was assigned to Pearlene, a comfy-looking forty-something with unlikely auburn hair. While Pearlene was giving her a wash and comb-out, Faye leaned back and luxuriated in being manipulated without having to invest anything in it but relaxation. Still sleep-deprived, she went into a shallow doze, and so missed the polygonal exchange of significant glances that ricocheted over her head. Pearlene gently broke the spell with a warm rinse and a cleared throat.

"That's a right nice scent you got on."

"Silken Rain. I've heard it well spoken of."

Pearlene smiled. "Seem like I've seen you, time to time, but I cain't seem to place the face, Honey. You new to town?"

"I moved here at the end of October." Faye realized what was being asked, and took the plunge. "My name is Faye Bynum. I work at the *Intelligencer.*"

"Well. Well my land, a celebrity. Mary-Deane, Ginny, this here's that Faye Bynum, writes for the paper."

There was a flutter of interest from other corners of the shop, and Faye found herself explaining how she'd come to move to Gabbro, from where, by what means, how she liked it, who she was related to (no one they knew, which apparently amounted to no one at all); and that, yes, it was her little pink Chevy they'd seen buzzing around town.

"Maroon," Faye said. "The dealer said it was Royal Maroon, was the name Chevy gave the color, but they didn't give a name for the color it faded to."

"Princess Pink, how's that? Pleased to meet you, Faye. I'm Mary-Deane Gaines, live out'n West Park. Sometimes I just love your little editorials, they're so … Help me out, Ginny."

"How about smart-face and snippy?"

"Why, nonsense, Ginny, what's the matter with you? I was fixing to say something like, oh … warm and pleasant. Perceptive, even."

"Well, I guess you're both right, mostly Ginny. I work hard on not being smart-faced and snippy, but sometimes it just gets away from me. I don't think I have a very good feel for how things work here."

Pearlene gently pushed her head forward. "Well, you took the right first step, coming in here." She snipped judiciously. "Hardly nothing goes on, work or not work, don't get talked over here."

Faye inhaled, relaxing. A tiny, tiny crack in the smiling face of Gabbro, North Carolina. "Well, could I ask a question?"

"See," Ginny said. "Asked like a Yankee. Go ahead, ask, and then I'll tell you how you might should have raised the subject."

"OK. How are colored folks supposed to improve themselves, if the County won't spend a nickel to give them decent schools?"

"Ha. Perfect. Examine your premises, young lady. The answer is, they are not supposed to improve. They are supposed to stay put exactly where they are. But we never, ever discuss politics here. Try something else. Ask me about that Travis Wayland you been running around with. Ask me what Forde Morgan thinks about it. Ask Mary-Deane if there isn't someplace you could afford to live, that wouldn't be a mile better than upstairs over the five and dime. And you might even ask where you could find a nice curtain for that front window, that doesn't give the old goats in the courthouse a look at you when you're getting ready for bed or changing your clothes. They're missing their suppers, staying late on the third floor for when you get off work, all hot and sweaty. With binoculars."

Faye, crimson, turned suddenly toward Ginny, causing Pearlene to snatch her scissors away. "Easy, Honey, we 'bout lost an eye there. Ginny, you apologize to Miss Bynum for that fresh talk."

"No, no," Faye managed. "Please call me Faye. It is so refreshing to hear something more deeply felt than 'Y'all have a blessed day, hear?' Thank you, Ginny. I'm not going to ask anything about Travis, because he and I are trying to manage to be just uncomplicated friends … all right, smile all you want, but we are. Mary-Deane, I want to talk to you about some other housing than on top of Woolworth's, but that sounds a little too close to politics to discuss here. And you can believe the goats are getting no more free peeks. Shame on them, anyhow."

Faye subsided into position for Pearlene to go back to her clipping. "All right, how's this? What do you know about a fellow named Claude Reynard, was supposed to have grown up here, but he's living out west Carolina somewhere now, teaching music?"

"Very good, Honey," Ginny said. "A perfect topic that we could fill your little ears brim-full with. But a direct question? You'd have to be on your *death*bed to short-cut it like that. Where'd you hear about Claude? When you went up to Greensboro with Wayland the other night?"

"That's right. And now are you going to tell me I ought to know better than to have four glasses of wine on top of the sherry I suppose the old goats read the label of, when I was taking a bath?"

"Nobody told me anything about that. But pay attention, now, how we do it: 'Say, Pearlene? Never guess who I run into the other night, up'n Greensboro.' "

"Not gonna try," Pearlene said.

"That Clode fella, his folks come from Canada somewhere? Left town kinda sudden after him and the Shaler girl got the divorce?"

"Thank the Lord they wasn't no children from that train wreck," Mary-Deane contributed.

"Oh, that was a blessing. Can you imagine, explaining to a little boy or girl about their Daddy liking boys better than girls?"

Faye looked from one to the next and burst into laughter. "I see. Never say it straight out. Say it slantways."

"No you don't see it all yet, Honey. Set up there and let Pearlene get you dried off, and listen. Two more things: One, we short-cut it something awful just now, so you could go on about your business yet today. I'd say it took 3-4 days, maybe a week to say all that, first time around; and that was after just about everybody here already knew the whole story. Second thing, once everybody you think ought to know about it knows, which in that case would have been the regulars here at the Salonnette; the Shalers, who left town over it, living outside of Wilmington, what I heard; and one other person, that I don't believe I'll share the name of, this afternoon ... Anyways, once ever one who should know, knows, you never refer to it again. Maybe look cross-eyed at someone you've discussed it with, if the name should come up; but otherwise, it pretty much drops out of existence."

Faye thought about it while Pearlene's dryer roared around her head. "Well. I can see that a nosy Yankee is not going to have an easy time prying information out of this town. Maybe it will help that Missouri is a Border State, so I'm only a sort of Yankee." Faye sat up and looked in the mirror that Pearlene was holding. "Oh, Pearlene, that is just amazing. I can't imagine how you did it, given what you had to work with. Thank you ever so much."

"Does real nice with the shape of your head, which is right handsome," Ginny commented. "Sets off your ears, which are also cute. And it makes you look maybe three weeks older, which you could use, if you're going to go on deviling us about the schools. You'll need to come in about every week, to keep it like that."

"Oh, goodness. I would be a fool not to come in here every week for the news, even if I was bald. Which I have been, less than a year back, and this is the first cut it's had since then."

"Bald?" Ginny's eyes opened. "Why ever?"

"Heavens, a direct question. Don't you know you'll never learn anything that way? It's a long story, Ginny, and I'll tell you all about it next week. This has been a marvelous experience, so thank you all very much. How much do I owe you, Pearlene?"

Faye walked back toward the *Intelligencer*, sauntering in the heat, glancing in shop windows to admire the new hair-do, and vowing to hang a towel over her front window, maybe with an insulting message on it that could only be read with binoculars. She encountered the assistant principal of West (equivalent to white, in this town) Elementary on the sidewalk, and persuaded her to fix an approximate dollar value to the new books, received and expected, courtesy of the bond issue. ($500, which meant that all the grade schools together couldn't have accounted for more than $2500, and probably much less.) Faye made a note, and a resolve to keep prying.

She walked in the door of the *Intelligencer* no more than 45 minutes after she left the Salonnette, and smiled at Sharon. Sharon smiled back with quavery lip and a brave tear in her eye. Some domestic problem, Faye thought, or Sharon's granny had died. She wondered if she would hear all about it next week while she got trimmed up. If she would count as a regular, on only her second visit.

10.

T HERE'S SOMETHING FUNNY going on with this bond issue money. I'm sure of it."

Custis pulled a face. "Be pretty unusual if there wasn't. Faye, Honey, you might want to take it a little easy, now."

"What?"

"Well, under the circumstances. You need to save your strength, sweetheart. You know we are all here for you."

"Um..."

"Dad?"

"Look, kids, I told Clay I owed him a lunch, and I'm already late. He's prob'ly sittin over there in the Terminal ... Oh, Honey, I'm sorry. Really, got to go, now. You'd never guess, to look at you in that pretty haircut. You rest up, hear?" Custis picked up his hat and walked out the door at a pretty good clip.

"Forde? Any idea what that was about?"

"Not the least. I'm starting to worry about Pop a little, how he'll say things you can't make any sense of, walks into a room and stands there looking around, walks out without a word. Plus, he vowed that he was going to stay away from the *Intelligencer* and go fishing, but he's in here for some silly little reason about every day. I tell myself, he's just getting on, and it's hard to give up your life's work, but ... " Forde shrugged, and picked up Faye's note about school funding. "How much do you really know about what's going on with the bond issue money?"

"Well, let me lay it out. But about your Dad, look, he's what? pushing seventy, he's probably entitled to a little absent-mindedness. The 'rest-up' business, he sounds like he heard I'm sick or pregnant or something. Maybe somebody heard me tossing my breakfast Sunday. *Or one of the goats saw it through the window. I have got to fix that.* I got a little lesson in how gossip works in Gabbro, down at the Salonnette, and it was an eye-opener. They never say anything straight out, apparently, so you could walk away thinking they'd told you that you had a week to live. I swear, I said nothing at all to that bunch that would lead them to think I was sick or pregnant. You didn't let anything slip about my being pregnant for a few weeks last summer, did you?"

"Nope. That whole business is buried six feet deep, as far as I'm concerned. You're not, are you?"

"Certainly not." *I'm pretty sure.* "Why on earth would you even ask?"

"OK, OK. Show me what you've got on the bond issue."

"Well ... OK. It's not complete yet, but here it is. As far as I can tell, the white schools got brand-new books and some other goodies, that we know about already. The black schools got nothing but hand-me-downs, and the Indian schools didn't even get that, since the books from the black schools are too old and tattered to pass down. From all I can tell, either the Indian schools are using clay tablets, or they have some other source of funding. Plus, of course, they don't have a high school, so even if they shared in the bounty, it would be at the grade school - junior high level, which is minimal.

"I don't have anything but a rough estimate on the money that Gabbro High got, but the grade schools - the white ones, that is - seem to have raked in maybe $500 worth of books each, and Gabbro Junior High maybe $800. Add that all up, with the fuzzy number from Gabbro High, it comes up to, mmm ... OK, maybe $35 thousand. Where's the rest of the $50 thousand?"

*   *

"Principal Evans, I appreciate your making time to talk to me again about the upgrades you all are planning with the bond issue money. First of all, have you been able to get all the new books and equipment?"

"Some of it's on back-order, but the bulk of the forty thousand has been committed. The new books are in, have been since last winter some time."

Forty thousand for the high school? Jesus. Faye scribbled random phrases in her notebook. "And the microscopes, and the other supplies?"

"Part of the back order, some on hand. We could walk up to the science lab, have a look at a microscope if you like."

"Surely would enjoy that. I haven't seen a science lab since I was in high school myself."

Raised eyebrow. "You didn't have a science requirement in college?"

"Not in my case, no, sir." *Watch what you say, idiot.* "Let's see. The gym floor refinishing is scheduled for over the summer, I believe? And how much of the new money will go for that?"

Anson Evans frowned. "Is that something your readers really need to know, Miss Bynum?"

"Oh, I reckon not. Just thinking of a picture caption, *'Gabbro High gymnasium gets thousand-dollar spruce-up,'* that sort of thing. It's not essential at all, no."

"I'd rather the number stay a bit under wraps. There was competitive bidding involved, where we didn't necessarily consider the lowest price to be the only deciding factor. I can say, it was some above the number you just now mentioned."

Huh. Something up, here? "Oh, certainly. Would you be willing to release the name of the successful bidder? Was it a Gabbro firm, for example?"

"See, that's just the sort of sensitive consideration we'd just as soon keep confidential for now. It will be public of course, once the work is going on."

"Of course. Well, I do appreciate your time. If you had time to walk me to your science lab? Are the new microscopes out on benches, where I could maybe get a picture?" Faye fished in her purse and flourished a Kodak that she'd charmed away from Peter Maribel, an awkward kid photo-nut who was even newer at the *Intelligencer* than Faye, having started with the new year.

Principal Anson Evans nodded a little impatiently, and rang a bell on his desk.

"Miss Squire, could you walk Miss Bynum here up to the science lab, and then return for dictation?"

Having duly admired, casually snooped make and model, and photographed a representative microscope, Faye went back to the *Intelligencer,* sweating in an early spring heat wave, wrote up her notes, and stuck them in a folder. She headed for Woolworth's then, and shopped materials for some necessary home improvement. Hating to do it, she climbed the endless staircase in the heat of the day, and banged into place on the lintel of her front window the hardware for a roller shade. She had it mounted before the courthouse goats could start their vigil. She left it rolled up for the sake of the breeze while she stretched out on the plaid couch to consider not just prevention, but punishment. After a troubled and sweaty doze, something Sister Penitentiary had said about Dante came to her. Simple punishment wouldn't be enough, and might backfire. They needed their dirty noses rubbed in it. She went to the meagerly laden bookcase and consulted *World Literature*'s boil-down of the *Inferno.*

On her way back to the *Intelligencer* she stopped at the Post Office to see about getting a box. She had virtually no friends or relatives in the world who might send her personal mail, but the check from the sale of her family house had come from a settlement agency in St. Louis to the *Intelligencer* office, to be routinely slit open by Sharon and admired as it sat on her desk for half a day while she was interviewing school personnel; and her life was now getting just that little more complicated - a bank account, a telephone, two sort-of suitors, a homosexual acquaintance that she nevertheless kind of liked - that she didn't much fancy having mail sit on her desk, or on the staircase at Woolworth's, which is all her apartment offered in the way of a mailbox, for hours at a time. Besides, who wants their address to be "3½ Church Street?"

"Them're getting somewhat scarce," the window-keeping clerk allowed. "What we got left open is all on the top row: 401, 501, and 701. Might be a little tall for you." - giving Faye a vertical survey. "Let's go an' see how it'd work for you. Got a preference?

"Yes, something lower. But if it's top row or nothing, I guess it's top row. Let's say 701 for luck. How high are they?"

"Uh huh. Five foot four inches to the bottom."

"Well, that's how tall I am."

"Yup, good, but your eyes ain't. No problem to reach up to, but above your sight line, if you wonted to check before you tooken the trouble to open it."

Faye found that if she stood on tiptoe and bounced a little, she could just see through the little window all the way to the back of the box. "That's good enough. Maybe I'll get some platform shoes just for mail."

The clerk, who'd enjoyed the little dance, handed her a form with her name already filled in. "Fill in the rest of this and sign at the bottom. It works with this here key, which if you lose it, there's a ten-buck replacement fee. Rent'd be fi' dollar for the first three months. We don't take no checks."

That evening promptly at five, she yawned and stretched, which got Rob Stoker's attention as intended, and drawled, "She-oo, I'm hot and tired. I bet the co'thouse clock says five. I know my tummy does. I'm gonna knock off, go home an' get cool." As she left the newsroom, she glanced back to see Stoker picking up his phone. Uh huh.

Back at the apartment, she sat on the couch and stripped down to a brassiere, panties and stockings, and, after some waffling, listening for cues from Dante, took off the bra, triggering a pang of daring in her belly. After some visualizing, she slipped her heels back on; sat trembling for a moment, and then stood tall, gritting her teeth. *Intelligencer* City Editor M. Faye Bynum took a deep breath and strutted through the bathroom toward the front window. Passing the rack on the bathroom door, she plucked off a towel and draped it around her neck, like a boxer coming in from road work.

As she entered the bedroom, she caught a flash of glass from the top floor of the courthouse. She walked to the window and stretched her arms to the frame on either side, hips cocked saucily, but keeping her body a couple of feet inside the opening to avoid a sight line from Church Street below; just enjoying the breeze that the exhaust fan in the kitchen provided, and letting the ends of the towel slip this way and that in the flow. Improvising a topper, she put a foot on the sill and peeled down one of the nylons. Then she pulled down the shade and let the watchers read the message she had lipsticked on the outside:

GO HOME AND EAT YOUR DINNERS, YOU DIRTY OLD GOATS!

11.

F AYE, HONEY, WHY didn't you tell me?"

"Tell you what?"

"About the … you know. That you'd been, um, you know. Sick."

"Well, I had that little 24-hour bug that was mostly hangover. You knew about that. Did you get it too, by the way?"

"No, I meant before. About the CANCER."

"What cancer?" Not whispering as Travis had. Heads turned, then turned back.

"Faye, everybody seems to know about it, I heard it from probably four-five people. But listen, Honey, don't get down. We're all here for you, and lots of people go on just fine for years."

Faye gave up on the chopsticks and picked up a fork. "Well, that's very supportive and - and encouraging of you, and I can't tell you how I appreciate it. But I don't have cancer. Never have, so far. Who told you I did?"

"You never? Really?"

"Travis, I'm your uncomplicated friend. It would be very complicated to hide something like that from you, and I'd never do it. Not doing it now. You'd be about the first one I'd run to, if you want to know. So where'd you get the idea?" She pushed away her plate of lo mein, full for now.

Travis sat back in the booth and finished off his wine. He seemed shaky with relief, looking around the China Clipper like a man reprieved … well, from cancer. "Jesus, what a relief. OK, you want to know, after about the third time I heard it, I did some investigation, like a good journalist. It seems to have started at the Salonnette. Ginnie Freeman, in particular."

"Huh. What on earth would have given … oh! Ha! I bet I know." Faye went bent over her own glass of Blue Nun and giggled. "Remember I told you about the time the Klan shaved my head? Why I had such short hair when I got here? I told the ladies at the Salonnette I'd been bald once, and I bet anything that's what started it. Oh, that's too much! See what comes of never saying anything straight out? Everybody has to inkle what they can, from what's not said. Leaves worlds of room for whatever you want to think. What say we split another glass of this sweet wine and see what lies ahead? Here."

She handed the plate of fortune cookies to Travis, shaking off his "Ladies first," and took the one he left behind. "See, my fortune depends on how you decided. You better hope it's uncomplicated. What's yours?"

He cracked open his cookie and pulled out the flimsy slip. "Huh. 'Avoid unnecessary complications.' How's that? These little guys really are on the case."

"Depending on what counts as a necessary complication, I guess. Wouldn't want to avoid that."

"I promise. What's yours?"

"Just a second ... 'You have a caring but rebellious nature.' What say to that?"

"On the mark, I say. Isn't that what's going on with the school thing?" He gestured at Faye's glass, and the waiter refilled it. Faye poured half into Travis's, and giggled again.

"Maybe it's talking about my window show." Faye having given Travis the highlights of the Goat Tease. "It was rebellious, all right. I'm not sure about the 'caring' part."

"Well, you were caring about your privacy."

"Furious, more like."

"That's hard to tell from 'extremely caring,' wouldn't you say?"

She smiled at Travis over a raised glass. "I guess. Thank you for putting a good face on it." She sipped, savoring the sweetness and the astringent impact of the alcohol.

"My pleasure. I doubt they were looking at your face anyhow."

Faye blushed, and patted his hand. "You know - just to change the subject, if we please may - I'm really beginning to think that somebody is coming out of that school deal a great deal better off, and it's sure not the kids. I made some simple phone calls, and got prices for floor varnishing and the same make and model of microscopes, that ran two thirds, three quarters what those guys are quoting in their budgets, which came out this week. And the crazy thing is, I didn't pretend I had anything to do with a school, meaning they didn't throw in whatever educational discount."

"There is one? How big?"

Faye wagged fingers and deepened her voice. "'Pencil runs you a nickel at Woolworth's don't cost us but three cent.' I have that straight from Mister Mack himself. Have to think a microscope might cost at least two cents less as well, wouldn't you? Not to mention 40% off."

"At the very least. Look, be careful if you go after Mack. He came to Gabbro from Florida somewhere in kind of a hurry, in the middle of the school year."

"Isn't that when they needed him, though?"

"It was. The old Superintendent, Clete Lewis, had a heart attack on a Tuesday, and died on Thursday. Mack seemed very qualified, lots of experience on his application. But notice that Mack was free to come in the middle of the year and on very short notice, thus not previously employed. It wasn't one of those Interim Superintendent - Pleased to announce - Expected to join us next fall, kind of things. We got a sudden opening, bam, we got a new guy. Mack was in office the next Monday."

"Huh. No nation-wide search, then. Or statewide."

"Not even Gabbro-wide. They totally passed over a couple principals that would have been at least qualified to be interviewed; including Anson Evans. The fix was in."

"Mm. Interesting. Is there a connection to the school board?"

"Funny you should ask. Mack is Ellice Laffler's brother-in-law, and Ellice is Chairman of the Board. The way it was given out, lucky us, we just happened to have this connection to an experienced and regionally prominent educator."

He stood and fetched Faye's jacket from the hook on the booth. "We better get you on the road, though. The finals are tomorrow, and I have to interview both coaches and both captains, and they're all going to say the same things about hoping the best team wins, while also praying that Jesus will help them."

"Wonder how many winners he's got to pick in the next two or three days. Forty-seven more state finals, not to mention the ones that are still back in the quarters and semi's. He must wonder sometimes if all the nagging that comes after was worth going through crucifixion."

"Rebellious Faye."

"But not much caring. Except that it keeps you away from ... from Gabbro."

"Uh huh. Well, thank you for driving all this way for Chinese with me. Maybe I can show you something fancier some time. Come on, I'll walk you to your car."

At the little Chevy, Faye turned to him, shrugging out of her jacket. "Is it always this hot in March? Thank you so much for caring about the phantom cancer. I'm sorry I upset you like that."

"That wasn't you. That was silly Ginny Freeman."

"Well, it was me being mysterious, to get back at her for calling my columns 'smart-face and snippy.' "

"Rebellious, again. You know, you really can't top a fortune cookie for dead accurate."

"Well. It also said 'caring,' and that's true too. I care a lot about you, Travis." The full T*r*.

"Oh, me too. God, I can't tell you how worried I was about that cancer business. I guess I cherish this uncomplicated friendship even more than I thought I did, which was greatly, already."

Wry smile. "Cherish. An uncomplicated term. Nobody writes music about the pain of cherishing."

"Kirschenleid."

"Sounds plausible, but I don't know any German. We better be careful."

"You be careful driving home with that wine in you. Sure you don't want to sleep on my couch?"

"Complicated." She gave him a cherishing sort of kiss, jumped in the Chevy, and flivved off, looking for US 74.

*   *

Sheriff Alfred Burns stubbed out a cigarette on the inside of Forde Morgan's wastebasket and shook his head. "Honest to God, Mr. Morgan. If we had the least clue who done that, we'd be on him like ticks. It just looks like a dead end, far as I can see."

"Call me Forde, Sheriff. It's the first serious, life-threatening crime that's happened in your first term as Sheriff, and you're already giving up on it?"

"What's 'already?' It's been more'n a month of hard detective work, around the clock."

Forde raised an eyebrow at the "around the clock." "Pretty quiet work, along three, four in the morning, I guess. I sure didn't hear nothing."

Burns had the look of a man easily irritated - a round face in a permanent scowl, a Julius Ceasar-style haircut that was pasted to his massive forehead with Brylcreem, and a stocky frame that, belying the Falstaffian good humor that often goes with such a look, was like an overwound alarm clock that was straining not to erupt. He was irritated, but knew better than to antagonize the editor of the local rag, in a county that elected a sheriff every three years. Christ, how was a man supposed to get anything else done, you got to spend half your time running? The *Intelligencer*'s endorsement carried a lot of weight at election time, and the crack about "first term" was clearly meant to rub that in. Burns sat back and pulled out another cigarette.

"You know, they was another issue come across my desk this week, affects you. Well, the *Intelligencer*. Where'd they come by that name, anyways?"

"Makes folks more intelligent. Couldn't be plainer, seems to me. Was that the issue?"

"Nuh uh. One of your employees was observed putting on a lewd display before a minor this week."

Forde grinned, guessing that Rob Stoker had got drunk again over in Bozlee. "Really? What'd he do this time?"

" 'Twasn't a he. That Bynum girl you got."

Forde grinned again, shocked. "Faye? You kidding me? What, she showed some kid her ankle?"

"Showed this fella about all there was to show, seems like. We can't have that kind of thing in this town, Forde."

"Huh. Gonna tell me who the minor is?"

"Young Robbie Pardee."

"That the simple-minded kid that's related to Anson Evans?"

"Robbie's a little slow. That don't mean she can get away with a strip tease in front of him."

"Shit, Fred, you couldn't possibly describe an act that would be more sheer impossible for Faye to carry out than that. Who put the kid up to it? Evans?"

"I'm not at liberty to share everything about this to a possibly interested party, Forde. You pull that girl in here, and you get to the bottom of it. I'll give you 48 hours, and you can figure I'll follow up on it."

"I'll talk to her. You tell Anson Evans, if I find out he's behind this, the *Intelligencer* will be on <u>him</u> like a tick. I'm going to need a hell of a lot more information before I believe anything of the sort."

Burns rose, and tossed his cigarette in Forde's wastebasket. "Past suppertime, I see. Your prejudice in this matter is noted. Good night, Forde."

*   *

"License and registration please, Miss."

Faye produced them, shiny and new, both acquired along with the Chevy, and handed them over with shaking fingers. The cop shone a massive flashlight on them, and tucked them into his tunic pocket. Scotland County Sheriff's Office, his badge read. *Thank God, not Gabbro County.*

"Mary Faye Bynum. Well, look who I got me tonight, the famous M. Faye Bynum. That you, darlin'? The newspaper lady?"

"I'm Faye Bynum, yes."

"Why you're a slip of a thing, big as you write. We do get a chance to read your blisterin' crap way over here, time to time. Miss Bynum, do you know why I pulled you over?"

"No, sir. I don't think I was speeding, was I?"

"Thank the good Lord no, Honey. The way you was weavin' down the road, you'd a spilled over for sure. You were doin maybe 30 in a 50 zone. Still, you like to clip my fender back there, where we first encountered one another. You been drinkin', pretty thing like you?"

Faye, conscious that she was still, incredibly, not yet of age, shook her head. "Oh, no, sir. I got sleepy, late as it is, and I suppose I might have dozed off. I'm only going to Gabbro."

"Uh huh, figgered you got more crap to write, that it? How many fingers am I holdin' up?"

"Two."

He moved the fingers down where Fay had to lean out the window to see them. "Now how many?"

"Three."

"Very good. How many now?" He ran his fly open and released an erection.

"One finger, one … one thing that is not a finger." Faye's heart pounded, and she felt like she might throw up on the thing.

"You're a very smart little girl, darlin'. No wonder you write so big. Now pay attention, here comes the interesting part. You want to suck my finger, I'll let you off with a reckless endangerment citation, which would cost you twenty dollars an' license suspended for a week. Suck the other one, this whole thing never happened at all."

"What if I don't care to suck either one?"

"Drivin' under the influence of alcohol, failure to keep right, reckless endangerment, an' resisting an officer of the law.

Hunnerd-'n'-fifty to two-fifty, a full month suspension, court costs. I think your easiest way forward is pretty clear here, don't you?"

"Sure is. I wouldn't suck your dirty finger or your dirty little weenie for a million dollars, so write your damn ticket. Are we finished here?"

The deputy drew a revolver. "Not by a mile. Step out of the car, smart-mouth bitch."

Faye opened the door, heart pounding, and forced her trembling knees to lift her out. The warm night was filled with the cry of roadside bugs; the cop's uniform dark with sweat. She closed her eyes and tried to pray, but couldn't think whom to target. "Sir, please don't … "

"Shut up. Taller'n you look, settin in that Chivvy, ain't you? Bet you got legs'd stop traffic on Broadway. Lessee you walk them down that white line, both feet on it at all times. … Stop. Turn around, and back here to me, same way. … Uh huh. You flunk. Open your blouse and kneel down. Do it, right now." Revolver big as a steam engine, pointing at her heart.

Caring and rebellious. She knelt in the roadside gravel, not feeling the pain as it dug into her knees. It brought the deputy's hand to her eye level. It was dirty, all right, with a wedding ring half-embedded in the meaty fourth finger. She looked up into the congested face. *Maybe he'll have a heart attack.* "Sir. Do you have a daughter?"

"None of your goddamn business. Blouse down over your shoulders, and get busy."

"How old? Old enough to drive?"

Without answering, he jammed her face into his crotch. Faye screwed her eyes and mouth shut against the rank musk and fought to turn her head, gagging and praying to pass out.

"… Shit. Now look what you done, I lost it." The pressure on her head eased.

"Lost … ?" But it was clear, what was lost. The erection deflated, and Faye sat back while he turned away and zipped up, grim-faced. She lowered her head to the gravel. *Thank you, thank you, God in heaven, Ave Maria gratia plena, thank you.* Slowly, she stood, buttoning her blouse. The deputy's face was streaked with tears.

"Oh … How old was she?"

The deputy turned without answering and stalked back to his cruiser. When the door slammed, he looked back at Faye still standing by the Chevy, her hand trembling at the top button. "Twenty-six. Cancer. Fuck you for being alive, you little bitch."

12.

F AYE COLLAPSED INTO the driver's seat, crossed her arms over her chest, leaned her head on the steering wheel, and wept until she fled into sleep. That sanctuary held her until an early truck thundered past, a thump of dusty air in the open window. Her defensive reflex brought her elbow onto the horn button, loosing a bray from the front. She woke whimpering, fleeing a dream of plunging down a snowy hill, trying to steer from the rumble seat, screaming, no one there to hold her or keep her from falling. The sky in her windshield was streaked with gray.

She opened the door and leaned to retch in the damp and the bug-song, and pray that the Scotland County deputy had been one more in the string of nightmares that had dogged her since Gordon's death. Had she been smart enough to pull over and sleep when the Chevy started to wander? When she stood, papers fluttered from her lap. Her license and registration, and a citation for failure to keep right, with a fine of $5, payable at the Scotland County courthouse in Laurinburg before 30 days from date. And a ripped-out notebook page on which was scribbled, *"Amy Lee had your eye browse and black hair before it fell out. You are a lucky little bitch."*

*　　　　　*

"Anybody seen Faye?"

"She called in," Sharon hollered from the lobby. "She's in Laurinburg, and she'll be in before noon, she said."

"Huh. What's going on in Laurinburg?"

"She din' say."

"Tell her I need to see her, when she gets in."

Faye at that moment was on a folding chair outside the Scotland County clerk's office with the citation and five dollars cash in her hand. When the office opened, she paid the ticket, and asked a few questions that a county clerk might be able to answer, and in those days cheerfully would to any stranger. She visited a florist just opening, located St. Mary's, and went there to visit a grave.

The stone she found was carved in polished gabbro, the letters filled in gold, bright in a lance of early sun. Above the name and "Safe with Jesus," an etched barefoot angel who looked about ten years old. She laid the flowers against it and knelt - enduring the stab of pain and memory that brought up - and thought for some minutes about what the stone marked, covered, and was about. After a time, she folded her legs under and sat on the sandy ground, not speaking or praying or thinking at all, but picturing a woman who looked like her, and lived only five years longer. Seeing the trees that arched like the dome of heaven over the stone and the coffin, all in the embrace of a single holy ellipse.

In the church, she found a nickel in her purse and bought a candle for the altar.

"In profound gratitude for the life of Amy Lee Windell, 1920 - 1946," she whispered, when the priest asked. "Thank you."

*   *

"Yes?"

"Come in and shut the door."

Forde grimaced to signal his reluctance to say, "Faye, Sheriff Burns was in here with some disturbing allegations, last evening. I told him the whole thing sounded ridiculous an' unbelievable, but I guess I have to bring it up."

Faye blinked away tears and turned her back. "Is this about that Scotland County ticket I got? I paid it, and it was … He … I'm too upset and embarrassed to discuss it, even with you."

"I don't think Scotland County came into it, far as I know. But maybe, I guess. And I'm afraid I have to discuss it, being, as you noted the other day, your supervisor. So here it is. There was a complaint, you put on a lewd display in front of a minor."

"<u>Me</u>, lewd display? He was no minor anyhow."

"Robby Pardee is definitely a minor, and none too bright for that. Who's the "he" you're talking about?"

"Wait a second. Who's Robby Pardee?"

"Robby Pardee is the kid, was passing your apartment the other evening, you was standing in the window, naked. Or I guess pretty near."

Faye's jaw sagged, and she leaned against the door. After a time, she managed a laugh. "A very serious charge, that. You want to come with me, we'll make just a couple of stops, I think I can put your mind at ease."

At the Salonnette, Pearlene was finishing up a customer. When they had her in private, Faye asked, "What's the latest from the courthouse, Pearlene?"

Pearlene giggled. "Them goats was fit to be tied, what I hear. You are a mean one, Miss Bynum."

"Got that Forde? Some goats, fit to be tied at the courthouse. Thanks, Pearlene. See you Friday. Come on, Forde."

At the Woolworth apartment, Faye went through the thing, fully clothed. Forde had to laugh, red-faced and sweating in the heat. Faye lifted the shade to show him her message to the goats. "I meant to clean that off, but as you can see, you're not going to be able to read it without a telescope, or pretty good binoculars, anyhow. Might be just as well to leave it there, for future reference."

"Well." Forde let out a snort of glee, and had to stop and mop his brow. "OK, but what about Robby Pardee?"

"Was he over at the courthouse too?"

"Supposably, passing by on Church Street out there."

"I showed you how I was standing well inside, Forde. Believe me, I was very aware of not letting anybody down there see me. And then after Church Street, it's all trees until you get to the courthouse. I suppose he could have been climbing one of the trees in the square."

"Not from what came to me. Passing by on Church Street, he said."

"Who said, anyhow? Not young Pardee, I bet."

"No. One more thing, though, and I'm embarrassed as the dickens to ask. <u>Were</u> you naked at any point?"

"No. I was wearing panties and stockings and a towel. Want a demonstration?" *But don't think you're about to see the full effect.*

"Don't guess that'd be necessary. Thank you, Faye. You understand, I got a fairly formal complaint through Sheriff Burns, and I felt like - "

"I completely understand, Forde. I hope you understand how furious and embarrassed I was by the whole thing. And don't worry, the shade will stay down until I find another place to live. I don't care to put you in a position to answer for any more of my follies. Now, who do you suppose put the kid up to it?"

"When I find out, I'm going to wring their neck, and you can help. What was the business about Scotland County?"

"Well. I'm still very upset about it, but you are my supervisor, so I guess if you ask, I owe you an answer. I don't think there will be any repercussions, and I already told you, I paid the ticket. But look, I'm wringing with sweat, and so are you. Let's get out of this hotbox and down to the cool old *Intelligencer.* Or better yet, it must be almost lunch time. Can we talk privately at the Terminal?"

"Not a chance. What would you think of joining me at our little cabin?"

Faye led him out to the sweltering hallway and turned to lock the door. "Well, … I guess. I've never been to your cabin."

"Well, it's nice enough. and it's in a cool spot, up on the river. I stayed there last night, matter of fact, so there's lunch fixings. Do you have a bathing suit?"

"For lunch?" *Now what?*

"No, before lunch, to cool you off. I'd be inside, fixing sandwiches, and you could have all the privacy you wanted. Though not so much you wouldn't need something to wear."

"I don't have a suit, it just hasn't come up as the next thing for moving in. I guess I'm not much in a mood for swimming just now, between the courthouse goats and what happened this morning."

They started down the long stairs. Halfway down, she stopped. "Oh, but I'm so dirty and sweaty, and I can't face the thought of taking a bath where the goats had such a good time staring. Maybe I can pick up something downstairs. This will not set a precedent, Forde."

"Goodness. Of course not. Just, you looked like you needed a nice, private place to cool off. That's what I'm talking about."

The swimwear selection at Woolworth's wasn't wide, and Faye didn't want to hold up the works by going anywhere else. She picked a mostly daffodil-colored one-piece that was modest enough in front, though deeply scooped in back, for the purpose, Faye figured, of lying around and getting a tan. It was trimmed in black, which she thought might go well with her hair; and besides, it was one of only three suits on the "slender" rack, and the other two were a little more daring.

Forde got his first ride in the Chevy, and was diplomatically admiring. "Next right, then the second left." They were on the north side of Gabbro by now, far into cotton fields, scrub oak, and pine.

"Gosh, Forde, I had no idea you lived so far out."

"Well, I have a place in town where I <u>live</u> live, but this little cabin has been in the family for a long time. I go out there to sleep on hot nights sometimes, since I got the DeSoto; it's kind of peaceful. Right, here."

"That track? That's the driveway?"

"Have faith."

The track ran down hill, surprising Faye, who hadn't thought there was much up and down to the country around Gabbro. It got bumpy, and Faye slowed. "Good thing nobody's in the rumble seat. I think we might have launched them on that last root."

"OK, slow down a little. You could park down next to the steps."

"Oh, my gosh, Forde. This is just beautiful!"

It was. The track looped in front of a rustic-looking structure that seemed to consist largely of screened porches. A lawn of centipede grass sloped to a wide pond that was shaded by live oak and pine, and disappeared behind a peninsula of rock and rhododendron. Faye peered out the windshield and let the Chevy coast past the steps to where a swaybacked dock extended into the water. She got out and looked around at Carolina wetland charm on all sides.

"It's so much cooler than in town, isn't it? Is it the water? Why is the water so brown?"

"Tannin from pine needles. It's perfectly clean. Come on in and make yourself at home, and you can use the bedroom to change, if you decided you wonted to swim." They climbed the steps and entered a screened porch cluttered with inviting-looking cottage furniture. Folding chairs, wicker chaise, a swinging glider, and a coffee table that held a citronella candle and a couple of ancient mysteries.

"Or, if you wanted, they's a canoe under the porch, paddles on the wall there. The water's right cool, but not too cold to go in and enjoy it. It's called Morgan's Eddy. There was a Civil War battle here. Though more of a skirmish, I guess, when Sherman come through after he burned down Atlanta. S'posedly still got some bones down in the bottom, Confederate home guard. Bunch of twelve-year-olds from The Citadel, all changed to fossils by now. Pyrite, somebody said, that fished one out, which they never should of.

"Anyways, it's really just a wide place - more of a bulge, really - in the Gabbro River, If you saw it on a map, it looks like a snake that swallowed a basketball. The bulge was carved out by springs, that come all the way up from the coastal aquifer, and when you get near one of them, you feel it. If you look across to the other side, you can see how there's flow over there, a little strip of rock - gabbro, in fact - sticking up in the current. They's a popular swimming hole down below there, if you just let yourself float, you'd get there in ten minutes or so. But I'd be standing here waving a san'wich at you, so … "

Forde ran down, and Faye followed him into a country-cabin interior. Forde toured her around the limited spaces of the cottage - the kitchen, with Coleman stove, bottled-water dispenser, kerosene lamps and the (literal) icebox that served as utilities, the back door reached through a mud/utility room off the kitchen, the living room with its rustic furniture built of logs with the bark still on. A stone fireplace with a slab mantel held a pendulum clock that struck the hours and had been a wedding gift to his grandmother in 1858. And finally the bedroom, where she could change in private. She shut the bedroom door firmly, noting with approval that the bed was neatly made. Forde could not have anticipated this spontaneous event, could he?

The daffodil swimsuit was a hit with its wearer and with her viewership of one. The front was orthodox mid-Century modest, with only a hint toward the crotch-clingy styles to come, in the form of a scattering of small black triangles at the bottom; deniably referring to what lay beneath, if, shame on you, you wanted to see it that way. Sometimes, the suit appeared to say, a triangle is just a contrasting chromatic element. The whole thing was finished off with a two-inch ruffled skirt, reasserting the modesty theme. From the front, the black-trimmed yellow-gold fabric against her pale skin, her stylish little black hairdo, and her very dark eyes, were very appealing. But as Faye passed toward the screen porch and its steps to the yard, with the graceful walk that bare-footedness occasions in the slender, Forde was stunned to see that the suit had *no back to it whatsoever.*

Well, no, he saw. A very deep scoop, though, just about down to her hips. She had a handsome back, he thought, when he could think again. Smooth, straight, spinally grooved, and lightly muscular from exercises that were the inalterable duty of a St.

Anne's woman. Forde had not thought of backs as a point to be considered in assessing a woman's looks, but he was prepared now to rank all others somewhere below this one.

"That looks very nice on you. Don't forget to take a towel, here, let me find you a clean one, boy, guess that's why they call it a suit, 'cause it suits you … your … Here, no, take this one, kind of matches the suit, lunch will be ready in ten minutes or so, but don't hurry. The ladder on the dock is a little shaky, mostly we just jump off."

Faye gave him a preoccupied smile, and exited. And as he heard her tread on the steps, he whispered, "Jesus Lord an' Savior," knowing that sleep would come hard this night. It was during that night, and increasingly over the following weeks, that he identified exactly the moment: As she opened the screen door to the steps, and he saw in the slender back, in its grace and in the lift of her head in the face of whatever had happened last night that was bothering her so, that Faye Bynum was a brave and admirable woman, and that he, Forde Morgan, was in love with her, and would remain so to the end of his days. It was a case of a body - bone and muscle without the distractions of feminine ornamentation and those triangles - speaking the language of bone and muscle directly to another body. Or to a heart, if you prefer. It was a moment to which he would remain loyal through all that was to come.

With the clatter and splash of her dive from the rickety dock, he turned, bumped into a sofa that had been there for twenty years, and limped to the kitchen to collect lunch materials.

*   *

On the screen porch Faye, out of the daffodil sensation and clothed again, finished her pimento cheese and white-bread sandwich and the ice-melt from the last of her tea, took the towel from around her hair, and said, "I think I found one of the springs, felt like you were piping it in from the South Pole. I needed the cleaning-off as much as I needed the cooling-down, as you will now hear."

She stood and walked to the screen. When she spoke, it was outward, toward the river, as she combed tangles from her hair.

"OK, here's how I spent this morning, starting around midnight." She drew a breath and at first seemed unable to put it to use, shaking her head, sighing. But, haltingly and to a series of shocked monosyllables from Forde, she told the entire melancholy story of her late and sleepy drive from Charlotte to Gabbro, and of Deputy Windell, his cruelty and his daughter and his pain, and the humiliation, fear and pain he had inflicted on her; and what she had done to encompass it all in Catholic solace.

Forde rose and came to stand next to her, careful not to crowd. He too addressed the river. "Faye, you poor … oh, Jesus, Faye, I am so sorry that happened to you." Forde blushed at his drooling over the daffodil suit, at the impact of its wearer revealed not just as a pretty girl whose affections he coveted, but as an admirable person. Who was still talking:

"If not to me, to the next woman he stops at night, when there's no traffic around. It will probably go worse for her, given what happened with me. I got a strong feeling from … I'm almost certain he must have abused his daughter."

"I don't know the guy, but I have heard stories like this, and I was never able to believe that they were common occurrences. That next woman may have her own comforters." Forde drew a breath through clenched teeth. "I want to be yours, Faye. On behalf of the whole state of North Carolina, I apologize to you from the bottom of my heart."

"Well." Faye smiled minimally, blotting the tears that talking through it had brought out. "Thank you, Forde. I hope some day you will have the standing to apologize on behalf of all four million of us. When you're Governor, I guess. But what is it down here, men brutalize women who are just trying to get along, and then think they can apologize, and it's all done with?"

"Um. Well, I'm not sure there's that much 'down here' to it. Men, and specially cops, are often mean to women, specially pretty young women, all over the world, and much worse - Yes, I understand, it doesn't get a whole lot worse than what happened to you. If it had happened to me … " His voice wavered, because in fact, something quite a bit like it did happen to Forde at the hands of a senior basketball jock when he was in 7th grade. Not quite as full frontal, no deadly weapons involved, and quickly broken up by other senior jocks, but humiliating and scarring all the same. He gathered himself and went on.

"But sometimes it does get quite a bit worse than what he done. He could have really raped you. Hell, he could have killed you afterwards, so you wouldn't testify. Are you going to testify? Anyways, I apologized, but *I* didn't do the brutalizing."

Faye sighed, and flipped a hand. "No, I know you didn't, Forde. I guess I'm still mad about Custis, who has actually been a lamb since the big apology. And you're being your usual sweet self, as usual. As for testifying, filing a complaint, what do you think would happen? I'd be patronized and called 'little darlin' and ogled up and down, unless I showed up in a nun's habit. Asked if I wasn't teasing and tempting him beyond bearing, by the mere fact of being female and having breasts. I'm not sure there's even any good to talking about it, though once through it with a friend was certainly helpful. I will simply have to learn to be more careful."

Forde nodded, rattled by the mention of breasts, teetered on the edge, and then went ahead. "Well, being careful is never a bad idea. Maybe starting out to drive over a hundred miles that late was kind of risky. Had you been drinking, in fact?"

She lifted her chin to address the pines. "Are you going to ask me to walk a line, Forde? I'll tell you exactly where and with whom, which I suppose you have already figured out. I had dinner - Chinese - at a cheap place called China Clipper on Tryon Street, with Travis Wayland, my good and uncomplicated friend from WGAB, who bothers you so badly. Dinner included a glass and a half of Blue Nun, which I could not admit to the cop who was about to shove my face into his crotch, because I'm under-age, and it would have somehow given him high ground enough to feel justified about his disgusting deed. Travis is stuck in Charlotte for the week for the damn high school basketball tournament, and being a friend, I went to spend an evening with him. I guess if Gabbro wins, they'll bring their trophy back and put it on their goddamn brand-newly varnished floor. OK?"

She put her head against the screen and burst into tears. "I'm sorry, Forde," she wailed. "I'm sorry, it's not your doing, but surely you can see how terribly this has upset and hurt me. So please, please back off." Nose wiped on the soggy napkin. "Think about what kind of questions your supervisor-ship requires you to ask, and maybe what kind you might do better not to ask, please?"

She drew a shaky breath, took his hand and placed it on her cheek. "I like you very much, Forde. I <u>don't</u> like what this supervisor - employee business is doing to our friendship. I'd be a better friend for you if I worked for Travis and dated you on the side, wouldn't I?"

13.

I N APRIL, Faye's analysis and exposé of the racism and graft hidden in the school bond issue was addressed in three successive editions of the *Intelligencer*. On Monday, a front-page editorial written by Forde but protectively bylined "Editorial Staff, the *Intelligencer*," reviewed the basic dimensions of the bond issue: How big, what percent of the bonds had been sold (over 95% as of that date, and still rising), what the annual cost of servicing the bonds would be, and - unprecedented information - what portion of that annual cost would be borne by white, Negro, and Lumbee Indian taxpayers. (70, 20, and 10%, respectively). Bar graphs were employed.

Wednesday's editorial - written by Faye - described the benefits that would be made possible by the bonded debt. It was explicit about the lopsided budgeting toward white schools, and among those, toward Gabbro High School, relative to the total (subdivided by school) going to the junior highs and the grade schools. The textbook pass-down was described, with photos of the new books and the wretched castoffs. Bar graphs once again, this time with benefits broken down by race, and compared side by side with Monday's graphs showing costs.

Friday's paper - selling out an extra-large press run - contained a "Staff" editorial written by Faye, describing the mismatch between the claimed and budgeted costs, and actual quotes for comparable work and assets that she had obtained; and calling for an outside audit - this having been the subject of intense wrangle among Faye, Forde, and Custis, carried out in the privacy of the river cottage. Custis had been dead against it, pressing Forde and Faye to take into account that "we all got to live together in this little town;" but in the end out-argued by Faye and overruled by Forde. He took it well enough, but Faye could see that it grated on him.

Finally, there was an "Our Town's Times" op-ed, signed by Faye, summarizing:

... Thus, in the first place, 100% of the benefits of the bond issue will go to white schools, with the lion's share of that going to Gabbro High; this in spite of the fact that between them, Negro and Indian taxpayers, many of whom contributed mightily to victory in the recent War and who pay taxes in proportion to their share of Gabbro County's wealth, bear nearly a third of the cost of issuing the bonds. It is true that a wholly false and arrogant case can be made that the Negro schools, by getting textbooks that until this year were good enough for the white schools, are benefiting in some measure. I have heard opinion by Gabbro citizens that even that pathetic gesture is more than good policy would grant. Let that go for now - though thinking about how you would feel if it were your child getting the worn-out books might help understand what is wrong with it; but families using the Indian schools - which in fact, do not even include a high school - get nothing at all for their 10% of the cost, since the Negro schools have nothing at all of value to pass on to them. We could have used a bar graph to illustrate this injustice, but the bar representing benefits to Indian taxpayers would have been invisible.

Second, it seems to The *Intelligencer* very curious that a newspaper staffer who holds no academic job title could get better prices for everything - by make and model - included in the bond issue but the textbooks, with a simple, un-accredited, cold phone call. Did Superintendent Mack's staff ask for competitive bids for the microscopes, supplies and labor involved in upgrading the science labs and the gymnasium? Or are they - and thus we - being robbed blind by the companies supplying the goods and services listed in Monday's paper?

Or, finally, is there something even more unsavory going on? As the reader can see by reading today's staff editorial, The *Intelligencer* calls for an independent audit of the entire project by a respected, outside party. It should be done before another expensive and hard-earned tax dollar is spent.

- M. Faye Bynum, City Editor

*　　　　　*

"My stars, Faye, you done put your foot in a cowpie this time." Pearlene seemed not at all alarmed at the thought, serene as she clipped. "You know, some a them same goats you done irritated back in March with your winda shade, is the same ones gonna be in there with you. Minor Mack for one."

"He was in the herd? I am not at all surprised. I hope he darn near had apoplexy, the old crook ... Well. He will be in a different cowpie than me, and a worse one, I think."

Ginny Freeman chipped in. "They are all much the same, in my experience. But speaking of bullshit, I have done a little research on something you asked me about back in March."

"Really? Ah, the leisurely pace of life in the Southland."

"Don't be smart with me, young lady. It required establishing a relationship with some ladies at the Kut-Kwik in

Laurinburg. Plus, I could give you lessons in asking indirect questions without going all around the barn like you done.."

"Sounds great. I could pay by giving you lessons in coming right out with things."

"Ha ha. See where that gets you. No, it's about Mr. Deputy Miles Windell of Scotland County."

The Salonnette grew silent. Scissors stopped snipping, and a hair dryer shut down. Faye felt a tickle, and not a pleasant one, to have the trauma resurrected. "Well, go ahead, though I am trying to put that whole ugly thing behind me."

Faye had, of course, resorted to the comforting of the Salonnette soon after her encounter with Deputy Windell; the ladies had come through handsomely, but only with general emotional support and the re-telling of similar things that had happened to them, or to women whom women they knew, knew. No one had ever heard of a Deputy Windell.

"Uh huh. And I'm not sure if this will be very helpful, Faye, honey. Anyways, seems like Deputy Windell was a hard case World War I veteran the Scotland County sheriff hired when they were going through some kind of crime spree after the war. Runaway littering on South Main, I suppose. He established a reputation as a go-getter, regard to speeders and drunk drivers. He met himself a Laurinburg girl name of Louise, and married her. They stayed married long enough to have one child, a little cutie named Amy Lee, which I think you already know about."

"I do." *The trees, the black stone, the coffin.*

"Well, Windell doted on her, and then some, all the more, the more she grew from a cute little tot into a pretty young thing of twelve or so. When it turned ugly, know what I mean, Louise booted him out the door and moved to Greenly. And took Amy Lee with her."

"Where is Greenly?"

"Oh, it's this little town, the far end of Scotland County, half the folks are named Greenly, and they marry each other like half-wits. Anyways, it was close enough by, that Miles Windell could still see Amy Lee. He'd run his County cruiser through

Greenly in the line of duty, swing by Louise's, just to get a look at Amy Lee if she was playing outdoors. If she was, he would invite her to sit in the car for spells that finally got long enough to drive downtown and get ice cream. Louise got a court order against it, which was a mistake, because, first of all, who was supposed to enforce court orders but the sheriff's office? And then he got a counter-order for visiting rights. Under supervision, for what that's worth. He'd used to take her and the social worker, was supposed to supervise the visit, fishing back in Gum Swamp, hours on end. Turns out the social worker had a bottle problem, which Miles would solve for him in exchange for a little privacy and a clean report. Louise wasn't fooled, the way Amy Lee kep' coming home a little mussed up, and eventually, she resorted to tucking little tell-tale things, like a flower petal, into Amy Lee's panties, which would come back moved, or missing. But in those days, you about had to catch a man with his dick in the wrong drawers, 'scuse my frankness, before a cop or a court would listen to a complaint either from a girl or her mother.

"Whatever, things went along like that for some few years, and Amy Lee grew up and got boy friends, which seemed to cool off the Pop romance. She eventually got married, which seems to me like a miracle, but again, in those days, it was the expected thing. Not that different now, matter of that. When are we gonna hear them orange blossoms ringin' for you and Travis Wayland? Or should I be asking about young Morgan?"

"Not on my to-do list for this year. I suppose in due course, something may eventuate. I promise, you ladies will be the very first to know, which is always the case anyhow, so what am I saying?"

"Uh huh. So in the eventual due course of things, Amy Lee had a little boy, but she never recovered too good from the labor, which was so hard they finally went in and done a Caesarian on her. While they were in there, they noticed a tumor on her ovary, and took the whole works out, but too late. She went through chemo and lost her hair, like you mentioned, but she was dead in six months. Louise was completely busted up about it, and she blamed Miles and his long history of fooling with Amy Lee. *In public, out loud*, right in the middle of the funeral. Seems to've been a world record ugly scene." Ginny, an appreciator of ugly scenes, smiled a little at the thought, like a Yankees fan contemplating Joe DiMaggio's 56-game hitting streak.

"Ever since, nobody in Scotland County hardly even mentions the name of Miles Windell. You don't cross him if you want a peaceful life. You got stopped by him and you got away more or less intact, you are one lucky little girl."

"Yes," Faye said. "He told me that too, though he didn't call me 'girl.' Why don't they get rid of him?"

*   *

(Marching music, fading) "And, welcome back to this edition of 'Gabbro Voices,' where we will be chatting with schools Superintendent Minor Mack, Gabbro High Principal Anson Evans, Douglass High Principal Abe Cousins, and the Managing Editor of the Gabbro *Intelligencer*, Forde Morgan. Welcome all, gentlemen."

Mack: "Wait a minute. Nobody told me we'd be setting here with a Nigra principal. That was definitely not -_"

Wayland: "Well Mr. Mack, Mr. Cousins is one of - "

(Crosstalk)

Evans: " … neither. You are of course within your rights to interview 'Principal' Cousins, but … "

(Crosstalk, followed by a slamming door.)

(Marching music)

Wayland: "Forde, I guess we are left with you and Mr. Cousins. So let's see if among us, we can put together some dialogue on a topic that has turned this town upside-out and inside-down.

Morgan: Fine with me.

Cousins: I got nothing else on my calendar for this morning. Let's talk.

Wayland: Very good. Let me begin with you, Mr. Cousins. First of all, I believe you are owed an apology for what just took place here in the studio. WGAB regrets very much that your Superintendent was not willing to share a round table with you.

Cousins: Think nothing of it. It's the first time I have been in the same room with Mr. Mack since I had my interview, and I suppose he was unnerved by the experience.

Wayland: … Very well. Let's get down to business. You doubtless read the three-part review of the bond issue in last week's *Intelligencer.*

Cousins: I did indeed. I was surprised and rather amused.

Wayland: Amused?

Cousins: Yes. It is amusing that our newspaper thinks it is news to point out that the white schools are superior to the colored schools, because infinitely greater resources are showered upon them. Everyone knows that. Now, I was surprised that it was actually mentioned in a public place.

Wayland: Forde? Old news is no news?

Morgan: Mr. Cousins has hit it. What's news about it is that this is the first time that the policy of budget discrimination has been pointed out in any public medium in Gabbro. Or, as far as I know, any other one in North Carolina. The law of the land states, children are to be educated in 'Separate but equal' schools. The *Intelligencer* is proud to be the first public medium in the state to point out that we are flouting that law 'across the board' to use a phrase dear to our Superintendent. The first step in addressing any problem is to recognize it for what it is."

Wayland: Isn't it true, Forde, and Mr. Cousins, that to offer truly equal education would finally involve integrating the races in the schools? Is that what the *Intelligencer* is advocating?"

Morgan: I believe our City Editor Miss Bynum addressed that question very thoroughly when you interviewed her on the air. The *Intelligencer* is taking no position on any question of school integration. We are simply pointing out that Gabbro schools, like nearly all others state-wide, are in violation of the plain meaning of the law of the land, in that they are unequal. And that the way the proceeds of the latest bond issue are being spent has made that inequality deeper an' more obvious than ever.

Wayland: Mr. Cousins?

Cousins: Please call me Abe, Mr. Wayland. Mr. Morgan has admirably summed up the tension between what is ideal, or desirable, and what is real. You must understand, sir, that for a colored person to question or attempt to eradicate that tension, was tantamount to a death sentence not so long ago in this state. You will excuse me from addressing that particular issue, in that I have plans and hopes for a long life yet before me.

(Silence)

Wayland: We'll be opening the phone lines after these announcements.

14.

F ROM THE GABBRO *INTELLIGENCER* for Wednesday, May 19, 1948:

INTELLIGENCER FOUNDER MORGAN PASSES

Custis Benajah Morgan, founder and long-time managing editor of this newspaper, has joined the immortals.

Mr. Morgan's son and present managing editor Forde H. Morgan found Mr. Custis Morgan dead at his desk in the early hours of yesterday, May 18. The exact time and cause of death has not been established as of the deadline for this edition of the *Intelligencer.*

Mr. Morgan founded the *Intelligencer* in 1898 "on a nickel and some high hopes," as he loved to say, using borrowed and mortgaged press equipment, to serve the infant community of cotton and tobacco farmers primarily at first as a market and exchange bulletin, in the hope of giving Gabbro County farmers a competitive information edge over rivals from other regions - and over those who chose not to subscribe. Under Custis Morgan's strong and steady hand, it grew to be a general-purpose newspaper, but kept the name and the mission of giving its readers an advantage in the form of information not known to others.

"Ol' Custis, my stars," mourned longtime associate Anson Evans, Gabbro High School Principal. Why, he's been essential to Gabbro for almost half a century ... "

Faye Bynum arrived at the *Intelligencer* late on that morning of Tuesday, May 18th after spending over an hour in conversation with the principal of Crispus Attucks (colored) Junior High School, to find the front door locked, and a shade drawn on which was lettered "CLOSED." Such a thing had not occurred in the half-year she had been there, including over the Christmas and New Year's holidays. She rapped, and an answering silence was broken at length by sharp footsteps and the voice of Sharon. "We're closed. Come by tomorrow."

"Sharon, it's me … Faye."

The door opened and Sharon stood in the doorway. "Din't he given you a key?"

"Yes, he did. I carried it with me on a key ring until last month, and never had to use it. I think it's still sitting on my dresser. What's happening? Why are we locked up like this?"

"Mist' Morgan done passed. Best you carry the key anyways."

Sharon had been a little short with Faye after the false cancer alarm had been explained, and apologized for by Faye in a staff meeting. Sharon's response had been as cool as her initial, wet-eyed reaction had been warmly dramatic, and Faye figured that Sharon had felt a little cheated by the deflation. Now, Faye felt a pang of shock.

"Forde?"

"Course not. Old Mr. Morgan. Mr. Custis."

"Oh, thank God. I mean, poor Forde. And poor Custis. What happened?"

It seemed unlikely to the point of absurdity that Custis could have died; he had appeared to Faye to be a permanent immortal old man, his spotted hands eternally poised to grab her somewhere; never more than when she had stood up to oppose his stubborn, casual racism, while he chuckled fondly, his eyes always on her butt, her legs, or her breasts. She had even had passing moments when it seemed almost endearing in him, that eternal innocent assumption that any kind of unilateral intimacy would always be welcome, in preference to Yankee-style formality. The racism, the assumption that women were put in the world to be looked at, handled, and disregarded as soon as they opened their mouths - less endearing by far. He alternately amused and infuriated Faye, and she was shocked now at her grief that he would be there to infuriate her no longer.

"I am sure that it would not be my place to discuss Mr. Custis Morgan's passing on in any detail. Perhaps you could discuss it with Mr. Forde."

"Of course. Thank you, Sharon."

"Pleased, I'm sure."

"I found him here first thing this morning, just setting at my desk."

Custis had been provided a desk at the end of a hallway that was converted to an office-like space. But he continued to show no inclination to stop showing up and inserting himself in editorial conferences; always eventually deferring to Forde's point of view, always with the same speech about not being one of these old geezers that has a problem letting go of his alleged power. Faye had never seen Custis use his pseudo-office. He preferred either to stand overseeing one thing or another, or sitting in Forde's office or Faye's alcove, on one of the new visitor chairs.

"He looked like he'd dozed off, setting there. But when I joggled him to wake him up ... " Forde shuddered. He looked dazed, and seemed to have been standing just inside the door of his office for some time, reluctant to sit where Custis had sat to die.

"Oh, Forde, how awful for you. Did he ... I mean, was he ... I don't know how to ask this. What was it?"

"No telling. Well, course, I expect we'll hear some time today or tomorrow. He didn't look ... you know. Injured. He was just sitting there, cold." Forde covered his eyes and shuddered again. "Probably a heart attack, I suppose. Or a stroke. Sudden unexplained death always calls for an autopsy." He sounded like he was quoting from a rulebook.

"Of course. Oh, poor Forde. Just that, that has to be hard." In fact, Faye was mildly surprised to hear of this relatively progressive policy in Gabbro.

"Uh huh. It's a North Carolina law. I'm OK with it. I want to know what took Pop away, of course. I just don't like to think about him being cut up like that."

"Of course. Then don't think about it, I'd say. Will you be taking some time off?"

"Well … That would present a problem, given that we got to keep putting out a paper. Fact, we're late getting tomorrow's paper started, everybody's just standing around, waiting for somebody to give orders."

"Look, I have gone through this. You are going to have to be available for the … for whatever needs done in regard to Custis. Depending on the autopsy, there could be Sheriff Burns to deal with. Funeral stuff, in any case. We'll need a really good obit, and that's on you, too. Will you let me take over getting the paper out? I think I've watched you doing it enough that I can take most of it off of you for the rest of the week. And if I mess it up, probably the press guys or somebody can help out."

"If everybody just does their job, it should go along fine. I will lay out the front page, I'm sure I can get that done before I need to pay attention to, you know." He sighed. "To arrangements. Thank you, Faye. You are a … Well."

From the *Intelligencer* for Friday, May 21:

Rites Set for Custis Morgan

Funeral services for Custis Morgan, who passed away unexpectedly overnight on May 17 - 18 will be held at Gabbro Baptist Assembly, Church Street, on Wednesday afternoon, May 26, at 2:00 PM. Services will be provided by Wegeman's Furniture and Undertaking Establishment …

*   *

Laudanum overdose. Mooted by the finding of a small bottle with residue under Forde's desk, and confirmed by autopsy. The words circled behind Faye's reverently closed eyes while the closing benedictory prayer soared aloft from the pulpit. *Tedium laudanum.* ... "In the name of him who came to promise eter-rnal life, A-men."

So Custis apparently had done away with himself, and though Faye doubted it was her place to wonder why, she could hardly think of anything else. She had asked Forde, gently enough, she thought, if Custis had been either ill or depressed, and Forde brushed off the question. Well, she thought, it was bound to be whispered among the *Intelligencer* staff, if not by the public at large. She looked forward to her next appointment at the Salonnette, in two days, and started practicing indirect ways to ask the ladies what they thought had been bothering Custis, before she realized that they would certainly broach the subject in their own expert way before she had a chance to open her mouth.

She stood to file out with the rest of the mourning congregation. *Audience, more like.* The service had been an endless celebration of a leading Gabbro light, a man without whom Gabbro would not have amounted to a very small hill of beans, the enlightener and "intelligencer" of a marginal farm community that had flourished around its minor stone quarry under his guidance; a very funny guy, a sport, a family man who left a fine young son to carry on his life's work, and so forth for two solid hours, not even counting the no-verse-omitted hymns that had been favorites of his, the no-detail-omitted prayers for the rest of his soul, the soprano soloing a wobbly boil-down of "Abide With Me," and the 9-year-old violin student playing "Jesus Loves Me," all carried out at a temperature of 90 and humidity that started there and climbed with every tear and drop of sweat that forced its way into a blanket of atmosphere that comforted and smothered the afflicted. Fans wagged hard, alternately advertising Perpetual

Care, and bedroom suites available through Wegeman's; stirring the air but powerless to cool it.

On the front stoop of the Baptist Assembly, Faye encountered Forde Morgan, shaking hands with men and getting kissed by ladies, and two steps down from him, Peter Maribel the photographer, and Travis Wayland murmuring into a microphone like a golf commentator. She shook hands with and kissed Forde, winked at Travis, and went her way, enjoying the relatively cool, relatively dry air. Before she had gone a half block toward the *Intelligencer* office, Travis was alongside. Faye turned to him, trying not to look eager.

"What, you not going to the reception and committal, doing a play-by-play?"

"I am, I got to, this is the biggest news since y'all's fire-bomb. I just wanted to catch up with you for two seconds, got PSA's running for the next minute and a half."

"Well, how've you been, Travis? Seems like I seen a little less of you, last couple of weeks."

"Uh huh, and that's what I wonted to discuss, real quick here. You like to hike, get up in the mountains some?"

"You know I do, didn't last Christmas convince you?"

"OK, but that was winter and snow, all that. I meant, cover some serious ground. What do you get for vacation?"

"My vacation time kicks in after nine months. That would be September the first. Up to then, I pretty much get Sundays off, and an hour here and there. You thinking about more than that?"

Travis looked dashed. "Well, I was, yes. Well, how about dinner in Raleigh next Sunday, then? At the Sir Walter."

"Sounds like almost more fun than I can stand. Tell me just a little about this hike. You meant go out in the woods and share a tent? Couldn't that lead to complications?"

"We could take two tents, I guess. Thing is - "

"Tents are heavy. Even one, we'd have to share the load."

"I'd be OK with that, if you would."

"I would have to think about it, and discuss some aspects of it with you. But still, I thought you'd never ask, Travis."

Travis blinked. "I got to go, they're pulling up the hearse. We'll talk about it over dinner."

"Call me, we'll make some kind of silly plan for leaving separately, so we don't give the Salonnette crowd hysterics."

*   *

"Lean back here, Hon, you gonna run this rinse right down the back of your neck, you don't watch out."

Faye leaned back. "Wait just a second here, Ginny. Mr. Morgan's death is a private and sensitive matter, as I'm sure you can understand, and there are feelings involved. It would not behoove me *What would it feel like to be behooved?* in the slightest - or ill, I guess - for me to discuss it before I know what y'all ladies already know about it." *I'm getting better at Salonnette dialog.*

"I don't know why you'd say a thing like that. All we know is what's in the *Intelligencer*, am I right, ladies?"

"Huh. How 'bout it, Mary-Deane?"

"Well, Honey, what sort of 'feelings' could be involved if the man had a perfectly straightforward heart attack? He was well up in his 70's, I believe. You got to expect a certain tendency."

"There was an autopsy, of course. Any time you have a sudden, unexplained death ... "

"Yes, yes. And of course the results of autopsies are confidential, and all."

"Yes, they are."

"So was it a heart attack?"

Faye sighed. "Now I see why y'all don't ask direct questions. I am simply not at liberty to discuss what the cause of death was. Might have been."

Ginnie Freeman smirked. "Don't need to, Hon. They's a pretty strong current of feeling hereabouts that there's more to it than a simple heart attack."

"Well, there you go. The wisdom of the community, never been wrong that I ever heard of. Mary-Deane, I believe we were going to have a discussion about real estate. I am like to perish in that garret over Woolworth's. Don't you have something a person could live in that's not an Indian sweat lodge?"

"Well, Hon, 'course you got that shade in place, cuts down the breeze, I expect."

Ginnie guffawed. "Ain't all it cuts down. You look along Church, South Main any more, it's full of pillars headin' home ever' evening dinner-time, like lambs."

"Of course, I will always regret being the one who spoiled any fun aspect of living in Gabbro, where fun can be like rain in the desert. Thing is, this fun was kind of one-sided. Except that last time. Too bad young Pardee got his eyeballs caught in the wringer."

"Well, he never done, of course. I give you credit, young Faye, for checking sight lines before you put on your little show."

"Oh, I did. If Robby Pardee saw anything at all, he was up there in the top floor of the courthouse, taking his turn at the telescope. And if so, had it coming. What's the likelihood?"

"Put up to it by somebody, likely his Uncle Anson. That's why you never heard another peep about it."

Faye recognized this as Mary-Deane's way of asking if in fact she had heard another peep. She didn't see why she couldn't oblige a bit, after stone-walling on Custis' autopsy. "Sheriff Burns did come to Forde with the complaint. Forde stiff-armed him on my behalf, for which I am thankful. I took Forde up and showed him - fully dressed - what I had done. I was glad to get the air cleared on that. What's that Bible story about elders peeping at a young thing?"

Silence. "You thinking of David an' Bathsheba?"

"No, there was a story about a couple of old goats ... wait a minute ... happened around dinner time, matter of fact, I remember that. Come on, surely you remember that? Wait, Susannah was her name. It's in the Book of Daniel, one of the sexy parts the sisters used to hurry us over - "

"Nuns?" Ginny sounded scandalized. "Honey, are you <u>Catholic</u>?"

Morgan's Eddy

Uh oh. "I was educated in a Catholic high school, that's right. The teachers were all nuns. Teaching Sisters, strictly speaking, of the Luminous - "

"But are <u>you</u> a Catholic? Is that where you getting all these ideas about the schools?"

"Well." Faye took a breath, praying for calm. "I hardly go to any church any more. My folks put me in a Catholic high school because my mother was Catholic, and my father didn't care one way or the other. One of the things I learned from the Sisters is that everyone - and I don't remember their saying anything about skin color on this - everyone is infinitely precious to God. Are we still on common ground here?"

Silence, and then Pearlene put down her scissors. "Set up here, Hon. I do believe that. I can't feel close to God, if He's gonna be no better than some ignorant sand farmer about loving us all the same."

"Huh," Faye said. "Good way to put it. Well, if all people are so very valuable, I just think it would be kind of cooperating in that, to give every kid the best chance we can to make something of themselves. That would involve giving every kid the best education we can. That's all."

"Well. I am going to have to think some about that notion. <u>Nigra</u> children? Are you sure?"

"Mary-Deane, I am not sure about one thing, except what the Sisters <u>didn't</u> say. And about roasting to death. Here we're getting into June next week, and it's just going to turn into the Amazon River up there over Woolworth's. Don't you have something that isn't up under a roof somewhere?"

"Honey, I have looked, and found nothing, and kept an eye out for you since you first brought it up. There's a handful of apartments open, and they are either a place I wouldn't put my worst enemy into, or they are just like what you got, second floor walk-up in a two-story building. And one of those is over Randy's Garage, they drop tools on the concrete floor all night, and cuss like longshoremen. Believe me, I'm aware of your needs an' hopes, and I am looking out for you as if you were my own

130

daughter. When I find what I think you would even half-way consider, I will drop everything and <u>run</u> over to th' *Intelligencer* to tell you about it."

*   *

On Sunday the 30th, Faye pulled the Chevy onto the apron of Northside Texaco, where Travis Wayland leaned on the fender of his Studebaker, chatting with Merlin, the Sunday pump jockey. When she had locked the Chevy and transferred herself and a pair of Sunday-dining pumps into the Studebaker, she slumped low in the seat to change shoes and evade Merlin's incurious glance.

"Darn it. I didn't think there'd be anybody here on Sunday. There goes our discreet exit from Gabbro. Aren't things supposed to be closed on Sundays?"

"No worry," Travis said, checking nonexistent traffic and pulling out. "First of all, Merlin only works Sunday afternoons, and spends the rest of the week drinking up what he just earned, not gossiping. Though of course your Salonnetters are missing a heck of a source, if they only knew it. Second place, that's right, we're mostly all locked up, so God-fearing Baptists, including the Salonnette bunch, are still in church, crankin' out the third or fourth of their Seven-fold Amens. They get their tanks filled during the week. And racists won't come here anyways, 'cause Merlin appears a little tan to be a real half-white, half-Lumbee like he claims, so his touch on the gas nozzle would be a form of race-mixing that would probably make their Packards run rough. It's practically a state secret, you and me slippin' out of town like this to break bread."

Faye laughed, and tried to put a little growl into it. "What could go wrong, then? And anyhow, whose business is it in the first place?" She had not seen Travis, except for the hasty conversation at Custis' funeral, for more than a week, and she realized now that she missed his glib chatter when it wasn't there to be deplored.

"A question never asked in Gabbro. We all expect to be fully Intelligenced on everything that goes on. And speaking of that, mademoiselle, what can you tell me about <u>why</u> Custis would drink a dose of laudanum big enough to kill a horse?"

"I can't - wait a minute. Who told you he did?"

"I protect my sources; it was Doc Everly."

"Good job. Who's he?"

"The Medical Examiner. Easy to remember, isn't it? The ME is Ever-lee."

"Isn't he supposed to keep that kind of thing confidential?"

"Sure. As it happens, I have bailed him out a few times on matters involving press access to his state accreditation, and this was the thing I chose to cash in on. Metaphorically. No actual cash changed hands. And anyhow, aren't you and I rather good friends?"

"Yes, we are, very good, I think. Does that mean we have no secrets from each other?"

Travis watched the highway for a moment. "That would depend, I guess, on whether the alleged secret would complicate or un-complicate our friendship."

"Oh, God, Travis. That keeps kind of … going in and out of focus. I <u>mean</u>, it … "

"I know what you mean. So, have you thought about it?"

"About Custis? Practically nothing else. Forde says he wasn't depressed, and wasn't sick, that he knew of. Well, I should say, when I asked him about it, he waved it away, like not worth thinking about."

"Hm. What about you? If you think back to the last few days he was around, what do you think of?"

"I … are you interviewing me for later use, or are we just conversing off the record?"

"I thought we had that conversation last Christmas, when you went through your recent history. Certainly not. I suppose we might or might not have secrets <u>from</u> each other, but in regard to the rest of the world, we are completely confidential <u>about</u> each other."

"Well, that's rather neatly said."

"As in, not spontaneous? Guilty. I have been thinking about it, and I have decided that, besides sex, the next surest road to complication would be for us to discuss each other to third parties … other people. I then spent some time, yes, thinking of how to phrase it, since that's what I do for a living. It kind of comes naturally."

"It's what I do, too, but I don't have to be as fast about it as you. Anyway, I completely agree. Good thinking. As a matter of fact, I have been asked to describe our relationship by just two people in the last six months, Forde and the Salonnette bunch. Counting them as one, because whatever one of them knows, they all know."

"And … ?"

"And? Oh. I clammed up completely."

"Good. 'Course, that's telling them everything, just by itself."

"I know. But I just always say the same thing. 'Travis is simply a friend, with no complications,' and they laugh. Sometimes I think a little addendum, but I never say it."

"Addendum."

"Yes. Usually, it's *Why can't you get that through your thick head?* but once it was *That I might have slept with last night.* That was after the Mateus fiasco."

"Good choice of words. Did you know that 'fiasco' is Italian for a wine flask?"

"God, you do know an <u>awful</u> lot about an awful lot of things."

"Comes of doing my homework, instead of trying to charm ladies."

She patted his thigh. "God, you know nothing at all."

After a humming silence a few miles long, Faye sighed, and said, "Anyway, about Custis. The last time I saw him to actually talk to, was a debate we had about calling for an independent audit of the school bond issue. He was against it, I was for it, and Forde eventually came over to my side. When he did, Custis looked kind of disgruntled, but in the end, he went along with Forde, which he always does. Did. He was very good about that, right up to the last. He never looked sick, or anything, that I could tell, but I wasn't giving him particular scrutiny. And anyway, after that conference about the audit, he got a good deal scarcer, seems like. Hm."

"And that conference would have been? Around the middle of April, right?"

"Good for you. The whole series ran on April 12, 14, and 16. So the conference was the previous Friday. The, uh, the 9th."

"A month and a bit before he died."

"Yes. What are you thinking?"

"I don't know. And you didn't see much of him during that month, after the bond issue series?"

"N..no, Not that he disappeared. He just wasn't around as much. He used to come in almost every day, and then it was scarce enough to notice, thinking back, but not so scarce that it occurred to me to ask Forde about it, for example."

"Can you think of an actual time, what he was like when he did come in?"

"Not a specific date, no. He was ... he seemed quiet, I guess, for him. Usually, he was always in and out of my space talking about stuff around town so he could stand next to me, check down my blouse for cleavage."

"It required regular checks?"

"Something did."

"Well ... can't say that sounds suspicious. But then it dropped off?"

"Definitely. And when he was in, he like to never gave me a glance, never checked my ass or anything."

Travis snorted. "You swear like a navvy."

"Well, I thought that was all the vocabulary men had about ladies' behinders. I was trying to make myself understood. What's a navvy?"

"You succeeded. A sailor, I think. So taking that into account, would you go so far as to say that Custis was depressed?"

"Or maybe scared. Like all of a sudden my behind was not so important any more."

"Your … ? Oh, your ass? Huh. On that grounds, we can't even rule out sick. Anyway, something was bothering him, sounds like."

At the Sir Walter dining room, Faye and Travis ate economically, and danced a couple of numbers, as much not to waste Faye's bringing dancing shoes as anything, though Faye was glad to confirm her Christmas-party observation that Travis was a good dancer. The Custis conundrum and another unspoken matter kept them silent on the dance floor, until Faye could stand it no longer. Under the influence of a not-half-bad, Benny Goodman-ish orchestra of keyboards and reeds, she whispered, "Travis, we said we have a matter to discuss."

"Yes?"

"Tents."

"Ah."

"I told you I was going to have to think about the whole matter of one tent, or two. I have done so, mostly while out of range of your ladies-charming manner. Nevertheless, I have to say, I have been charmed. So here is my thought-through position in regard to tents: I would be OK to share one with you, whatever complications that might lead to."

Faye felt an immediate twitch against her tummy, which pleased her. *I am a loose, loose woman. I am so loose, I'm floppy. And glad of it.* She let her fingers play with the curls on his neck.

Travis pulled her closer. "Talk about 'neatly said.' Have you been thinking that through, in your slow, print-medium way?"

"Yes, I have. That is what I came to, word for word. The nice thing about print media is that you can go back and read something again, if you're not sure you got it all the first time. Would you like me to say it again?"

"Not necessary. Us mercurial radio types are trained to catch things as they happen. 'Live,' we call it. Want a demonstration?"

"Well … OK, go ahead."

"You said, *'Here is my thought-through position in regard to tents: I would be glad to share one with you, whatever complications that might lead to.'* How'd I do?"

"I didn't say 'glad.' "

"No, you said 'OK.' I guess you will have to chalk the 'glad' up to hopeful hearing. Or wooing, looking at it another way."

"I always thought 'wooing' was a silly word that does no justice. But it does please me to think that you and I were thinking carefully about each other, during that rather long separation, when I didn't see you for days."

"That's neatly said too, even though I suppose you have not been pondering it for more than a minute or so. The blink of an eye, for print media folks. Still, though, we have this problem about your vacation time. Lack of."

"I am capable of quick thinking when needed, and here's another piece: The Woolworth Arms is getting just completely unbearable, now that we're into summer. I am going to put a classified in the *Intelligencer* looking for a decent, cool, private place I can move into before the real heat comes. I don't care if it's way out in the country, or in middle of the Baptist cemetery. If it is cool enough and private enough, we could put a tent in the back yard on Sunday afternoons."

They danced on for a thoughtful few minutes, and the appeal of that idea became so evident that Faye did not dare jostle him too urgently. But she could not resist murmuring, straight into his ear, "Or, hell, we could just skip the tent."

15.

PROFESSIONAL WOMAN seeks affordable, private, 1-BR lodgings to rent for indefinite time. Furnished desirable, but not required. Box 141, the *Intelligencer*.

"What's Box 141? We don't have boxes here."

"I know that, Forde. It's just my sneaky way of not putting my name on it for all the world to see."

"Cute. 'Course, all the world will figure it out anyway, in about two seconds. You could count the number of other professional women in Gabbro on one hand. Well, there is that new vet, moved in last year. You and her, couple of grade-school principals, I think that's about it."

"If she gets her hair done at Salonnette, they'll know it isn't her. And besides, Mary-Deane Gaines already knows I'm looking. I hope she doesn't get her nose out of joint, I'm going around her like this."

"Well, see, I'm not sure you have to. With Pop passed, I have to get where he was, which is our old family place, fixed up, to sell or keep, I'm not sure which. I'm living there full time, so I'm never out at the cottage. Would you want to rent that for a few months, till Mary-Deane finds you something more permanent?"

"That beautiful place where we had lunch? Oh, my gosh, Forde, I'd love it! Except … "

"What?"

"Well, I could never afford it, a nice place like that."

"Pooh. Right now, it's bringing in nothing. I ought to pay you to house-sit it. Tell you what, let's split the difference, and say nothing a month."

"Oh, no, uh uh. Think about what folks'd think about that; first you hire in your floozy friend, and then you put her up in a beautiful cottage out in the woods."

"Not that anybody has to know. And we've already discussed 'floozy,' I think."

"OK, but are you foolin' me? Everybody knows everything, Forde, I shouldn't have to tell you that."

Forde fumed a little, and then: "Aw right. How about the same as you're paying for the Woolworth's place. I'm not going a nickel higher."

"Well, all right, then. Forde, you are a handsome, generous friend." She threw her arms around Forde's neck and kissed his cheek so scarlet, you could hardly see the lipstick until later, when he cooled off.

Faye had scruple pangs of course, when she thought about accepting Forde's generous offer to let her live in the river cabin, knowing perfectly well that he had to have seen it as a way to bring her closer to him; while she could not help thinking of it as a private place for herself, the quintessential "room of one's own" that she had sought since leaving home. Woolworth's attic did not count; Faye could not for a moment imagine Virginia Woolf putting up with it. And of course, she did not fail to think of the cottage as a potential trysting place for herself and, well, anyone. Forde, she supposed. But also maybe Travis Wayland. And she could not deny to herself that the thought of sharing that beautiful, secluded spot with Travis was, oh God, much more exciting, than with Forde. *Or, hell, if two, why not three or four? I might add another dozen suckers to the string if I ran an ad in the Intelligencer. Make some decent money on the side. Floppy slut.*

She somewhat pacified her conscience by arguing to it that the two questions were not necessarily inextricable. That, for example, although she had irreparably complicated her friendship with Travis by declaring herself ready to share a tent - or anyplace private - with him, still, no one can predict the future. So she argued, while Sister Penitentia stood upright by Custis' desk at the end of the hall and glinted rimless glasses at her, unrouged lips pressed. A muted trumpet in the pit band laughed out loud.

*   *

The move out to the river cottage was accomplished quickly, since Faye owned no furniture, and the possessions she had acquired since coming to Gabbro - mostly clothes, a basket to carry them to Sudsies or the dry cleaners and back, toiletries, and food - fit neatly into the basket and a couple of grocery cartons from the Piggly Wiggly. She moved to the cottage on Friday afternoon, June 4, and Forde came out that evening to help her get settled, show her how the icebox, propane water heater and the toilets worked, and how to manage the fireplace, and who sold firewood for what price; and take her back in to Gabbro to get supper. It was all easy enough, but there would be a thousand little things: cleaning out the mouse-infested cupboards before she could put groceries in them, airing sheets to put on the - ah, blessedly roomy - bed, finding the pillow cases that fit the enormously wide pillow, sweeping the sand and pine needles from the porch and the living room. She did the bed first, fell into it, and woke ten hours later to dedicate Saturday to all the rest, and to stopping by the WGAB transmitter to give Travis the news. Travis was on the air, so she left him a note, written to be read by whoever would of course snoop it.

She rewarded herself with a solitary swim off the dock in the late afternoon, her backless daffodil-and-black suit dazzling no one, since she was alone. She dried, dressed in a nightie and bathrobe, and fixed herself eggs, bacon, toast and jam for supper, the toast produced from white bread and a stove burner. *I should open another bank account. Oh; but no electricity.* She washed them down with a glass or two of Blue Nun on the porch while a full moon rose through the woods across the river, cheered on by cicadas, katydids, and crickets, and the lonely tedium of a whippoorwill.

Lulled by the beauty and the wine, she considered whether she would be bored or lonely way out here by herself - assuming

Morgan's Eddy

she did not in fact run a string of boyfriends through - and recognized again what she had known all along: that Mary Faye Bynum was a loner who could and would be perfectly happy with her thoughts and with the beauty of Morgan's Eddy for as long as possible or needed. Maybe she could think of getting some writing done. *Border-State Yankee: A Catholic Girl Among Baptists. The Adventures of Faye Floozyface. Poems 1948 - 1949. On the Air: A Broad, Casting.*

In fact, being a loner was why she had not said anything to Travis about her encounter with Deputy Windell. He would have wanted to talk about it, and the thought was distasteful. She had unburdened to the Salonnette ladies, and she had been obligated to tell Forde, but it had led to no improvement in her life, and a considerable change, not for the better, in the balance of their relationship.

When she had cleaned up the dishes, she crawled glorying into the big, cool bed with Friday's *Intelligencer,* to count typos.

After midnight, the full moon had westered enough to slant through the bedroom window and progress in a slow sweep up Faye's twitching body to shine at last on her face. It fell on an eye, closed and trembling, and illuminated rapid movement within, a frowning brow, and the slightly open mouth. Like an apologetic child, it woke her and brought to her notice the smother of the bedspread that covered her. She threw back the covers and turned over; and when she had pulled smooth the wrinkled nightgown under her body, she tried to remember what the rapid movement had been about, but only nonsensical truncates remained. It had been important in its own world, she remembered.

She sat up, and saw moonlight lying in her lap like a sleeping baby. She whispered, "Oh," not knowing what else to say to it. The window glass was old-timey and wrinkled, and the little square of light rippled like water, though unmoving. The Grandmother clock whirred and struck twice, both notes rising lonely and interrogative. The light showed sparkles of dampness on her skin: perspiration from the dream and from the smother.

140

When she lay down to sleep again, no sleep came. Her stubborn mind ranted about the schools, Travis danced in and out of her thoughts like Fred Astaire; her pulse drummed in the ear on the pillow. Faye stared into the dusk that gathered under the rafters above her. One of them, hewn cross-wise, looks for all the world like the dock below the cottage. Just enough moonlight reflects from the white sheets to imagine almost anything among the edges and angles and knots below the ceiling, from the peaks and angles of Sister Rose Penitentia's habit to the solemn angularity of Amy Lee Windell's tombstone. After a quarter-hour, she gave up and rose to pee, and wandered then to the screen porch to assess the night.

The moon, visible silence, lies across the lawn and the water. The chorus of insects is nearly silent now, their joint stillness brought into relief by the chirr of a single cicada. Faye steps onto the porch, holding the door frame for support, still dizzy from her restless sleep. There is no breath of wind; the night lies inert, and Morgan's Eddy is a swaying mirror to the trees on the far shore, where the current makes a moonstruck vee around the gabbro outcrop, and sends slow oscillations across the surface.

Bare feet cross the porch, nightie swirling, waiting for her tentative hand to open the screen for them; down the stairs to the lawn below. Still more than half asleep, Faye drifts to the dock, a nightie anchored by a hard-cut black shadow, a rag of cloud across the sky beneath. She breathes warm moonlight, and exhales silence. At the end of the dock, she sits and wraps her arms around her knees, her nightie bound about her. The whippoorwill, waked by the muffled slap of the screen door, takes up his tedious condemnation, seconding the hypnosis of the moonlight. She curls on the dock, watching the sway of the moon in the water. The water speaks of breath and flight.

Waking; the moon has slid west to illuminate the far shore where the current runs, looking cool and content. Nearly inaudible under the whippoorwill, the call of a Confederate bugle: *The water's fine.* Faye strips off the nightie, drops it on the dock, and ventures to the ladder to lower herself into the Eddy. The water receives her, not into her day mind, but aslant into hallucination in which nothing has its day meaning. Enchantment held within by daring, fear, and surrender. *I am in this river alone, and no one else is even awake.* After a minute or two, the water feels warm. Holding the ladder, she feels the stretch of water at her back and its lap on her shoulders like a living thing, hospitable, sisterly. The tiny filament of fear makes her shiver and smile.

She pushes herself from the dock, trying to make no sound at all, to be only a thought, a current of water. To become entirely the same as the silent water. *I am 95% water. Can't I dissolve?* She spreads her arms and legs, inviting the water to dissolve her. So silly to put the daffodil thing between them this afternoon. Floating on her back in mid-pond, she submerges her face and opens her eyes to see the moon drowned and shattered like Ophelia through an inch of water. She makes herself hold perfectly still while the ripples subside until the moon heals itself, intact for an instant, as round as her own eye; then she is out of breath, and it flies apart, a cold and silent explosion.

Rising, she breathes, then sinks herself again, disappearing into water and light, feeling the cool springs on her feet. The wavering moon fades to the color of tea, to blood, fades again nearly to eclipse as her toes find the sandy bottom. She feels the pressure of deep water in her ears and the unsleeping spring at her back, and pushes off to flee. A single downward stroke brings the moon, but not the night. She reaches for the tan circle, strokes again and her head beaks the surface.

A gasp of thankfulness, a deep breath, and the chill touch of the springs merging with the fear that she has nearly joined the Confederate fossils. She lies back in the water to let her heart return to normal, relaxing into the warmth of the surface water, into a softness that cradles her nakedness like a new mother. She smiles, believing that she remembers this, a new-born in the arms of her own mother. The trees overhead are her father, smiling remotely, moving away …

The trees moving away, the mother-faced moon walking and then running behind them. So she herself is moving, embarking on a tide that carries her away, as she once carried herself away from mother and father and never saw them again, and she is on the far side of the river now, where the current will take her south, headfirst all the way to Gabbro. The rock that marks the outflow current sails past on her right. … *swimming hole down below here, if you just let yourself float, you'd get there in ten …*

Oh, no. Not down that dark tunnel of forest naked as a jay at three in the morning, into the blackness that lies downstream, concealing horrors and disgraces. Faye can not swim against this current that is carrying her away from the dock, away from her nightie, away from safety and life itself. She raises her head and looks about, fighting panic as she sees bushes gliding past her in dappled moonlight.

"Gabbro River?" It can't be …   A little over knee deep, is the answer. Really awake now, Faye stands in the stream, water clamoring around her legs, toes digging into the sand bottom, laughing and shivering in the flow of air that the water brings with it. Behind her the little stream enters a thicket of blackness where water noisily parts around some obstacle. Someone there? Shreds of a Rebel drummer boy? Shapeless Nothing?

Fearing to look behind lest Deputy Windell stands in that thicket, she begins to walk back against the current, staggering in the shifting sand, urgent, listening for the sound of water roiling around the legs of the Other. After a dozen yards she steps on a submerged branch and, thinking of Confederate bones, recoils, loses her footing and is carried back, all arms and legs scrabbling for a purchase in rushing sand, toward what waits below. Upright again, slogging to make up the lost ground, *So we beat on,* she whispers, a charm against the blackness behind her, *boats against the current, borne back ceaselessly into - something, something.* Sister P, Modern Lit. But now as she beats on, the river becomes deeper and not so rushed, so she makes progress while the water rises around her, Faye now a pre-Raphaelite water nymph with plastered short hair and beating heart.

Slowly at last, the moon tarrying to help, she emerges from the darkness of the flowing river. And the moon holds still while she stands panting waist-deep in slowly moving water, still not daring to look behind. The pond gleams in moonlight not perfectly white. Looking down, she can see her legs braced against the gentle urge of water, moonlit and tapering into the universal tan of the river. Straight in front of her is the rock and the vee of water that marks the beginning of the flow.

She swam on her back toward the dock, keeping her eyes on the black tunnel, the devouring current that urges her back. The Eddy lay gentle as a sister under the moon, absorbing the ripples of her passing and covering the bones. *Nothing to be afraid of. What if you invited Travis to come and swim with you?* Her swim became less urgent, toward languorous, and she was imagining Travis with her in moonlight, lean and warm, the water beading on his naked chest, when her head thumped the ladder.

*   *

On Sunday morning, Forde Morgan sat in one of the guest chairs behind his desk, morose, fingering a brochure from Dixie Office Furniture. It had proved impossible for him to sit comfortably in the swivel chair in which his father had died, and he had given it to the Gabbro Presbyterian rummage sale, without burdening them with its history.

Tell the world you're The Boss! with the Imperator chair. Choice of ✓*Wood Finishes,* ✓*Upholstery,* ✓*Leather,* ✓*Filigree,* ✓*Coat of Arms.* Forde paged on, looking for something like the one Faye had found at the Fayetteville Good Will to replace her fire-damaged one. A chair that a Christian might sit in without going to Confession for the sin of pride.

Which was where, his imagination unable to follow, Faye has told him she is off to, when she stopped by around nine. Confessing what? Faye had committed no sins in his presence, worse luck. He hoped to hell she had not, in his absence. What had she been up to, that she needed to confess, all of a sudden? Forde, who had matured considerably from the pudgy blusher Faye still thought him, ran a trembling hand through his hair. Beyond the mourning, he was uneasy about his father's suicide. Custis went quiet and preoccupied right after the bond issue series of editorials, and Forde was astute enough not to miss the implications.

Faye awoke for the second time at dawn on Sunday morning, rested and snug, and looked back on her small-hours adventure in the river with a shiver of relief. It was just the kind of thing that fools did who are found on a riverbank somewhere, bloated and pale. The song of a church bell in Gabbro came through the open window, mellowed by distance. It sounded so goddamn rural and peaceful that she stretched, yawned, and drifted off again, snuggled under a spread - a bedspread, of all things, where anything heavier than a Kleenex had been unbearable in the swelter of the Woolworth Arms - and slept until after eight. She jumped out of bed then, and dressed herself soberly from one of the grocery boxes.

Her aquatic-tryst fantasies about Travis had tweaked her conscience enough to make her stop by the *Intelligencer* to leave Forde a note of burbling gratitude about the cottage. Finding Forde actually there - *What about Sunday School, Forde?* - had led her to the fib about going to Confession rather than getting into a long conversation, which then piqued her conscience again, and she decided finally to seek out St. Ann's - even though it was spelled wrong, what was the <u>matter</u> with Southerners and spelling? - and convert the fib to truth.

She found the church, not on Church Street, which was dominated by Protestants, but on a little cul-de-sac off of Greenly Street, tucked among tract houses. A dozen early-service parishioners were straggling out, and when the last of them disappeared, she asked the tired-looking priest - Father Kenneth, said the signboard - about when he might be hearing confessions.

"Right now, child," he said, "But cover your head." Faye did not leave in a huff just because of that familiar priestly arrogance. *He can't help himself, he is a product of his times and his training.* But it took a little of the edge off of the morning's euphoria.

Inside St. Ann's, the smell of Catholicism, compounded of flowers, wax, and incense ambushed Faye and threw her to the feet of Sister Penitentia; who told her it was about time, and that she, Sister P, hoped that this was not just some one-time guilty-conscience thing, which of course it was. No, wait, Faye protested. It comes from how peaceful and at one with life I felt when I woke up this morning.

Life, Sister sniffed. *At one with life. How pleasant for you.*

When Faye left St. Ann's, she had no intention of doing the penances she had earned. She did penances enough at Mount St. Anne to fill a phone book, and if the BVM was still unclear on whether humble little Faye Bynum considered her blessed among women, well, she obviously had not been paying attention, so what was the point of saying it all again? Besides, she had Hailed her good and hard when delivered from the hands of Deputy Windell, and again last night when she returned dry and safe to her bed.

But when she confessed to what she felt was the sin of encouraging Travis and Forde to consider themselves 'special' friends, which she admitted was no different from encouraging them both to sue for her permanent affections, Father Kenneth seemed unimpressed. He administered no penance, but pointed out the unfairness of keeping both on the string. He strongly advised her to inform one or the other, preferably both, that there was no possibility of more than friendly acquaintanceship. He gave no guidance as to how to decide which, and Faye left the church dissatisfied and un-counseled.

The solipsistic ritual of Confession was another matter. It fit with the serenity she had felt on waking this morning, and added to it. Confession, she decided, really is good for the soul, even when one's confessor is a dope. She felt as clean as she had on exiting the river this morning. She felt now that the stage on which she moved no longer necessarily framed a cheesy operetta, but a world in which she belonged, and within which her hand had found something to do that she could do with all her might. That by itself was worth a couple of Aves, not that she had any definite plans to render them.

Fine, but still, there was the matter of Forde v. Travis. If she were to be honest with herself, she honest to God fancied Travis more than she did Forde. He was clever, and exciting, he had that slender, muscular body that had held her on the toboggan, and that made her breath deepen when she thought of it; and he didn't have to have everything spelled out for him. She realized that she was closer to loving him, and certainly closer to taking him into those snug, peaceful sheets out by the river. That could be so …

She sighed with frustration. The sheets on the bed in the house by the river, that Forde Morgan had generously made available to her, <u>damn</u>!

16.

THE NORTH CAROLINA PRESS ASSOCIATION in those days supported a program of annual awards, with categories for coverage of state-wide issues, investigative journalism, features and humor, editorial writing, and small-town papers. Based on issues published over the course of the preceding July 1 through June 30, the awards were made on August 5 of each year. After the state Attorney General got wind of questions about the Gabbro schools bond issue, and after the resulting audit showed clear evidence of skimming by Minor Mack, Anson Evans, and an un-named co-conspirator, the *Intelligencer* was widely felt to have legitimate hopes for either the investigative journalism or the small-town award.

"Heck," Ginny Freeman said, "why not the humor prize, considering the clowns we got running the schools these days. Anyways, good going, Faye. I'm tickled to death that we got this hot celebrity as one of our regulars."

"Well," Faye said, making Pearlene jump back with her scissors. "Sorry, Pearlene. Anyway, what I wanted to say is, being called a 'regular' at the Salonnette means more to me than any of their dumb awards. And besides, it's not for individuals. The award goes to the whole staff, and Forde will accept it and hang it in the lobby for the world to see. That's if we even get any award, mind. It's just a possibility."

"When's it get announced?"

"Forde will go up to Raleigh next week. Some reason or other, they don't make a big public announcement. You get called up there if you're a finalist, which we are, us and a dozen other papers, and they have this cocktail party where they practically sidle up and tap you on the shoulder to sit at the head table with last year's winners, who actually make the presentations. Then afterwards, they let each paper make their own announcement, and they run a list of them after that. If we even get an award, our circulation is around three thousand, and that's who'll see the big news first."

"Huh. Who's this un-named co-conspirator? Please tell me it's Al Burns."

"Ha. Well, we could wish, I suppose. 'Course, if I knew, and I spread it around, then he wouldn't be un-named any more, would he? They are keeping it tight, and they are not about to tell us at the paper."

Faye knew well enough that the un-named one was Custis Morgan, not named because deceased, and what would be the point of naming him now, Custis in his grave for a season and his memory among the townspeople intact? *De mortuis*, Sister Penitentia added, *nil nisi bonum.*

*　　　　*

From the Gabbro *Intelligencer* for Monday, August 2, 1948:

Mack Resigns, Will Make Restitution
Bonds Sold, Improvements Will Continue
Former Gabbro Schools Supt. Minor Mack has pled "No Contest" to charges of improper use of public funds, agreed to restore all funds improperly assigned to his discretionary fund, and pay an undisclosed fine to avoid a trial. The School Board has accepted his resignation. The *Intelligencer* has learned that Principal Abraham Cousins of Frederick Douglass …

Faye smiled at Acting Superintendent Abraham Cousins, crossed her legs, and pulled her skirt over her knee. "Congratulations on your promotion, Mr. Cousins."

"Heh. A highly temporary Hobson's choice, you can well believe. However, I believe that it will last long enough for Mr.

Acting Superintendent Cousins to order up a mess of textbooks for Douglass, Attucks, Carver, and Banneker from Mr. Mack's ill-gotten discretionary funds. I'm looking at a very modest request from the Indian schools for salary supplements, which may or may not be legal, given the terms of the bond issue. Might even be enough left over for a microscope all around, I'm hoping."

"Your appointment, I understand, is to last until a permanent replacement is hired. Will you be applying for the position?"

Cousins snorted. "That would be forgetting my place, Miss Bynum. What they want is somebody to do the dog work, sign papers, sort the mail, till they find a white candidate that wants the job." He paused. "Could take some time, come to think, given the black eye this county got from that mess. Might be a chance to do a little more good than them school board folks was counting on."

"Well, Mr. Cousins, The *Intelligencer* and the fair-minded citizens of Gabbro County all wish you well in this new position. Who will replace you as principal of Douglass?"

"Assistant Principal Farney been nipping at my heels as it was. She will be Acting Principal until I come back, do her job as well as mine, see how she likes it."

*   *

When Forde returned from Raleigh, he strode through the lobby of the *Intelligencer* and past Faye's rebuilt alcove with barely a glance in her direction. Sharon, Rob Stoker, and Jenny McCall exchanged what Ginny Freeman had once called "cross-eyed" looks and tiptoed to their workplaces. Faye missed the whole thing, being at the moment of Forde's passage hunched over her telephone, trying to make sense of what she was hearing from Travis Wayland.

The call was interrupted by a pair of toots over the line. "Travis, let me get back to you. I just got a beep from Forde, and I think it might be something ... well, it might be something. I'll call you back. Keep it simple."

"Keep it simple" had become their motto and code over the months since their discussion of tent-sharing at the Sir Walter. Keeping it simple meant in practice avoiding acts or speech that would unduly and unfairly arouse feelings in the other that could not be relieved under the immediate circumstances. Keeping it simple was proving difficult for both of them.

Faye presented herself at Forde's office door and tapped.

"Come in. Shut the door, if you don't mind."

Faye did, trying not to look as tense as her gut felt. But Forde did not look ominous, or jealous, or as if, really, his mind was in any way agitated. He sat back in his mid-range Boss Chair, and contemplated Faye as if she were a lavishly illuminated manuscript that he had discovered but could never afford to own. He was smiling sadly and shaking his head.

"Faye, Faye."

"Forde? What is it?"

"You know when I wrote you about coming down here, I said I thought you could help me make a difference in this town, get people to think new thoughts, all that?"

"Yes?" *Why is everything so mysterious and significant with him? What ever happened to routine and boring?*

"You know where I've been."

"Yes. So, come on! Did we get one?"

"Y - No."

"Oh ... Well, darn. Still, it was an honor just to - "

Forde smiled and shook his head again. "Shut up. We got two."

"Aaahh! Two? Both of them?"

"Shh. Don't let them blabbermouths out there know about it yet, but I just had to tell you, because it was your doing, top to bottom."

"Oh, Forde, oh, my gosh ... " Faye tracked around his desk and yanked him out of the Boss Chair. She then violated her self-discipline by wrapping herself around him and kissing him hard. "Forde, oh, you are the most generous, lovely ... Really? Small-town <u>and</u> Investigative?"

"No. Small-town and State-wide. Investigative went to our old friends at the Charlotte *Star-Dispatch*."

"State-<u>wide</u>? Really? Isn't that the big deal, top award? What's state-wide about some petty graft in a piddly school bond?"

"Please don't call it that, even if it is. I am pretty sure it's why Pop killed himself." Forde paused and looked at the floor. "Typical of a pattern, anyway, and our coverage put the icing on the cake, 'cause nobody else actually went from school to school and checked bids and budgets like you done, until the auditors - that <u>we</u> called for, thanks to you - unwrapped the whole thing. The rest of the districts were so big and had so many schools, that the reporter manpower just wasn't there to check it all out. Our good luck is, we're so 'piddly' that one person, namely Faye Bynum, could go to every single school and look at every single budget and bid.

"Apparently, they was collusion between banks and school boards from here to Boone, and it was the *Star-Dispatch* that broke that part of it. They did all the really complicated digging, but we got a lot of credit when they wrote it up. They mentioned us - and you personally - by name. If we had some kind of linkage between newspapers other than just mailing each other copies of our print run, we'd of seen it."

"Well, <u>dang</u>! Oh, my God, I think I'm going to explode. Or cry."

"Well, don't make a mess, either way. Here." He sat, opened a drawer and handed her a packet of Kleenex. She sat in the nearest visitor chair and blew her nose, while Forde wiped his lips, admiring the crimson residue. "Now. I'd like to have a kind of special, private occasion to let the rest of the staff know about it. Any place here in town is a no-go. I was thinking, wondering if you'd mind if we put it on, out at the river cottage? Isn't your birthday coming up?"

"August tenth. Of course, we can use the cottage. It's yours in the first place."

"Huh. How'd I miss that last year? Your birthday?"

"That was the day I heard about Mother and Daddy. I left Charlotte that day."

"Oh. Well, we got something in common, then. Anyhow, yours is the first birthday to come along since Pop died. I will announce that we're going to have a cookout on your birthday, and give all the staff a little birthday bonus to mark the end of my mourning. And when they're all out there, and we're by ourselves, we'll pop the award thing on 'em at the end. How's that sound?"

"Lovely, though how we're supposed to keep something this big from them for five days is beyond me. Or why. Look, first of all, August tenth is next Tuesday, and we'll all be busy with the Wednesday paper. Why not have it tomorrow? It's Saturday, I can have the place cleaned up by then, and if you wanted to come out ahead of time, we could get set up. Maybe go for a swim. If you 'wonted' " Wiggling quote-fingers.

"You gonna wear that yella bathing suit?"

"Y - I wouldn't have to, if it bothers you. I mean, just not swim." Flustered.

"Well. There's different kinds of bother."

"I know. Also, I want to have a serious talk with you about all that. If you're free Saturday, and want to come out, I'll fix something, and we can talk it over, over lunch."

" 'It?' "

"Being a 'Thing,' like we talked about at the quarry. Thing-ness. I have owed you a serious talk about that for some time now."

He saw that her eyes were bright, and knew that what she had to say could not be good. He nodded, waved her toward the door, and she turned to go.

But she thought of something and looked at Forde suddenly. "Oh - but does all this mean that Custis' name will get out in connection with it? I don't even believe that business about co-conspirator."

Forde sighed. "Well, that's the thing, isn't it? It's gone on here in North Carolina for years and years, and part of the method is, you grease the local media to sell the package to the taxpayers, who end up getting screwed. I guess they set it up before I took over. His share of the take was maybe $500. How's that for a mess of pottage? 'Course, I'll give it back, out of the Estate. But it's not beyond imagining, by the way, that good ol' WGAB got greased too, and we just haven't heard about it yet."

"Oh." *So that's what Travis was talking about.* "Forde, I'm so … Oh, my gosh. What a mess, huh?"

"Well, it's pretty complicated, morally and all. Ironic that Pop's paper gets an award for exposing graft that he was sharing in. 'Course, that's why he killed himself. He knew it would all come out from the audit."

"And that's why he didn't want the audit." Her eyes widened. "Oh, Forde, he killed himself rather than try and over-rule you on the editorial about it. Because he really meant it about keeping hands off."

"Yes."

"Because he was proud that he'd made a newspaper out of nothing, and his son was running it now."

"Apparently so."

"And I'm the one who insisted on an audit. Oh, God, Forde, I as good as killed him, didn't I?"

"No, now, don't - "

"Oh, don't what? I'm a goddamn angel of death, everything I touch …"

"Stop that! First of all, he killed himself, not you. And he did because he stole public money and he was about to get caught, which he knew would reflect on me, his son, and on this newspaper, which was his life's work. All you did was come along and ask for the truth to be told, which you were exactly right to do."

"Let justice be done, though the heavens fall. Let the truth come out, though it kills a sweet, hard-working old man and compromises his life's work. Damn truth, damn justice! Why don't I learn to think before I open my mouth?"

"Think what, Faye? You would have caught on to his involvement before there was an audit? You know you wouldn't of. Why does this have to be all about you? You did the right thing, and it just happened to be a thing that led him to kill himself. He put himself in the position where it did. For five hundred dollars."

Faye saw how this hit Forde, and she did the only thing she could think of. She went to him in his Boss Chair and drew his head to her body and patted his shoulder, saying, "There, there," and "Don't cry," because he was crying, overwhelmed by the loss, his insight into its reason, the fact that the newspaper Custis created was being noticed and rewarded for the first time in its long life for exposing him, among others, and that the agent of it all was this woman whom Forde worshiped and whose breast now pressed his ear. And who wanted a 'serious talk' about them, about his worship. He stood up, blew his nose, wiped off the lipstick, kissed her on the forehead, and walked out to the newsroom.

"Folks," he said. "I got a little announcement for you. We're gonna have a cookout."

*   *

Faye looked around the nearly deserted Terminal Café, and leaned forward. "OK, well, <u>you</u> didn't get in on the dirty money, did you?"

"Nope, sadly. I'm fired for it, but I didn't do it. Matter of fact, the guy that fired me did it. He's covering his … you know. His ass."

"His … ? Oh, his behind? Well, heck, Travis, that's not fair."

"Life's fair? Nobody told Rafe." Rafe being the WGAB station manager, Rafer Penfold.

"Well, can't you complain?"

"Who to? God?"

"There's nobody above Rafe?"

"Nope. Rafe started the station back in 1928. He's our version of Custis. Only instead of killing himself, he figures he can claim I set up the deal without his knowledge, and skate. Here's the only redeeming feature: I have a standing offer to go out to Boone and catch on with a little station there."

Faye's smile drained away. "Where's Boone?"

"Well, it's a little town out in the mountains. It's got a little teachers' college, and some resorts, but it's only got a 200-watt radio station, WBON. They've raised the money to build up the juice and go to 24-hour broadcasting, which they only do from sunup to sundown, now. I'd come in as head of scheduling, with a show of my own. I'd still have to do some sports broadcasting, play-by-play. But it's twice what I'm making at WGAB anyhow."

"But ... how far away is it from here?" She knew she sounded like a 3rd-grader. But he was sounding like a Daddy getting ready to disappoint a 3rd-grader.

"It's I guess about a six hour drive. It's still in North Carolina, after all."

"Travis, I'll never see you! Who'll be my friend?"

Travis startled Faye then by taking both her hands and looking straight into her brimming eyes. "Faye, I thought about that, believe me. There's one solution to it. I know this is skipping some steps, but we don't have months and months to go stepwise. What if you married me, and came out to Boone with me?"

Something transfixed Faye then, and she dropped her head over their joined hands. "Oh, Jesus, Travis. I'm not going to say 'This is so sudden,' because it's a horrible cliché. But it is, really. Skipping steps, my Lord! One minute we're uncomplicated friends, and the next, you just pop up with the biggest complication anybody ever heard of. What are you thinking?"

"I'm thinking I love you, Faye. I'm thinking it's going to be horribly lonely out there with nobody who knows me but Jeff, the station manager, and Claude."

"Claude? He's there?"

"I told you that when we met him, I think. He's on the faculty of the teacher's college, training kids to be music teachers. Is there a problem?"

"Oh … " *Can you imagine, explaining to a little boy or girl about their Daddy liking boys better than girls?* "I guess I heard something not very nice about Claude."

"Huh. At the Salonnette?"

"I protect my sources. Yes."

"Well, you know Ginny Freeman is Claude's ex's cousin."

"Jesus. Somebody told me once, the whole state is as inbred as canned cockroaches."

"True. Still, there it is. A biased witness."

"Well, let's let that go, 'cause we're ignoring some very serious complications, worrying about Claude. Travis, you … I will tell you something. Even though it's immodest, and probably a strategic mistake in the war between the sexes."

Faye sighed and shook her head. "This is going to sound stupid. But sometimes, when I think about you, I get this pang, and my knees go all funny. That's a big fat complication, seems to me. But I am not going to say I'll marry you just on the strength of that. I've been through wobbly knees before, and it turned out very badly. I want to know all about you before I say I'll spend my life with you. How am I supposed to do that if you move a million miles away up in the mountains?"

"Faye, it doesn't sound stupid, for gosh sake. I adore your knees. I hope they enjoy going all funny. But I can't live on love and air. I need a job, and this is a great one. I've offered to keep you very close to me indeed."

"Wait a second. Wait. This conversation is getting out of the line of what can possibly be carried on in public, even in a bus stop café. Let's get somewhere private."

Travis rose suddenly and headed for the door, Faye trailing behind and blowing her nose. Out on the sidewalk, the Raleigh bus had just pulled up. A Negro girl emerged from the rear door, carrying a small suitcase.

"We can't go to my place. The sewer's backed up, and they've got plumbers and cleaners all over the place. What about yours?"

Faye considered. "I suppose. You know it belongs to Forde Morgan, and it's not out of the question that he might pop in. Also not at all impossible is that we could end up doing what we agreed would lead to chagrin, and that in a bed that belongs to Forde. That would make me feel sneaky and cheap. Oh, shit, Travis. Life in a small town, huh? Look. I think the best thing would be for both of us to take some steps back and think about all this really carefully. When would you be leaving for Boone?" Just saying it sank Faye's heart.

"Next weekend. I start the following Monday, the 16th. I don't like stepping back; half the time, I trip on something. But, on condition that we step forward again before the end of the week?"

"I guess. We can surely figure out something by then. Please give me a little time and space to think about it, Travis. I'm closer to saying Yes than to anything else, if that helps. But I want to be really careful about it. I just got myself clear - mentally, I mean - of that horrible mess from last summer. I need to take a breath, but I promise to give my knees a voice in the discussion. You're a very lovely man, Travis. It is a wonderful, dazzling thing to be proposed to by somebody like you. I love being with you. That's as far as I can go for now."

She pecked him on the cheek and stumbled around to the Terminal parking lot and the Chevy.

17.

T HE WHOLE *INTELLIGENCER* PAYROLL sang "Happy Birthday," and Rob Stoker remarked that now that Faye was 21, it was probably legal at last for her to occupy a management position; and come to think of it, other fun stuff might be legal now, too. On that cue he, Sharon, and the press mechanics rushed her, took the new Mont Blanc pen out of her hand and gave it to Forde to hold, and lifted her over their heads to run to the end of the dock and throw her bodily, shrieking with fake glee, into Morgan's Eddy of the mighty Gabbro River.

Faye, knowing what was coming - when was a secret ever kept in Gabbro, North Carolina? - was wearing the daffodil bathing suit under a loose and easily shucked dress, and had gotten out of her sandals in anticipation. She rose from the water appropriately clad and boosted herself onto the dock to take a bow. "Now," she said. I believe that Mister Morgan has an announcement that will be of interest to all of y- us."

Forde announced the North Carolina Press Awards, beamed at the resulting cheers, thanked everyone for all they did to make them happen, and claimed that he had sat down and calculated what the awards would mean in the form of new revenue from advertising and circulation, and had divided that number by the total number of staff, and come up with the amazingly even number of $100.00 per employee regardless of rank, which sum he stood ready to distribute in cash. And he hauled from his seersucker jacket a wad of new bills and an alphabetical roster that began with Chief Press Operator Clay Abbott, and ran to Mary Zecharias, a pleasant-faced 50-ish Lumbee who cleaned the offices at night.

"Forde, you are the best dang boss in North Carolina," Faye announced. If y'all will excuse me a second, $100 all in one place - a nod to the five crisp twenties peeking from the top of the daffodil suit - is a little scratchy. Must be from how even it come out. I made us some peach cobbler, so don't nobody go away."

*   *

In Travis' Studebaker, on the way to the Sir Walter dining room on Sunday afternoon, Faye was silent through half the trip, looking at the familiar passing humdrum and worrying at a hangnail. As she recognized the thickening of settlement that marked the approach to Raleigh, she pulled a knee onto the seat and turned to Travis.

"Travis, I … "

"Me too."

"You too, what?"

"I think we forgot to keep it simple back on Friday. I should not have sprung that on you, and if I can do so without being a rat, I would like to ask you to put my proposal of marriage up on a high shelf somewhere where it will be safe, and return to it when things have settled down a little."

"What made you think I was thinking that way?"

Travis smiled. "You didn't say '*Trra*vis.' It was a very controlled 'Travis.' "

Faye thought about that. "And are you a very controlled Travis?"

"Well. With some wiggle room within limits."

"Whatever that might mean. What limits?"

"Oh … for one, I'm not going to ask you to marry me again. I did that, and I don't regret it, but I consider it done. No need to repeat, until you're ready. At the other extreme, I don't intend to go to sleep or sit in a corner and suck my thumb."

"Uh huh. So, that sounds like you intend to go back to charming and flirting, and doing all the charming, flirty things that drive me crazy, but not moving us in any direction that we might be free to move, short of my dropping everything and moving to Boone, for Pete's sake. I thought Gabbro was already as Boone-y as it got."

"Could we set that question aside for now, and talk about those other directions? For example … ?"

"Oh, well … Faye's knee, on the edge of the Studebaker seat, got a sinking sensation, and would have wobbled if it had been load-bearing. "Let's work our way back from the premature question-popping. Back before the Boone … thing. Business. Where were we?"

Travis spooked his voice into contrabasso register. "Back into the mists of the past. Back past your birthday. Backward through time to when you were a minor, and I had a job… Wait, a voice approaches from the past, ass-backward from the time reversal." He covered his mouth to squawk his voice into sci-fi mode. "*Tent the skip just could we.*"

"What?"

"You think that romantic little whisper didn't bounce around my skull for days? Until I knew it forwards and back, it did. Always in that growly, sugary voice that about rips the pants right off my mind."

"We could …just … skip … the tent. Did I say that?"

"You know perfectly well you did."

"Well, true. I remember. Your mind wears pants?"

"So do all men's. Put a man's mind in a skirt, he'd start thinking like a woman."

"Tell it to the Scots."

"Wouldn't dare. Can we get back to the crux of it?"

"I'm already there. Yes, that would be a possible developmental direction in which we could move. To keep it simple, and just, I guess … have an affair. Is that what you're hinting at?"

"Yes, you bold thing. I guess it is."

She was silent until Travis peered at her, assaying her reception of the notion. She laughed, not merrily. "An 'affair.' What a perfectly weightless word. And descriptive! Half air. An affable airy affair with Faye. You hardly feel it leaving your mouth. A light-hearted adorable little …"

She opened her fingers, *poof*, like a magician. "Fling! We could banter and kid and smooch, and hire somebody to fade the lights when things got a little sweaty. Like these movies that have started coming out, with titles that give a big wink, but no actual sex on screen? No ring, no ceremony, no papers, no house, no mortgage, no children, no messy complications. Keeping it simple, by simply … " She sighed, and went up a half-octave. "Fucking, from time to time."

"Ye gods, Faye! But, OK, yes. That was what I understood you to mean by 'skipping the tent.' Or, what did you?"

"No, you're right. I certainly did. I was drenched in sweat and hormones by the time I said that. My knees were wobbling so bad I could barely stand up, let alone dance. I wanted you, I was dying for you to take me, right there and then on the dance floor of the Sir Walter, waiters tripping over us trying to serve tables while we ripped at each other's clothes. To have an *affair* so hot, we'd float up like fire balloons and bump against the chandeliers, doing it for all we were worth upside-down on the ceiling, while cops and priests yelled themselves hoarse. Whatsoever thy hand findeth to do, do it with thy might. And not just thy hand, it seemed to me then." She looked out the window. "And might again, I suppose."

"Jesus, Faye."

She grinned up at Travis' sweaty face and punched his arm. "C'mon, Travis. Can't you tell when you're being flirted with?"

*   *

Forde poked his face into Faye's domain on Monday afternoon.

"Hi, Emancipated Lady. I got an errand to run that you might find kind of interesting. Want to come along?"

Faye looked up from her desultory scribbling. "Sure. I'm having writer's block or something, anyway. Thank you so much for restoring my lovely Mont Blanc. It's so beautiful that I don't feel like I have anything worthy of it to write."

"This might solve that. C'mon." Forde led her out through the pressroom, where monster machines were putting together the day's edition. "You believe Pop used to do that on an offset letterpress, back the turn of the century? He must have sweated through a dozen shirts a week."

"Are you getting over … Not sure how to say this. Are you feeling a little better about Custis these days?"

Forde was silent, scratching his head, until they emerged onto a loading dock. "He was … whatever he was, I guess. He was my Pop, <u>and</u> all the other stuff, not all of which was so admirable. Irony is ironic until somebody points it out, and then it's just part of the way the world is. But he's the only Pop I had, and he was very loving to me. Thanks, Chuck." He nodded to one of the press technicians, who straightened up and sketched a salute after he'd put something massive into the trunk of the DeSoto that made it creak lower on its springs.

"You didn't have brothers or sisters? I never thought to ask you about that. Custis didn't strike me as a one-child kind of guy."

"Momma had some kind of condition that was supposed to rule out children at all. I think I was a slip-up somewhere, which I hate to think it shortened her life, but it probably did. But funny you should ask. I have a half-sister, and we're going to meet her."

"Oh. Goodness."

They drove east on Church Street, and once they had passed Woolworth's and the courthouse park, it became new territory to Faye. Church Street became weedy, and then gravel, and they passed what looked to Faye like sharecroppers' cabins, except that they were lined up side by side, unpainted or showing remnants of whitewash. These past, they crossed a small creek and drove between cotton fields toward a pine-and-laurel woodland.

"Runs into Indian Girl Swamp," Forde commented as they crossed the creek. "There's this legend about a disobedient Indian princess who got lost, or killed, or both; supposably, she's still in there, and if you take a boat in, you'll hear her singing to the boyfriend that her mean Daddy killed. If you try an' follow the voice, you'll get lost and never find your way out. 'Course, kids always went in part-way, and then scared each other into believing it. You about never go back in a second time, which is a good thing, since it is easy to get lost, even without help from a ghost."

"Gosh, Forde. Dead Confederate teenagers and Indian ghosts. This must be what they mean by 'Southern Gothic.' It kind of piles up on you, doesn't it?"

"If you let it. Lumbees don't seem to believe in it, and they fish an' hunt in there. I think they made the whole thing up as a joke on the white folks. Maybe all of that Gothic stuff is a joke, too. Anyways, here we are."

He turned the DeSoto onto a track that plunged through an alder thicket and between towering pines. As soon as they had gone a few DeSoto-lengths into the woods, it seemed to Faye as if they were hours of impenetrability from even the mild urbanization of Gabbro. She grew quiet as the gloom of pines thickened around them. But after a few minutes they emerged into a sunny meadow dotted with low bushes, and a few brown goats browsing. In the center was what appeared to be a feeding station for the goats, with bales of cut hay and a wooden manger arrangement, all of it in the shade of an enormously tall live oak. At the far end of the clearing, a small house trailer - little more than a camping caravan, Faye saw - stood in the center of a wide ring of metal scrap. The night cleaner Mary Zecharias and a younger version with an oddly familiar face looked up as Forde rolled the DeSoto down the grassy track.

"Hey," the older woman said. "Hey, Forde. How do, Miss Bynum."

"Well, hey yourself, Miz Zecharias. What a beautiful place to live." Faye came forward for a formal hug from the night cleaner, whom she had never seen at the office - Mary Zecharias cleaned the *Intelligencer* after a stint at the courthouse. Faye's first acquaintance, other than seeing things moved, tidied, and cleaner than the evening before, had been at the cookout.

"Thank you, Miss."

"Oh, please call me Faye. Then maybe I can call you Mary? That's my first name, Mary Faye."

"Mary Godfire, properly. I married an old bastard name of Zecharias when I was fifteen, which he's gone to his proper reward, I do hope. Zecharias is the name I pay my social security under, but that's about it for him. This here's my daughter Annie."

"Hi, Annie. Faye Bynum." The younger woman came forward for a handshake that felt to Faye like greeting a hay baler. She looked to be late teens in age, darkly tanned, broad-shouldered, hard of hand, narrow of hip, and closed of countenance. Her hair was black and short, in the style known in those days as a DA. She wore oil-darkened overalls that bristled with tools and a bundle of short wires, and a man's undershirt that rippled with muscle and taciturnity. When she gave a brief, social smile, Faye saw the connection. "Oh. Custis was your father?" *I done things I wouldn't tolerate another man doing to my daughter. Huh.*

Forde beamed his way into the conversation. "Annie Godfire, my very esteemed baby half-sister." Annie looked at Forde with reciprocal fondness that darkened a little on 'baby.'

"Pop was always very clear about how proud he was of Annie, and has always supported her in whatever she chose to do. Which reminds me."

He brought an envelope from his shirt pocket and handed it to Mary Godfire, who hesitated, and then tucked it away. "Don't know that your going on with the support money makes much sense now that Custis is passed, Mr. Forde."

"Got to, and glad to. Pop's will set up a trust, and what you'll see from now on will be the income from it. Annie comes in to the body of it whenever you say, or when you pass, which we all hope will be a long time off."

Mary Godfire blinked, and blew her nose. "Well, the old poop. He didn't have to do that."

"I don't think it was a case of 'have to,' Mary. Pop wanted y'all to feel as much a real family of his as Momma and me. Don't think Gabbro Presbyterian ever got used to it, but it's always made sense to me. Now, lemme show you what I got, and you see what you think."

Forde walked back to the DeSoto and opened the trunk. "These things are heavy as sin, so have a look before we rassle them out."

Annie Godfire walked over to peer in to the trunk. "What are they?" Her voice was gritty, in the cello range.

"Rollers from the *Intelligencer* press. Month ago, one of them got a little out of balance, and that shook the others out of true before we could stop the press. We've had to run that one press half speed since they went off, till we got in the replacements, end of last week."

"Made out of?"

" 'Bout eighty pounds of steel each. They'd still be true within less than a ounce. It's only when they spin that you can see they're not balanced."

"How many you got there, an' how long did they run before you tooken them off?"

"Five, and they are the original ones that came on the press, which went into operation in 1936."

"So, twelve years times fifty-two, times three runs a week?"

"Close enough. I done the number last night, taking into account, it's not exactly twelve years, and there was special editions, and some days we never published, like when Christmas come on a publishing day. Exactly 1,871 editions of the Gabbro *Intelligencer*, good times an' bad, through the Depression and Pearl Harbor, Mr. Roosevelt's death, atom bomb, V-J, all that. Their last full-speed run was when Faye, here, tore the top off that bond issue business."

Mary's eyes sought Annie's, and they smiled at each other. "A prime number. Perfect," Annie said, and she reached into the trunk and flipped the rollers, two at a time, onto the grass. Mary made a pass at picking one up, and gave up. "We was figuring to start this week, yet, and these will get built in right at the ground level. Thanks so much, Forde, hear?"

Annie picked up one of the massive rollers in each hand, and walked off toward the circle of scrap around the trailer, accompanied by her mother, who was hesitantly dividing 360 by five, writing numbers in the air.

"Seventy-two degrees. Honestly, mother."

Faye turned to Forde. "What?"

"Well, of course they want to space them out even around the - "

"I got that part. What's the circle of junk about?"

"Oh. Well, they're building a new Spirit Catcher."

"Of course. What's that?"

"You'd have to get Mary or Annie to explain it. Has to do with the way Mary makes a living besides night cleaner, which is by spiritual counseling."

"Oh, for goodness sake, Forde. Palm reading?"

"I'm about to get defensively Southern here. Yes. Mary is very good at advising folks in trouble, or baffled about their lives, or having marriage problems. She claims she gets help from the spirit world, and the Catcher is to ... well, not so much catch spirits, as give them a nice place to gather, and chip in advice when Mary needs it. She's training Annie to do it in her footsteps. That and welding."

"To build the Spirit Catcher."

"Uh huh. Mary left me a pitcher of it, what it'll look like, got it in my desk somewhere. It'll be about ten stories high when it's done."

"Good God. What was all the rigmarole about how many editions of the *Intelligencer* they've run?"

"Well. A Spirit Catcher can only be made out of stuff that's had some form of life into it, or the spirits don't care about it. The first one, which Mary's grandmother and momma built, was made out a pine logs, seven stories high. Bunch of Klan yahoos burned it down, and Mary's been working on a replacement, designing, collecting fireproof material, for years. I guess she figures she's got enough now to start."

"Steel has life built in?"

"Well, that's the thing. With pine logs, it was no problem, they're full of life. Steel isn't, at first, so you have to use steel that's been used hard for a long time, and soaked in, which is a slow process with steel, all the life and pain and joy that's been … "

Forde looked at Faye, and flipped a hand. "Aw, well. I can see I'm wasting my breath here. You're never gonna understand, Yankee sense of things, saints and nuns and all. Don't let me waste your time."

Faye put a hand on Forde's sleeve. "Don't jump to conclusions, Forde. I'm more likely to believe in this than I am in saints. Do you think Mary and Annie would be offended by a little feature about the Spirit Catcher in the *Intelligencer?*"

Forde looked to where Mary and Annie were pacing off a circumference around their trailer. "Not exactly community news," he said. "Last time anybody tried to interview Mary, it was almost funny. He come away with a notebook full of ideas, which when he set down to write the story, none of it made any sense at all to him. And he swore it was clear as crystal in his mind when he left here. I guess you could try."

"Huh." Faye walked to one of the rollers that Annie had left behind, squatted next to it and took a breath. Somehow, she got it into her lap and stood with it cradled in her arms, gasping. She staggered over to the builders, who were huddling over something scratched on the ground. She stood panting for a moment, until Annie looked up and saw her.

"Don't let me interrupt. I was wondering - "

"No interest in no publicity or interview. Of course, you're perfectly welcome to write up what you've seen today, can't stop you there. But those as need to know about this project already know, and those as don't, will never understand it in the first place. Save your trouble, I'd say. You could drop the roller over where you see that little flag."

"All right. Thank you."

Mary Godfire stood up then, and walked toward Faye, crooning in the base of her throat. "Annie, hold your tongue, if you can manage it. This little sister has some doubt and puzzlement in her heart, and we would be heartless to turn her away."

She glanced over at Forde, shutting the trunk of the DeSoto. "Why don't you come back and see us ... oh, Wednesday evening, wouldn't you say, Annie? About six, Hon. Thank you for fetching that heavy thing."

*   *

The replacement Mont Blanc glided across a sheet of Multigraph paper. Faye could, and should, have been typing, but she was still in love with the feel of it:

OUR TOWN'S TIMES
Wednesday, August 11, 1948
by Faye Bynum, City Editor

Gabbro's Sister City of Bozlee was struck by Nature at her very cruelest this week, in the form of a tornado that demolished the historic Old ...

... Caledonian Methodist Church and tore into Bozlee Elementary School, luckily empty at that hour. As the storm exited to the northeast, it took a final cruel swipe at the Pentland Hill neighborhood, damaging seven homes, injuring twelve, and killing US Army Staff Sgt. Milo Hayes, who was home on leave from his duties in occupied Berlin. The hearts of all Gabbro County go out to the displaced and bereaved of Bozlee. Monetary donations as well as blankets and clean used clothing are pouring in to the Red Cross collection center on North Main. Anyone wishing to contribute can send donations of money or canned goods to the VFD, care of Jim Hendley, Church Street Road, East Gabbro. Bless you all for your kindness and caring. *And rebellion.*

Faye passed the Hendley mail box - it was surrounded by bags and blankets - as she drove out Church Street Road on her way back to Mary Godfire's crazy project on Wednesday evening, as directed. She was dressed in dungarees and a tee shirt, influenced by how she had found Mary and Annie. The sun was behind her, glaring in the rear-view mirrors, making it hard to recognize the track through the alders that led to the Godfire project. Only when she found herself crossing a steel-truss bridge over the Gabbro River - and wondering if carrying traffic for thirty years would qualify the steel to be part of the Spirit Catcher - was Faye sure that she had overshot the mark. Cruising back slowly, she spotted it, and saw that she was five minutes late. She hoped, and suspected, that the Godfire household was not finicky about punctuality.

When the Chevy emerged from the bumpy track into the clear, the meadow was suffused with sunshine the color of the daffodil swimsuit. The ring of scrap steel had partly transformed into a circular knee-high fence that wove cutter bars, train couplers, box wrenches, the ink rollers, and dozens of other cast-off steel objects into an airy, symmetric and weirdly handsome circle some 40 yards across. Two of the *Intelligencer*'s massive rollers defined the beginning of a portal between the meadow and the trailer yard.

The goats were gathered around the feeding station by the towering oak, and Faye saw Annie lifting a fork of hay into the manger. Something in Annie's stance warned Faye to keep a quiet profile.

"Hi, Annie. Sorry I'm late."

" 'S OK. Mom's not feeling too good, though. I think you might have to reschedule."

"Oh. I'm sorry. Anything I can do?" *Run an errand, bring medicine through a snowstorm. Bake a cake.*

"Doubt it."

"OK. Would it be OK just to peek in and give her my best?"

"Can't stop you."

Faye doubted that. Annie looked like she could stop a Sherman tank with one hand, and was clearly in a foul mood. Faye walked through the portal to the little trailer, and tapped at the door.

"Eah."

"Mary? It's Faye."

"Come in, Hon."

The inside of the trailer was cramped and dark. Mary Godfire lay on a pallet of blankets opposite the door, with a cloth over her eyes. Her cheek below the cloth was swollen and bruised. She didn't turn her head to acknowledge Faye's entry.

"Oh, gosh, Mary, I'm sorry you're not feeling well. What, an accident?"

"Not exactly. Sorry I won't be able to chat with you tonight. I had a bad night last night."

"Oh, goodness, Mary, don't let it bother you. We can think about another time when you're over this."

Annie spoke from behind Faye. "Yeah, in a couple years."

Mary snorted. "Don't be silly, Annie. What happened, happened. Goes on all over the world, women get over it and get on with it."

Faye turned to Annie, who turned aside abruptly, and motioned Faye out of the trailer; Faye went to Mary, knelt, and kissed her unhurt cheek; then rose and went to the door. A weak voice followed her.

"G'night, Hon. Le's give it a week, say. Same time next week OK for you?"

"Certainly. See you then, and thank you."

When Faye walked out of the trailer, Annie took her arm and walked her back toward the Chevy. "Don't count on no week. She's hurt worse'n she knows."

"Gosh, Annie. What happened?"

Annie choked with fury. "Rape. Rape, is what happened." She slammed her work gloves on the ground and squatted over them with her hands over her face. "She was coming back from Rockingham, picked up a couple trannies from the dirt track, some son of a bitch dressed like a cop stopped her on 74 and dragged her out of the truck at gun point, slammed her a couple times, and threw her down in the ditch and raped her. In the ditch! She's 53 years old. She had to sit in the truck for two hours, before she could drive. I was going out of my mind, where is she, what's happened, when she finally made it back. Then it was another hour before she could talk enough to tell me. The guy was in a pickup truck with a magnet flasher stuck on the roof, how he got her to pull over. If I find out who the bastard is, he is gonna wish he'd never been born."

"U.S. 74?"

"What other one is there?"

"Don't ask me. Was this in Scotland County?"

"Don't ask me. She didn't take no readings. Between Rockingham and Maxton, she said. She remembers going through Maxton afterwards."

Faye turned back to the trailer. "I bet I know who it was. Come on."

*   *

Annie Godfire closed the trailer door and put an arm around Faye's shoulders. It felt like an 80-pound ink roller. "Same one?"

172

"I'm pretty sure, yes. A Scotland County deputy sheriff named Miles Windell. All the same tough talk, counting fingers, walking the white line. The gun sounded the same. Same moves toward oral sex, but going past that when she resisted."

"I'll pound the piece of shit to dogmeat."

"Wait." Faye stopped on the path, and held her head. "God, I would love to tell you, go to it. But I can't do that. I can't let you fight my fights for me. I did that once before, and I've regretted it ever since. Oh, shit."

"What's your problem? I'm not going after him for what he done to you, which you have my sympathy for. I'm going to pound him for what he done to Mom."

"Well, that's it, though. We don't know for sure it was the same guy. If I tell you it was, not knowing for sure, I'm just using you to get even for what happened to me, not what we know about your mother's thing."

" 'Thing,' shit! He raped her, he as good as raped you. You know Windell's got it coming, so what the hell?"

"Well, think a minute. What if it wasn't Windell that raped Mary? I just said it sounds like him, but the things he did, about anybody that was up to it might do the same. Probably would. You go after him, you about kill him, and the real rapist goes loose to keep on raping."

"He still has it coming, for you."

"And you walk off, feeling like you did the world a favor, is that it?"

"Damn right."

"And the other guy, the one that actually raped your mother?"

" … Well, how's this? I find Windell, and I talk to him about Mom. I have Mom's Gift, I know what people are really thinking, whatever lie they tell me. Why I'm even talking to you, by the way. I can't see that you even know how to lie. Anyways, I will know if he's lying about Mom. And if it wasn't him, I'll just give him a little dusting for you, whatever, OK?"

"No. Not OK. If you figure out about Mary, well, that's up to you, what you do about it. Don't kill him, you'll be sorry your whole life. But don't lift a finger about what happened to me. I can go on and live with being humiliated and terrorized. I <u>can</u>. I couldn't live with thinking I killed him by siccing you on to him."

Annie opened driver door of the Chevy and looked over it at the trees, and at the two-foot beginnings of the Spirit Catcher. "You think too damn much, my opinion." She stepped out of the way. "But you're right, all the same. I'll let you know what I find out. If it wadn't Windell that done it to Mom, I'll let him off."

Faye nodded, climbed in and pulled the key from her purse. "I thought your Mom looked a little better by the time we finished talking." She turned the key, and the Chevy started, after a show of reluctance.

Annie grunted. "Come back next week. She wants to talk to you. We could look at your timing, carburetor, too."

18.

S HERIFF AL BURNS rapped at Faye's alcove on Friday morning. " 'Scuse it, Miss Bynum. The boss sent me ask, could you spare a moment of your valuable time down 't his office?"

"Certainly. Can he wait, oh, thirty seconds while I finish a paragraph?" Saccharine smile.

"I will inform your boss that you are busy, but will be along in less than a minute."

But the train of thought was gone, and Faye rose grimly to follow him out to the newsroom.

Forde sat behind his desk, straight-faced. Burns preceded Faye in the door and adjusted its Venetian blind for opacity. Faye took what she knew was the better of Forde's two visitor chairs. Burns paced.

"Word come to my office, your girl here was interfered with by one of our Scotland County colleagues, few months ago, and never reported it to nobody. Why was that, Miss?"

"I reported it to my supervisor, Mr. Morgan, there. Right, Mr. Morgan?"

"She did, Al. What brought that up?"

"What I heard, she was next to raped. Why wouldn't a lady look to the law to seek redress for that kind of thing?"

Faye snorted. "I suppose you have some theory, but if I take your question at face value, Sheriff, I still have to ask you: Are you kidding?"

"I certainly wouldn't kid about that kind of thing. What makes you ask?"

"Could y'all excuse me for just a moment? I need to fetch my notes on the night I was 'interfered with.' I won't be a minute."

When she was gone, her footsteps tapping across the newsroom, Burns turned to Forde. "Nice lookin' little piece, cute ass, decent stack. Too bad she got such a mouth on her." Forde didn't reply, but went to the blind and re-opened it.

Faye returned with a manila folder under her arm, and a notebook in her hand. She sat, smiled at Sheriff Burns, and opened the folder.

"Ella Beason, complaint of rape, June 23, 1939. Charge dismissed. Elaine Cromartie, July 29, 1947. Complaint of molestation of her 12-year-old daughter Diana, charge dismissed for lack of evidence, since no one in the office of the Sheriff of Gabbro County on July 29 of last year, Sheriff, took the girl's black eye, bruised arms, and missing underwear as evidence of anything much but 'typical kid fantasy.' Fran Custer, September 15, 1945, beaten and raped, charge dismissed because Miss Custer was judged to have behaved in a sexually provocative manner and, in the words of the presiding judge, "asked for it.'

"I have summaries of twenty cases in this folder, which is all of those in the last fifteen years in which the complainant and defendant were both white. I did not include any cases involving Negros, because I didn't want to muddy the waters by mixing in race matters. Though believe me, it would have changed nothing. They are in alphabetical order, from Beason to Williams covering the last fifteen years, starting January 1, 1933. Of the twenty cases, the charge was dismissed in 19 of them, and upheld in one, Minnie Perdue in 1937, because a passer-by observed the entire incident - without intervening, by the way - and testified as to Miss Perdue's demure and un-provocative appearance and behavior, and her attacker's 'aggressive bestiality.' Shall I go on?"

"Don't see why you should. None of them cases has any bearing on your allegations against Deputy Windell."

"You don't get it? Then let me spell it out for you, Mr. Sheriff. Unless a girl who is about to be raped in Gabbro County is lucky enough to have the act watched by some spineless peeping-tom while it's happening, she has a zero percent chance of her story being believed, and a 100% chance of being verbally assaulted and humiliated all over again, quizzed by a drooling lawyer about what she was wearing, and accused of behaving so brazenly that no red-blooded American could possibly be blamed for 'raping the shit out of her,' to quote one juror. And besides, I made no allegations, except to report to Mr. Morgan what had happened to upset me, on being asked."

"So you went ahead an' let yourself be molested because you didn't think nobody would believe you about it? Aren't you the same Faye Bynum that pranced around naked in front of a half-wit boy last spring? Sure you didn't just relax and enjoy it?"

Faye's face went white, then red. She turned to Forde. "Mr. Morgan, will you be so good as to respond on my behalf? I do not trust myself to do so without calling the sheriff of Gabbro County a jackass."

Forde smiled thinly. "Al, just between us, off the record and in private here between friends, you're talking like a jackass. If you weren't somebody I know and respect, I would add some other words that I might guess Miss Bynum was considering, such as … oh, well, stupid asshole? I know I did. Excuse me, Miss Bynum."

Faye nodded.

"In any case, Miss Bynum did not 'let' anything happen. It was forced upon her. If I credit her account of the incident - and I certainly do - she saved herself from anything worse by appealing to Deputy Windell's better nature. I give her the honors due a saint, for even imagining that there was such a thing to appeal to."

Forde leaned forward. "Now, in that stupid matter of 'prancing naked,' Miss Bynum and I have reviewed the question thoroughly, and I find it to be entirely without merit, which I expect is why no further complaint has ever arisen from it. Miss Bynum, while admittedly partly unclothed in the privacy of her own home, was having a bit of fun at the expense of some degenerate jerks over at the Courthouse, who had been spying on her in said privacy with high-powered binoculars. I note in passing that the Office of the Sheriff of Gabbro County is located in the

Courthouse. Have I represented your thoughts accurately, Miss Bynum?"

Faye took a breath, adjusted her skirt, and grinned at Forde. "Mr. Morgan, you could not have hit it more accurately with a hunting rifle. Also, I might have forgot to mention the business about the Sheriff's Office. Was this degenerate peeping going on under your nose, and you didn't notice, Sheriff? Or were you running late for dinner yourself, for a few weeks prior to the incident in question?"

"Never mind, Faye. Now, Al, what in God's name brought you here to review that matter at this late date? As you pointed out, the thing happened last March."

Burns stood rigid, examining Forde's BA in Journalism on the far wall, while his right hand played with the butt of his Police Special. "You folks certainly know how to walk the edge of a razor. I will take into account that we are speaking privately and off the record, and overlook your smart-shit wordplay. I'd like to remind you that most incidents of so-called police brutality occur in private and off the record, and nobody is able to establish guilt or innocence, for lack of witnesses.

"But to answer your question, I am here to interview you both about Miss Bynum's unfortunate alleged incident, because Deputy Sheriff Windell was found shot to death next to his burnt-out cruiser this morning. The cruiser was barely warm, and Windell was not, in the least. Evidently, the killing occurred last night some time. Can you account for your actions over the last, oh, twelve hours, Miss Bynum?"

"Well." Faye tried not to look guilty and rattled, though it was not on her own account that she in fact was. "That would include some ten hours during which I came home from work, took a swim, fixed myself supper, and slept, all of those alone. Since eight this morning, I have been here at the *Intelligencer*.

"As for what you're getting at, I would have loved to set fire to Deputy Windell's cruiser, but I didn't, because I would never be able to get myself within a half-mile of the unfortunate son of a bitch, much less somehow overpower him and shoot him.

My thoughts and prayers go out to the Scotland County sheriff's department, and to whoever it was that killed Windell, because it was almost certainly one of his other victims."

She rose, and smiled a Southern smile at Alfred Burns. "But I surely do admire 'smart-shit wordplay.' That's good, strong English composition, Sheriff, and I would ask permission to borrow it, if I could ever use it in a family newspaper. Are we finished?"

"I want a word with your boss, here. You can go."

"That girl wants to watch her mouth, Forde. And you, too, damn it. You had no call to rag me in front of her."

"Sorry you took it bad, Al. Miss Bynum is a very valuable employee here, and I won't have her harassed by that crude talk about 'relax and enjoy it,' is that clear? From what I hear, the world is a lot better place without Miles Windell in it, not that I think there is a chance in hell that Faye had anything to do with pushing him out of it. Best you took your search for the culprit in other directions. Like those other victims."

"Ain't my search in the first place. I come here as a courtesy to Scotland County, and to you, so you wouldn't be answering to some cop you never met before. I got one other place to go in Gabbro County, which is another employee of yours, that Mary Zecharias that does the cleaning here. I'll catch her tonight, or out at her trailer today yet. See if you can't put a muzzle on that girl of yours, Forde. I'm asking for her own safety, here."

"Wait a minute. Mary run afoul of that bastard too?"

"Th'other night, and he got her good. One I'm really looking for is Mary's daughter Annie. Mary's a little too old an' gentle to murder somebody, but her kid's strong as an ox."

*   *

Faye did not wait for the official end of the week, or for her appointment, but drove as fast as she dared out to Mary Godfire's meadow. The Spirit Catcher had not advanced since Wednesday; Mary was alone, moving slowly, lifting and discarding small pieces of scrap steel. Her face was still swollen and livid.

"Annie ain't here."

"Oh, dear. Did you know that Deputy Windell was murdered some time last night?"

"No. Why would that bring you out here in a rush, Miss?"

"Well, I ... " Faye straightened and looked at Mary Godfire. "I am worried that Annie may have ... well, had something to do with it."

"Kilt him, you mean?"

"Yes. That's what I mean. People find it hard to lie to you, don't they?"

"I suppose that is my Gift. It is not so much a gift to me, as to them that was thinking about lying. Why would you?"

"Because it is not an easy thing to suggest to a mother that her child might be capable of murder. I suppose I was tiptoeing around coming out with it."

"And yet <u>your</u> Gift is that have no trouble telling the truth about other things."

"Is that a Gift? It certainly has caused me a lot of trouble."

"I have noticed that the kind of gifts we're talking about pretty often cause trouble for the folks that have them. Would this be a good time for you to talk a little more about it?"

"Well. I rushed out here to warn you that Sheriff Burns is likely to come looking for you, in connection with the murder of Windell."

"Looking for Annie, more likely."

"Yes."

"Annie did not kill that man."

"Well, good. But I don't want to take your time, tire you out, while you're still recovering from ... " Faye straightened, and then reached out to Mary Godfire. "From being raped. Oh, that hurts me even to say it. That wretched, lousy ... "

"I'm not going to insult you by spinning some lie about how I hold no hard feelings toward a dead man. I'm glad he's dead, on both of our accounts. But I can see that there's some other matter, longer ago, that is weighing down your spirit. Tell me about it."

"Oh … Well, can we sit down where it's shady? You have such a beautiful place."

Mary Godfire led Faye to the goat feeding station, and sat on a bale of hay, gesturing at a neighboring bale in the shade of the giant oak. "A little better than the ground. It's another death, I think?"

"I was engaged to a soldier at Fort Bragg, that I'd known when we were both in high school, back home in St. Louis. While I was pregnant with his child, he had sex with another woman who was much more rich and beautiful than me. I was so angry that I killed him by provoking a bunch of Klan thugs to get into a fight with him. I was hoping they would beat him up; well, I got what I wanted, except that they killed him."

"And you are angry at yourself about the setting-up for him to be beaten to death."

"Yes."

"Not much point in saying that <u>you</u> didn't kill him, that they did, I suppose."

"No. If we'd been standing by a railroad track, and I pushed him out in front of a train, it would be stupid to say that I didn't kill him, the locomotive did. Wouldn't it?"

"Locomotives got no choice what they do, people do, even Klansmen. But you're right, anyways. We kill each other indirectly many more times than ever appears in the newspapers. We drive each other to drink, so somebody dies early of cirrhosis, or a car wreck. We badger and criticize, or we whine and cling, and the next thing, somebody's come down with cancer. We drive each other to suicide, sometimes. We claim that all men are created equal, and half a million of them die in a war about it. Killing each other this hands-off way is something you don't see so much in Nature. Humans are the experts, at it, aren't they?"

Faye covered her face. "Yes."

"Most of us don't have the truth and courage in us to admit it. In your case, to insist on it."

"Small comfort."

"I'm not here to comfort. You would have to find someone you love, and loves you, for that." Mary Godfire drew back. "That's a troublesome thought for you too, I see."

"Yes. Another potentially lethal tangle I've created, by encouraging two different men to think they have an inside track to my affections."

"Do you want to discuss it?"

"I'm not sure I should. It involves … " She gestured toward where Forde had parked the previous week.

"Young Forde. Well, that does present a few complications."

"Yes. I've already confessed it to a priest, and what he said is probably exactly what you would say."

"To resolve the situation by choosing one or neither, and telling any leftover fella that he can never be more than a simple friend."

"Yes. It all sounds so simple and boring when you say it in simple English."

"The worst kind of tangles are almost always simple if you boil them down. But in the boiling, you lose so much of the volatile flavors, don't you? Everything turns to the same brown sludge. In this case, the complexity is in the problem of choosing one or the other? Or, as you say, neither."

"Yes."

"Please tell me their names. There is no need for being guarded with me. I already know the one, and the other will be known to me, since Gabbro is a very small town."

"He no longer lives in Gabbro."

"Travis Wayland, then."

Faye laughed and clapped a hand to her head. "The joys of small-town life."

"Yes. I don't see how anyone manages to live a meaningful life in a big city. But go ahead. Say their names."

"Forde Morgan. Travis Wayland."

"Well. There is no mistaking your affection for Wayland, but it sounds very different from your affection for Forde. You evidently don't know yourself which one is best for you, so you can't be as truthful as you'd like to with them. Plus, given that I know and love one of them myself, and don't know the other one, I'm not going to be a good advisor on this problem. But generally, something happens in the course of time that reminds you of what you have known all along. I would be very surprised if this time next year comes around, and the situation is still the same. My best advice would be to let some time pass."

Faye sighed. "As it will, with or without my permission. But thank you so much for taking the time with me. How much do I owe you?"

"You already paid. Annie came in from her talk with you very much comforted."

"Really? Comforted how? I just begged her not to go off after Miles Windell on my say-so."

"She said you talked good sense to her. And that she felt like she had found a sister. She has been wanting a sister since she was old enough to talk."

"Well ..."

"Annie has the Gift that I have, but much more so. I don't doubt her on this kind of thing."

19.

G ABBRO'S PRE-WAR COUNTY CRUISER sat at the foot of the cottage steps when Faye returned. When she entered the screened porch, Alfred Burns was sitting in the wicker chaise, looking out over the Eddy.

"Nice place."

"Thank you. It belongs to Mr. Morgan's family."

"Belongs to Morgan himself, then. He's pretty much the family now."

"I suppose that's true. How can I help you today, Sheriff Burns? Other than accepting your apology for making that silly crack about relaxing and enjoying nearly being raped?"

"He charging you rent? Or you paying him some other way?"

Faye went white. "Well, I was about to say, what he's charging is none of your business. Now, I guess, just between us and off the record, since Forde's not here to say it for me, I guess it's up to me. You're back to talking like an arrogant jackass. Want to try for 'stupid asshole?' You're half way there already."

Burns looked out over Morgan's Eddy for a time, while Faye wondered if she could get all the way back down the steps and safely into the Chevy before Burns could catch her.

"You know, little girl, one of these days, somebody's going to do what your Daddy should have done, and paddle your ass. You never get told to address your elders and betters with respect?"

With respect to what, redneck? "No, they taught me to tell the truth when my elders asked for it. I believe I just did that. If you disagree, you could stop talking like a stupid asshole, and maybe it would change my opinion. Also, please never refer to my Daddy again, he died a year ago and I'm still in mourning. Did you have some actual reason for coming here beyond trying to get even with me for what Forde said today?"

"I don't have to get even with nobody. I - "

"Literally true."

"I come here looking for you, tell you not to pass on nothing you heard at your office today."

"Oh. OK, got the message. Us journalists are good at protecting our sources, which usually annoys officers of the law. Anything else?"

"Yep. Have you seen Annie Godfire?"

"Yes. But not recently."

"When did you last see her?"

"May I ask what this is about?"

"Sure. None of your business. When did you last see Annie Godfire?"

"It was yesterday afternoon. I had an appointment with her mother to talk about that Spirit Catcher they're building."

"Bunch of jigaboo mumbo-jumbo. Did you talk to her about that Scotland County business?"

"When I was 'interfered with,' as you put it? I think that would probably come under the heading of privileged information. Doctor-patient confidentiality, though I admit she's not a regular doctor. 'Jigaboo mumbo-jumbo' is pretty good too, by the way, though it's another thing I can never use in the paper. You're a doggone poet, Sheriff. Anyways, I'm sorry, but I cannot discuss what I spoke to Mary Godfire about. It's personal."

"Yes, you can, God damn it. I'm an officer of the law and of the courts of Gabbro County, in which we are now located. I can make you talk."

"Yes, with a subpoena, I suppose you can. Come back when you have one, and I'll be happy to cooperate, but I already told you it was personal. Was there anything else?"

"Well." Burns shifted in the chaise, to a chorus of wickery, and heaved himself out of it. "One more thing, I guess. I'm reluctant to bring it up, but a man's gotta do his duty as he sees it. Remember what I said about allegations of so-called police brutality?"

"Yes." Faye's heart contracted, and a rush of fear exploded in her belly. "You said they usually occurred in private and off the record. Like we are now. Are you threatening me?"

"No, ma'am. A threat is usually what they call a conditional transaction. For example if I was to say, 'You tell me what you talked to Mary Godfire about, or I'll warm your britches for you, and don't think I won't,' that would be a threat."

Burns rose to look out over the Eddy. "But what I'm about to say is more in the nature of advisory information, like a road sign. You didn't tell me what I need to know, when I asked you nicely, acting as an officer of the law. So I am going to warm your britches, you little smart-aleck, and see if that improves your attitude."

He lunged at Faye, who jumped back and turned toward the screen door. But there was porch furniture in her way, and she barked a shin on the coffee table, knocking two Agatha Christies and a citronella candle to the floor. It slowed her enough that Burns could grab her arm and yank her back. He sat on the table and slung Faye across his lap.

Faye struggled, arms pinned in front of her by his knees, while he lifted her skirt and smacked his hand across her panties twice. Tears jumped to her eyes, and she was vowing to stay silent and see him dead, when there came a sharp sound like a well-hit softball. Alfred Burns collapsed across her back, knocking her wind out, and rolled to the floor. Faye, trapped under his bulk, struggled out, red-faced, stinging, and yanking at her skirt, to find Annie Godfire leaning on a canoe paddle and shaking her head.

"Shit, I barely tapped the son of a bitch."

Faye, still struggling for breath, managed, "Ann - Annie, Jesus. Oh, Annie." She threw herself on Annie, who stood as solid as oak, and kissed her cheek. "Oh, thank you. Where'd you come from? That miserable bastard, I am going to sue him so hard he'll never ... " She collapsed to sit on the table, wincing.

"I come to see you an' thank you for talking sense to me last night. I was here when he got here, so I laid low. And think nothin' of it. I owe you anyways, you straightened me out on that rat bastard deputy from Scotland County."

"Well, did you … You know. Did you kill him?"

"Long, strange story, that I'll tell you in a minute. Let's figure what we're gonna do with shithead here."

Faye wiped her face with the hem of her skirt. "Mm. First of all, is <u>he</u> OK?"

"Far from it. But if you mean, is he alive, seems so. He's breathing, anyways." Annie put a boot on Sheriff Burns' hip and pushed him onto his back. Burns began to snore.

"OK, good. Annie, he's looking for you, about the Scotland County … about Windell. You've got to get out of here, before he comes to."

"Yeah, and leave you here with him. Don't think so."

"We could both leave. No, wait, he knows I was here, and he'll figure out there's no way I could have hit him over the head." Faye passed a hand over her buttocks, which seemed to be recovering. "And he'd guess it was you, maybe."

"Yep. What if we loaded him down the steps and into his damn cruiser, drove him out somewheres and left him?"

"Fingerprints in the cruiser. They'd know who did it."

"Gloves." Annie pulled a pair out of her hip pocket.

"What if he comes to while we're driving him?"

"Put him in the trunk."

"He'll suffocate."

"Probably not, but serve him right."

"Probably's not good enough. How bad is he hurt?"

Annie lifted Burns' head, none too gently, and probed the back of his skull. "Mm. Kind of a dent back there. I prob'ly shoulda used the flat part of the paddle 'stead of the edge. 'Course we don't know if he already had a hole in his head. He kind of acted like it." She probed the shallow groove in the skull, and Burns muttered, but stayed out. Annie stood up, letting Burns' head thump onto the floor. "Look, we stay here and wring our hands all day, he will wake up, and then we'll have twice the problem. I'll wire his ankles together, and you take that end."

They horsed Burns out the screen door and down the steps, Annie taking most of the weight under one arm, and looking as if she were carrying a small cat. "Throw him in the back seat, and let's go. I'll drive the cruiser, and you follow in your Chev. We'll leave him on some back road, and you can bring me back home."

"What if he comes to while you're driving?"

"I'll put him out again. Come on."

Annie had detailed knowledge of the Gabbro County backwoods, and drove the cruiser over dirt roads to a place by a sandy creek deep in Indian Girl Swamp, where the only way out was to back it over fifty yards of twisting track. Faye, following, was at a loss to do that, so Annie did, with casual skill. At the dirt road, she swung the Chevy around and let Faye drive back the way they'd come.

"How is he?"

"Still snoring in the back seat when I left. I tooken the ammo out of his gun, and his pants off, and threw the whole mess in the crick, so he won't come knocking at anybody's door till he goes home for another pair."

She turned to Faye. "OK, you wanted to know about Mr. Deputy Windell. Well, I did burn his cruiser, for sure, and I suppose I owe Scotland County for it. I didn't shoot him, though. He shot himself ... Left here, then the next right."

"Really? My God, Annie!"

"I went after him by speeding up and down 74 until he pulled me over. I have Mom's Gift, I think I told you." Annie seemed to run out of words.

"Yeah? Seeing the future, listening to spirits?" *Listen to me. I'm a redneck now for sure.* But Annie Godfire had a presence that eradicated doubt.

Annie put a foot on the Chevy's dash, leaving a smear of mud, which she wiped off with the tail of her wife-beater shirt. "Nobody can see the future. But I can see the past and the truth real clear when I talk to people. Mom can tell what people are really thinking when they talk to her. Me too. But ... with me, it's like <u>they</u> know, too. Like if I was kind of a mirror for what people are thinking. I remind them of what they already know, but don't want to think about. So after Windell's gone through the license-and-registration-please, and the fingers business, I sort of calmed him down and got him talking. And he's telling me no-o, he'd never rape a middle-age woman in a ditch, it'd get his uniform muddy, and anyhow, there's plenty of good-looking young things on the road - he's telling <u>me</u> this, mind, as if I'd understand. As if, long as I didn't think he'd raped Mom, anything else would be OK.

"But I can see he's lying, that it <u>was</u> him that raped her, and then, guess what, he can see I know he's lying, and he can feel what I'm feeling about the lie. The disgust, the sick feeling I've got about this subhuman asshole, and all of a sudden he gets that from me, and then he feels the same way. He steps back, and stands there for a second, and I hope I never see a face like his again. Then he pulls his big fuckin' pistol, and I think, Uh oh, and he's raising it up, I'm ready to try and jump him, but I know I'll never get to him quicker'n a bullet will get to me."

Annie stopped, and blew a breath at the ground, looking sick. "But then he puts it under his own chin and pulls the trigger."

"Oh, God, Annie."

"Well, it was a mess, of course. Whole top of his head come off. But bad as it was, he come out looking better than just before. And that's all I'm gonna say about it."

"Don't go in our lane. Burns is just smart enough to pick up your tire tracks in the mud."

"There already. I came by to talk to your Mom this afternoon."

"Which you already told Burns about before I whaled him. OK, but still. Drop me here, and get gone, before he comes around and finds us together."

"All right. I still never saw you today. Where were you?"

"F'etteville, picking up a couple firehouse slide poles that was next in line to get built in. All them fires, folks getting their lives disrupted, babies rescued, rookie firemen sliding down scared to shit their britches. That's plenty of life to help the spirits. So that's the story, anyhow. They're already built into the portal, along with a couple a your press rollers. How's your britches, by the way?"

"Just between us girls? A little tight. I think I got kind of a swollen butt, which I intend to treat with a cool dip in the river. Want to come along?"

"Hell, yes. But I better get on, see how Mom's doing, get her up to speed on Burns. And Ex-Deputy Windell."

"Well, come on over any time. You busy over the weekend?"

"Sunday morning be OK?"

"You bet. Night time's fun too, so mark your calendar next full moon."

20.

F ROM THE GABBRO *INTELLIGENCER* for Friday, September 3, 1948:

Burns Out of Intensive Care

Gabbro County Sheriff Alfred Burns was transferred from Intensive Care to a recovery ward at Gabbro Memorial yesterday, and seems on the road to a full and cheerful recovery. He suffered what doctors called a "severe concussion" after being attacked by an unknown assailant while on duty two weeks ago. Burns continues to suffer from amnesia as to the circumstances of the attack. He was found in his cruiser …

Vacancies Continue as Schools Open

Acting School Board Chairman Ellice Laffler reported "little progress" in the search for a qualified replacement for fired Superintendent Minor Mack. Abraham Cousins, Negro, formerly principal of Frederick Douglass High School will also continue as Acting Superintendent of Schools, a situation characterized by Mrs. Laffler as "Unprecedented, and I will say frankly, undesirable" …

Morgan's Eddy

*　　　　*

Faye Bynum, having authored these stories in a pleasant welter of human glee and Catholic guilt, lay in starlit dark in a tent on the flank of Grandfather Mountain in the Pisgah Forest, some twenty miles south of Boone, North Carolina, and reviewed the events of the day. By her side, as naked, exhausted, and sweaty-cool as she, Travis Wayland snored gently with an arm flung over her belly, having achieved only a temporary and incomplete waking when Faye, unable to resist, turned toward him and buried her fingers in his hair to pull his head to her breast and kiss his irresistible taffy curls. That accomplished, she stretched luxuriously, and listened to the chorus of applause from the night bugs that surrounded their tent. Somewhere some kind of owl, Faye hoped, sent a shivery ghost-voice over the forest.

Travis had been a little hesitant at first when she called to follow through on the discussion of tents and hikes, but warmed when appeals to 'Travis,' surviving a crackly long-distance line from Gabbro to Boone, hit their mark. Faye reminded him that, as of September 1, soon coming, she would be entitled to three days of paid vacation, that would later swell to five, eight, and ten as the months rolled by. He invited her to join him for a hike ("Overnight, I mean, of course.") the Labor Day weekend of September fourth.

"… No, don't come here to the station. There's a little coffee shop on Watauga Street, I can meet you there. I get off at noon on Saturday, so do you think you could be here close to that? We'd have time to get pretty high up Grandfather, where the leaves are starting to turn."

"Goodness, already? I'll be there."

"OK, great. Bring a nickel, you could call me from their pay phone, it'd take me three minutes to be there, and I'll have all the stuff."

Faye had risen at five, downed some corn flakes, and pulled out of the river cottage's lane at 5:30, and turned west toward a sky that held the last of the night. The Chevy ran like a Cadillac after Annie Godfire spent an afternoon reasoning with it last week. Faye hosted a tingle in her belly that was kin to the enchantment that had led to her dead-of-night dip in Morgan's Eddy. She tried not to think of Morgan or his eddy; or of the late Deputy Windell as she drove west through Scotland County on U.S. 74, passing a burned spot on the shoulder east of Laurinburg.

It was a good deal more than three minutes after she called Travis from the Watauga Street Diner, but there he was, as slender and delicious as she remembered him, grinning and graceful. They executed a circumspect hug, and Faye pulled at his arm.

"I'm so glad to see you, Travis. Come on and sit down for just a minute, I'm starved. I ordered a bowl of soup that's just now come. Want some?"

They ate, they split a piece of chess pie; Travis talked about his new job, his apartment, and finally, about where they needed to get to before dark.

"We can drive to within a few miles of it, but once you start up the trail, it gets to be virgin-forest wilderness pretty quick. You feel up to carrying a sleeping bag and a little food? I'll have the tent and the rest of the food, and drinks."

"Well, heck, Travis. You don't have to give me some kind of ladies' load. I can carry as much as you, I bet. Almost."

Travis snorted. " 'Ladies' load.' God, how I've missed you, Faye."

"I'm taking lessons in wordsmithing from Sheriff Burns. How do you like 'smart-shit wordplay?' Or 'jigaboo mumbo-jumbo'?"

"Well, I love smart-shit wordplay when it's you doing the playing. Burns actually said that?"

"Literally."

"What was the mumbo-jumbo about?"

"Mary and Annie Godfire's Spirit Catcher." She saw that Travis drew a blank on this subject. "I'll tell you about it while we're hiking. It's been on my mind a lot the last couple of weeks. Oh, Travis, you've been gone so long, and left me with nobody to share things with. I've missed you, too."

The hike stressed Faye, despite her claims of rugged capabilities, and she was glad when, with the sun aslant though enormous oaks and hickories, Travis walked through a screen of rhododendrons - 'I think this is it ... yup' - into a grassy clearing. Faye followed, panting and immediately enchanted.

"Gosh, Travis. It's like something out of Bambi."

"Yup."

Having achieved it, they realized that this particular hike was more about the destination than about the journey. Here is where they would share a tent and, as Faye put it, "all that." The realization put a damper on talk. They busied themselves with wilderness housekeeping, neither of them experienced campers, but with some originality and sense of seemliness. By the time they finished, sunlight was only grazing the circle of treetops above the clearing, and they had a tent, a circle of stones to echo the trees, a stack of firewood, runny noses, and four cold feet. After Travis built and lit a fire, and they ate some Dinty Moore, talked about the Spirit Catcher, and had a second glass of wine each, they sat in silence while the darkness grew and the crickets and katydids tuned up around them.

"Travis," Faye said at last, blowing her nose. "You know, you are under no sort of obligation."

"Obligation?"

"In regard to our sleeping together. Well, of course, we <u>are</u> going to sleep together, unless one of us sleeps on the grass. But I meant ... Well. You know ... " She sighed and looked at her feet, stretched toward the fire. "OK. Sex."

"Synonyms came to your tongue rather more easily on a couple of prior occasions. Are you talking in your blushing-maidenly way about fucking?"

Faye laughed. "Wordsmith. Yes, that was the one I was looking for. Anyhow, I would be lying to say I have no expectations, but I would be OK with … oh, shit, Travis. Please help me out."

Travis nodded, stood, and gestured. "Come here a second."

She did, and he enfolded her. "I never honor obligations. When I do something it's because I damn well please, and usually because it's something I've been wanting to do for months."

When they had kissed sufficiently to run out of breath, when they had wiped their noses and begun to fumble with buttons on each other's hiking clothes, Travis stepped back, keeping a hand on her cheek. "Wait, though, by the way. You know I said this was virgin wilderness."

"You did say something about that. I'm afraid I don't qualify."

"Well, I forged you a certificate that I will have handy, in case we get inspected."

"Can I see it?"

"Certainly, officer, but I'd probably have to get out of my underwear to get at it."

"C'mon, then."

*   *

Lying now in the printer's-ink darkness of the tent, Faye relived in memory the whole, and each separate stage, of their love-making, and scored it on a scale that was entirely subjective, relative to reasonable expectations, and dominated by the dictates of a nerve somewhere in her belly that might have been a toaster filament, given its tendency to warm and cool, depending on what was passing externally:

(1) <u>Setting and ambience:</u> The wilderness hike was a brilliant idea, far better than beginning a sexual relationship (Oh, hell, an 'affair') in some hideous motel or in Travis' alien apartment - Faye recognized with a small shock that, while Travis had visited her poky garret over Woolworth's more than once, she

had never even known his address in Gabbro. Whatever that might mean, or nothing. The beauty and intrigue of the virgin forest, the views of miles of hardwoods touched by the first colors of autumn, the sky crammed with stars that accompanied them to their bedding, the very fact that they had climbed upward for hours to reach this enchanted spot, all added in to the delight of the occasion. Score: A solid 10 on a scale of 10.

(2) <u>The initial stages</u>: Had been dizzying in the way Travis seemed to care so much about her particular pleasure, and to make a little ceremony of each stage of undressing and touching, which had been mutual, and had taken hours (objectively, she supposed, maybe twenty minutes) of slow revelations and admirations, until Faye deliquesced into a barely sentient puddle of desire, stunned beyond speech - this articulate woman - at his smooth, muscular, lanky completeness, his obvious delight in her, and the sense he gave this foreplay of some hilarious secret never before revealed to humans. Score: 20+ on a scale of 10.

(3) Actual intercourse: Nothing to complain about, really, and maybe nothing short of bursting into flame and rising to the stars could have matched the perfection of the setting and the foreplay. The business of the condom was a little off-putting, and Travis was expert at it, which was - well, at least thought-provoking. But he was considerate, gentle, patient, and strong when strength was called for. It was a different species of experience from the hasty and no-frills deflowering she'd received at the hands of Gordon, that left her pregnant and largely unsatisfied. She had an odd sense, though, that before they shuddered to a mutual and vocal climax, Travis had turned inward, and absented himself to parts unknown, his intricate, sexy body wholly present, his mind continents away. Score: 7 or 8 on a scale of 10.

(4) Summary: Hm. Faye found herself too cold and sleepy to do numbers in her head. She burrowed herself and Travis into

196

the double sleeping bag, laid her head on his chest and her knee over his slender, furry leg to listen to the cricket lullaby and thought, before she merged with the darkness, *Well, it was a very good start.*

Some hours later, Faye emerged from a dream in which she held a wooly lamb that had run away, and had to be trained to stay at home by grooming its curls of fleece, and found that she was nuzzling the curls of Travis Wayland instead, his head bowed to lick at the gentle valley between her breasts.

"Oh," she said, muzzy with sleep, cradling his head. "How nice. Travis, my sweet, my lovely. Ah, Jesus. You think Adam and Eve woke up like this on Monday morning?"

"Not dealt with in my Bible. Boy, that's a nice perfume, meant to say something about it last night. Goes real good with sweat." His tongue traced a path down her belly, tasted the dried sweat at her navel, and became busy at her groin.

"Silk - Hhh…ah, Jesus, *Trrahhv* … Silken Rain." She arched to meet him and, from within the half-conscious fog of that pleasure, listened to the dawn chorus of birds, the day being barely begun in gray tones of mist and mystery. She thought of floating half-asleep in the mothering waters of … oh, damn. Of Morgan's Eddy. This time, it was Faye who was only partly there as they coupled.

Scoring:

(1): 15 (Still in the forest; dawn, mist, birds, arousal straight from sleep).

(2): 15+ (Tongue; second go in less than twelve hours; that amazing thing of sitting coupled in each other's laps).

(3): 8 again, her fault this time.

(4): It occurred to her later to wonder if a distraction like hers might have taken him away from their coupling the first time.

* *

Later still, they stood panting hand in hand in clarity and sunshine at the peak of Grandfather Mountain, while Travis pointed out other peaks that rose above an encompassing low cloud. "Gets this way in the fall, they tell me, like there was a sea of fog. I guess this is what they mean. There's the Blue Ridge all along there. That's Mount Mitchell, highest point in the eastern US. Boone lies that-a-way from Beech Mountain, over there. But it's all down hill from here."

"Boy, do I believe that. Travis, I don't know but that my whole life isn't going to be all down hill from here … I think; I never did handle multiple negatives very well. What I mean to say is, I have never been so glad in my life as I was to find you all over me when I woke up this morning."

"We could give it a few more shots, see if we could live up to this again. Willing to try?"

"Purely in the spirit of research?"

"Of course not. Purely in the spirit of seeing if we can make each other pass out. Think that's possible? For both at once?"

"I'm willing to try if you are. If we're both going to faint, we'd have to find some place where nobody could get hurt."

"Atta girl. Why don't you work on the logistics side of it? But not now, alas. I'm on the air at six tomorrow morning, so I've got to be back to Boone some time tonight, and you've got to get yourself back to dear Gabbro, I presume."

Halfway home, Faye passed a north-pointing sign, *Greensboro 46*, and seeing it brought back perfectly the sound of the cello octet and the bittersweet harmonies of *Liebesleid*. Love's sorrow. She knew something of that sorrow, from the time she discovered Gordon's betrayal; and she could only hope and pray that it would never again be as intense as that, or as the pleasures just past, in which the yearning was so strong that it was in itself a kind of sorrow. *Maybe that's what they mean by Liebesleid. That would be OK.*

"But do I actually <u>love</u> him?" A big question in a small voice, under the roar of air from the windows. She turned off the staticky radio to think about it. Everything Sister Orian had ever said about love in Health class (not counting Jesus-involved kinds of love invented by churchmen whose lives could not possibly have included being licked awake to birdsong at dawn) - all that curriculum insisted that sex came only after love. Well, according to that, she logically must love Travis, or how could she have <u>made</u> love with him so whole-heartedly?

Well, she certainly had strong feelings about Travis, but if she were honest, those feelings bore little resemblance to the love that Sister O taught on Friday afternoons: chastity, wedding mass with Eucharist, marriage for life without possibility of parole, babies galore to be raised in the arms of the Holy Mother Church, fidelity to hubby through thick and thin, more babies and beatings and bitterness. And if she examined in retrospect what her mother must have felt about her father, whatever pleasures there were in that marriage had surely been diluted and alloyed with the patience to follow him on his barnstorming rounds. Faye shook her head. Her feelings toward Travis had a good deal more to do with pleasing and being pleasured, as had just happened without benefit of any of that other stuff; and, frankly, with when she could possibly go back for another helping.

Nor was the question of marriage reintroduced during the weekend, and that was fine; there was that about Travis that did not really fit with the idea of a bread-winning hubby in a tie and fedora. What Faye wanted now was simply to banter, to tease, and to enjoy life, including sex, with him for quite a while yet, and then see where they were. And she was pretty sure that was what Travis wanted too. It was annoying that Travis lived and worked so far away, a good six-hour drive over slow roads.

But here it is, she decided. *Your attention please, everyone:* Precocious little Miss Mary Faye Bynum is at last a grown woman at the beginning of a very pleasing affair with a very sexy lover, in which thrilling wicked acts are committed that make her laugh, and jelly her knees in the remembering. 'Love' as such might have to wait upon developments.

Still, it seemed to her as the Chevy hummed along the slow roads to the flatlands, mutual fainting would not be a danger until they managed to get that low third score up closer to a ten. She gave the next hours, which brought her to Morgan's Eddy at last, to thinking about what that might involve.

21.

W HAT'S THE TOWN'S TIMES ABOUT this week?"
"Hm?"

"Town's Times? About?" Forde stood at the entrance to Faye's alcove, leaning on the wall, looking oddly to Faye like Errol Flynn in an executive mood.

"Oh." Faye flourished the Mont Blanc. "Still thinking about it. I thought maybe an, um, a collection of little things that have been piling up. Prospects for the Quarrymen under their new coach. Friends of the Library book sale. Resurfacing West Church, when East Church is in much rougher shape, but it's on the dark side of town. No one big thing."

"You could probably leave the Quarrymen to Rob Stoker. That's his beat."

"Yes, sir. Rob Stoker is kind of a nitwit."

"Faye, don't take advantage of our friendship to run down a fellow employee."

"No, sir. Sorry … Am I a friend, or an employee?"

Forde, on his way to his office, wasn't particularly intended to hear the question, but he did. He turned back. "Faye, you're both, as you know. As far as I'm concerned, you're a very dear friend. But as your employer and supervisor - "

"Oh, Forde … " Faye's voice, airy with boredom, fell a diminished fifth on his name. She shrugged, hoping to dismiss the subject and get back in spirit at least to the virgin wilderness of Grandfather Mountain.

"What?"

Faye recognized the danger. "Nothing, Forde. I'm a little tired this morning. I'll get you the column in … well, by noon."

"Didn't get much sleep on your vacation?"

"No, as a matter of fact, I slept very well."

"And your uncomplicated friend Mr. Wayland? How did he sleep?"

"What on earth leads you to believe that I would be in a position to answer a question like that? You are starting to become offensive. Please don't push it, Forde."

But it was too late. "Push it? Push what? Me, push anything? Not me, God, no." Forde pivoted and headed for his office. Faye heard a slam and the clatter of the Venetian blind, followed by a giggle from Jenny McCall, presumably at some miming by Rob Stoker. She rose, knowing she shouldn't, and followed him, entering his office and shutting the door gently. Forde was at his desk, white-faced and trembling.

Faye decided she could be generous. And must. "Forde, you know how much I like you. I hate to see this."

"Yes? Please don't upset your self about anything."

"Look, I have owed you a serious talk for a very long time, and it appears that the time has come for us to have it and get it behind us."

Forde shrugged, and Faye pressed on.

"You appear to have some knowledge, or theory, about how I spent my vacation time. Well, that is of course entirely my business, and none of yours. However." She raised a hand against Forde's looming outburst. "This is not a great place for us to talk. Why don't we … oh, look, join me for a glass or two of wine at the cottage this evening? We could maybe iron out a few things."

Forde inhaled - rather ostentatiously, Faye thought. He sounded like Osgood Conklin on "Our Miss Brooks."

"Well. All right. What time, and what can I bring?" Gritted teeth.

"Mm. Well, six? No, 5:30, bring a nice bottle of wine, we can relax on the screen porch. I'll fix some snacks. I do like you ever so much, Forde, and I can't stand to see things get … well, crossways between us.

Forde waved a dismissive hand. "All right. See you then."

"Good." Faye opened the door. "Thanks Mr. Morgan. See you then." - for the benefit of Jenny and Rob.

*   *

P.O. Box 701 had been more a luxury than a necessity for Faye, once she moved out of the Woolworth attic. Mostly it yielded flyers, and once a month her phone bill and a dunning note from Hubbard Chevrolet. She had given the address to Travis for anything he might not want to discuss over the leaky telephone, and he had used it a few times for remote flirtatiousness that was a pale imitation of the close-up thing. On this evening, there was a piece of real mail there, neither the window envelope of the phone company, nor Travis' scrawl.

Faye noticed that, of late, her hopeful tiptoe dance to see into the top-row box had become less necessary; it was as if her new sense of herself as a mature woman *With a lover!* had rendered it both less seemly - jumping on tiptoe felt like a six-year-old at Christmas - and for some reason less necessary. In fact Faye had, like relatively few of her age cohort, actually added some fractions of an inch in height in the last year, entering her 22nd year at nearly 5'5". She keyed open the box and extracted an offer to buy her house sight unseen, a mass-mailing ad for the Salonnette, and a crisp long envelope with an unfamiliar logo in the return-address corner:

Miss Faye Bynum
PO Box 701
Gabbro 1, NC

Dear Miss Bynum:

The publishers and staff of the Asheville Exchange have been most impressed by your work as City Editor of the Gabbro Intelligencer, in particular your investigative work in regard to recent school bond issues. We applaud the perspicacity of the North Carolina Press Association in rewarding the courage and diligence of the Intelligencer in breaking that story, while recognizing that you, personally, were principally responsible for the award.

Miss Bynum, we are writing to inquire whether you would entertain the idea of accepting a similar position as that you now hold, with the <u>Exchange</u>, an independent daily newspaper serving the Asheville, NC city and region, with a circulation of over 20,000. Your responsibilities would be similar to your current ones, but would include a larger area - substantially all of western North Carolina - and a larger city. Pay and benefits would be more than comparable to your current compensation, and you would be able to call on the services of a full-time reporter who would serve under your direction.

If you are interested in pursuing this possibility, please contact the undersigned ...

It was signed by a Clement Atkins, Jr. - presumably the Custis Morgan of the Asheville <u>Exchange.</u> Faye closed her eyes and slumped against the wall of mailboxes.

*   *

On the screened porch of the cottage at Morgan's Eddy, Faye poured a refill into Forde's glass, to which he neither objected nor assented. Beyond the screens, crickets and a whole chorus of peepers filled the dusk with flickering white noise erected on a bullfrog foundation. A low sliver of moon showed a crescent worthy of a Krazy Kat panel, and laid a golden track across Morgan's Eddy. Faye leaned back and crossed her ankles on the table with the Agatha Christies and the citronella candle. *I should light that. Also, I have a beautiful lover who makes me feel like Cleopatra, minus the snake. I must not think of him now.* She looked about vaguely for matches.

"Forde, you are my oldest friend. Longest-standing, I mean. I am everlastingly grateful to you for giving me this job, and this opportunity to prove myself as a writer and a journalist. Without you, I would still be working at menial jobs and trying to keep my sanity."

"Which sounds like a lead in to telling me that I have no business asking you about your private ... doings. And, of course, that's true. Just, you seem different since you came back. Like you're in another world. How can I keep from wondering?"

Faye rose and walked into the kitchen, returning with a fat box of strike-anywheres. "Well, no, you don't. Have any business. But that's not what I was going to say. The fact is, I have an offer to join a newspaper in Asheville, which would be a step up for me. I am seriously considering taking them up on it."

Forde exhaled and leaned back, shaking. "Asheville. Is that where you were over the weekend?"

"No. Do you really want to know where I was? Because if it's terribly important to you, I'll tell you." Faye lit the citronella candle. "In fact, wait a minute. I'll tell you anyhow, because it's important to me, too. To both of us." She blew out the match and remained poised over the table. "Forde, you know that I have been seeing Travis Wayland."

"Well. I thought he moved away."

"He did. He's working in Boone now. I'm still seeing him."

"Way out there? Oh, boy." Forde bowed and put his hands to his eyes. "Sounds serious," he said, at last. "It sounds like your uncomplicated friendship got complicated all of a sudden."

"Yes. Forde, there's no easy way to say this. I'm very much ... attached to Travis." *Particularly sometimes.*

"Uh huh." Forde sighed, and rose. "It's going to take me a while to get used to this. Let's talk about your Asheville possibility tomorrow morning. Maybe there's a way I could make it attractive for you to stay at the Intelligencer. My feelings aside, you are very valuable to the paper."

"All right. Maybe."

"Not likely, though, huh? Asheville's a sight closer to Boone than here. Is. Is that a consideration?"

"Well." Faye rose and put a hand on his arm. "Yes, honestly, I'm afraid it is a consideration. I didn't see this coming, Forde. But I like you so much that I'm not going to deceive you."

"Well. Thanks for that. I appreciate it. Too late, though."

"What does that mean?"

Forde didn't quite snarl, but his face became set and angry. "It means I'm already deceived. I thought we might have a future, you and I. But that's obviously me, deceiving myself."

22.

FAYE LEANED BACK to let Pearlene rinse. Ginny Freeman piped up from beneath a dryer helmet.

"Where you been, Honey? You been patronizing some Yankee outfit?"

"I would never patronize a Yankee clipper," Faye said, grinning. "Last time I was due, I was on vacation. For a trim, I mean."

"Ladies, I ask you. Don't she look different somehow? What have you been up to, young lady?"

Faye blushed. Damn all small-town women and their snoopy noses. "I love all my respected elders way too much to say, None of your business, Ginny. Pearlene, would you be willing to say it for me? … Anybody?"

"I said it, I'd probably get fired. Anybody else said it, I might agree."

Ginny sniffed. "Well, good land. I'll say it to myself: None of your business, Ginny Freeman. But where does that get us? The only things worth thinking about in this hick town is stuff that's none of our business. How else would you have found out about that courthouse crowd peekin' at you?"

Faye smiled while the warm water washed over her head. "You make a good point, Ginny. All right. Let me ask a question, and maybe y'all can fill in from what I'm not saying, which you are all so good at: How do you know if you actually love somebody?"

Universal laughter. "Oh, stuff! That much was obvious just seeing you walking down Church Street this week. And I'm fairly sure we can all fill in the name of the lucky fella, seeing Forde Morgan kicking rocks down the road yesterday. What we don't yet know is, what happened? If you see what I mean."

Mary-Deane Gaines waved a dismissive hand. "I believe we should do our little sister the favor of addressing her question just now, and get off the other. Even for the Salonnette they's some things that really are none of our business. So. Anybody here remember ever being in love?

Universal silence, broken by Pearlene's snipping and underscored by the dryer. "There ya have it," Ginny smirked, resuming the speakership. "I do recall one time thinking, Dang, I must have been in love to do such a damn-fool thing. But I don't remember how it felt, except the nauseous headache all next day. So, how was it? ... Never mind, you're as pink as Pepto-Bismol. That good, huh?"

"I had a lovely, very pleasant visit with Travis over Labor Day, and that's all I'm going to say about it."

"Don't fret, Hon, that's as much as anybody ever says. We'll take it from there."

*   *

From the Gabbro *Intelligencer* for Monday, September 20, 1948:

OUR TOWN'S TIMES
By M. Faye Bynum
City Editor

I had a chance to catch up with Sheriff Alfred Burns this week, the first time I've seen him since his traumatic run-in with an unknown assailant a month ago. Sheriff Burns is still suffering from the after-effects of a serious concussion, and handled himself carefully in chatting with a visitor.

Gabbro Intelligencer: Sheriff, thank you so much for agreeing to talk with us today. The whole staff of the *Intelligencer* has asked me to pass on their good wishes and prayers for a speedy and complete recovery.

Sheriff Burns: Thank you very much.

GI: Have you made any progress in learning who it was that ambushed you and left you pretty much to God's mercy out in the swamp?

SB: The whole incident is a nearly complete blank to me. As you know, the last thing I remember before I woke up in the ICU is talking to you about crime statistics in Gabbro County since I assumed this office.

GI: That's right. That was earlier that same week, over lunch at the Terminal. I recall that there was some good news on that front, isn't that so?

SB: That's right, the incidence of ...

... so much for your time, Sheriff, and please take it easy and get well soon.

SB: Your readers can count on this: If and when I figure out who done this to me, you can believe that the full and righteous force of the Law will descend ...

*　　　　*

"Oh, gosh, Forde. That's a very generous offer, and I frankly don't see how the *Intelligencer* can afford it."

Forde shrugged. "Not something you need to worry about. Would you be interested?"

Faye sighed. "You would be taking a salary cut, wouldn't you?"

Forde shook his head. "Not your department, Faye. That's my counter-offer, take it or leave it."

Faye leaned out very gently, and kissed Forde's cheek. "I would feel like a ruthless mercenary wretch to take a penny more than the salary I'm already making, not to mention the generous raise you already promised for the second year, and the lovely bonus that you gave me for the journalism award. Money just isn't a factor here, Forde."

"You know, you could be running out there after a fella that you might end up not in love with after all."

"Well, that's so, Forde. But I'm not going out there primarily for that personal reason. The *Exchange* is a daily, and the job is more … well, substantial. Responsible. It's a real step up in the world of journalism, and it could lead on to bigger things yet. I'd have the whole Blue Ridge area, five counties, as a beat, instead of one - now mind you, charming, lovely - little town."

"Well. I can't make Gabbro any bigger or more important all by myself. All right, Faye. When were you planning to leave?"

*   *

The Spirit Catcher was waist high to Faye now. She stood against it and listened to it hum and whistle in a stiff breeze that was blowing solid clouds over Mary Godfire's meadow.

"That is just amazing, and amazingly beautiful, Mary. And a little bit … well, is it already attracting spirits? Because, I swear, there is something a little spooky about it."

"If you feel it, then I expect it's there, Hon. 'Course, it could be just your own spirit taking an interest."

"And these things are all … all part of it, contributing?"

"We got these lawn mower reels from a development up by Aberdeen that grew up and went bust when the water supply turned out to be full of typhoid."

"Huh. Did you think of taking off the cutter bars, and let the blades spin? They'd go around pretty well in this wind, I'd think."

"We did. Sperrits didn't think much of it."

"Frivolous, I guess."

"That's right." Annie spoke up. "This isn't some kind of circus toy. Take those parts away from what they done over the years and make 'em into whirlygigs, you're making a joke of all that work."

"Of course. Well, I came out to see how you all were getting on, and to let you know, I'm fixing to leave Gabbro." Faye found herself clouding up at the thought.

"Sorry to hear that. Let's go set down a minute - Annie, if you'd give us just a little time? I see you've got some things you want to go over with Faye, and I'll call you when we're finished."

"OK, Momma."

Annie picked up a welding torch and got it hissing, and Mary led Faye to the live oak and sat on a bale. "Getting a little chilly, like weather coming in."

Faye pulled her jacket closer around herself and nodded. Mary's swelling and black eye were about gone, but something about her stance told Faye that the psychic damage from the rape might linger for years. She pictured Miles Windell minus the top of his head, burning in Hell, and uttered what Sister Penitentia once called a prayer of assent. "Yes, Ma'am. I wanted to ask you about a couple of things, if I could."

"Always. But I should tell you, love is a very tangled subject, and my record in helping people with it is some good, some bad. What is it?"

Faye smiled. "Gosh, you have to ask? Yes, love. I'm leaving Gabbro to take a very good job in Asheville, and Travis Wayland is in the picture, since he lives in Boone, which is not that far away."

"Almost a hundred miles."

"Yes. But compared to here. Maybe this is that 'something that will happen in the course of time,' that you talked about."

"Well, Faye. Which do you think is more important, the job or Travis?"

"Oh, gosh, Mary. That's it, isn't it? How do I separate them out?"

"Maybe you shouldn't. Right now you live in a nice little town with a nice little job, working with a nice boy, and the thought of leaving them makes you cry. That's all one picture, and I bet if you tried to pull them apart, they would boil down to nothing much. Now, the other picture, tell me about it."

"Well. Start with the job. It's like the job I have here, a kind of regional-editor beat, but with a bigger region. I'd have a reporter working under me. I kind of feel almost a duty to myself to take it on. I think I could do a good job."

"All right. Add in Travis."

"I could see him much more regularly. I could leave work and be in Boone in three hours, in time to, well …"

"In time to go to bed with him?"

"Yes, Ma'am."

"Maybe even some day, marry him, or at least live with him, and drive back and forth every day."

"I … I haven't thought that far ahead."

"Would you want to marry him?"

"Oh, how do I decide such a thing? I suppose if we continue … well, as we are, I would about have to, wouldn't I? I don't mind the thought of a - " Faye puffed out her cheeks and looked Mary in the eye. "An affair that would go on for a while. A pretty good while. But at some point, you have kind of a duty to fish or cut bait. Make a commitment."

"Why is that?"

"Well. First of all, it's not impossible that I would become pregnant. Then there would be a third party involved, the baby, and there would be a duty to provide him with a family."

"You're quite dutiful, aren't you? Duty to yourself, duty to marry, duty to this theoretical baby."

"I … yes."

"What happens if you don't do your duty? Just let it go?"

"I would not respect myself."

"Huh. No problem to sleep with a man who makes no commitment to you, but you wouldn't respect yourself if you passed up a better job. And a marriage that would be for the sake of the baby."

"Yes."

"Are you religious?"

"I was brought up and educated in the Catholic church. By religious Sisters."

"Not surprising."

"I guess not. But here I am, and I can't go back and be raised differently."

"No, you can't. You might have to ask that raising which direction it is really pointing you in this situation. I have to say, the presence of a love affair really muddies the water for me. It appears as if this is a matter between you and your nuns. Annie?"

"Just one thing," Annie said, handing the acetylene torch to Mary and walking Faye into the goat meadow, where a west wind sent silver waves across the grass. "And you don't have to answer, 'less you want. What is sex like?"

Faye glanced at Annie, who smiled and said, "That good, huh? Wow."

23.

I T WAS LIKE WHEN TRAVIS HELD HER on the toboggan with his arms and legs, but even more exciting, and the other way around. Faye held Travis with arms and legs, grasping and gasping while the dark waves rolled through her and broke against her heart.

"Ohh, *God!* Oh, Jesus, Mary an ... a-an ... anh..." She closed her eyes and subsided a little, trying to feel every inch of herself, and of him. *Morning sex. So much sexier than the night before.*

Travis looked down at her, smiling. "Still conscious?"

Eyes closed, murmuring, "Barely. What about you?"

"Can't tell. I think I might have fainted back there."

"I have a new attitude on that. I refuse to faint, because I am not going to miss <u>any</u> of what I'm feeling. Oh. Oh, wait, don't go. Give me another little time to hold you. Morning sex is just *so* perfect. You think it's because it's so lazy and cozy? Or 'cause we're rested up?"

"Probably. Feeling good?"

"The only way I could feel better would be if I could bundle you up and take you home with me. Fold you completely into myself somehow. Enfold you forever, because I love you so."

"Play hell with play-by-play broadcasting."

"Oh, well, never mind, then." She let him go, and shuddered at the feel of his leaving. "I can probably last a week on what we've accomplished this weekend. Next weekend?"

"Of course ... Oh, no, wait. I'm on a basketball trip to Tennessee next weekend."

"Oh, damn. Really?"

"Yes. That's part of this racket. Basketball is big out here, as you will find. Congratulations on the new job, by the way."

"Hey. I was saving that for a surprise when I was leaving."

"Word gets around."

"Huh. … Wait a minute. They wrote to my PO box, which only you and Forde and the phone company know. And Murray Chev. Very few people. Did you have anything to do with this?"

"I admit. I know a guy there, and he said they were hiring. I thought it was a job you'd like, and you'd be so much closer. When do you start?"

She rose and wandered to look over his half-shutters at the frigid stream from the neighbor's leaking gutter, cozy in her nakedness, listening to church bells with lazy nostalgia.

"Friday. For, you know. Orientation, Sign here, Here's your key to the building, all that. I really start the next Monday. The 25th."

"You have a place to live?"

"The editor and his wife are putting me up for a couple of days over the weekend, while I look. He says there are lots of reasonable places."

Travis opened a drawer in the bedside table, and sorted through the pencils and condoms. "So speaking of keys to the building. You talked one time about how an affair involves no ring, no ceremony, all that. I guess for an affair, like we're having, the equivalent of exchanging rings would be having a key to each other's place. What would you think about having a key to this place, and giving me one to your new place?"

"Goodness, how advanced. That would bring down condemnation from any Catholic church in the land. So, fine."

"If you wanted to keep things here … I don't know, a toothbrush, some clothes? That would give me something to remind me of you when you're not around."

"Well. I brought a change of clothes that I guess you could tuck away for me. No fooling around with my underwear."

"Not my idea of fun. Anyhow, here you go, courtesy of Mac Hardware." He tossed her a key on a rabbit's foot chain, and she surprised herself by catching it. She stretched and yawned, and sent a wink out the window, in case Boone had peeping toms in its courthouse too.

"Do you think Adam and Eve liked morning sex? And was it better than after the Fall? Or did God let us keep this one divine thing, just to remind us of what we gave up to eat apples? I'll tell you, when we're well, you know. Making love. I certainly feel like I'm in a state of grace."

"And thus ignorant of the difference between good and evil, which would account for your complete lack of inhibitions. I like the idea, but I guess I missed Sunday School the day they talked about that."

She turned toward him, posing a little. "So, you know what? Today's Sunday, so here's a piece of school for you: What if all of living in Eden, like walking, eating, naming the animals, mowing the grass around the Tree of Life, what if all that was as wonderful and ... and <u>radiant</u> as sex for them, before the Fall. What if Adam and Eve took as much joy in fixing lunch as you and I do in sex - which, speaking for myself here, is rather a lot. And, ha, know what else? I bet all those things even had their own, special, um, you know. Feeling. Climax."

"The technical term is 'orgasm.' "

"Ick. Really? Is this another one of those things you learned by doing homework?"

"Pass."

"Well, it just sounds dirty, for something so lovely. But OK, the point is, what if everything they did back then was like sex, and had its own kind of *Oorgazum*" - drawing it out, mock-scientific - "all different, each for the part of your body that you've used to do it. A foot orgasm for walking, an arm one for, oh, gardening, I guess. Holding hands. They might have been in this kind of bliss all the time."

Travis cackled. "Foot orgasms! Man, I want one of those. How about a mouth orgasm for talking my arm off? So to speak."

She walked toward him, twirling the key, letting her hips do as they pleased; purring, "Sure. But now, since the Fall, all we have left is the one for ..." Voice down another register, hissing it like the Snake: "Sex."

Travis held up the covers. "No wonder they went out of their minds. Aren't you cold out there? Get in here and get cozy. That is, if you're ... you know. Inclined All that slinking around and sex talk has got me all steamed up again."

She crawled over him to straddle his hips. "What do you think it was for, dummy?"

*   *

Driving back to Gabbro, Faye began to score her first visit to Boone:

1 (Setting and ambience): About a 5. Rain all weekend. Travis' apartment was poky and cluttered, and located on the second floor of a glum two-story apartment house, in a town that made Gabbro look like Atlanta.

2 (Initial Stages): 10. Travis, maybe realizing that the setting was a drawback, reprised the charm he'd shown on Grandfather mountain, greeting herself, her body, and every stage of undressing as old friends for whom he had pined for years.

3 (Actual intercourse): Oh, Lord, a thousand? A billion? How many grains of sand ...

Childish silly game. Numbers do no justice.

4 (Summary): No more score-keeping. If this isn't love, then I have no idea what love is.

*   *

From the Gabbro *Intelligencer* for Monday, October 18, 1948:

OUR TOWN'S TIMES
by M. Faye Bynum
City Editor

This column will be my farewell to Gabbro and Gabbro County, as I have accepted an editorial job at the Asheville *Exchange*. I will miss all of my friends (Hey there, Salonnette ladies!) and all of you who have made me feel so welcome and at home here, and have borne with me as I ranted about schools and school bonds, street repairs, and so forth. Thanks and goodbye to all of you whom I have interviewed, and who made Gabbro come alive for me. And a very warm 'so long' to my co-workers here at the *Intelligencer*, particularly my friend, Managing Editor Forde Morgan. And of course, a special bye-bye to my gallery of fans at the County Courthouse. Sorry I spoiled your fun by moving! But there has hardly been a day here in Gabbro that has been anything other than warm, thrilling, fun, and entertaining. I will miss the town, its people, and the beauty of its fields and rivers. Farewell!

*   *

After lunch, and while Mrs. Atkins was busy in the kitchen supervising the cleanup, Clement Atkins, Editor of the Asheville *Exchange,* held Faye's chair as she rose, and let the knuckles of his left hand graze her breast, so lightly that Faye could not be sure that it was anything but purely accidental.

"Martha, I'm going to run Miss Faye downtown, let her look over a few properties she might be interested in renting."

Mrs. Atkins' voice fluted from beyond the swinging door. "All right, Clemmie. Miss Bynum, we will expect to see you here for dinner. It was right pleasant meeting you."

"Yes, Ma'am. Likewise, and thank you so much for your hospitality. Oh, and please call me Faye."

"All right, Honey."

Between rising from lunch at 1 pm, and entering the seventh vacant apartment a little after five, Clemmie's hands had been on her more than a dozen times, some of them in relatively innocent ways: taking her arm on a particularly steep stairway (too much like Woolworth's) or draping a hand around her shoulder while introducing her to the mayor, after encountering him on the sidewalk outside a Victorian with a basement apartment (a real possibility, except for having almost no windows) - but most of them directed at brushing contact with more intimate areas. Faye, as she tried to picture herself in each place, and to picture Travis with her in each bedroom, began to anticipate when Atkins was likely to paw her, and to back off or pivot to present him with the least possible and most neutral surface. Even so, he got in pretty solid gropes on her butt, her thigh (in the car) and her left breast (holding the car door for her in a way that she had to duck under his arm).

At the end of the afternoon, she had had enough. Standing in the empty dining alcove of another Victorian basement, she turned to him, vowing to maintain a pleasant conversational tone. "Mr. Atkins."

"Clem."

"Sir, I will begin by saying how very much I look forward to working with the *Exchange*, and with you personally. But I have to add this: it will not be possible for me to do that if you persist in pawing and touching my body at every opportunity. I don't like it, and I don't much like the relationship between us that it seems to imply. I am here to investigate, write, and edit for you, not to be your plaything. Am I making myself clear, here? Can we go forward on that basis?"

He pushed his fedora to the back of his head and grinned at her, looking like Spencer Tracy after he was too old to make movies. "Cuss Morgan said you could be a little spitfire. I see what he's talking about, rest his soul."

"Spit - Jesus, Mr. Atkins. Cliché. And if Custis Morgan is going to be a model for your behavior in regard to me, we have a very serious problem."

Atkins shrugged. "Hell, OK, girlie. Jesus, yourself. You one of these lesbians? I didn't mean no harm."

"Well, you caused it, just the same. How do you know Custis, anyhow? You mean you discussed me between you way back last winter some time?"

"Yeah, we talk about things - talked, that is, pretty regular. I known him at Chapel Hill."

"Huh. Well, look. Maybe the women you've worked with up to now have been OK with this kind of dumb-ass behavior, but not me. Keep your hands to yourself, and we'll get along just fine."

"Dumb-ass? You actually calling me a dumb-ass, your employer that's gonna sign your paychecks?"

"No, sir, of course not. I was calling your behavior dumb-ass. Far as I'm concerned, you are one of God's precious children, like anybody else."

Atkins turned toward the stairway that led to the sidewalk, and paused at the bottom step. "G'on ahead, Honey. Not sure I trust you behind me, you might kick my dumb ass on the way up."

Faye, knowing what he was planning, said nothing, but ran up the first three steps to establish a buffering distance. A mistake, evidently, because Atkins called out, "Stop."

Faye stopped and turned. "Yes?" Heart beginning to pump, at something she heard in his tone.

"Come down here, please."

"Um. I'd rather not, sir."

"I didn't ask what you'd rather, ya little pisspot. I'm your boss. Get down here."

"No. And don't call me stupid names."

Atkins lunged for her arm, but she dodged and ran up the rest of the steps, slamming the door at the top to slow him down a little. And lo, he had left the key in the lock. She turned it before he could twist the knob.

And there he was, locked in a cellar apartment whose slit-like windows would never have let Travis Wayland wiggle through, let alone a fat old editor. She leaned on the door and shouted, "I quit, and you're locked in, you dumb-ass old goat. I hope you rot there."

And there <u>she</u> was, on the outside, homeless and unemployed with an empty feeling under her ribs.

She left the Victorian and stood on the sidewalk, trying to establish directions and to reconstruct where she had left the Chevy. By the time she found it on the street a block from the *Exchange* offices, darkness had fallen. She sat behind the steering wheel, mopping her cheeks and blowing her nose. Wonderful. Homeless, unemployed, and lost, with night coming on. She drove at random until she ran across a cruiser marked "Buncombe County Sheriff," outside the Patton Street Eats. She pulled in beside it and started to get out, but as she unlatched the door, a lanky guy in uniform exited the Eats and headed for the cruiser. Faye had a cruel flash of Deputy Windell, but desperation won out.

"Sir? Sir?"

"He'p you, little girl?"

"Yes. I'm meeting my, *(lover)* my <u>brother</u> in Boone, and I seem to have got lost coming through town. Which way is it to Boone?"

"US 19 what you want, goes most the way there. How 'bout I lead you out t' 19, get you started. Wup, but hang on, listen here: you get about 20 miles north on 19, hit's gonna fork, 19E and 19W. You want E, W's a mountain road, take the rest of your life to get anywheres in that ol' Chivvy."

"Oh, that's very nice of you. So, wait. At the fork, 19 which?"

"19E, Honey. Hell, I got nothin' better than he'p out a pretty little thing, I'll take ya up there, point the way."

Oh, Jesus. "No, don't bother yourself. I got it now. 19E."

"Folla me."

There was no choice. Without this likely rapist, she could not even find the way out of town. Faye climbed into the Chevy with pounding heart, and waited until the cruiser had backed onto Patton Street, and fell in behind him.

Hail Mary, full of grace, the Lord is with thee....

*   *

Forde knew it was stupid to move out to the river cottage after Faye left. All it did was reinforce the hateful fact that the girl - no, come on, the *woman* he thought would be his wife, was in love with someone else. Was gone for good, and had left a tiny bottle of Silken Rain on the bathroom sink to torment him. Nevertheless he stayed, telling himself that it was important to clean the place up and get it ready to sell; sleeping hardly at all as he tossed on the bed she had occupied, and finding other small traces of her, even down to the tracks of the Chevy's tires in the dirt. He went out of his way to avoid driving over them. In the evening, he lit the citronella candle, and dragged himself through the memory of their breaking-up, while he tried and mostly failed to produce a replacement for Our Town's Times; and the Grandmother Clock ticked away the silence.

His anchor in this sea of despondency was the memory of the moment when Faye exited the screen door of that porch in her daffodil swimsuit, her beautiful naked back carrying her into her life after the humiliation at the hands of Deputy Windell. Forde renewed his vow of loyalty to that singular moment, promising it never to forget, and never to think ill of Faye for the choices that she made after it.

He was careful to extinguish the citronella candle when he went in, not to waste its memories on the void night air.

*   *

... *now and at the hour of our death.* Faye was finishing the 180th Hail Mary when the cruiser's flashers went on, and he pulled to the side of the highway. She pulled alongside and lowered the passenger window. *Hail Mary, full of grace...*

"This here's the split. You want the right-hand fork up where you see the sign."

"19E."

"Good for you. Now listen. Another 10-15 mile, you'll hit North Car'lina 194. Take it right, go 4 mile, then lef' on US 321. Take that ten mile, you'll hit 105 t' the right, runs past Grandfather Mountain. That runs you straight into Boone. I wroten it all out for ya."

"I've been on Grandfather Mountain. I can get it from there."

"C'mere, then, Honey."

Faye gave up all hope, and stepped out of the Chevy, walking to the cruiser on shaking legs. *Hail Mary ...* When she walked around the Chevy, the cop rolled down his window and pushed something out. Not a finger or a pistol, Oh, thank you, Blessed ... "

"Honey? You been up to something? I never saw a pretty little thing as jumpy as you."

"No. I haven't been drinking. I didn't ... I just had a bad experience this afternoon."

"What, with a cop?"

"N - Yes. He raped me."

"What, this afternoon."

"No. Last March."

"Huh. Well, Jesus Lord. Sorry. Here, look." He pushed a folded paper out the window. Faye saw that it had a naked woman on it, and almost fainted. The cop looked down at the paper and blushed. "Wait. I confiscated this calendar from my boy this morning, and it's all the paper I got. Turn it over."

On the back, the cop had written, *'19E 15mi, 194 right 4mi, 321 left 10mi, 105 right to Boone.* Faye sagged against the cruiser.

"Oh, Jesus. Thank you, you sweet, sweet man." She leaned in the window and kissed the cop's cheek.

"Hey. Looks like it was me needed to watch out, wannit?"

Faye was three miles up 19E when she remembered that she had left her overnight case at Clem and Martha Atkins' house. She was not in a position to throw away even a small handful of clothing; she pulled into the next gas station and fished in her wallet for nickels and dimes to call.

-Hello?

-Mrs. Atkins? It's Faye Bynum. I need to tell you that your husband is locked in the basement apartment at 218 Patton Avenue.

-No he's not. He's right here. Where on earth are you, Honey?

-Oh. May I speak to him, then?

-Yes. Here, Clemmie.

-Bynum?

-How did you get out?

-Yelled out one of them little windows. You're fired, of course.

-Too late. I resigned when I left you down there. I need my overnight case.

-Where are you?

-I'm some distance from Asheville. I just remembered it.

-Huh. Not that smart after all, are you?

-I'm about average, at best. But I won't be trifled with like -

-Let's forget it, shall we?

-... Ah. Is Mrs. Atkins on an extension?

-Yes, I am, dear. What on earth is going on?

-I'll let Mr. Atkins explain it. But I won't be joining the Exchange, I'm sorry to say. Can you put my overnight case on your front steps?

*   *

On this same evening, Forde woke from a much-needed doze, saw that it was nearly nine, and extinguished the citronella candle. Behind the forest across the Eddy a gibbous moon, orange with haze and humidity, rose to greet the frog songs. Forde picked up one of the Agatha Christies and tried to figure out from the first page whether he had read it. Maybe some weekend when he was ten or twelve, and came here with Custis to lie around and resist suggestions that he get out and do things. The book smelled almost pleasantly of mildew. It was about Miss Marple, but that didn't narrow it down enough. The hypnosis of the brief sleep had demolished his defenses, and the sight of the screen door felt like a rapier gliding through his chest. He stumbled through the living room and sat on the edge of Faye's bed to unlace his shoes.

*   *

When Faye came within range of Boone, she heard Travis on WBON doing a play-by-play for a team called the Mountaineers, she supposed somewhere in Tennessee. Just his voice was enough to make her cry with relief at the thought of seeing him. She hated that he would not be here for her, but she composed a loving note as she drove, breaking the news that she would not be moving to Asheville, and in fact had no idea where she would be living. Having nowhere else to go, she decided to settle in and wait for him to return. Maybe do a little cleaning up, though Travis was really neat enough, for a man. Still, some flowers, a woman's touch. She pictured herself in a frilly apron, and laughed.

With the driving back and forth, and rain during the homestretch on NC 105 that slowed her to let the headlights and wipers catch up, it was past eleven by the time Faye found Travis' apartment house. Numb with fatigue and emotion, she climbed the stairs, fishing in her purse for Travis' key. There were four apartments on his floor, and she was not perfectly sure which door was his. She walked up and down the third-floor hall, eliminating two possibilities because the occupants had put their names on the doors, but completely unsure as to whether Travis' was the corner door on the left after turning right at the top of the stairs, or on the right after turning left; and emotionally unwilling to take the fifty-fifty chance, and meet another stranger, who would ask who the hell she was, trying to break in. In the end, she went out into the rain to compare what she saw at each corner of the apartment block to what she had seen last Sunday when she peeked over his half-shutters. When she had been employed, housed, naked and comfortable.

Oriented, she returned, climbed the stairs once more, dripping and exhausted; and turned right.

*　　　　　*

At the river cottage, Forde rose from Faye's bed, disgusted at the unequal struggle to get back to sleep. He began to clean out some of Custis' things that had been locked away while Faye was living there; even this was preferable to boring himself with Agatha, or tossing fruitlessly on the heartbreaking bed. In a shoebox held shut with a man's garter, he found Custis' bottle of laudanum. The label said *Tinct. Opii Ent. 10%* It was still more than half full.

*　　　　　*

She was disoriented and embarrassed at first, entering the apartment and heading straight to the bedroom to throw herself face-down across the bed. And knock her wind out across a line of knees. A woman screamed, and someone gave a bark of outrage.

"Aah! Oh, my God, I'm so sorry, I must have the wrong … the wrong…" *No, but, the key fit.* A light flared, and Faye squinted against it. "Claude? … Travis!"

"Oh, sweet Lord Jesus," Claude said. "Here's a fuck-up fit for a French farce. Well, come on, Hon, get those wet things off. Snuggle in and meet our pal Brenda. Brenda, Faye. Faye, Brenda. I believe you know Mr. Wayland. Ever done a four-way?"

*　　　　　*

Forde sat on the edge of Faye's bed and stared at the bottle. When he swirled it, flakes of something dark rose and orbited against the glass walls. That darkness was the prospect of living here without Pop, without Faye, with no prospect of happiness. He rather envied Pop, whose heartbreak was at an end. And here Pop had left him the means to follow.

He tried, self-conscious and skeptical, and in the end, he could not do it. He raised the bottle to his lips and lowered it twice; then steeled himself, and took a slug. It was so bitter that he spat it ten feet across the bedroom and ran to the bathroom, coughing. It was possible, he thought, that he might have swallowed some of it, but he could not see how Custis could possibly have gotten down enough to kill him.

Or, wait. Maybe the little that went down was enough to kill him. Maybe he was already doomed, ready to join Pop in a brigade of the disappointed. Well, he would leave it in the lap of the gods. He had had enough for one night.

*   *

The rainstorm accompanied the Chevy as together they hurled themselves and Faye down the mountainsides toward the flatlands, averaging about twice the posted speeds. Driving it was like riding the toboggan, and Faye burst anew into tears at the memory, astounded that she had any left. Her lap was wet where they had dripped from her chin. Her wet and swollen eyes gave her a smeared approximation of the empty road that rushed at her in a rainy and structureless blur while the wipers dabbed at the windshield. The 1936 headlights were intended as much to show other drivers roughly where to look for the Chevy, as to show its driver the road, and she was overdriving their sepia glow by furlongs. Her mind was pretty much absent, and she drove on last-instant reflex to keep the Chevy somewhere on the wet road. When towns loomed up, she hurtled through them at the same speed that carried her on the open highway.

Where her mind might have been, there was only the horrible image of Travis, silent and hostile next to this woman Brenda whom Faye had never seen before, who was next to leering Claude, all of them naked to the waist and doubtless beyond. Except that Claude was wearing on his oily head the panties she'd left with Travis as a down payment on a Boone wardrobe.

Her scream still rasped her throat, her arm ached with the half-second satisfaction of turning on her way out and throwing the unlucky rabbit's-foot key in Travis' face and slamming the door. Running down the stairs while the full horror of her situation unfolded, and kept unfolding with every step she took. By the time she had driven two blocks, the radio warmed up and thanked her for listening to a delayed rebroadcast of last night's Mountaineers game. Being recorded, WBON would not be taking any further call-ins.

Good. I have no further questions. A homeless, jobless, friendless, loveless schoolgirl with no place in this world, she had been toyed with, laughed at, and debauched by a playboy who gave not one fig about her fantasies: *Ayy, God,* her *vanities* about being a grown woman with a lover - how she had preened herself over the word - who loved not at all; about her giddy and feckless notion of enfolding into herself a viper who would eat her heart. Her prattle about *varieties of orgasm in the Garden of Eden, Oh, God in Heaven!*

Her face burned through its mask of tears at the memory of chattering like a kindergartner holding Daddy's hand, marveling about the beauties of sex, to Travis - Travis, who had seen it all, done it all, doubtless in the company of goddamn Claude, who liked boys better than girls. God knew what diseases she now harbored. The cleanest thing would be to terminate the affair, terminate love, and …

And while she was at it, to put an end to her hopes, her career, and her rotten, wretched, hollow so-called life. Faye knew the way to only one other destination from Boone, and it was back to Gabbro. Fine, she drove hell-bound for Morgan's Eddy, where she could drown herself in the freezing depths she had already visited, and wherein she was known and welcome, not abused, mocked, and made a fool of.

Whether to drive the Chevy off the end of the dock and drown trapped in it, or to dive in and drown on her own, she had not decided. Deciding was beyond her entirely. Whether to drive all the way there, or simply to flatten herself at eighty miles an hour against a bridge abutment and thus to smash forever the image that rode the hood of the Chevy - the expressions of surprise, fear, and finally of contempt, that had paraded across Travis' face - this was all that her mind could manage. So far, she liked the idea of dying in Gabbro better than on a piece of civil engineering. When she had concluded that, Sister Rose Penitentia appeared on the Chevy's hood, not disapproving, but displacing the horror of Travis. With the rain and the fogged windshield, it was hard to see, but it seemed to Faye that Sister P. might be crying.

She passed the "Greensboro 46" sign, and knew in full Love's Sorrow, next to which the pain she'd had at the hands of Gordon was barely an annoyance. As she wailed anew, the gas gauge showed less than a quarter tank. Faye, still navigating by the gross shapes of things, could not read it.

*   *

At Morgan's Eddy, Forde, tranquilized by the jot of laudanum that had filmed the inside of his mouth, slept dreamlessly for the first time in a week.

*   *

Faye made it to Gabbro a little after five in the morning. The Chevy, pretty much out of gas, sputtered and roared out Church Street, the engine fed only by the sloshings of the last hatful of gas and condensation water, and down the track to Morgan's Eddy. Confronted by trees coming at her and teeth-rattling bumps in the track, Faye eased back on the gas as the last of it siphoned up the fuel line. The engine coughed and died; Faye kicked it out of gear to roll down the sleeping lawn. The sight of, and reflexive swerve to avoid ramming Forde's DeSoto sent the Chevy into a slither on the wet grass and out onto the dock. It managed a final, prodigious backfire, and its left front tire slid off the edge, leaving it canted over the Eddy with its right rear a foot in the air. The driver's door opened; Faye tumbled straight into three feet of water and dashed into the Eddy, yanking off her blouse.

*　　　　*

Inside the cottage, Forde was startled awake by the backfire. He threw off the sheet and stumbled toward the porch, thinking of shotguns or lightning.

*　　　　*

Yes, this was right. Sinking to the sandy bottom to lie there forever, Morgan's Eddy her pool of tears, the cold springs her preservative. She stripped out of the last of her clothing, planning that in a hundred years, her body would have turned to pyrite - Fool's gold, perfect! - joining the Confederate bones, to be glimpsed by other wounded maidens as they sank to their deaths; forever hiding the fool within.

She turned onto her back, still holding her breath and waiting for the moment when she would have to breathe water, and saw a figure in the wavelets of her plunge, in the shattered light of the gibbous moon. Not a dead Rebel but a fantastic thing of horns and flying capes - Sister Penitentia in full regalia, apparently come all this way on the Chevy's hood to escort her to an eternity of damnation.

"You owe that boy an apology. Get up there and present yourself to him. Beg for his forgiveness if you have to, but don't dare come back until you have it. I will wait."

Faye sank deeper. "No, really, Sister. I am dead already, and it's too late for forgiveness. Please don't make me."

Sister Penitentiary drew the ruler from her habit, but instead of whacking Faye's hand, she pointed it over her shoulder. A cold current lifted Faye and pushed her toward the dock. Faye emerged, rejected by the Eddy, coughing and gagging, and began obediently to wade toward the shore. She called out to Forde, her voice a wretched croak of misery.

Forde stumbled down the cottage steps, clad in boxers and a bathrobe, doped on opium and a dozen other alkaloids. He saw the Chevy canted suicidally across the dock, and started across the centipede grass toward it; stubbed his toe on a pine root that had been there for fifty years, and fell to his knees. What he saw then convinced him that the laudanum had won, and that this would be his last sight on this earth: Faye Bynum, sleekly naked against grey streaks of dawn, emerging like Venus from the depths of Morgan's Eddy - though without the cockleshell and the tapestries - and calling his name in a voice that quavered like a spirit's.

"Forde! I'm sorry, I am horribly sorry." And as she spoke, she kept wading, emerging from water that was waist, then knee deep, illuminated by the moon, the infant dawn, and the fading cockeyed headlights of the dangling Chevy as she came onward, shivering, splashing now in the shallows. "Fo-orde!"

Forde breathed her name in return, and flopped facedown on the grass.

24.

F AYE'S RECOVERY TOOK months, until Christmas and beyond, starting from the moment when Forde's eyes opened in response to the left-right slaps impatient Faye gave him, kneeling over him, dripping river water on his face to make them sting.

"*Ow*, dang it. The hell you think you're doing?"

"I'm hitting you to make you wake up and forgive me, you stupid ... stupid angel, you redneck darling, Oh, God, Forde, please forgive me. And make it quick, I'm freezing."

"Well, shit, OK. For what?"

"For making you sad. For like an egotistical ass, preferring goddamn Travis, I guess. I don't know! I don't kno-ow, I just know you have to forgive me so I can kill myself. Come on!" She began to sob.

"OK, fine, Jesus, you're forgiven. Now c'mon and get inside, you're nek - you got no clothes on. Here, take my bathrobe."

"Nope, don't need it. Thanks f' the forgive ... ness. I am so ... h-huh... sorry I hurt you, but now you've forgiven me, all ... h-h-huh ... done, right? G'bye, Forde."

"No, wait! I take it back, then. I <u>don't</u> forgive you, damn it! Stand up here." She stood, but fell against him protesting the bait-and-switch at Voice Level 40, and tried to push him away. In the end, he had to lift her off her feet from behind and carry her squalling up the porch steps with his arms locked around her waist while she kicked her heels into his crotch and banged her head into his face, starting a bloody nose. When he put her down to open the screen door, she squirmed past him and headed for the dock. Long-legged and a good runner, she almost got away, and he had to tackle her onto the centipede grass, giving her two or three strawberry marks, and himself a skinned elbow to go with the bloody nose. He was less circumspect this time, and threw her over his shoulder, dangling down his back and whacking his butt with desperate fists, but leaving him a hand free to deal with the screen door.

*   *

A tiny rural town in the South in 1948 is not the best place to find treatment for humiliation and self-hatred. On the other hand, it was far from being the worst. For example, it was not Vienna, New York, or anywhere in California. Her treatment began with being wrapped confiningly in Forde's flannel bathrobe with the zigzag Plains Indian motif, and carried to the bedroom where Forde, still half-sure the whole thing was a merciless hallucination brought on by the laudanum, nevertheless sat Faye on the edge of the bed, dried her hair and feet, and as much of her body as he could decently reach with a beach towel while she wept and pounded his back. He sang to her all the songs he could think of that fell within a "There, There" tradition. Slowly, gently, he managed to persuade her that the imperative self-murder did not have to be done that night, and could be left to morning, when it might look different. By degrees, he managed to extract from her sobbings the gist of the trouble. When he thought she was a little quieted, he picked up the thank-God handy bottle of laudanum and tipped a jot into the cap.

"Just put this in your mouth, and then spit it - There you go, that's the way."

"Agh! Jesus, what *was* that?"

"Um ... *Tinct. Opii Ent. 10%.* Just what the doctor ordered, Faye. I just tooken some of it myself, and right away, there you were. Like Romeo an' Juliet, right? Except nobody's dead yet."

Under the mercy of the laudanum residue in her mouth, Faye's weeping subsided a little, and she began to wilt toward the pillow. "Forde, Jesuh Marian Jos'. Don't bother yourself, I'm a snotty-nose kinnergarden brat, so full of myself. I'm not worth bother, tha's a fack."

"We'll talk about it in the morning, Faye. Lie down, my dear little girl, my little darlin'. Go to sleep. I will be here with you all night."

And - while she snored and woke to weep and gnash, and muttered in sleep that was plainly a struggle - he was.

*   *

The woman in Travis' bed, unfamiliar to Faye but not to Travis or Claude, was Brenda Benson, the sister of Travis' ex, the former Alice Freeman, and some kind of cousin-in-law to Ginnie Freeman of the Salonnette. Brenda and Alice had always shared the fun things they had gotten into when they were schoolgirls, and they still did.

Alice lived in Bozlee, Gabbro's baby-sister city, and thought the whole thing was a scream, particularly the part where the apartment key, hurled by Faye as a parting gesture, caught Travis in the eye and damn near blinded him. Alice was still on speaking terms with Travis because Travis was a buddy of Claude, whom Alice fancied. Alice had followed and advised the whole Travis - Faye romance at a remove, thinking it might give Claude the idea. She also thought it might be fun to alert all of Gabbro to its smash-up through Ginnie, who always counted as one who Needed to Know, and who, we have seen, was a connoisseuse of romantic crashes.

That Travis even had an ex and, despite his boyish appearance, was 32 years old, came to Faye as a further devastation. Consequent to all this circulating, Faye's reputation as a ruined libertine was cemented for the next decade, occasioning censure, amusement, and awe respectively among the wives, gentlemen, and adolescents of Gabbro County.

After some days of Forde's nursing, Faye's Liebesleid began to shade toward plain English melancholy, with a side of anger, both of which were quadrupled when Forde sat her down to fill her in on what was buzzing all around Gabbro.

"Did you know about that when I was dating him?"

"Of course not. Don't you know I would have brought it up?"

"Brought it up is right. It's the stinkiest kind of puke."

"Well, unpalatable, for sure. Faye, when I heard it, it shocked me as if I was you."

"Well, I doubt that. But Ginny knew I was dating Travis. Why the hell didn't she have the bare decency to tell me about him?

"I reckon you'd have to ask her that. What I want to talk to you about, is coming back to the *Intelligencer*. I made you an offer that you turned down to go out to Asheville. Maybe, what with all this, Asheville doesn't look quite so attractive? I understand, it was a more responsible job and all, so the offer I made is still good. What do you say?"

"Asheville is a dead issue. I am currently unemployed. Oh, I don't know, Forde. You made that offer under duress, and I can't take advantage like that. I suppose I could consider coming back to the *Intelligencer* at exactly my old job, with or without the raise that you already built in before all this came up. Not a bit more."

"Heck, with the raise, of course. That was in the cards all along. What happened to Asheville?"

"Well … Can we just say that Clement Atkins was some kind of fraternity brother of your father at Chapel Hill, and he had your father's pre-apology attitudes toward myself and my body, with about one tenth of his character and intelligence. I was in his employ for four hours, and he had his hands on me - and I don't mean my shoulder or my elbow - a dozen times. I finally blew up at him and locked him in a cellar apartment."

Forde grinned and shook his head. "That's the old Faye. I would be pleased to consider this whole incident nothing more than a piece of the vacation time you had coming anyhow. How's that sound? Oh, also, your clothes washed up under the dock, except for the panties, which are still in the Eddy, I guess. Unless the current took 'em, which case, they'll be down by the dam at

Riverbend. I run the rest through the laundry, which probably wrecked some of the wool stuff. Sorry."

"Forde, Jesus. You once denied being a saint. After this week, you can't keep that pretense up any more. I'm writing the Pope this afternoon. I would be so glad to come back to the *Intelligencer* on any basis at all, I can hardly stand still. Look, don't panic, but I'm going to kiss you good and hard, as long as you don't take it as any kind of promise about - you know, that 'Thing' thing. This is strictly in recompense for the caring and generosity you've shown me in the last few days. Not that, in spite of my new reputation, I consider kissing some kind of quid pro - "

"Oh, shut up."

She did.

*   *

From the Gabbro *Intelligencer* for Friday, October 29, 1948:

OUR TOWN'S TIMES
by M. Faye Bynum
City Editor

Well. Those of you who may have read my "Farewell" column last week may be a little surprised to see an un-Farewell column this week. I can't say much about it in a newspaper that is meant to be read by the whole family, but suffice it to say that my intended move to the Asheville area and newspaper turned out not to have been as good an idea as it looked from the other

side. I am so grateful to Editor
Forde Morgan for keeping this
desk open for me, and for the
opportunity to take part in the
ongoing life of Gabbro County
that ...

... I could just kill myself. Faye found her melancholy
deepening rather than fading with time, with opportunity to
reflect, and with her return to the *Intelligencer*. On Hallowe'en
afternoon, she drove the rescued and refueled Chevy to check on
progress on the Spirit Catcher, on Annie vis-à-vis Sheriff Burns,
and to wail at Mary or Annie, whichever would listen. Mary was
there, standing on a hay bale and welding a bicycle frame onto the
still waist-high structure.

"H'lo, Mary. Can I help?"

"Don't reckon. Have a bale, I'll be with you in a minute."

Faye wandered to the goat-feeding station, and discovered
Annie when she stood from behind a stack of bales. "Hey, Annie."

"Hey, y'self. How's your butt?"

"OK, I guess."

"Usually not something a body has to guess about. What's
- Oh, wow, Faye. How bad is it?"

"It's not my butt, if that's what you're asking."

"No, I see that. But something's got you hurting. Got time
to talk?"

"I guess."

"Hm. Lot a guessing. Gimme a word you're sure of."

"Fool. Brat. Promiscuous - no, scrub that. Fool. Fool. *Fool*.
Object lesson to young maidens. Laughing stock."

"Huh. What can I tell you?"

Faye looked up from the shoe that had been rearranging
dust.

"I don't ... " She saw herself in Annie's face. "Oh. But
Annie, you don't know what a fool I've been this time. I'm not
who you're thinking about, at all."

"Not true. You're exactly the same as you were, though I reckon you've been a little down on yourself. Far as I can see, you're still smart, strong, and pretty."

"Well - "

"But also, you put yourself out there in the *Intelligencer* every week, and Mom and me, we read that. Hell, everybody does."

"Well, I'm sure Forde would be glad to hear that. Not to mention the advertising department. Any more, they're just looking for sensational true confessions."

Annie shrugged. "Hi, Mom."

"Hi, Hon."

"Mary, Annie's trying to tell me what a swell woman I am, and she's just crazy. You need to take her in for - "

"Pipe down a second, would ya, Honey? Lemme have a look. Annie can read folks while they're talkin', but I never learnt the trick ... She reached for one of Faye's hands, and led her to one of the client bales.

"Let's get where it's quiet. All Soul's Day, big day for sperrits, you about can't hear yourself think. So ... Well, shoot. I got - lemme tell you what I got, you tell me what's wrong with it. I got a young woman that's had some ideas that didn't work out so good. You're sad as hell, I see that, and you don't think so much of yourself. Fact, you come damn close to closing it down, didn't you? That'd be a waste. You take all that sad shit that's sticking on to ya, you tooken a good bath, I mean real thorough, down the bottom of that Eddy place you're staying, and stay down as long as you can."

"You know there's dead Confederate soldiers down there. Supposedly."

"That's so. But just bones. Bones is all that's left when spirit and flesh are gone, and they can be a little simple-minded. But no harm in 'em."

"Let's hope."

"Never a bad thing to do, honey. You wash off that bad stuff on your own spirit, you'll start to hope, yourself. It's just a kind of a crust, useta be something else, I can see that. More joyful, like, but something happened, like you burn the crust on a loaf a good bread, and now it's hard and stinky. It hurts, and it's making you sick. But it's still good bread underneath."

"But - all that. What you just said. That's what Annie said, word for word, just by looking at me. She never opened her mouth, but she … it's as if she reminded me of something I believed once. And then you said the same thing, but in words."

Mary Godfire smiled sadly. "Don't know how Annie does that so quick. I'll tell you, that girl's got the Gift so bad, it's like to make her miserable one day, if it don't kill her outright. Gives me the whim-whams."

"Well. You advised me to let time pass, and something might happen to remind me what I'd known all along. Something happened all right, but darned if I can see what it was supposed to remind me of. I'm just sick and miserable, where I wasn't before."

"Not that you knew of, anyways. More time, Honey."

"I have to go through another disaster like the one with Travis? It will kill me."

*   *

Luminous Mysteries House
1 Luminous Mysteries Place
Greensboro 10, NC
All Souls Day, 1948

Miss M. Faye Bynum
C/O The Gabbro Intelligencer
Gabbro, NC

Dear Miss Bynum:
Greetings from your old - but not yet elderly - friend and advisor. I have been sent to one of our convents in the Greensboro, N.C. area, to assist the Sisters

there in their preparations for the season of Advent and the coming of Our Savior, in the absence of their recently deceased Mother Superior.

While reading a newsletter about secondary education in North Carolina, I ran across a short notice about the corruption scandal in regard to school bond issues, which notice credited your newspaper, and yourself specifically by name, with uncovering the evil-doing. I would love to have a chance to talk to you and get further information about it. While I will be quite busy before Christmas, I will have some time between Christmas Day and New Year's before I have to return to Mount St. Anne's. I wonder if you would be available to come to Greensboro to meet during that week, just to catch up on things?

I was thrilled, but not surprised, to see how well you have done as you begin your career in journalism.

Yours Faithfully
Sr. Rose Penitentia SML

*   *

Morgan's Eddy
RR 1, Box 10, Gabbro NC
November 7, 1948

Sister Rose Penitentia
Luminous Mysteries House
1 Luminous Mysteries Place
Greensboro 10, N.C.

Dear Sister Penitentia:

You could hardly be more thrilled than I am - though very surprised - to hear from you. Of <u>course</u>, I would be so delighted to see you again. I can hardly begin to tell you how important your teaching and example have been to me both in Charlotte last summer, and here.

It occurs to me that you may not have anywhere to live during the week between Christmas and New Year's, if your work will finish on Christmas. Perhaps you would like to come here to Gabbro and live with me for that week. I have a very comfortable house with a spare bedroom, that should serve your doubtless austere needs (just kidding) very well.

Oh, I so look forward to seeing you!
Your always grateful student,
M. Faye Bynum

Dear Miss Bynum:
Most delighted I am sure. There is a bus from Greensboro to Raleigh, and another to Gabbro from there. I will arrive in Gabbro at 7:47 PM on the 26th of December.
Sr. Rose Penitentia SML

Dear Sr. P:
Bus travel that close to Christmas will be difficult and tedious. I have ridden the Raleigh bus, and it is no place for a Woman Religious. I will be delighted to pick you up at Luminous Mysteries House on the 26th and drive you here. I look forward very much!
Love,
Faye

*   *

Faye stepped out of her robe and cannonballed, getting as much noise and splash into it as she could. When she surfaced, she was met by sunlight and a face full of water at the hands of Annie Godfire. It was a brisk and windy afternoon in mid-November, and the normally chill water felt warm by contrast. A mist hung over the Eddy, and Faye was determined to follow Mary Godfire's prescription that she immerse herself thoroughly and for as long as possible in the deep waters of Morgan's Eddy. As a precaution, because she was still depressed, she invited Annie Godfire to share the swim, without saying in so many words that she did not completely trust herself not to follow another and fatal agenda, and remain on the bottom forever. She did not deceive herself about the likelihood that she could deceive Annie in regard to any unspoken agenda. She simply wanted a lifeguard, without necessarily thinking that her life held anything worth guarding.

So, after some time of horsing around in the water, of lying in the sun on the dock and getting chilly - November in Gabbro County is rarely more than that - and with the sun now westering into the pines, she turned to Annie as they bobbed in mid-Eddy.

"I am going to do what your mother said I should. I will go to the bottom of the deep part, and stay for as long as I can, to wash away this crust of sadness and hatred for myself. Can you take the time to do that with me, and make sure I don't stay down too long?"

"Sure, of course. Very wise of you. Momma's gone overnight to pick up some cast-iron reddiators from the orphanage at Knoxville, so I got all the time you like. How do I know what's too long?"

"When I begin to leak air out of my mouth, the next thing would be to breathe in water. I should be in the air by that time."

"OK, go ahead."

Faye paddled into the mist until she judged that she must be about in the middle of the Eddy. She looked around to locate Annie - right behind her, and giving her a thumbs-up - and took a breath. She pushed herself down through the pale tea of the Eddy, watching the wavering sun fade to a caramel disc. She found the bottom, alive with dancing stripes of sunlight, and prepared to wait there until she was desperate for air. But she had landed above one of the springs, and its cold updraft constantly moved her about and forced her to spend energy to keep herself down. After two or three such excursions, her lungs aching, she gave in and stroked for the surface, looking for the sun.

It did not reappear.

She stroked upward again, and found her cheek scraping the sandy bottom of the Eddy. Disoriented by the spring currents, she had lost track of up and down, and she drifted now in tannish disorientation, air leaking out of her mouth, desperate not to inhale. Strong hands seized her leg and shoulder and set her upright on the bottom. Faye pushed away from it with all the strength of her legs, helped by a massive push on her butt. Another stroke, and now she had to let the old air go, there was no help for it. The light became yellow, while her lungs clamored for air and her diaphragm retched to pull it in, where there was no air.

When her head broke the surface at last, she drew in breath before her nose and mouth were fully clear, and it was a mix of air and water. She coughed and gagged, and nearly sank again as her body jackknifed into a spasm. She whooped and pounded the water with the flat of her hand. And with a final paroxysm, she cleared her windpipe and breathed. And looked around for Annie, embarrassed at the uproar she'd made.

No Annie.

"Annie?"

Silence.

"Annie!"

She spun around on the surface of the Eddy, looking for Annie's head to break the surface. All that rose was a cluster of bubbles.

"Annie!!"

Faye took a breath, which set her coughing again, and then another, and plunged beneath the surface. Far below, she saw a flicker of paleness, either a fish or a weed. Or a hand. She dove, and found Annie Godfire, her eyes half-closed, and sunk over her knees in the sand of the bottom. Faye grabbed her wrist and heaved upward, which only pulled Faye downward to the bottom. She spread her feet into the sand as far away from whatever had trapped Annie as she could, and heaved upward again. Annie's shins appeared, then her feet. Faye, gagging again for air, put her hands on Annie's butt and shoved her upward. She pushed off and stroked for the air.

*   *

In view of Mary Godfire's absence, Faye persuaded Annie to stay with her overnight. Fed and rested, they lay side by side in the big, cool bed in the fade of daylight. "Quicksand shouldn't work when you're submerged," Faye objected. "You're weightless."

"Not me. No fat, big bones. Feel me. I don't float."

Faye probed, finding bone and muscle. "Huh. Guess there's a little advantage to fat. I float just fine. I suppose that's why I've never had that problem down there where the springs are."

"You're not fat either."

"Not really. I've got what Travis used to call 'lady fat,' supposed to make us smooth and soft. Pain in the ass, up to now."

"Well, anyhow. Thank you an awful lot for coming back to get me. I stayed down when I saw you was having difficulty, and when I pushed you up, I just sank into the bottom. I felt something with my foot, way under where the spring comes out. Prob'ly just a stick, but I was thinking about them Confederate kids' bones at the time, and I yanked my foot away, which sunk the other foot deeper yet. I was sinking past my knees when I felt you hauling on me."

"How did you keep from breathing water and drowning?" Faye shuddered at the thought. She'd come too close herself.

"Shut myself down, quit breathing."

"Huh. You can do that?"

"Anybody can, that wants to work on it. So anyways, how did the cleansing work?"

Faye spooned herself around Annie's sturdy butt, noting the absence of lady fat. It was a little like spooning with Travis, but … Well. She snuggled against Annie and yawned. "I feel just fine. Just perfectly clean and fine. Thank you for saving my life too, Annie."

Faye pulled the sheet over them and they settled concentric into the twilight, dark heads sharing the wide pillow. From her damp hair, as from Annie's, there rose a faint clean scent of the tannin of Morgan's Eddy. Underlying that, a vanishing few molecules of Silken Rain; underlying Annie's, acetylene and welding flux. In both cases, the secondary aromas were so faint as to be subliminal, and they each appeared to the other instead as some inexpressible, delightful personal essence.

After a little time, Faye said, "I got to admit, I was thinking about the dead Confederates down there too."

"Pooh. Nothing there but bones, about a mile down in the sand by this time. They can't hurt nobody. Though they do say ever so often the biggest spring will spit up a bone. Sinks down in the sand again in a couple days. One of my so-called brothers, one of the Zecharias boys, tooken one an' put it on his mantle. I seen it, a leg bone all changed to pyrites, you couldn't hardly tell what it used to be. Dumb ox come down with blood poison inside a month."

"Jesus, Annie. Didn't you just say they were harmless?"

"Course. Won't no fossil give you blood poison. It was his stupid attitude, done that."

Faye smiled. "Mary said you were always wanting a sister. D'you think I would do?"

Annie twisted around to gaze at Faye in the last of the twilight. "You did do, or I'd be dead now. You got yourself a sister, if you wont one."

"Wonted one all my life. Good night, sister."

"Good night."

25.

G INNIE FREEMAN, you snake, why didn't you tell me Travis had been married and was twelve years older than me?"

"Whoa now, Faye. First of all, you know how we react to direct questions here. Also to name-calling, you little hellion. Second place, you made it perfectly clear when the subject first came up, that you did not want to discuss Travis Wayland. You were gonna be ... wait a minute, let me get it right ... 'uncomplicated friends,' wasn't that it? Don't see how his age and marital status was anything against that. And then by the time your friendship had become - ha ha, 'complicated,' new word for it - it was too late."

Mary-Deane cleared her throat. "Shall we once again have some mercy on our little sister? Faye, Honey, there wasn't a one of us here that wasn't some mix of sorrow and giggles when we heard what happened with you and Travis. Just, the mix was different for different ones of us."

"I bet. Well, I certainly had the giggles coming, and you know I'm always happy to entertain my friends. As for the sorrow, you can let me take care of that."

"So is it all over between you and Travis? No chance of a reconciliation?"

"Gosh, Ginny. It's not so much Travis as all the friends he seems to squeeze into bed with him. No. I have never been as miserable as I was that night, and I hope I never am again. If Travis Wayland was on fire, I wouldn't squat down and pee on him." Faye surveyed the shocked faces. "Sorry, I guess I'm supposed to say 'spit on him,' but that just doesn't do justice. Pearlene, I apologize for staying away so long. As usual, you've done the impossible, and made me look like a Christian lady."

"Well, you given me a little more material to work with this time, stayin' away. Thank you, Miss Faye."

*   *

And then it was time for the Gabbro media Christmas Party, which Faye had sworn to forswear. But Rob Stoker smirked that he supposed she would be skipping the Christmas party this year, and she responded with a whatever-gave-you-that-idea that was intended to shut him up, though not to make it impossible that she not attend. Thus she trapped herself into attending, all the while wanting to get back to the Agatha Christie she'd found under the coffee table on the screen porch at Morgan's Eddy.

It was an altogether more subdued affair, with no Custis to offend the ladies and no Travis to charm them. Lacking Custis' devious touch with the Baptists, Forde neglected to see to it that the punch was spiked. The two-geezer orchestra, incredibly a year older and still functioning, gave out the same tunes in the same order. Faye, after one taste of the punch, took the Chevy downtown, got into the ABC store thirty seconds before closing, and returned with a gallon of terrible gin. Which was fine, since the Sunkist-based punch would have overwhelmed the taste of any additive in any case.

Things warmed a little then; a couple of middle-aged men danced with Faye to thank her for the lubricant, and possibly to see what it was like to hold a Ruined Woman in their arms; Forde gave her what he called a 'quid pro quo' under last year's mistletoe that the Baptists had not bothered to remove from the ballroom chandelier, and danced with her until Rob Stoker started causing a ruckus that he felt he had to quell. While he was busy with that, Sharon the receptionist approached Faye by the snacks table, clearly thinking rapprochement, which Faye was glad to embrace.

"Merry Christmas, Sharon."

"Merry Christmas to you. Reckon you got some un-merry vibrations from this time last year."

"Indeed. It was the last time Custis Morgan ever grabbed my ass in this life."

"Oh, you. I'm grateful, though, seeing until yours come along, he was after mine all the time."

"Well, I apologize if I - "

"No, it was no fun after a while, and I got to admit, yours is more the shape that got him going. Mine was too, 'fore I got that reception job, which involves about nothing but sittin' on it all day. Not to mention, you're ten years younger. Oh, my … "

Sharon was looking over Faye's shoulder, and grabbed her arm. "Don't look, but look who just come in the door."

"Don't tell me."

"Sure's you live."

"Damn. <u>Damn</u> his eyes … Well. Look, Sharon, would you do me a huge favor? Would you go to him quick now, before he spots me, and tell him I have nothing to say to him, and if I see his face I will be in danger of vomiting all over his shoes. Got that?"

Sharon's eyes sparkled. "Shoes. Nice touch."

"Go."

Sharon went. The two-man band wheezed into "All I Want for Christmas is My Two Front Teeth," with most of the harmonies wrong. Faye kept her back to the door by admiring a faded lithograph of Jesus at prayer in the Garden of Gethsemane. Jesus looked about like Faye felt.

"That's why I wore galoshes."

"Faye, I'm sorry. I given him your message, and he just pushed - "

"Never mind, Sharon. Thanks for trying. All right, Travis, for God's sake, let's get it over with. Ready? Here goes, and this is as gently as I can put it: Drop dead, jerk."

"Faye, no, wait. Just listen to me for one minute."

"Life's too short. I had other plans for this minute."

"No, come on. Look, I don't blame you for being sore…"

"Sore? I'd have been sore for a millionth of a second if I'd crashed into a bridge abutment on the way home, which I was sorely tempted to do. I suppose if I'd succeeded in drowning myself, that might have left me sore in the Eternal Fires of hell. 'Sore' doesn't begin - ”

“Honey, people are beginning to look.”

“Agh! Good! Let 'em. Let them see how a lady brushes off a no-good, slimy, worthless - ”

“Asshole,” Travis whispered. “I know. That's what I have got to make you understand.”

“You needn't bother. I thought I understood it pretty well already, but a lady would not use the term, even in speaking to one.” She looked over Travis' shoulder. “Oh, good, here comes Forde. All right, come on … no, wait. There's a kind of cloister out the side door. I will meet you there in five minutes for the sake of cutting short this public spectacle, on the absolute condition that you turn around this instant and leave this hall without looking back. If you so much as say one word or turn around and look, it will be like Orpheus, except it will be you, going back to Hell for good, not me.” Faye smiled to herself a little at that. Must be the recent correspondence with Sister P, stirring the ashes of her tiny campfire of classical allusions. And it avoided her casting him as Lot's wife, and thus herself as Sodom and Gomorrah.

Travis turned and left. He said nothing, but there was nothing Faye could do to wipe from his face the smirk that he displayed on the way out. Don Juan triumphant.

Sharon put a hand on Faye's arm. “Faye, Honey, be awful careful. He's like quicksand, and believe me, I know.”

“Oh, Sharon! Did I … you know? When I showed up?”

“Yes, and that's why I been a little cool with you for the last year.”

“Oh, dear, I am <u>so</u> sorry! Still - ”

“Oh, you don't have to say it. You saved me from getting tied up with a louse. Just, at my age, even louses don't come along all that often no more. Lice.”

“Uh huh. Well, but I think Rob Stoker has some ideas.”

“I'd sooner go in a convent, thanks. You better go.”

“Yes. I don't want to keep the Louse Laureate waiting, do I?”

Sharon giggled. "No wonder Forde thinks you're the bee's knees. I'll keep him busy while you're dealing with louse-boy."

The cloister was built originally to give Sanatorium patients a sunny place to rest and enjoy the illusions of health that a good hot spring can induce. The deck chairs and end tables were long gone to dust, and the stone architecture was left to supervise moonlight, a swirl of dead leaves and the gum wrappers of the Scripture scholars. A series of dim windows gave onto the merrymakers within, who seemed to be making themselves plenty merry over the drama just past.

Faye appeared from the shadows and slipped through the stone pillars that defined the cloister. She looked around, but Travis was nowhere to be seen. She entertained a brief hope that he'd had time to internalize her contempt, and slink away.

No such miracle. Travis sauntered from the parking lot, humbly jaunty, and leaned in all his grace against the pillar Faye had just abandoned.

"Faye, bless you for a good girl, for seeing me. Please let me explain that ridiculous scene you walked in on."

"Go ahead." Faye grew up with level black eyebrows that all her life had rescued her from the curse of being another beautiful woman. She used them now to pin Travis against the pillar.

"Sure. It was a silly thing, a bet Claude suckered me into. That Brenda, who was the girl who was there, naturally means nothing to me. Nor Claude, of course, good Lord. It was just … " He waved a hand at the impossibility of expressing -

"Oh, God. Poor Travis. It was just a silly thing, wasn't it? Fit for a French farce, I believe Claude called it. And he should know, speaking from under my panties."

Travis relaxed even further. "That's right, Faye. That's exactly right. It was nothing, it - "

"Let me save you some trouble. I have gone through exactly this scene once before in my life, so I know most of the lines, and in particular I'm sure I know what you are fixing to say about your silly thing. Do you remember that childish life-history confession I trusted you with on the way back from our romantic snowy weekend in Asheville? Gordon's 'silly-thing' defense was so unconvincing the first time that I accidentally killed him - who was worth three of you, by the way, and would never have allowed himself to get into such a nasty 'silly thing.' I don't want to have another accident on my conscience, so let me explain as clearly as I can how you have forfeited any hopes for my love, my friendship, even my passing goddamn <u>acquaintance</u>, damn you, by participating in that 'silly thing.' And no doubt many others."

Faye saw that the windows were now lined with spectators. She lowered her voice. "Travis, when you and I made love, when we slept together, you transported me to another place, another life, another... everything. I was another Faye Bynum altogether when we made love, and in that other person, it felt as if I were better, wiser, more loving and complete than I even <u>suspected</u> I, or anyone, could ever be. That's why I made up that stupid blather about the Garden of Eden, why I wanted to merge myself with you and carry you around inside me. It felt like - whatever it was that we have lost now, back when Adam and Eve were the apples of God's eye. When they were basically spotless angels.

"Now, I'm not silly enough to take that story literally, but I know it is meant to show how angelic and charged with God's grace human nature can be. That's how I felt when I was with you, and that's what you did for me, through a whole courtship that started with uncomplicated toboggans and flirting and 'Keep it simple,' dancing me step by step to heaven, until my knees buckled, and I was so soaked in love that I thought God was holding me on His lap."

"Faye - "

"Shut up. Now I find out that the same Travis Wayland who did that for me, the same angel who used sex to make me feel transfigured and holy, is someone who will just hop into silly bed things with anyone and everyone. That you and I were all along having completely different experiences. While I was in a state of grace, deliriously incapable of sin, you were just ... You were just

251

getting laid, weren't you? Now that I see that, there is no way I can go back to loving you. That horrible moment in Boone when the light turned on and showed you in that 'silly thing; and the anger and contempt on your face ... that is the flaming sword between me and the paradise I imagined."

"Faye, listen, you and I - "

"Shut up, I said. I'm almost finished. I have been a fatuous idiot in imagining myself a mature woman with a dashing lover, God help me. After what you did to me, I have had to work very hard at even beginning to respect myself. Some day in the future, when I can actually love myself, I suppose I may be fit again to have a lover, maybe a series of them. I doubt that I will ever again be transported to Eden; that's gone. But, whoever those lovers may be, at least none of them will be Travis Wayland. So please, just go away and get laid, you and Claude and Brenda. I'm through with you."

From Travis Wayland, silence; a shrugging turn to the parking lot. From behind him, through the window that one of the revelers had opened - Faye can only hope, after she finished with the sex and murder parts - a burst of applause, whistles, and organized cheering from the *Intelligencer* contingent.

From Faye, bitter tears and a shuddering feeling, as of something loose from its moorings.

26.

S ISTER ROSE PENITENTIA was smaller than Faye recalled - about Faye's height, really - and at first only a little more human. The bony judgmental face had aged a little, lost some of what little color it had. She walked out to the Chevy on Faye's arm, her wheat-colored woollen habit clutched about her knees, lips tight against the cold and glasses even more grimly octagonal than Faye remembered. Greensboro had experienced a snowfall the night before, that had thrown the city, and certainly all the custodians of its infrastructure, into a panic that somehow precluded any shoveling of sidewalks. Neither Faye nor Sister Penitentia could conjure galoshes to deal with the situation, but by the time the Chevy was an hour north of Gabbro, the snow cover dwindled to a half-inch that was further dwindling under the touch of fifty-degree sunshine.

"Well. A very benevolent climate, I must say. Are the people as lacking in moral fiber as their reputation would imply, because of it?"

"Sister, whatever lacking there may be is difficult to assign to any single cause. They are even more racist and oppressive than Missouri, if you can imagine, but they are more relaxed and genial about it. Their attitude seems to be, your Nigra is happy in his place, and his place is and must remain at the very bottom of the social order. Given that, they claim to have the best race relations in the country. I would be at a loss to attribute that to the benevolent climate, or any other single cause.

"But you asked about moral fiber in general. There is that song, 'Summertime, and the livin' is easy.' Summertime lasts pretty long here, and what you might think of as real character-building winter almost never happens. Mind you, this is only my second winter in North Carolina, so what do I know?"

"And moral fiber?"

"I judge not, lest I be judged."

"Hm. Are you attending mass regularly?"

"No, to be honest with you, I am not. Mass, as such, holds no magic for me any more. Bread is bread, wine is wine. I did go to Confession a while ago."

"Really. How long ago?"

"Oh …" Faye thought back, pink-faced. "It was in the summer. Let's say six months."

"Honestly, Miss Bynum. And how many murders had you committed, to drive you to that act of desperation?"

Faye laughed. "No more than one or two. Look, I'm happy to answer your questions, because I very much value your opinions. But I am now 21 years old and no longer a Mount St. Anne's student. So as your hostess for this week, I am allowed to set some ground rules. I will answer all the questions you like, if you will agree to answer one from me in return for each."

This was greeted austerely, and then by the wave of a pale and undecorated hand. "Of course, the life of a Sister of the Luminous Mysteries holds very few actual mysteries, or events of any kind beyond observation of the sacred offices, so you will have poor pickings. But I've asked you three questions, so I'll give you three to get you started, before I ask any more. Oh, wait, one codicil, if you please. Practical questions, such as where you keep the kitchen wastebasket, don't count."

"Sure. OK, here goes: How old are you, actually? What's it like being married to Jesus? How's the BVM as a mother-in-law?"

Sister P. smiled. "Forty-one. But you wasted two questions on a frivolous topic. It's 'bride of Christ,' not 'wife of Jesus.' There's a big difference. But to address your impertinent question indirectly, do you imagine that we have not thought up every possible variation on that line of blasphemy during late-night giggle sessions?"

Faye put back her head and laughed. "The gently smiling mask cracks again! I swear, there were girls at MSA who were convinced that you were in your sixties. When does a bride become a wife?"

"When she marches out of the church, which never happens for us. You asked your three questions - no, four, your second was compound. I have two coming before you get to continue your raillery."

"All right. I will be generous to a guest and not count the question you asked in answering mine."

Sister Rose Penitentia sat in silence for a good five miles, and then, amazingly, stripped off her headgear and ran her fingers through an ashy blonde bowl cut. It was as if she had removed her head, to reveal a younger, ruddier creature underneath. Faye was startled.

"Very poor sleeping accommodations in that place, even by convent standards. Faye, dear, you have turned very quiet and thoughtful. Is there something on your mind you'd like to share?"

"No, no, just thinking about … Yes, of course, there is. I could never lie to you, Sister."

"You could never lie to anyone, if I recall rightly. That and your quick mind made you the extraordinary person you were, and still are, I believe. What is it?"

"All right. You are curious about the state of my soul, which I certainly appreciate. But piecemeal questioning about religious observances will never make any sense of it, without context. Do you really want to know it all?"

Sister Rose Penitentia let a small Sandhills village go by before she answered. "Faye, you were the most interesting and able student I have encountered in fifteen years of waving a ruler at adolescent girls. I was actually gloomy when you graduated and left St. Louis to start your career. I had once thought of trying to recruit you to join the Sisters of the Luminous Mysteries, but I realized that you would never consent to being confined that way. Now, talking to you, I can see that the young woman I knew has endured some vicissitudes in the short time you have been out in the world. If my listening to them would help you to move on, then by all means."

"Well. You may be getting more than you counted on, so if that turns out to be so, please tell me when you've had enough. I will go through the highlights of the last year and a half - and it seems impossible to me that it's only been that long - on one condition: that you simply listen and not judge and condemn. I've already done a thorough job of that, including the condemnations. Can you do that?"

"What am I, a Spanish Inquisitor? I am your former teacher and advisor and, I hope, your present friend and admirer. As for the passage of time, how many days or years do you think Adam and Eve lived in a state of grace before they were ejected from the garden for cause? If you read the Bible, it sounds like only a few days. And maybe that's how it would feel to them. Can you believe that church fathers have wasted years on arguing about it?"

"Of course I can, what else do they have to do? But does that count as a question? Funny you should ask, though. I've given some thought lately to what Eden must have been like. But I suppose the days do tend to blur together when you're in a state of grace. All right, here goes. When I left Mount St. Anne's, I was all but engaged to a slab of muscle named Gordon Simmons ... "

The recitation continued through the rest of the trip to Gabbro, broke for lunch, and continued down to the confrontation with Travis at the Christmas party. The afternoon was half over, the sandwiches that Faye had risen at five to prepare reduced to crumbs on the screen-porch coffee table. The front that brought snow to the Piedmont had passed, and the afternoon was cool and blustery. The pines that ringed Morgan's Eddy crooned under sunlight that waxed and waned as a sky streaked with cloud dimmed the sun, then bustled on to let it sweep the Eddy with a new moment of brilliance. "Goodness, what a lovely place to live, Faye."

"I'm very lucky. I rent it from our editor."

"Do you swim in the pond?"

"Yes, in warm weather. It's actually part of a small river, but it's spring-fed, and rather chilly lately. You'd be welcome to come back when it's warmer, which will start any day now."

"Mm. Faye, I will need some time for contemplation before I can possibly respond to your - I suppose we could call it a confession, but lower-case, since I am not authorized to hear Confession or to offer absolution. If there <u>are</u> any offenses to absolve, I may add. But … well. How much of the drama that has disrupted your life since leaving Mount St. Anne would you be willing to attribute to your habit of provoking and challenging others?"

"Smart-facedness, you mean? That's what they call it down here. By the way, that certainly counts as a question."

"Of course. Are we still keeping track? What I'm getting at is this: a pattern of behavior that served you well as a precocious student might be more troublesome when you are talking to people who are not … oh, dedicated to the free and healthy exchange of ideas."

"Goodness. Travis used to ask me if I had spent time rehearsing, when I asked questions like that. But of course you're right. It's a hard habit to break. The whole incident of last summer's pregnancy was not caused by repartee; on the other hand, I certainly talked myself into a very serious and dangerous situation with Gordon. And Travis, far as that. I could have killed myself driving back here in the rain to kill myself. I might claim that I have just been unlucky, in stumbling into crises. Maybe I need to learn to read situations better."

"Not possible that your way of speaking might push situations toward crisis that might otherwise have passed peacefully?"

"The peace that passeth unchallenged. Boring, wouldn't you think? Oops, sounds like we have company."

Sister Rose recovered her shoes while Faye went to the screen door to watch the unwelcome car feeling its way down the track through the pines.

"Oh, Jesus, Mary and Joseph. It's Sheriff Burns, d - darn."

"Forgiven. Is he the one who spanked you on this porch?"

"Yes, but he's still blacked out about it, from the concussion. We above all don't want to jog his memory. Here, switch seats, quick. Think you could charm him, please? Tuck that blouse a little tighter."

"Really, Faye, what do you take me for?"

"A sister of luminous mystery. Get luminous, please, Sister, really, it's terribly important. I haven't told you everything about that episode, but we are not dealing here with a man dedicated to the free and healthy exchange of ideas. I'm not asking for seduction, just regular charm. No rulers, either."

"I will do what I can, consistent with my oath of chastity."

Burns was climbing the steps by now, and Faye whispered, *"Thank you. I'm obviously desperate.* Sheriff Burns, hello! Come in and meet one of my teachers."

Alfred Burns wore a truculent look as he climbed, that changed to non-plus when he saw Sister Rose. "Oh," he said. "I could come back later."

Faye opened the screen and beamed down at him. "Nonsense. You've come all this way, and down that terrible bumpy lane to get here. Come and take a load off your feet. Sheriff Alfred Burns, may I present my former teacher and advisor, Sister Rose Penitentia of Mount Saint Anne High School?"

"How do, Ma'am? Naw, Miss Bynum, I was wanting to talk to you about Annie Godfire, not somethin' to be discussed in front of a lady of the church, har'ly."

Faye could see Sister Rose girding herself. But she burst into an arguably luminous smile that did well with the blonde cap of hair and eyes that Faye now saw for the first time were piercing green. How had she missed that, behind the rimless glitter all those years?

"How do you do, Sheriff Burns. How interesting to meet a real Sheriff. I suppose your duties are very taxing, are they not? I'm sure you're quite busy preventing evil, but can't you sit down for just a few moments?"

"We were just about to open a bottle of wine, Sheriff, and, tell you what, sharing it three ways will keep us from getting carried away. Here, the glider is real comfy, and it gives you a good view of the river. I'll be back in a flash." As Faye exited, she heard Sister Rose asking Burns if he had a family, and if so, how they dealt with his life of danger and adventure. Her eyes clouded with fond gratitude. Sister P. unto the breach!

By the time Faye returned with a tray holding a bottle of Blue Nun, three glasses, and a plate of Ritz crackers, Burns had his Sheriff's hat off and his arm flung across the back of the glider, and was talking about techniques of high-speed car chase.

"Oh, my. I don't suppose you'd consider taking a passenger along? I'll be here until New Year's."

Faye intervened. "Oh, Rose, I know it sounds glamorous and exciting, but probably too dangerous, wouldn't you say, Sheriff? Here you go… And you, Sister. Chin-chin!"

By sundown, Sister Rose Penitentia was on the glider next to Burns, the second bottle of Blue Nun was drained, shaken over the last glass, and Faye was beginning to talk about dinner.

"No, nonono, doody calls, ladies. Don't know when I passed a nicer aft'noon, gotta tell you. Faye, I'll check with you later about … about whozit. You know."

"Sure do, Al. Hurry back, hear? Sure you're OK to drive? Not that we're any better off."

Burns hooted, standing by the cruiser door. "Who's gonna flag me down? Answer me that."

*   *

Nine thirty in the evening. Sister Penitentia has finished clearing the supper dishes, and River Cottage drowses in the glow of three kerosene lamps: one on a bracket over the kitchen sink, one on the living room mantle, and one floater that can be used to seek out one's bed when the time arrives. Faye's crossed feet, now bare, and Sister P's, in white religious socks, occupy a split-log bench side by side in front of the fireplace, next to bowls sticky with the scrapings of butter pecan ice cream cranked by hand with local pecans by the chef at the Terminal Café. The wind-bluster of the afternoon has subsided, and Morgan's Eddy lies dark under the reflection of the circling trees. On the mantle by the lamp, the Grandmother Clock ticks over a dying fire. Both Faye and Sister Rose Penitentia would like to be in bed, but can't muster the energy to rise from the rustic sofa.

"Sister Rose, I can hardly find the words to thank you from the very bottom of my heart for the p'formance you put on this afternoon. I know it must have stressed you to … well. I know it did not come naturally to you. At all. You were very convincing."

"My pleasure, Faye. I could see that the urgency was great."

"Well, the deed met the, the… " Faye brightened. "Deed met the need. Howzat?"

"Elegant. You are skilled with words, even when you're half in the bag."

Faye snorted. "Not so bad yourself. Where'd you hear that espression? Not around Luminous Mystery House, I doubt."

"I wasn't born in Luminous Mystery House."

"Yup, well, my turn for a question then. How'd you become a numb? A nun?"

Sister P. stretched and wiggled her toes in the religious socks. "Oh, my. You're asking for a tale as long as what you laid out this afternoon. Can I give you just the short version?"

"Or none at all. I don't mean to pry, if it's personal information."

"Could hardly be anything else, you know. But I don't mind; since you were very frank with me, I will be frank with you: I was given a choice of postulancy to be a teaching sister, or to remain a prostitute."

After a silent two seconds, Faye leaned forward to stare at Sister Rose Penitentia. "<u>What</u>?!"

"Do you need me to say it again?"

"No, no. Oh, my …" She flung herself at Sister Rose and embraced her. "Oh, you poor thing! Oh, dear God, I can't stand the thought of you, my beloved Sister P, of <u>all</u> people … "

260

Sister Rose began to stroke Faye's hair. "It was a horrible life. I was very lucky to have the choice. And your reaction is generous and loving. Most of your peers would have recoiled."

"My peers were a pack of … " She stopped at a severe look from Sister Rose. "Sorry. But who gave you the choice?"

"A Catholic rescue mission in downtown Baltimore. They had a program, with rare openings available, depending on the willingness of various convents to accept a new postulant. The Church was experiencing a downturn in girls who wanted to become women religious, so they recruited where they were likely to look like a safe haven. There was a long waiting list, and of course the madams and pimps discouraged it violently. And most of the girls who did get the chance, washed out in the first month or two. The Sisters of the Luminous Mysteries was the one that was accepting when my turn came up. The girl before me had lasted three days."

"Oh, my. Tough, huh?"

"You could never believe. First, you had to convert to Catholicism, with all that involves in the way of instruction, questioning of sincerity, confession of every single instance of sin - which I leave to your imagination - catechisms, rituals, and what not. While that was going on, I still had to eat, and I only knew one way to earn it. Of course, I couldn't let the Luminous Mysteries Sisters suspect that, so I led a double life for six months. Some days, I showed up for instruction stinking of the cheap perfume that I used to cover the sweat of customers. The priest who ran the confirmation class luckily did not know which of us were from the Program. Though I suppose he had his suspicions.

"Then there was an extensive period of trial by ordeal, known as 'discernment,' that broke women who had prevailed in knife duels. But really, most of the girls washed out of Luminous Mysteries because it was a teaching order, and the preparation for teaching was harder than the prostrating yourself on stone floors for hours, scrubbing them on your hands and knees, all that stuff you hear about postulants and novices. I was good at school things, so all I had to get through was the conversion and the stone floors.

"But I'll tell you what saved me from throwing it up. I wasn't a regular streetwalker, with a pimp. I was in a house on Hanover Street in Baltimore with a madam, and I flattered myself that I was a performer, an artiste and a girl who liked her fun. In fact, I was a tank stripper and a prostitute, in a company of strippers and prostitutes. For a price, gentlemen in the audience could have a shot at the girls after the show. There was this certain john - a certain customer who always asked for me, because he liked how I reacted to being ... well. Mistreated. When I got really sick of sore knees and wrinkled fingers in the convent, all I had to do was remember that guy, and I would dip my brush and keep scrubbing."

"I hate the very notion of somebody mistreating you, and I refuse to even try to imagine it." Very quietly, then: "What's a tank stripper?"

Shrug. "The house had a stage with a big glass-fronted tank. I would do an underwater act that included a lot of fake seaweed, fan corals, and a tame octopus. I got very good at holding my breath, which was useful for afterwards."

"Hard to picture. And is that where the "Penitentia" comes from?"

"All the girls who got out through the Program had to take it as a religious name. I was born Rosie Dawn Satterfield, and I performed as Rosie Aspen. The Sisters let me keep the Rose, because of its association with the Blessed Virgin. 'Penitentia' is kind of a Scarlet Letter, if you know about the rescue program."

Faye groaned. "And we thought we were so funny and clever when we called you Sister Penitentiary. Oh, what a bunch of privileged little snots! And I thought I made it up and all the rest of the girls copied me. Sister Rose, please, please forgive - "

"Oh, for heaven's sake, Faye. St. Anne girls started calling me that some time in 1935. The new girls this year picked it up by the second week. And I doubt I'm the only ex-prostitute in the parochial schools who goes by that nickname. It isn't that easy to commit an original sin."

"Well, I ... Heh. I won't commit the cliché of asking how a nice girl like you wound up in a brothel. I'm sure it's a sad history. But, so, not too much of a stretch to entertain Al Burns today?"

"On the contrary. I may have relaxed into the role so far that Mr. Sheriff Burns got a whiff of my earlier profession. Your sheriff is a lot like the john who encouraged me to keep scrubbing. He gives me the creeps."

27.

W HEN FAYE ROSE on Monday morning from a sleeping bag on the screen porch, she found Sister Rose Penitentia at prayer before the fireplace, so she tiptoed out the back door to bucket some face-washing water up from the dock. Returning, she saw that the Rosary was continuing, so she washed in cold water - waking herself thoroughly - and lit the propane heater for Sister Penitentia. While she was dressing, Sister P. entered, looking tranquil.

"Slept well?"

"Perfectly. Faye, there is no reason for you to be sleeping on the porch. That bed is so enormous, I could share it with you and still have twice the room I had at that dreadful place in Greensboro, and a better mattress at that. But most of that bed is wasted when I'm in it."

"Well, fine. I shared it before - with another lady, I hasten to add. I'd be glad to share with you, if you're sure. On another note, small newspaper staff don't get much in the way of time off for holidays; I have an editorial meeting this morning for Wednesday's paper, and then I will have to knock out whatever stories land in my lap from that, so you will be on your own for a time.

"As a big city, Gabbro is undetectably small. There's the public library, and a Catholic church, St. Ann's - spelled wrong - on Greenly Street. Farther afield, the gabbro quarry and a Baptist junior college, and farther yet, Indian Girl Swamp, in which the spirit of a murdered Indian maiden still lures the unwary to their doom. Sound good? Or, you for could stay here and take a walk, and I should be back by mid-afternoon or so. There's some leftover meatloaf in the icebox."

"That sounds fine. I missed several offices yesterday, and I might be able to repair the damage if I apply myself earnestly today. If I'm praying when you return, you don't have to pussyfoot around like you did this morning. The Godhead is very cordial to latecomers."

"Good to hear. See you around noon, then. Sure you don't want me to run you into town?"

"No. I will relish the solitude."

"Relish away, then. See you later."

Faye was buoyant at the editorial meeting. Something about re-connecting with and hosting Sister Rose Penitentia overcame the bitterness that had lingered, in spite of the cleansing in Morgan's Eddy, and in spite of her telling-off of Travis. For weeks after the disaster, she could not think his name without a feeling that was a raw hybrid of nausea, lust, and shame. As the lover and enfolder of a man who could do what she had discovered him doing, her body and her being felt tainted from within. Now, reminded by Sister Rose of a sunnier Faye, she began to feel that a recovery might be possible, in which some scrap of self-regard might be smuggled through the seasons of trouble to the brisk winter. She was cheerful in suggesting and accepting assignments that would have bored her at the height of her fever.

"OK, sure," she replied to Forde's request for a routine re-survey of the impact, one year later, of the benefits of the bond issue as re-administered by Acting Superintendent Abraham Cousins and his reluctant manager, Mrs. Ellice Laffler of the Gabbro County School Board. "Why don't I make a round of all ten schools, and see where we are."

"I thought the Indian schools weren't part of it."

"That was before Cousins took over as administrator of the goodies. I think he was leaning toward some kind of formula based on our article about who exactly was paying how much for the bond issue."

"Great. I hope that's so, but find out. If so, we can pat ourselves on the back. Take Peter along with you on one trip, he's been pestering me for some assignment more thrilling than the Jaycees."

When Faye returned to River Cottage, she found Sister Penitentia sitting in sunshine at the end of the dock, with her feet in the water.

"Re-baptising your toes?"

"I have made the acquaintance of a dozen minnows, who wanted a bite, but went away satisfied with a glancing nibble."

"Little devils. Want to come along for some investigative journalism?"

Sister Penitentia retrieved her feet and swaddled them in a towel. "Faye, I hope you do not think less of me because of the things I revealed to you last night. It came to me during Terce that I might better have been more modest, and protected you from my past."

"Sister, listen. If anything, being half in the bag - thank you very much - kept me from being as clear as I wanted to be. At the very depths of my despair after I discovered Travis in that threesome, it was you, your face, and your voice that appeared to me and kept me safe. You kept me from killing myself straight away, when I had thrown myself into this river. There is nothing you could say about yourself that would prevent me from loving you with all my heart. So ... " She raised an open hand. "Well, that's all, I guess."

Sister Penitentia placed a hand on Faye's shoulder and her forehead against Faye's. "The Sisters of the Luminous Mysteries keep their distance from Sisters Penitentia. Thank you, with all <u>my</u> heart."

"Come here and hold me tight, and I'll tell you what we're about to investigate."

*   *

Chavis Elementary was the Lumbee Indian primary school, and contained, Faye recalled, the Lumbee junior high school in its basement. Abraham Cousins, using the bar graphs in the *Intelligencer* editorials, had shamed Ellice Laffler and the School

Board into granting the building five percent of the whole bond issue to spend as they chose. That they chose to use half of it on chalk, erasers, and coffee pots and the rest on a portrait of the Lumbee hero Henry Berry Lowrie in no way, Faye decided, lessened the psychological impact of their first dollop of luxury funding since the founding of separate schools for Indians back in 1880. She began to sketch out a non-judgmental paragraph or two as she walked down the dirt path back to the road; and found the photographer Peter Maribel leaning on her fender.

"Forde sent me."

"Good. Go in there and get a shot of the painting of that guy. Lowrie? That's in the front foyer. That's their big photogenic prize from the bond issue. We're off to Carver Elementary; see you there."

"Next stop," she said, when they were back in the Chevy, "George Washington Carver Elementary. One guess which segment of Gabbro society it is designed to serve."

"Well, you really are thorough-going here, aren't you? Even Missouri doesn't have <u>three</u> separate school systems. How ever do you afford it?"

"Missouri doesn't have three separate populations, or I bet you would. As for how we afford it, you're about to see. Oh, and I should have mentioned the fourth school, the Baley school. That is a family of mixed Lumbee - Negro blood that is outcaste from both communities. And don't even ask about whites, who mostly use the Baleys as material for jokes. Since no other people will associate with them, they are even a bit more inbred than the rest of the population. They run a kind of jackleg primary school that apparently teaches addition and subtraction, and the alphabet up to about J, from which no Baley child has yet graduated to knock on the door of a junior high school. They generally give it up to work in the fields, or as janitors somewhere."

She glanced at Sister Penitentia and shrugged. "I know. All of God's children are infinitely precious. I had occasion to mind that teaching more than once, the summer I was in Charlotte. But honestly, Sister, if I manage to have any kind of good impact on the Negro and Indian schools, I will be doing more than I just now think I can. If you'd like to take on the Baleys, we can try to find their school."

"Goodness. All that, without my saying a thing."

Faye snorted. "Then you see how you've conditioned me. All of us."

"That was not I, but the Holy Spirit speaking through the voice of its humble servant."

"Regular burning bush, are you?"

"Strictly speaking, the Holy Spirit had not been conceived of in Moses' time."

"Ha! But is nevertheless co-existent from everlasting, and has spoken through the prophets, as I recall. But I suspect you made that elementary mistake on purpose to test me. Unless you wish to posit that the Holy Trinity is nothing more than a notion that was patched together to settle a squabble among theologians."

"Once again, the student confounds the master. I suppose we can leave the Baleys for another time."

The children of G. W. Carver Elementary were at recess in their dusty schoolyard, playing crack-the-whip and tossing an improvised football made of wadded-up *Intelligencers* and adhesive tape. Faye, having called ahead, was ushered into the Principal's office. There, she introduced Sister Penitentia as her teacher and mentor, occasioning a faintly mocking look from Principal Legare.

"How do, Sister Pen'tentia. You acquire that name the same way my brother's girl done, up in Baltimore?"

"I expect so, since I acquired it in Baltimore as well. How is your niece doing?"

"Teaching at a Sisters of Providence school in Baltimore, thank you for asking."

"Please offer her my greetings in Christ, the next time you speak to her."

Principal Legare gave that a brief *pfft* and waved a hand to let it lie. "How can I help you ladies this afternoon?" A slight ironic emphasis on "ladies," and Sister Penitentia rose.

"I'm afraid I would only distract Miss Bynum by attending; shall I wait for you in the car, Faye?"

Faye was inclined to stand on principle and join in the walkout, but she had agreed to this assignment; and besides, Sister P. was giving her the heavy eyebrows, meaning that the spoken guidance accompanying was not to be disobeyed.

"All right. This will not take very long, evidently."

When Sister Penitentia had executed a meek and anti-inflammatory exit, Faye turned to Principal Legare, who looked possibly a little apologetic. "Never got along with that niece, never was surprised when she ended up in a whorehouse, and never had much use for Cath'lics, let alone nuns. I'm sure your friend is a perfectly nice lady, but not my sort, any number a ways."

"We all have our ways of seeing things. Let's get down to business, then. The *Intelligencer* would like to run a one-year follow-up on how the bond issue has affected Gabbro County schools, so I'm talking to all the principals. I won't go behind your back and talk to your teachers, unless you recommend that I do. I will quote you only with your express permission."

"Can I see your article before you publish it?"

"I understand your asking, but no newspaper in the country would say yes to that. I'll do my best to get it right, and you'll just have to trust me. You're always welcome to write a clarifying letter to the editor, if I get something badly wrong."

Miss Legare nodded. "Well, we done a good deal better than we or anybody expected us to, and I suppose I have to thank the *Intelligencer* for that. We actually went out on the open market and used regular white money to buy brand-new textbooks for reading and math that had never been opened before and - if you can imagine it - were entirely free of torn pages and profanities. I had a job to get some of the teachers to hand them out and use them, instead of putting them up on a shelf."

Faye smiled dutifully. "And did you see any impact on the students that we could report?"

"Folks read the *Intelligencer* give a crap how 'Nigra' kids do?"

"Many of our readers are colored themselves. And before I'm finished, Miss Legare, I will see racial attitudes in Gabbro County brought to the point where everyone does."

"Heh. You an' John Brown, that's a-moldering in his grave. Well, bless your heart."

"Which I have lived here long enough to recognize as about the most dismissive thing you can say about anyone. But I don't believe you had a chance to answer my question."

"Fourth grade math scores up 15%. Fif' grade reading up 63."

"My land! Really? Can I quote you on that?"

"Nobody gonna care."

"There's where you're wrong. I already care, and my reporting those results to the readership will just be one more step on the road … Oh, never mind. Nice going on the scores."

Back in the car, Faye turned to Sister Penitentia. "Sister, she was that way when I came out here a year ago."

"Hostile, ironic."

"Yes. A real chip on her shoulder. I am so sorry that she brought up the 'Penitentia' business."

"Don't be. Many of us consider it a badge of honor, as I expect her niece does as well. More to the point of your investigation, I took a roundabout way back to the Chevy and spotted health and safety violations in that school that would have shut down any school in Missouri five times over. Luckily, your photographer drove up as I came out, and I took him in to get documentation."

"Huh! Well done! Missouri is not exactly Minnesota, but as far as I have been able to see, North Carolina is a mile down from there, maybe five steps behind Mississippi for the most backward, filthy place in the country. What you saw is what I have become used to. There were hardly any cockroaches to be seen in the kitchen when I was here before."

"But there were some, and they looked very much at home. There were mouse and rat droppings on the stove-top and the counters. There was food waste on the floors, where it will attract more vermin until someone slips on it and breaks their hip. The rear door to the cafeteria was chained and padlocked, probably to prevent theft of food by the children, but also very effectively preventing children and kitchen staff from escaping a stove fire. There were flies everywhere. I didn't see any sign at all of fire extinguishers."

"Goodness. Do you think we should go back and warn Principal Legare?"

"We would be telling her what she already knows, and has chosen to live with or, more likely, has no budget to fix. The question is, could we live with ourselves if we said nothing, and children died in a fire or were sickened by food poisoning?"

"If we make a stink about it, the authorities will shut down the school."

"Yes, pity. Then all those children would either have to stay home, violating state law, I bet, or be accommodated somewhere else while repairs were made."

"They would ship them all to Banneker, the other colored elementary; it's already crowded, and no better maintained than Carver."

"No doubt. Will we be visiting Banneker yet today?"
"Yes."

"And if Banneker were also to be in violation of state health and safety laws, what remedy would then be available to insure that all those children from both schools be educated in accordance with state laws?"

Faye drummed on the steering wheel for five seconds, and her jaw dropped, and then framed a delighted smile. "Once again, the master confounds the student. Banneker Ho!" She gunned the Chevy toward northeast Gabbro under a grey sky.

*　　　　　*

They finished with Benjamin Banneker Elementary around four, too late to start another visit. Banneker was if anything, more ragged than Carver, and unmistakably deteriorated in the year since Faye visited it in early 1948. But Principal Mayfield had used the bond issue money in similar ways, and had similar improvements to report; and was more welcoming and more articulate in recognizing the good influence of the *Intelligencer* in helping to bring these things about.

"A very heartening experience, Faye."

"I will quote him extensively in reference to the colored elementaries, since he was so generous in recognizing us. If it miffs Principal Legare to be apparently overlooked, oh, well. What did you see in your wanderings?"

"Squalor. Mostly in the form, though, of what appeared to be structural problems, and not so photogenic as at Carver. Some cracked and broken windowpanes. The floors creaked very loudly underfoot, and I could feel them bouncing. A crowd of full-grown adults or tenth-graders would crash through to the nonexistent basement, so having only malnourished moppets passing is all that saves it. No ventilation, beyond the broken windows. No fire extinguishers. Plaster missing, exposed laths and studs. Sinks in the kitchen with only cold water. Not so many vermin, but some."

"What would happen if the entire population of Carver were to be added?"

"Chaos and catastrophe."

"Oh, my. I will have to run all this by Forde, and see what he wants to do, after I decide what that should be."

"Good for you. Are we finished for the day, then? This has been very interesting."

"I'd like to take you one more place, which will take us no more than ten minutes out of our way. Be prepared to add something to your view of the world."

*　　　　　*

The Spirit Catcher was another row of debris higher, up to Faye's shoulder now. Annie Godfire was fastening a ten-foot angle iron in place with lengths of baling wire, preparatory to welding it permanently, and greeted them around a mouthful of them. "Be with you in a secont, soon's I get this piece welded."

Sister Rose P. was at first not clear on the purpose of the Spirit Catcher, and then seemed to lack the categories to give it sympathetic consideration.

"But, Faye, what earthly use is it?"

"You didn't feel it?"

"Sort of a chill, maybe. It is nearly sundown."

"Hm. What if you thought of it as a cathedral, without the Nave or Transept?

"What would be left?".

"The spire."

"Decoration."

"Maybe the spire is all that distinguishes a cathedral from an auditorium."

"Nonsense. It is the consecration that makes a difference."

Annie Godfire walked to them, straightening scorched-looking pieces of baling wire and bundling them into her bib pocket. "Let me take your friend around to some of the new pieces we're fixin' to build in, tell her a little about them. See if that amounts to consecration. We're focused on barber chairs and straight razors this week."

"Hundreds of haircuts. I love it."

"Tens a thousands, more like." Annie took Sister Penitentia's arm and walked her over to a jumble of steel, and Faye turned to Mary Godfire. "I took your advice about trying to soak off the crust. Almost got Annie drowned in the process."

"She told me. Said you come through right nicely. She wou'nta drownt, though, hardly. She can shut herself down to almost nothing until she figures a way out."

"Of ... ?"

"Where she's at." Mary held Faye's hand and looked into her eyes. "Well," she said. "Still some work to do, don't you think? You feel kind of … ?"

"Numb. Yes. I've felt better since the cleansing. But still … well, I've felt better. I still feel dirty about Travis. How have you been? Since, I mean … "

"Since I got raped?"

"Yes, Ma'am."

Mary Godfire looked over the meadow at the woods beyond. "Leaves you empty, like an ol' paper bag somebody used, and crumped up and th'ew away. My age, it's not a good feeling. But every piece I weld on, and Annie here with me, I can feel a little bit more like myself. It'll take a good while. We've got up to where we'll be working from scaffolds, and then from the structure itself. That will slow things down considerable. But Annie's getting right good with the torch, can't hardly tell her welds from mine.

"Now, Miss. I can see you feel somewhat the same, far as being thrown away. Come on down here where we can talk."

*   *

"You're very quiet."

"I am trying to understand the Spirit Catcher. Whether I come at it as Rosie Dawn Satterfield or as Sister Rose Penitentia, SML, it eludes me entirely."

Silence for a half-mile of gravel road, while Faye got up her nerve. "How would Rosie Aspen come at it?"

More silence while Faye drove into town and to the ABC store, and emerged with a clinking paper bag.

"I was ready to say that Rosie Aspen never thought anything, but that's not true. Rosie would have thought it was a wonderful thing, and felt the 'sperrits' like a trooper."

"And since all of God's children are alike infinitely valuable, and since 'unless you become as a little child' …"

Sister P. gave that an indulgent smile. "You bring nothing new. Also, Annie Godfire saw Rosie Aspen as soon as she began to talk to me. And rather liked her. And it brought to mind - as I swore would never happen again - the grimy, unlikeable prostitute covered in lipstick, bruises and cheap toilet water, and possessed by a demon, who nevertheless swore that she would become a nun and never go back to Hanover Street."

"You have just seen what Mary Godfire calls 'the Gift,' and says that Annie has it so bad - her word - that it will make her miserable some day, if it doesn't kill her."

"Do you remember the story of Jesus and the pious young rich man?"

"Dragged his feet at selling all that he had and giving it to the poor. That guy?"

"That guy. But before that, Jesus hears him out, and loves and understands him, just from looking at him. The guy walks away grieving, because he sees himself too. It sounds very like what Annie has. It certainly made Jesus miserable, and killed him in the end."

"Do you love Rosie Aspen?"

"You won't get me that far. But I suppose I admire the part of her that vowed to escape her demon, and I am glad to have been her. Emphasis on 'have been.' I haven't thought about her for years. On purpose."

"That's the Godfire Gift. She gave you a piece of yourself back, just by reminding you. Look, I bought three bottles of Blue Nun, since you're going to be here three more evenings. Are you hungry?"

And now while they lie side by side in the big, cool bed at the River Cottage, and Faye can hear the Grandmother Clock keeping watch over the blue-bleak embers of the fire as they whisper *gall and gash*, (Sister Rose P., Modern Poetry II). And while that same Sister Rose Penitentia in her Rosie Dawn Satterfield avatar whispers dawn-like gentle snores, Faye feels, like the air that Annie Godfire learned to live without, the emptiness within herself: that hollow where Travis - or love for Travis, or perhaps only the love of being in love with Travis - once dwelt.

*   *

The three bottles of Blue Nun lasted two evenings, and had to be supplemented by a couple of Moselles. On Thursday of Sister Penitentia's visit, Faye brought her in to Gabbro proper on the way to a visitation at West Elementary, and introduced her to Forde Morgan and the Salonnette ladies. Ginnie Freeman was a little frosty at first, but eventually unbent. *Why is it called that? Surely it should be 'bent.' Still, she was decent enough, for an ignorant bigot.*

Forde blushed, of course, mostly on behalf of the prejudices of his late father, which Custis had never uttered in Faye's presence. Forde allowed that Faye had sung Sister P's praises since the first days of their acquaintance, and registered her for a complimentary mail subscription to the *Intelligencer.* "There you go, how exciting," Faye said. "The un-newsworthy news of a tiny town, a week late. Bet you can't wait to read it."

"You win. I will read it with pleasure."

On Friday evening, with Sister Penitentia already packed for an early Raleigh-to-St. Louis train, they sat in the glider, feet sharing the coffee table, gently tired, rocking a half-inch to and fro. "Well, Faye. This has been a perfectly delightful visit, and so full of discoveries."

"I hope you are not just referring to my long, unofficial confession on Sunday."

"Of course not. You know, I seem to bring out such stories whenever I meet a graduate. I suppose they are anxious to show how much they have grown once out from under Mount St. Anne's oppression. Some of them cover decades of headlong growth, error, achievement, and foolishness. Not one of them, not all of them rolled together, can be mentioned on the same page as yours. But, no, I meant the richness you have discovered in this - I cannot but call it insignificant - setting. What a gift you have for revealing the hidden glories of a perfectly ordinary place. I am thirsting to know how the schools deal with their apparently insuperable anomalies. I want to come back to the Spirit Catcher and watch it grow. Rather, Rosie Aspen does, and I suppose I will have to make some accommodation for her whims from now on. Rosie Satterfield is on tiptoe about Sheriff Burns and Annie Godfire. And of course, Faye, my dear friend, I want to see how you recover from your unhappy love affair with the Wayland fellow."

"Presuming that I will recover, which feels iffy just now. Part of me is completely over him, and another part is still aching. Still, hearing him referred to as 'the Wayland fellow' is comforting. I shall make it a point to do that from now on."

At six the next morning beside the looming coaches of her train, Faye embraced Sister Rose Penitentia and handed her the tiny travelling case. "Goodbye, Sister. I hope you can come back some day soon; I'll miss you terribly. Oh, I really do feel that you are my sister now. If that is not presumptuous."

"A delight, Faye. There may be a chance that I could visit for a short time this summer, if you are really open to it. And of course the Rosies will press for it. But in any case, I will follow your career with great interest. Thank Forde again for the gift subscription. I suppose I will be your first subscriber west of the Mississippi?

"The first west of the Gabbro County line."

"Wasn't West Elementary clean and roomy, though?"

"I'm sure they will find they have plenty of room for their brothers and sisters from Carver and Banneker. Please, please do come back next summer. We'll have good weather for swimming, so time it for the full moon. Goodbye, I love you so!"

"And I - "

" 'BOARD!'"

28.

F ROM THE GABBRO *INTELLIGENCER* for Friday, February 12, 1949:

Schools to Face Inspections

All schools in Gabbro and four adjacent counties will be subject to inspection and re-certification following unannounced drop-in visits due to an anonymous tip to the North Carolina Department of Public Safety regarding several schools in the area. Public Safety Assistant Commissioner Cindy Lou Railsback declined to specify particular conditions or schools that may have triggered the short-notice inspections ....

Adorable Puppies

Border Collie mix, wormed, free to good home. Call SAndhills 4405.

OUR TOWN'S TIMES

By M. Faye Bynum,
City Editor

... and may all of us find that special Valentine in our mailboxes tomorrow!

We can look forward to another Jaycee light bulb sale beginning the 20th. So if any of those bulbs you bought last year have burned out - which I'm sure can't be so - here is your chance to re-stock. Beachum Prothroe again has promised that proceeds will go toward continuing renovation of Gabbro Memorial Hospital, this year directed at refurbishing the pediatric wing.

And that may be a good thing, if alleged dangerous and unsanitary conditions at some of Gabbro County's elementary schools should sicken or injure any of our children in the new year (see 'Schools to Face Inspections' on Page 2).

*   *

"I don't suppose these surprise inspections have anything to do with your visits?"

"Forde, the problems were there for anyone to see. It could have been some kid's mother, after a parents' visitation night."

"I notice you don't specifically deny that it was you, though."

Faye picked up her chunk of gabbro - the two halves rubber-banded together - and twiddled them into closer alignment. "That is correct. And it would certainly be in accord with this paper's avowed mission of serving as a force for improving public life in Gabbro County if it <u>were</u> I. Please note the subjunctive. Those schools are deathtraps as they stand."

"Have you given any thought to what would happen if the two colored grade schools would be declared unfit for habitation, condemned, whatever?"

"There's nothing wrong with Carver that a good cleanup and some elementary hygiene and safety practices wouldn't fix. Banneker is another story. The place is slowly collapsing to dust."

"That's your opinion as a certified building inspector?"

"Why are you so negative about this? Those schools are disasters waiting to happen, and if you wanted to get off ... out there and look at them, you'd think the same."

"Thank you for not saying 'get off my duff.' I'm just trying to see the whole picture."

"Well, OK, good. Let me help you out. The first thing you'll see if you look at the whole picture is that Gabbro County schools are segregated - sorry, divided - into a group of handsome, modern, well-equipped educational institutions, and a bunch of dirty, inadequate, and dangerous disgraces. It's like something out of Dickens, except here we are in the middle of the Twentieth Century.

"Then if you look a little closer, still seeing the whole picture, mind, you can't help noticing, gosh, the handsome schools are full of white kids, and the disgraceful ones are full of colored kids. A coincidence, I guess; who'd have thought? Or, I guess, the colored schools used to be just as nice as the white ones, but them lazy Nigras don't take no care a nothin'. And then, when the colored schools by accident got the teeniest bit of justice, in the form of actually being supplied with decent textbooks, look how their scores improved, in both Carver and Banneker. It's practically a Science Fair project: Can Negro Children Do Better When Given Decent Textbooks? A Controlled Experiment." Duh!

"Faye, don't take that tone with me. You know I basically agree with you, but there are other considerations. The school bond issue about tapped out the County's credit-worthiness. Not to mention people's ability to pay the taxes it will take to meet the debt service. So where's the money going to come from for your cleanup and either repairing or replacing Banneker?"

"Is that the problem of the Gabbro *Intelligencer* to solve? Or is it our duty to point out a massive and dangerous injustice when it's right under our noses? I guess you'd be just as happy with the *Intelligencer* as the fearless clarion of the Jaycee jelly and light bulb sales."

Forde had to grin at that. "OK, tell you what. The inspections are supposed to happen next week. Why don't we wait and see what qualified building-safety folks have to say, and take our cue from that?"

Faye recognized that as stalling, but stalling with some sense to it. "All right. Good idea. I will hold my fire until we see the report; but if it supports what I already know from personal experience, don't expect me to hold back, or go at this slantways. We're just darn lucky some kid hasn't come down with ptomaine or fallen through the floor at Banneker."

*   *

Mount St. Anne High School
St. Louis 5, Mo.
March 1, 1949

Dear Faye:
Just a quick note to let you know that the Archdiocese has granted my request for a brief vacation during the summer holidays at Mount St. Anne. If you are indeed agreeable that I should return to Gabbro for a visit, it now appears that it may be possible. I realize that circumstances change unpredictably, so if you are not in a position to entertain company, please feel entirely free to say so, and we will cancel or reschedule.
Affectionately your friend,
Sr. Rose Penitentia SML

Morgan's Eddy
RFD 1, Gabbro NC
March 5, 1949

Dear Sister Rose:
I am nothing short of ecstatic that you will be able to join me again this summer. Let's set dates over the phone when

summer is closer, but in any case no later than the end of next month.

Meanwhile, I have an enormous favor to ask, that only you can grant. Feeling lonely after your leaving, I - probably foolishly - acquired a puppy who is a very good companion to me as the evenings become longer with the advancing season. She is a Border Collie mix, for whom I have not yet settled on a name, but it would be a considerable comfort to me to name her "Rosie." Would you be offended by that? After all, she is a female dog, technically therefore, a bitch. I am asking by this letter that you consult both Rosie Dawn Satterfield and Rosie Aspen before you reply. Miss Canine Bynum and I await your reply, and your most longed-for presence with -

Love,
Faye

Mount St. Anne High School
St. Louis, 5, Mo.
March 10, 1949

Dear Faye (and Rosie):

Rosie Satterfield was a little dubious, perhaps sensitive to the technical objection to which you referred, but Rosie Aspen and I, honored by your request, have overcome her scruples. By unanimous vote of all present, we endorse the name "Rosie" for your new friend, and look forward to meeting her this summer.

Affectionately,
Sr. Rose Penitentia S.M.P.

*   *

From the Gabbro *Intelligencer* for Wednesday, March 23, 1949:

SCHOOL REPORT IS ALARMING

NC Assistant Commissioner of Public Safety Cindy Lou Railsback stood before a press conference yesterday and defended as "impartial and thorough-going" a damning assessment of the state of certain public schools in southeast North Carolina, including several in the Gabbro County School District. Gabbro schools singled out were G. W. Carver Elementary School ("lax hygiene, failure to provide adequate fire egress, failure to provide fire extinguishers in all frequented spaces"); Benjamin Banneker Elementary ("irreparable structural decay, no hot water in kitchen"); Gabbro High School ("Lax hygiene, slippery floors in boys' locker rooms"); and Douglass High School ("Severe structural decay"). Several schools in adjoining counties were also cited for structural and hygienic violations. The Gabbro District has been put on notice that all violations will need to be addressed and plans for long-term structural remedies approved by the State before school opens this fall, or the named schools face a state mandated shutdown. A preliminary response listing likely strategies is due in Raleigh by the end of the present school year in June.

*   *

Faye slept badly on the night of March 31. A booming front passed through some time after midnight, and woke her by blowing the citronella candle off the porch table, causing a clatter that sent Rosie, who had been uneasy and clingy all evening, into mad barking. Faye, knowing it was an indulgence that she might regret forever, allowed Rosie to jump onto a towel on her bed and snuggle against her, while the trees around the Eddy moaned and bent under the wind, and wind-chop chafed the shoreline.

Faye was glad enough of a companion in the roomy bed, and she slept with Rosie until a knock and a gruff *"Faye?"* came from the porch as the Grandmother Clock bonged four. Rosie growled and jumped from the bed to race to the door.

"Who's there?"

Footsteps. "Faye, it's Annie. Momma done passed."

Faye bolted out of bed. "What? Rosie, quiet!"

"Momma done passed. She set up in the bed an' called me, and give me such a sad, loving look, and she laid down and shut her eyes. Time I got across to her, she was gone."

"Annie, oh, my God, I had no idea … I thought she was doing better, last time I talked to her."

"She were. I don't know what it was, heart, maybe. But a course, we know what it really was, was that slimy bastard that raped her. She was never right after that, however she talked. I oughta go back an' dig him up, shoot him again."

"I thought … Never mind, come in. Can I fix you some coffee?"

"Nope. I come over here, need to borrow the Chivvy. I can't find the keys to Momma's truck, take her over't Red Springs. Hey there, little fella."

"That's my new friend, Rosie. Rosie, my sister Annie. Oh, Annie, I'm so sorry! That's just so terrible! Your Momma was such a sweet lady, and she loved you so. My Lord, you put a hateful jerk into the world, he does hateful things, and the hate just goes on working after he's gone. That was something Mary led me to see. But, sure, about the Chevy … well, I need to get in to work early today. Could you drop me off?"

"Momma needs to be in Red Springs, time the funeral parlor opens. Tell you what, you drive us to Red Springs, an' go on. I'll hitch home after I drop her off."

"OK … well. You know, that Chevy doesn't have much cargo space. Have you thought about how you want to carry her?"

"You drive, I'll set in the rumble seat with Momma. Least I can do for her."

"OK, let me get dressed."

By the time they had transported Mary Godfire's body to Eternal Services in Red Springs, rigor mortis had made it impossible to remove her from the rumble seat. Rather than struggle with it, Faye took Annie, now distraught, into the mortuary and explained the problem to the staff, who were still yawning and putting their lunches into the embalming refrigerator.

"Drive 'er own round the back, let us take care of it, Ma'am. Park by the big double doors."

"Can her daughter sit down while I do that?"

"C'mon with me, Miss. You, Jacob! Anybody in th' Eternity Room?"

"Nope, got ol' Miz Locklear comin' in yet this morning, be a while."

"Right this way, Miss."

"I'll be right back, Annie."

By the time Faye had the empty Chevy parked in the visitors' space and returned, shivering, to the reception area, Annie was recovered and waiting.

"Nothin' I can do here. Run me back home?"

"Sure, Annie. We can come out this afternoon. Did they say when they'd be finished?"

"I'm not having her embalmed. She hated the thought of that. They'll have the Robeson ME do a quick autopsy, 'cause that's the rule. I told him, make it quick, I need to get her taken care of before 24 hours, which would be about half-past three in the morning. I want to get it done before dark if I can. Be a lot easier. Think you an' Forde might wont to be there?"

"Absolutely, speaking for me. And I expect, Forde, too. He was very fond of your mother."

"Hell, everybody was. I don't want but family, and that's the two of you. That is … you know. You still my sister?"

"More than ever. I'll be there. Come on, let's get you back home."

29.

S HE WANTS THE FAMILY THERE an hour before sunset. That would be you, of course, and I guess I'm still an honorary sister. Are you OK to participate?"

Forde nodded. "Of course. I barely remember my real mother, so Mary is who I think of now."

"So, poor Forde! First your Dad and now this. I'm so sorry, Forde. Do you have any idea what Annie has in mind to do? She wanted the autopsy done with by mid-afternoon, which sounds like she's planning to bury her today, yet - is why she wants us there. Maybe next to the Spirit Catcher? Or inside it, maybe. But can you just do that? Doesn't the Health Department or a funeral parlor have to be involved?"

"I expect there's a law about it somewheres, written to please the Funeral Directors' Association. Practice is something else, and around here, it's pretty much whatever the next of kin wants. And that's Annie."

"Well, good. She said to wear rough clothes, jeans and such. I guess we'll be pitching in on the grave-digging. We should have a marker made, I'll look into that. There's something to be said for playing without so many rules."

Forde grinned. "Like about cockroaches and mouse poop in the food?"

"Not about those, thanks. We've really started something with that haven't we?"

"*We* sure have, Pandora."

*   *

Forde's DeSoto eased down the lane to the Godfire meadow about an hour before sunset. Annie stood at the big live oak and goat feeding station, next to Mary Godfire's corpse, which was lying across a line of bales, wrapped in a sheet. Faye felt a pang; probably the same bales Mary had used as a reception area. She could see no sign of a grave.

Annie stepped forward and opened the passenger door. "Hey there. Thanks so much for coming. I couldn't hardly do this by myself."

"Our ... well, our sad pleasure, Annie. Where did you figure to lay her down?"

"You're looking on the wrong floor. We're going to give her a sky burial."

"A ...?"

"We're gonna carry her up the big tree and lay her out for the birds to take care of. I put together a sort of platform up there, 'safternoon. Nicer than a bunch of worms, don't you think?"

"Oh, my gosh, Annie. Fine, whatever you want."

"It's what she wanted, she told me last week. I should have known from that, what was coming. Thing is, I got a set of directions for it from a pastor over'n Red Springs. But it's writ out in longhand, that I never learned to read. Would one of you be willing?"

Faye peered up into the giant tree, past an extension ladder that disappeared into the branches. "Of course, I'd be glad to. Up there? But how will we get her up?"

"I'll take care of that. Ready? We need to get this done before dark, or we'll have to stay up there till it gets light again."

"Say no more."

Annie bent and cradled Mary's corpse in her arms. "I'll go first, y'all just watch where I climb. After we get done with the ladder, it gets right easy."

I got through near drowning, and Annie didn't let me. I can get through this.

Forde glanced at Faye, and grimaced. "You go next, Faye, and I'll be right behind. If you slip, I can catch you, but don't, OK?"

"OK. Guess this was why the jeans, huh?"

"C'mon, y'all. The sun's about to get behind the woods over there." Annie slung Mary's corpse over her shoulder - still tenderly - and bolted up the ladder as if on the way to a ringing telephone.

The ladder was the hard part, Faye saw. It jounced not only with her steps, but with those of Annie ahead and Forde behind. At the top of it, Annie stepped onto a series of branches that wound upward around the trunk. She had cleared away the interfering branches, so it was like climbing a spiral staircase. As she climbed in Annie's wake, Faye could feel the branches and the trunk becoming skinnier and more limber. An alarming distance overhead, she saw where Annie had nailed and tied a low-sided wooden platform that looped half-way around the trunk and rested on a pair of branches. At that height, neither trunk nor branch was more than four inches through.

Arriving at the platform at last and stepping down into it, Faye saw that Annie had cleared the branches overhead; the platform was open to the sky, and to a 180-degree panorama of Carolina low country. She scooted close to the trunk as soon as Forde had cleared the space.

Annie laid Mary on a tarp across the center of the platform, and opened the shroud to reveal Mary's face. She seemed tranquil, Faye thought, and happy to indulge this elaborate business. A puff of wind left over from last night swayed the top of the live oak and drew a groan from the platform; Faye grabbed Forde, and Forde grabbed the trunk. Annie smiled in the direction the wind had come from, and winked at Faye. "Late-comers." She pulled a folded sheet of 3-ring paper from her shirt pocket, and handed it across.

"Before you start, Faye, I just want to say grateful thanks to the two of you for being such good friends and helping with this. It makes my heart so much more restful to have you here."

Forde nodded. "Thank you for including us."

Faye opened the paper and began to read. *"A Liturgy for Sky Burial according to certain Pentecostal sects."*

Annie smiled. "Swamp Pentecostal Lumbee. Never had much dry ground for regular burial, so they developed this.

Momma's Momma was one. I don't believe Momma paid it much attention, but she did love her Momma. My Grandma."

Faye nodded, took a fresh grip on Forde's sleeve, and cleared her throat. *"The following liturgy is designed to be led by an ordained minister. In case of pressing need, the nearest of kin may be substituted as leader after instruction by an ordinate.* [How about an abscissa, Rev?]

The party of family or friends will gather around the deceased on the platform, which shall be no lower than four rods from the ground. Huh. Are we four rods up?"

"Five an' a half. Go on."

"Suitable prayers may be said, or a hymn sung if a musical instrument is available. The leader may designate one or more speakers to eulogize the departed."

"Forde, that's you. I done eulogized Momma all I can. And I don't see as anybody brought a piano."

Forde hemmed and spoke of Custis' affection for Mary, and of the - admittedly offhand - gratitude Custis felt for Mary's provision of a loving haven after the premature death of his lawful wife, a few years after Forde's birth. "She was like a second Momma to me, and a friend an' lover to my father, which meant a great deal to him, and to me, too. That's about it."

"When the eulogies are completed, - Wait a minute, I'd like to add something. Mary helped me so much when I was wrecked about - " Faye glanced at Forde, who turned his eyes to the landscape. "About the Wayland fellow. She was a counselor and a mother to me, too, when my own mother was gone. So - " Faye took a breath and looked out at the suddenly graceful landscape, and sang in a clear voice to a melody that any Mount St. Anne girl would have recognized. *"Hail and farewell, Mary Godfire, very full of grace art thou. The Lord is with thee, and with the Lord is where thou art. Blessed art thou among women gathered here. And the man, as well."* The silence that followed was unbroken by the fall of Annie's tears.

"OK ... *When the eulogies are completed, each member of the family shall step forward and thank the remains of the deceased for faithfully carrying the now departed soul through his or her life. The corpse may be touched or kissed, in token of this gratitude."*

Faye thanked the corpse for being a good home for a wise and gentle soul. She cradled Mary's icy cheeks between her hands, and was glad she had not tried to kiss them. Forde murmured something unintelligible, and put his cheek against her hair. But Annie, waiting until last, did kiss her mother and dropped tears on her face to ease the deathly chill. Faye let a little time pass, while Annie stood and blew her nose.

"All attendants but one, a lady or gentleman according to the kind of the deceased, shall depart, and the remaining person will remove the shroud and any clothing to expose the remains of the deceased to the birds of the air who will carry away and scatter them over the surrounding earth and rivers, to return to the Nature from which they were formed."

"That's me," Annie husked. She gestured at the last glimpse of sun filtering through the forest to the west. "Y'all go on down, it'll be getting right dim shortly."

Faye stared down the descending spiral of branches. "Forde, could you please be so good as to go down this tree ahead of me so if I slip I can fall on you? *When all have returned to the ground, a final prayer for the departed soul may be offered."*

They reassembled in dusk at the foot of the ladder; a white moon, brilliant against the darkening sky, looked on them in silence. Annie took from a goat manger a leather sack, and from that drew three glasses and an unlabeled bottle containing a sky-blue liquid. "This here's a lightly fermented sort of a cordial that Lumbees make from berries that only grow way back in Indian Girl Swamp. Far as I know, no white nor colored folks ever managed to find the place and get back out of the swamp. So it's death to hunt for unless you've been taught. But it is right soothing." She poured an inch of the swamp berry cordial into each of the glasses, passed them around, and raised hers.

She recited something in a language opaque to Faye, and then, "A toast of farewell to my mother, Mary Godfire, and a pledge of friendship and gratitude to my brother and sister. I love you both."

Forde raised his glass while Faye was sniffing at the cordial. Even the vapors were soothing. When she tasted the cordial, an essence like sharpish vanilla blossomed through her head and into her lungs, bringing a gentle burst of contentment.

"Your brother and his friend, your sister, pledge their permanent friendship, baby sister."

"And a prayer of gratitude - no, of <u>deepest</u> gratefulness - for the life of Mary Godfire," Faye added. "We are all lucky to have had her; and to have each other because of her."

"Yeah," Annie said. "Specially me."

Riding back to Morgan's Eddy with Forde, Faye felt flushed and relaxed. "That is some stuff. I see why they call it that. I feel so cordial you could bottle me. It must be about a million proof."

"I think you'd taste the alcohol. 'Lightly fermented,' she said. I think there must be something else that the berries contribute. Some natural, you know, relaxer, that a little alcohol brings out."

"Well, it's a good thing only Indians can find it, or next thing everybody in Gabbro's too relaxed to do any work."

"Yup. Some big company would come in, put in a road for trucks through the swamp to dig up all the bushes, whatever, that make it, and make up a cute name for it. Lumbee Lullaby. Swampland Serenity. And sell it for ten bucks a bottle."

"Uh huh. Duckweed Dreams. Did Annie tell you anything about the autopsy?"

"Cardiac aneurysm. A pretty peaceful way to go, she said the ME told her. Some pain, but you bleed to death internally, pretty fast. You pass out and you don't wake up."

"A broken heart, you might as well call it."

Forde nodded. "Damn whoever raped her to hell. You ever hear who that was?"

"I heard indirectly, it was the same guy that tried to rape me."

"And got shot, and his cruiser burnt? That - what was it? Windell?"

"That's the one." As Faye scrambled to remember how much Forde was supposed to know about Deputy Windell's death, they reached the track to Morgan's Eddy. "Forde, why don't you stop in and have a glass of wine? I think I can fill you in on some of that, now that Mary's gone."

When she had, and they had their feet paired on the coffee table, and were listening tranquilly to the frog chorus, Faye said, "What was that thing Annie said when she poured out the swamp stuff?"

"I only heard it once before. I think it's something you're supposed to say before you drink it. Get you ready for it."

"Sure worked. I'm ready as can be. Also, a very impressive ceremony for the sky burial. Impressive idea."

"Rednecks have some good ideas? Faye, you're going native. But, ready for what?"

Faye blushed. "Oh, my. Sister Penitentia asked me if my smart mouth didn't get me into a lot of the problems I ... well, sometimes get into. I'm ready to say good night, Forde. And to say ... Well. I owe you more than that. I was so wrong about Travis Wayland and about you. You are a heck of a guy."

Oh, shit. ... Well, go ahead. Be a fool for a change.

She looked up at Forde from where she was slumped beside him on the glider. "All right, here. Here is a fairly carefully considered statement that I admit I will be making up as I go along: After my time with Sister Penitentia, and after what we've done today, and seeing you in a family-like setting, not to mention thinking back on how kind and ... and manly, what a perfect gentleman you have been all this time, I am a bit advanced in the, the sensibility with which I can consider that 'Thing' thing that we talked about when I first came here. I <u>so</u> very much regret whatever pain I may have caused you by my ill-fated, ill-considered affair with Travis. The Wayland fellow. If by some miracle you were still interested, I am nearly to the point where I could imagine re-opening discussions of - "

Some time later, she emerged. "Rosie! Down! And you too, Forde. Discussions, I said. There are still the same problems involving our work relay ... relshnshp ... oh ... "

Some ninety seconds after that, she stood up from the glider. "Boss, you had better get your butt down the steps and into the DeSoto. We can continue this discussion when we are not under the influence of Lumbee love potions. Now get, OK? It's time I gave Rosie her walk."

*   *

April 2, 1949

Dear Forde -

I want to apologize very sincerely for my behavior last night, which was under the influence not only of that crazy potion, but also the sadness of Mary's sudden passing, and the drama and emotion of the sky burial. It was wrong of me to 'lead you on,' as the moralists put it, when we were both under all the above influences.

Forde, I like and admire you very much. I am still recovering from the emotion and pain of my love affair with Travis Wayland. Also, the questions around conflict between our business relationship and any other, remain. So it was very unfair of me to - Oh, how to put this? I have been staring at this half-sentence for ten minutes - well, to encourage your - Damn. To neck with you, and then to cut it off suddenly. There. Plain language is always best.

- Faye

PS - Only a very superior man would have stopped so quickly without trying to force the situation. Thank you!

*   *

"Miss Bynum, could you come into my office for a moment?"

"Yes, Mr. Morgan. Shall I bring a notebook?" *Or a gun?*

"That might be a good idea."

Forde eyebrowed a message to leave the office door open. Faye did. "I think we owe the community and the school board some suggestions about how they can respond to the inspections. A series of editorials, laying out a set of options for working out of the pickle we - or somebody - put them in."

"They were already in the pickle, given the actual conditions at those schools. They just didn't want to acknowledge it or think about it."

"Hindsight, Faye. The question is, given the mandates to clean up the pickles, how can they do that? Since you've taken a lot of interest in the situation, I'm going to ask you to be responsible for our editorial stance on fixing it. With an appropriate amount of detail."

"Goodness. OK. Do you have guidelines in mind for appropriateness of detail?"

"The sort of detail you'd find in a responsibly written newspaper analysis of the problem, not by an expert in educational administration or an architect. An example of something that would not be an appropriate solution would be immediate integration of all schools. I admit, that would solve a lot of their problems, but still. Not our call, and not realistic, so no point in even mentioning it."

"I can't live with that."

"I'm not asking you to. I'm just asking you to work with it."

"Well. I'm not going to argue with you, yet. But you can expect that what I come up with is likely to include some form of integration <u>as an option</u>, and for that to be so obviously the best option that only a fool would choose any other. Bu-ut, hear me out here: I admit that I have done almost no research on it, and I'm forming my opinion on the state of things in December of 1947, not now. So, thank you for the confidence you show by giving me this assignment. When did you want to go to press with it?"

"Let's say three or four weeks, before school lets out, and nobody wants to think about it over the summer. If that turns out to be rushing you, we can give you some more time, but before the last week of school, which is the first week of June. You could probably start by asking Ellice Laffler what the School Board's thinking, if anything. Oh, and one other thing, if you will." Forde held up Faye's note and whispered, "Thank you."

"Lord, don't leave that where anybody can see it."

*   *

Ellice Laffler was a steely woman of sixty or so, and she received Faye in her back garden.

"Set down, Miss Bynum. Lacy ?… you, Lacy!"

A leathery Negro looked around the kitchen door they had just passed through. "Ma'am, Miz Laffler?"

"We could drink a glass of tea, please."

"Yes'm. Some a them ham biscuits too?"

"I think not. Miss Bynum will not be staying long enough to snack."

"Yes'm." Lacy pulled his head back into the kitchen and Ellice Laffler arranged herself on a stainless-tubing chaise.

"Lacy's a nice boy, but he's not very bright. Now, then, Miss Bynum. Some on the School Board have noised about the idea that it was someone from the *Intelligencer* that sicced those idiots from the state onto us, and put us into this very unpleasant situation. Would that have been you, Miss Bynum?"

"The inspections took us all by surprise, Ma'am … Mrs. Laffler. I did hear someone speculate - *It was me, but I did hear it* - that perhaps the parent of a student might have been the source. In any case, no one external to the schools themselves brought about the violations that the state found. Some of them sound to us at the *Intelligencer* as if they might be dangerous, and let the School Board in for some actual liability in case a student is injured or sickened. Our readers include many school parents and, of course school tax payers."

"Dangerous fiddlesticks. Those schools are as sound as a dollar."

"Mm. I wonder, then, is there an appeals process you could follow about it?"

Clearly, a brand-new idea to Ellice Laffler. While Lacy distributed iced tea and supplementary sugar, she could see that Ellice was taking this new thought into her scheme of things.

"The report was their doing. I'm not sure why it would be up to us to make some kind of appeal."

Who else would appeal, *nitwit?* "Well, I suppose you could not expect the inspectors to appeal their own rulings."

"No, of course not." Ellice Laffler looked regretful at the thought. "The Board is considering filing an appeal, under the … the procedure."

"I see." This was kind of fun. Faye scribbled in her notebook. "Have you contacted Miss Railsback about it?"

"Miss … mm. Not yet. We expect to be calling her this week, yet."

Faye took a token sip of her tea. As she expected, it was viscous with sugar. "Well, Ma'am, may I call upon you again when you have, so our readers can follow what is sure to be a matter of very great public interest?"

"You may be sure, Honey. Oh, before you go, would you happen to know how she spells her first name? This Railwood person?"

"Yes, Ma'am. Cindy Lou. Let me write it out for you."

*   *

"The School Board, if we can judge from Mrs. Laffler, is tackling this complex, costly and potentially deadly situation by sitting around in their garden, sipping tea and blithering. She has obviously not lifted a finger to even call a meeting to discuss it. I suggested, indirectly, that she explore any appeals process. A novel, even stunning thought to Lady Ellice."

Forde smiled, reminiscing. "She taught Little Disciples Sunday School when I was six. Never made much sense then, neither. What's next?"

"I'm going to talk to the only one in the whole nuthouse that has a working brain, Abe Cousins."

Faye was on the glider that evening, writing up notes from her interview with Acting Superintendent Abraham Cousins when Rosie snapped to attention and barked at the screen door. *Oh, please. Forde? Burns? Damn, please not Burns.* Faye walked to the door, regretting the puny hook-and-eye that stood between her and the peaceful gathering of darkness. *Pop that thing with a good push.* She sidled up to the door frame, trying to read the figure that wavered in gloom at the foot of the stairs.

"Faye?"

"Annie! Thank God! Get up here, my gosh, how great to see you. How are you doing?"

"Aw right, I guess … Well, no. The birds are doing what they're supposed to do, but it's bothersome. At least worms are quiet about it. I was wondering if you might be able to put up with me for a week or so, till things settle down over there?"

"Oh, of <u>course</u>, Annie. Why didn't I think of that? Come here to me right now. Far as I'm concerned, you can stay forever." Faye pushed open the screen for Annie, and pulled her up the last step. "Come on, I'm just writing up some notes from an interview."

Annie entered the porch, ruffling the fur between Rosie's ears, and suddenly buried her face in Faye's shoulder. "You are a swell person, Faye. I seen that the first second I laid eyes on you. I wish I could be a woman like you."

"But Annie! You're ten times … forty … a million times the woman I could ever be. You're strong and you know a million things I'm completely ignorant about, and you have this wonderful Gift with people. You'd be coming down a good ways to be like me."

"Yeah, I'm strong. I'm stronger'n a grown man. I got the Gift. ' Nother words, I'm a freak. I'm a complete freak, and when my Momma needed me, I didn't do nothing at all."

"Now, take that 'freak' idea and kick it right out the door. You're as close to a perfect woman as I ever met. But nobody can fix a cardiac aneurysm, Annie."

"Naw, I meant when that ratshit was raping her. I *knew* something was wrong, right when, come to find out, it was happening, I could feel it, but I couldn't … there just wasn't …"

"No, of course there wasn't. What, you're going to fly to her like Superman or something? It was a horrible thing, and part of the horribleness was that no one was there to help her. He figured it that way, Annie, that's how he operated. Listen, I talked to Mary after it happened, and she told me how every piece you added to the Spirit Catcher made her feel better and better. You were helping her heal, just with your welding. Oh, Annie, don't beat yourself up, you're just feeling that man's hatefulness still sloshing around the world, stinking it up. But you are good and solid and healthy, and that will win in the end. Come in here. Did you bring some things with you?"

"Seemed kind of like nerve, I show up with a suitcase an' say, kin I stay with you."

Faye waved that off. "How did you get here? Don't tell me you walked."

"Isn't but a little under a mile. I come on that path that goes along the river."

"Huh. I never took the time to follow it and see where it goes. Well, you want to go back and pick up some things?"

"Maybe in the morning. I can sleep in my underwear."

"No need, I have extra nighties. Come on, let's have some ice cream and tuck you in. You've been carrying a load that would break a mule, and you don't have to do that."

Annie stayed with Faye for two months, off and on. In the morning, she walked back to the Godfire meadow with Rosie by her side, shutting her mind against the flapping and bickering in the live oak, to work on the Spirit Catcher. She hot-wired Mary's truck to haul used steel from demolition sites and junk dealers, and she became Rosie's favorite because she was always around - something Faye could not be - and took frequent walks along the river path between the meadow and Morgan's Eddy.

After a few weeks, Annie noted diminishing activity on the lofty burial platform, and one morning in May, convinced herself that the work was finished at last. The only bird to be seen was a mockingbird, sitting on the edge of the platform with his back to the scene, singing something he had picked up from a Florida scrub jay. A crew from Eternal Services came over then and gathered the scattered bones into a body bag for cremation. Annie cleaned out a drive cylinder from a Southern Railroad switcher locomotive, placed the ashes inside, and welded it shut; and put it aside to be included at some lofty place of honor, when the Spirit Catcher was near completion. The process was witnessed by Faye and Forde, and sealed with tots of the swamp berry cordial. Faye watched herself carefully until the next day.

30.

F ROM THE GABBRO *INTELLIGENCER* for Wednesday, May 11, 1949:

THIS TOWN'S TIMES

By M. Faye Bynum, City Editor

The not-so-flattering report from the State Department of Public Safety on Gabbro County schools has placed a heavy burden on the School Board and on Acting Superintendent Cousins to come up with a reasonable response before the end of this school year, less than two months from now. Gabbro taxpayers are rightly bracing themselves to take on new spending. The first thing everyone can see about the situation is that, while some of the critiques can be met easily by changes in hygiene and safety-related practices, there will be no free or cheap fixes to the virtual condemnation of both Banneker Elementary and Douglass High School. When I talked to him this week, Mr. Cousins acknowledged that he had been aware for some time that the two colored schools were many years past their design life, and needed to be replaced. "You always think," Mr. Cousins said, "Well, I reckon we can get away with one more year

*in the old buildings. But now we're
brought face to face with it."*

*Face to face, indeed. The
<u>Intelligencer</u> is planning a series
on various options to meet the
problems with Banneker and
Douglass; we can already see that
no option will be cheap to put in
place, so we are turning to our
readers for your creativity, which
is likely to at least match that of
the School Board. If you have an
idea for meeting the State
mandates for correcting safety
violations other than the 'brute
force' option of simply tearing
down the old school buildings and
replacing them with new ones,
please send us a letter. We want
to hear from Gabbro citizens on
this!*

Forde leaned back in the Boss Chair and looked at Faye over the top of the *Intelligencer*. "A little heavy, don't you think?"

"What, about the creativity? Have you talked to Ellice Laffler? And she's the brains of that operation."

"Yes; but remember, we have to live in this little town, so we try to speak gently even to idiots. But the whole tone. Kind of, 'Well, folks, you sure loused this up, and what you gonna do about it?' I thought you were on an assignment to offer helpful suggestions."

"I certainly intend to do that, Mr. Morgan. I will go to heroic lengths to avoid embarrassing you by even referring to the obvious best solution. But you will be interested to know that a group in South Carolina - <u>South</u> Carolina, mind you - is putting together a lawsuit arguing that schools there, which are separate and unequal like ours, violate not only that "separate but equal" fiddlesticks, but in fact deprive citizens of equal protection of the laws, which violates the United States Constitution."

"My. Well, we will follow their activities with interest, but let me remind you that your job description requires you to confine your contributions to matters taking place within Gabbro County, <u>North</u> Carolina."

"Occurring within, or directly affecting, the City and County of Gabbro, North Carolina. I looked it up. In my opinion, a Federal court case regarding schools that are an exact mirror of the ones here, affects Gabbro County."

"And in my opinion, that affection … affect<u>ing</u>, is indirect, not direct. Faye, I hate to do this, but if you can't keep an open mind on this subject, I will have to relieve you of the assignment, and either do it myself, or give it to somebody else."

"Really! You talk to me about - " Faye interrupted herself to shut the office door, as gently as her trembling hands would permit. "You talk to me about keeping an open mind, but you rule out of consideration the obvious best solution to this mess, which is to integrate all the students - and teachers, by the way - into the sound, modern, whites-only schools, which have plenty of room for the colored student population. That's not what I would call an open mind. It's a closed and prejudiced mind."

"I don't know why you have to get so upset about this every time we talk about it."

Faye turned and opened the office door hard enough to jam it into her right foot, which was wearing one of the ballet slippers she'd bought in Charlotte almost two years ago, and never were very much protection. It took enormous self-control not to yell and slam the door behind her, which she mustered. But not in time to stop herself from re-opening it and grating, "Life consists of getting upset about the right things at the right time. And by the way, isn't this an excellent example - an excellent <u>illustration</u> as a matter of fact - of the utter conflict between your ambitions in regard to a 'Thing' status with me, and your ambition to be some kind of conservative tough-but-fair Editor-in-Chief?"

And not so quietly either, that every word was not easily audible to Jenny McCall and Rob Stoker. Again.

Morgan's Eddy

*   *

Dear Miss Bynum -

I do not understand why school buildings that have been perfectly all right for colored children for many years are suddenly not all right. When I was a girl ...

To Miss M. Faye Bynum:

My solution would be to have all the white students transfer to the Colored schools, and all the Negro children transfer to the White schools, for a year. You can bet there would be an immediate outcry to fix up the Colored schools better than ...

Dear Miss Bynum:

I have a solution to the schools problem, but I do not see why I should give it away for nothing. What would the Intelligencer or the School Board pay for a guaranteed ...

To the Editor:

I have never understood what is the purpose of attempting to educate Negro children in the first place. ...

To the City Editor:

What if all the colored children were sent up to Raleigh on buses and we let this Miss Railsback figure out how to give them an education?

Faye tossed the last letter onto the pile of rejects. "Except for the one who wants the kids to switch schools, there's not one letter in that pile that wouldn't get the School Board sued for violation of the United States Constitution if they took it seriously. You realize, if you keep spoiling that dog, you will have to adopt her."

Annie lowered Rosie to the porch floor. Rosie wandered to a spot equidistant from Faye and Annie, and thumped herself prone, her chin on the floor. Her eyes switched from one to the

other and back. Annie sat back on the glider and turned to face
Faye.

"You're worried and upset. Maybe it's hard to see the
good in anything at all."

"Right on the first part. I had a row with Forde about this
stuff. But you can believe there's not much good to be seen in this
batch of … well, to put it as politely as I can, male cow manure."

"Momma's Gift ran to seeing the good person behind the
bad talk. She was probably seeing the good in Mr. Deputy
Windell while he was rapin' away at her."

"She said you had the Gift better than she did. But she put
it that you had it bad. What's that like? Is it bad?"

"If you let it be. The trick is, don't be thinking you are
responsible for what the person is. You askin' what I'm seeing
right now with you?"

"Y - not necessarily. Just in general. People put up these
crazy fronts, and you just see right past them. That would bother
me, I think."

"You do right good at that, yourself. Didn't you ever feel
like, the other person was lyin' to you for no good reason?"

"Quite a lot. But that's easy. You've got this extra piece,
where the liar sees himself lying. Is that hard to watch?"

"Oh … I guess. Not as hard as it is for them, a course. It
bothered me some when Windell saw himself. Bothered <u>him</u> so
bad, he killed himself." Annie squared herself back away from
Faye, placed one hand against the other, and looked at Rosie over
them. "Listen, though. I have got what you might call a life
problem that I need some talking about."

Faye raised a brow and cleared away the letters to the
editor. She was startled that Annie Godfire, of all people, could
want to play younger sister. "Yes?"

Annie gave Rosie a transcendently earnest gaze. "Yes.
That Sperrit Catcher was awful important to Momma, and I am
determined to see it finished. But it is gonna be a long haul.
Momma knew she would never live to see it done. Heck, we only
just started it, and it will take years an' years. Probably my whole

life. But Momma didn't worry, 'cause she knows I am a hard worker, and that I will stick with it. I think about her spirit, wherever it went, still watching, and hoping for me to finish it like we planned. Sometimes, when I'm there working on it, and when I make a nice weld, and some piece a steel fits like I know it should, I can feel her, and lots of other sperrits, kind of patting me on the back. So it would kill me to think I might not be able to finish what she needs me to. Trouble is, something happens, I might not live long enough to see it through, and it would help a lot if I had a daughter myself that I could bring up to work on it after I'm gone, like she did. And so forth, long as it takes, I guess."

"Well, you're pretty young, yet, to be thinking about having babies."

"I'm seventeen. Momma was married when she was fifteen, to this Zecharias fella, so she knew about … you know. Sex and babies and all. I never knew Mr. Zecharias; apparently, Momma couldn't stand him. They had two boys, live over toward Wakulla, never amounted to nothing. Came by one time when I was little and Momma was doing consultations with some of the farmers around here, had themselves a time laughin at her. Her own sons. It upset me something awful, young as I was. But when Custis come along, pining about Forde's Momma, or -

Annie broke off, looking puzzled. "I guess he was just after somebody to have sex with. Now I think back on it."

"Looking to get laid," Faye said. "I know all about it."

"Uh huh. But maybe Momma was already beginning to think about the Sperrit Catcher that her Grandma built, and about doing a replacement. She knew she'd never get it done by herself, so she would need a helper, and not just anybody. It would have to be somebody with the Gift, that would understand the logic of it, how it would need to be built, from the point of view of the sperrits. So she went ahead an' cooperated, and that's where I come from. I don't think Mr. Morgan was planning on another baby, but he come through handsomely when I come along."

Annie shook her head and shuffled her feet in frustration. "Oh, I know it sounds completely crazy to somebody - well, somebody like you, Faye. That's had a lot of education. Thinks about big things. Writes like you were hearing sperrits already, and didn't need this kind of back-country … hick stuff."

Faye shook her head. "Annie, I'm completely on board with all this. I stand in complete awe of you and your mother and your Gifts, because I've seen them work. And with the whole Spirit Catcher idea. Even that you know how to do a good weld. But I don't see how anything I know about can help you. That you don't already know more about than I ever will."

"Well, that's it. There is one big thing you know a lot about, and I don't know the first thing. That's sex. Momma taught me welding, but she never got around to sex."

"Sex? Oh, wait; for making the helper baby?"

"That's it."

Rueful laugh. "Well, right off the top, based on my vast and brilliantly successful experience, I'd say that the way to succeed in the line of sex is, you completely ignore what your Gift and your common sense is telling you about the guy, and let yourself go."

Annie snorted. "Well, fine. But, see, if I told you that the way to make a solid weld that looks smooth and good, and won't crack when it's got a hundred tons of steel depending on it and all the other ones, was to let yourself go, you might be looking for a little more detail."

"Well. I don't know anything about welding, but making a baby is almost certainly a lot easier. You want the real how-to?"

"For one thing, yes. Then, what I hear, not every time you do it makes a baby. What makes the difference between making a baby and not? What little I know about sex and having babies doesn't sound to me like something I'd necessarily want to go through for nothing, either end of it. But for another thing … now, this is going to get kind of close, so shut me up if you don't want to talk about this part."

"Go on."

"OK, look. I have the Gift stronger than Momma did, even though Custis seemed like about as far from having the Gift as you can get."

"No argument there. The man was as ignorant as Rosie, and a lot less sensitive to other people."

"Uh huh. By the way, don't be too hard on Rosie. That dog has some understanding of things, and that is just something you might have to take my word for it. But anyways, seems like Custis had something, that didn't get in the way, at least. Maybe helped, even. The babies she got with Mister Zecharias didn't amount to hogwash. So Custis had something that Zecharias lacked, in spite of how he didn't seem to. So."

Annie ruffled her hair and looked an appeal at Faye. "Do you think you could talk to Forde about it?"

"Forde? I guess. About what? You know I just had a big fat argument with him about this school stuff, but I think he'd still listen to me about something else. But what, exactly? Is this something you couldn't talk to him about yourself?"

"Not about this, hardly. Out of the blue."

"Well, what ... whoa, wait a minute."

"Talk to him about standing in for his father. About giving me what his father given my Momma."

"Annie!"

Annie nodded. "About being a father for my baby."

*   *

Forde flipped a typed draft onto his desk in Faye's direction. "I guess this is all right. Pretty good idea, really. OK, I think you could offer whoever picks this up, oh ... a couple dollars an hour, up to some maximum for each design consultation. The veto on integration stays in place."

"I have given that question some thought, Mr. Morgan. We will be asking simply for the costs of a variety of physical structures, without regard to how they will be occupied."

"OK. Why the PO Box?"

"We don't want the whole world to know what we're doing, that's why." *Also, I don't trust you to edit or manage any stage of this, Mister Managing Editor.* "This way, it could be anybody in town, or thinking of coming here to build something. Specially if we run it in the Fayetteville and Lumberton papers at the same time."

The following Classified thus appeared in a week's worth of *Intelligencers.* as well as the Fayetteville *Observer* and the *Robesonian* of Lumberton:

> **CONTRACTORS** A Gabbro enterprise wishes to research approximate costs and timelines for a series of building designs, in consultation with a reputable professional designer - builder. Consultation will be compensated at reasonable professional level. Aspects of the work will be confidential. Submit inquiries to P.O. Box 701, Gabbro, N.C. by May 20, 1949.

By the end of May, Faye had collected some twenty responses that showed varying degrees of seriousness and impressiveness. Setting aside the stiff-paper architectural firms and the those who looked like jackleg country handymen, she winnowed it down to those who seemed to be serious, competent, middle-rank contractors.

"Did you tell them we're talking about school buildings?"

"No. Converting a general-purpose office building to a school ought to be roughly the same price regardless of the particular form of building we're talking about. Don't you think?"

"It's your project. You use your own judgment on that kind of thing."

"Gladly. Thank you."

"Entirely my pleasure."

"To a man - and they were all men, of course - they spent about half of the interview checking out my behind and estimating the size and shape of my breasts, while they were interrupting me to say exactly what I had been saying. Nevertheless, four of them were able to focus enough to impress me as capable and experienced in public-building construction. I paid off everybody for their time, and took - in my judgment - the top three firms to submit complete estimates, so we might be able to catch any dumb mistakes or trickiness on the part of one of them; and after it's finished, we'll be able to say 'average of top contractors,' something like that. I have boiled down and simplified their final reports and averaged their numbers, which were pretty similar anyhow, to this summary." And she laid a single page on Forde's desk:

COSTS OF POSSIBLE RESPONSES TO NC SCHOOLS REVIEW:

I. Rebuild Banneker Elementary and Douglass High School buildings, standard construction quality:
A. Frame construction:$400,000 Lifetime: 50 yr.
B. Masonry construction: $600,000 Lifetime: 100 yr.+
C. Temporary (Quonset or trailer) :
New construction: $75,000. Lifetime: 15 yr.
Rental from Defense Dept: $4,000/mo.

II: Shore up and repair Banneker and Douglass buildings: $300,000 - 375,000. Lifetime: 10 - 20 yr.

III: Move colored students from Banneker and Douglass to West Elementary and Gabbro High School, and build quality replacements for white students (100-yr.+ masonry construction only considered): $900,000.

IV. Expand and partition West Elementary and Gabbro High to accommodate separate additional 40% occupancy, masonry construction: $250,000. Lifetime: equal to or beyond the lifetime of the original buildings.

Forde read through it and tossed it back on his desk. "You only have the two worst cases here. What about the other buildings that were reviewed badly?"

"Those were just cleanup jobs that will have to be done anyhow, whatever we do about the condemned buildings. You can see that Option Four, which is almost cheapest and looks like the best value, amounts to almost the same thing as integration, but it's not, because of the partition. Actual integration would be even cheaper. Of course, nobody will want to go with the obvious cheapest and fairest option, because goodness knows, those partitions might leak or even be removed some time in the future. Also, it would be so darn hard to maintain the 'separate-but-equal' baloney, when they're right there next door."

"Mm. There'll be an element that will push for the Quonsets, but I think they can be won over by asking if they want to go through the whole thing again in fifteen years. Why was option four so cheap?"

"Because both Gabbro High and West Elementary are under-occupied, so not much expansion would be needed. Really, you could just about partition the existing buildings."

"Gabbro's growing. It would be short-sighted to do something that would fill the schools chock-full right away."

"How true. Have you looked at Douglass? It's chock-full right now. And I suppose Banneker would be, if you taped off the unfit-for-habitation parts. But even doubling the expansions of West and Gabbro High would only add $50,000 to the cost."

"Well," Forde said, sounding alarmingly like Custis. "Faye, you have done a fine job on this messy and complicated project. I believe there is material here for the *Intelligencer* to guide community thinking in a positive way."

Faye said nothing, but nodded rather formally. *You must have spent solid minutes on that speech. I guess there's no excuse for not raising the next big topic.*

Faye sat in a visitor chair and softened her face for the next topic, which was something she had stalled about for weeks.

"Forde, I have something I promised someone to talk to you about. It's kind of touchy, so could we declare a cease-fire for humanitarian purposes on the school thing?"

Forde was willing, pending what "touchy" might mean. "Humanitarian" sounded kind of promising. "Of course, Faye. What is it?"

"I have a very personal question - or request, I guess - from your half-sister."

31.

F AYE! FOR GOSH SAKE, THAT'S INCEST!

Faye nodded. "I'm tempted to say I didn't think that was a big deal down here, but I won't."

"You just did."

"OK, true. Listen, don't think I didn't try to talk her out of it when she first brought it up. And that was weeks ago. I've been stalling, but she's so sweet and earnest about it, I just couldn't put her off any longer. So … I can't believe I'm saying this; but still, it's not hard-core, like marrying your mother or your sister."

Forde shrugged. "Half-sister."

"True, again. Believe me, I pointed this out to Annie when she asked me to talk to you about it."

"What in hell gave her that crazy idea? This isn't some notion of yours is it, to get me married off?"

"Forde, for God's sake! … Don't flatter yourself. And there's no 'marrying' to it. She just wants a crack at your, ah. Your, well, genetic material." Faye tossed a hand. "Your sperm. But there's actually a sort of reasonable idea behind it. Well, understandable. Sort of."

And Faye went through Annie's reasoning about the need for an heir to the Spirit Catcher project, and the importance thereto of continuing the apparently benign effect of Custis' germ line.

"She doesn't love you, or anything. Well, of course she does. She's not <u>in</u> love … Look, she's not hot for you, OK? She just doesn't want to take a chance on leaving the Spirit Catcher unfinished at the end of her life, and she doesn't want to gamble with anybody but her own daughter, with a father she is pretty sure will be reliably likely to allow the daughter to have … " Faye sighed. "Listen to redneck me. 'The Gift.' "

"Yeah, well, she's nuts. We'd be lucky the kid didn't have two heads."

"Well, it surely wouldn't be that bad. You only share one ancestor."

"Father. Don't make him sound like our ninth great grandfather."

"You don't have to convince me. I don't know why I'm trying to convince you. Except I promised Annie I would. Listen, I went through it with her, and I used some arguments against it that you haven't even thought of yet. She just sticks to the Spirit Catcher thing." Faye grinned. "She says they did it all the time with the goats, and never had any bad results."

Forde laughed, reluctantly. "With goats, wonderful. Don't know when I've been more flattered. I'll do her the compliment of assuming she meant <u>between</u> the goats, and not <u>with</u> 'em. You just run back to Annie for me and tell her nothing doing."

"Uh uh, know what? I'm not cupid's messenger, and I want out of the middle of this. You can tell her yourself."

"Aw, Faye, please?"

"Nope. The next thing would be, she'd give me six arguments to bring back to you, and there'd be no end to it. All that's going to convince her is, you tell her yourself."

"Well, awright, I will."

When Faye drove the Chevy down the bumpy lane to the River Cottage that evening, she drew a sudden breath through her teeth, and jammed on the brakes. Alfred Burns' county cruiser was parked at the foot of the steps to the screen porch. But she knew that she could never back up the lane again without hitting a pine tree. She let out the clutch and rolled on. Burns was sitting on the top step.

"Hello, Sheriff. Haven't seen you here for a time. Can I help you this evening?" Faye debated whether to even get out of her car; but what was she going to do, lead Burns on a high-speed chase down East Church?

"Hey, Miss Bynum. How you been?"

"Fine, thanks. What is it?"

"Why, I just was wantin' to see how you was doin' out here by yourself." *Uh oh.* "Plus, I had a question."

Faye tried to be casual about not getting out of the Chevy. "Doin' fine as frog's hair, Sheriff. I do enjoy the quiet, I must say. What was the question?"

"You goin' get outa that car, or spend the night in it?"

"I just remembered something I needed to pick up at the Piggly Wiggly. Not wanting to look inhospitable. Was that the question?"

"Nuh uh. Look, seems like I fired off my mouth a while back to you an' Forde about so-called police brutality. That was out of line, and I'd like to apologize."

Really. "Think nothing of it, Sheriff. We didn't take it all too seriously." *Hail Mary, full of grace ...*

"Good." His face darkened a shade. "Maybe you shoulda, at the time. But I been a changed man lately, since I had that concussion."

"Well, good for you." *... The Lord is with thee.* "What was the question?"

"You know, I don't blame you at all for bein' shy about getting out of your car."

"No?"

"No, ma'am. You done had that bad experience with the Windell fella. But I ain't him."

No, but you're about as bad. Blessed art thou among lawmen ... "Well, land, I'd hope not. Thank you for understanding, though." Faye felt her heart starting to pound. *Blessed is the fruit of thy loom ...* "You know, in some ways, I've never really gotten over that thing with Windell. I do hope you don't take personal offense. But it's late, it's getting dark, and as you pointed out, I'm here - we're here by ourselves. I believe I'll just go on around and do my groceries."

Burns rose and bounded down the steps, hollering for Faye to wait - the steps, Faye recalled, down which she and Annie had carried him concussed and unconscious. *Wholly married, other than God, playful as sinners ...*

"Wait!" It sounded bad and wrong to Faye. She floored it, and killed the motor. While she was frantically cranking, and the gassy smell of a flooded engine rose through the dash, Burns reached the Chevy and put a hand on the windowsill.

"Whoa, little lady. My land, don't get all hysterical. I just wanted to ast you … "

"Get your hand off my car," Faye screamed. "Get your hand off! Right now!"

And Alfred Burns did. He stepped back, not reaching for his pistol, not unzipping his fly, but grinning unconvincingly. "Sweetheart, I'm sorry. Easy does it. I just wanted to ast…"

"Well, what?" Faye cranked up her window, and opened the little quarter-window to talk.

"You OK?"

"Obviously not. Was <u>that</u> the question, then?"

"No, Honey. The question was, I was right charmed by that lady you had here visitin'. Can't seem to get her out of my head. Do you know how I could get in touch with her?"

Faye collapsed over the steering wheel, ready to weep. "For God's sake, Sheriff. You do realize she is a nun, right? She's a bride of Christ. You got some competition if you want to charm her back."

"Well. That does change things a bit, I s'pose. Is that the kind of thing, once you're in it, you're stuck?"

"I believe that's the way it works, yes."

"Uh huh. Oh, well. I don't wanta get into a triangle with Jesus, sure enough. OK, well, thanks."

Burns looked around the peaceful place, the cottage, the Eddy. "Funny thing. Something about this place kinda haunts me, like I dreamed about it once. Like what's happening now, happened just the same before. You ever had that kind of thing?"

Faye rolled down her window and gave Burns a shaky smile. "Sure did. It's a common experience, they call it *déja vu*. Very creepy. People get it for no reason that anybody can figure out, what I hear. If they think back, they realize they were never really in the exact same situation, after all. I know it gives me the creeps when it happens to me."

*   *

From the Gabbro *Intelligencer* for Friday, June 16, 1949:

SCHOOL OPTIONS MULLED

On p. A2, the reader will find a display of four options for the Gabbro County Schools to consider in response to the critical State review of local schools. The *Intelligencer* has come up these options after canvassing reader input and obtaining cost estimates from local …

"Which is not an out and out lie, Forde. We came up with them after the canvassing readers who turned out to be a pack of numbskulls and racists. But what the heck."

Forde dipped a Terminal fry into a puddle of ketchup. "Uh huh. Maybe just not as sophisticated as you."

"OK, OK. Sorry if I drove you into 'defensively Southern' mode."

"Faye. I'm sorry this has been such a … contentious - is that a word?"

"Yep. I'm sorry too, Forde. I was doing fine, I thought, after I began get the Wayland fellow out of my head. Now I can feel myself turning into a sourpuss old maid, hour by hour."

"My stars, Faye, you're 21 years old. You're not a *old* anything, let alone sourpuss. Ask any male in the county, you're a heck of a good-looking woman. But, you know, a good, solid relationship with an eligible fella could solve your problem."

"If you're putting yourself forward, I'd say you've got quite a big 'relationship' on your dance card already."

Forde shook his head, chewing thoughtfully. "What am I going to do about that?"

"Have you talked to Annie like you said you would?"

"Well. Kind of. Yes, I talked to her. She scares my pants off sometimes."

"I'd think that would be a good start, right there."

"Shut up. You know what I mean."

"Annie's formidable. Glad I'm not in your position, Mister Stud."

"Well, guess what: I tried to tell Annie that I was ... well. Inexperienced in that kind of stuff. Trying to get her to see it might not be as simple as she's trying to make it, seems like based on how her and her Ma bred their goats."

"Uh huh. She took that line with me, too."

"Well, here's her solution to my inexperience: She considers sultry an' dashing Faye Bynum <u>highly</u> experienced, and therefore qualified to ... um..."

"Yes? Now what?"

Forde turned as red as the end of his fry, and leaned forward to whisper, "You know. Give me lessons."

"What!"

Forde started to laugh, and Faye joined in. Eventually, people craned around to stare, and they made an undignified, scarlet-faced exit. People who had an *Intelligencer* open to page A2 pursed their lips.

*   *

On Friday morning, June 30th, Faye stood mournfully miffed at the side of the Seaboard Air Line tracks in Raleigh Union Station, checking Sister Rose Penitentia's letter. *Friday the 30th, 9:37 in the morning,* it said. And there was the train, all right. But no Sister P. *Gosh, she could have called.*

As she exited into the waiting room, snapping the letter against her leg, a woman in slacks and a sweatshirt, her hair pouffed atop her head with a silk scarf and - despite the gloom of the place - wearing sunglasses, stopped her. "Excuse me, Miss Bynum?"

"Yes?" *Now what horrible -*

"The clothes make the woman, can't we say? I'm sure we can. Miss Bynum, Rosie Satterfield. Would you be driving south to that charming little village? And may I have a ride?"

"Sister P! Oh, my … " Faye launched herself at Sister Penitentia. "Oh, you certainly may." She stepped back, still holding the sweatshirt sleeve. "So is this is the long-abandoned Rosie Dawn Satterfield? Did you quit? Resign, whatever they call it?"

"Not at all. If Mother Superior heard of my being in public out of habit, I would be on my knees with a scrub brush for weeks, so my fate depends on your silence. I thought your young friend Rosie deserved to see her namesake without being terrified by the get-up."

In the hurtling Chevy, Faye gathered her nerve. "What really, um, prompted you to dress down?"

"I simply could not say. I handed in my grades, I finished evaluating my younger colleagues, and left St. Louis as Sister Rose Penitentia. But I had purchased these other things in case I might have the opportunity to help you with some work around your place, and this morning, rattling along through Virginia, it seemed virtually imperative that I become a different person. Looser, less careful. More open to things."

"The South does that to me, too. But I only have one identity to choose from. You have this abundance."

"It was your heathen friends the Godfires who reminded me that there is more to me than the old stick. As I think you once called me in a note I confiscated."

"Oh, my. I apologize, of course. That was back when I thought I was the smartest person in the world. The last year has gotten me over that."

"But you were right. If escaping Rosie Aspen and all she represented required me to become an old stick, I was happy to do it."

"Well, you were - and are still - the smartest, dearest, most challenging old stick in the forest. Don't please change her in any way. Did your bring clothes for Rosie Aspen too?

"Rosie Aspen is not a matter of dress. She was Rosie Dawn Satterfield, possessed by a demon. She was a stone wall six feet thick with an inch of paint on the surface, and orifices for rent. You could put her in the full habit of a Mother Superior of the Sisters of the Luminous Mysteries, with a rosary from the Vatican in her hand, and she'd be spotted instantly as a whore in a nun suit."

"But that's not what you are!"

"Thank you very much. No, much as I hated and resented the trial by ordeal that the church imposed on me before I was accepted as a Sister, it did have the intended effect. It overcame Rosie Aspen, cast out her demon, and made a new person of her."

"Huh. Didn't change you back to Rosie Satterfield?"

"A half-measure. Rosie Satterfield is the kind of woman who could become a prostitute."

"Goodness. I'll have to watch you, then? And am I that sort of woman as well? I have a reputation as a fast and ruined woman, in Gabbro."

"I would say no, to be polite, but it seems to me that no one, if events happen to so conspire, is immune to prostitution. As for your reputation in Gabbro, from what I saw and from what I read in the *Intelligencer*, it is that of a formidable, if sometimes too daring, whirlwind and scourge of the self-satisfied."

"Really. You get that from boosting the Jaycees light bulb sale and news of the Library Board meeting?"

"I get it from other stories of course, mainly the articles about schools; but even your boosterism and local stories are the result of impeccable writing, and a kind of loving irony. You would need to read flaccid, clichéd, juvenile writing for a living to appreciate the difference."

"Well. As usual, here we are smothering each other with praise. Why do you have to live so far away?"

"As I recall, we used to live in the same town, and one of us moved a considerable distance away."

"Only too true. That wretched Forde Morgan was the siren who lured me onto this rock. Speaking of which, here we are. I need to do a little shopping at the ABC store. Blue Nun still OK? I don't think there is a Blue Satterfield."

"Of course there is. It's a rosé."

32.

S ATURDAY, JULY 2 was a half-day for *Intelligencer* staffers, provided their contributions to Monday's paper were written, edited, and typeset. That was the case for Faye, and she stopped in on Forde to check out before heading back to River Cottage.

"Yeah, sit down. I think your four options for the schools are gonna be a referendum. Nobody came up with anything else, so the Council approved a motion from the School Board to put your list up for a vote. Want to put down some money on what wins?"

"I'd be betting against all common sense and citizenship if I bet against the one that keeps the colored folks as far away as possible, namely shoring up Banneker and Douglass. But I bet that's the one that wins."

"I wouldn't necessarily bet against new white schools and let the coloreds move into West and Gabbro High."

"Really? For a million dollars, which you can bet it will be, by the time you figure in finance costs and overruns. A million plus."

"Very erudite, Miss Bynum. You been studying up. But on the new white schools option, first place, doesn't it feel familiar? Use up what you've got, buy a new replacement and give the worn-out one to the colored kids. Where have we heard that before? But also, the Chamber's got everybody in a froth about this new towel factory that's going in. Merrydown money, and nobody's ever seen the bottom of their pockets. Council and the School Board is willing to bet a new bond issue will pass for more than half of it, and the banks will come up with the rest."

"At a million percent, sure. We haven't begun to pay off the first bond issue, and now they want to float one for ten times as much? Are they nuts?"

"Pretty much."

"Huh. Well, fine. You'll be raising the rent on the cottage to pay for the tax hikes, you watch. Meanwhile, I'm hoping somebody will watch the arithmetic this time around, so we can at least not pay to line Ellice Laffler's pockets."

"So jaded an' cynical, and barely emancipated."

"Live fast, die young, I think they say."

"The rest of that is 'Leave a good-looking corpse.' You reading that trash?"

"No. I think I got the line from nauseating Claude Reynard." *Noseating Clode.* Faye grinned.

"You getting over all that? The Wayland fellow, you called him the other day. I thought that sounded like progress."

"Not necessarily. I just thought of something funny. But I can't stand the thought of having to do the elementary arithmetic on another bond issue. Once through that was plenty. Hey, though, isn't it time for the next round of awards?"

"The jury got hung on the investigative award between the Fayetteville *Observer*, story about communists in the army quartermaster corps, and - guess who? The Asheville *Exchange*, a story about contractor shortcuts that's like to make that Biltmore place fall down around Mister Vanderbilt's ears. Here you could have had a hand in it two straight years."

"Not worth the price of Clem Atkins having a hand on my butt for twelve straight months."

"Huh. Anyways, they had to push the awards party off until September some time. Far as I know, we're still invited to coronate the eventual winners in state-wide and small town."

"Uh huh. 'We?' "

"Sure. I was planning to ask you about it, but this big delay come up. Don't you want to go and crown your successor? Bound to be some big paper like the *Star-Dispatch*, Raleigh *News and Disturber*. They wouldn't dare give State-wide to a little paper two years running."

"Well, sounds like fun, sure. Would you be going?"

"I'll crown the small-town winner. Think I'm going to let you have all the fun?"

324

"Guess not. I'm in, long as they don't sit me next to Clem Atkins. Anyway, I just came by to check out. Are you about to leave?"

"I'm going to drop out to the Meadow and see Annie. Just check in, see how she's doing. She's out there by herself, she could kill herself on that Spirit Catcher, and nobody would know but the spirits."

"Well, watch yourself out there, stud."

"Not funny. That silly idea is coming between me and a little sister I love. That's half the reason I'm going out there; I haven't seen her for at least two weeks, because of that. I'm just going to have to stand up and put my foot down."

"Trying to picture it."

Faye, knowing that Sister Penitentia would be busy with Offices and Rosie the dog, tarried to pick up groceries to provision the visit. *Rosie Satterfield might be a bigger eater than a Religious.* She went by ABC for a fresh supply of Blue Nun; hard to stay ahead of demand in that quarter. She stopped back at the *Intelligencer* office to pick up the proofs for Monday. One thing and another, it was early afternoon before she set off for home. The Blue Nun was merrily audible behind her elbow in the open window, clinking in the rumble seat.

*   *

When Sister P. finished Terce, she felt acutely the fact that she had not bathed since leaving St. Louis, not counting a spit bath in Seaboard's one-to-a-coach toilet. After cleaning up her things, making the bed she had shared with Faye, doing the breakfast dishes, and reading some Thomas Merton, she took herself - in her Rosie Satterfield clothes - and a cake of Ivory to the dock and washed up, hanging off the end on her stomach, and managing to refresh herself a little. The day was warming, the water inviting in spite of a snappish breeze that ruffled its surface, but by this time, Sext was no more than twenty minutes away. She resolved to return after Sext and do a thorough bathe, when in any case, the day would be warmer yet, and the water even more welcoming.

*   *

Forde sat on a bale, watching Annie weld a sewer grating across the entranceway, marquee-style. The acetylene torch hissed, a blue-white spot of brilliance that threw occasional sparks against her face shield. She had been at that place, doing that weld, for the past ten minutes. Forde was no welder himself, but he thought he could see that it was not going well.

That was confirmed when Annie finished the weld, waited for it to cool, and jiggled the grating to test it. It snapped off and slumped against the baling wire that was holding it in place. Annie let fly a gritted obscenity, and threw the torch onto the ground, where it started a small grass fire. Forde leapt up to stomp out the fire, but Annie yelled at him to stay clear.

"You stomp wrong, you could detonate that torch. I'll be right there." She let the grating sag against the baling wire, and jumped from the ladder to rescue the torch.

"See, that's why I need a helper, dang it, Forde. I can't see why you are being so obstinate about helping me with that."

"I done offered to help, and you told me, go sit down."

"You know what I'm talking about. Help with a baby, to be my future helper when I get old."

"I told you about that, Annie. Brothers don't make babies with their sisters. It tends to make unhealthy babies. You don't want that, I think. Besides, you're what, 18 now? If I helped you now, even if she was fine, your baby would be less'n 19 years younger than you. Why don't you wait till you're 25 or 30, so your baby can go longer into ... well, when you're too old to work any more. Plus that gives you time to find the right fella who wouldn't give you some kind of freak baby."

Annie stood kicking the dirt with her work boot. "What it is, you don't care about me none at all. You think <u>I'm</u> a freak, and you're right."

Forde stood in shock. "What? <u>Wait</u> a minute, here. Annie! Of course I care about you. I love you like a sister, which you are. I thought this was supposed to be a breeding project, not a love affair."

"What difference? Don't matter what you call it, if you don't want to make a baby with me. Oh, to hell with the whole thing, I'm sick of it." And she burst into tears.

Forde stood stunned. "Well ... But, Annie ... "

*   *

Sister Rose Penitentia stripped to her underwear, covered the Satterfield clothing with a towel, and lowered herself shyly into the liquid embrace of Morgan's Eddy. The Ivory's characteristic smell blended with the sunshine and birdsong to remind her of summer afternoons in Baltimore, of being six and seven years old, unacquainted with the disasters that would ticket her for a life of stress and disappointment, beginning a decade later. She lay back in the water and let the sun play on her belly, and felt the cool presence of the springs below her. She thought about the years when she was as smart and unbounded as Faye Bynum, a girl she knew she would have loved when loving girls was what she dreamed of and did not reveal or discuss. The Ivory bobbed beside her in the breezy chop, following her slow progress with the lazy rotation of Morgan's Eddy. She used it to wash herself, and put it back to follow her like a tiny satellite.

*   *

Sheriff Alfred Burns bumped down the root-crossed lane and tooled the cruiser to a stop at the foot of the cottage stairs. By God, he would not be distracted by nuns, blue or pink, or by sweet talk by smart-ass Faye Bynum this time. Awaking at 5:30, his bruised brain had closed the last synapse in reconstructing the events of that day nearly a year ago when his memory stopped functioning. Burns was no naturalist, and had no curiosity about how such a reconstruction of mental mapping had occurred, nor had he the humility to thank Whoever for the miracle. Because what it revealed was humiliation, beginning to end.

Bynum could not have hit him while he was spanking her - he did pause a moment to thank Jesus for the returned memory of her fanny in daisy-printed cotton panties, squirming between his hand and his lap - so there must have been somebody else there. He had no idea who it might have been, but - some confusion remaining here - seemed like that nun friend of hers might have been there at the same time. Knocked silly for months by a nun, by God! Well, he would get to the bottom of that, too, and if it meant turning a damn nun over his knee, so be it, Jesus or no Jesus. Burns found the thought kind of stimulating.

*   *

Sister Penitentia heard Rosie Bynum barking remotely, and ignored it until the slow Eddy brought her into the current upstream from the gabbro outcrop by the far shore; then righted herself in the water.

Oh, no …

*   *

Forde walked beside Annie Godfire with an arm around her shoulder. The arm had been shrugged off, then accepted when Annie turned to Forde and laid her head on his shoulder.

"But, Fordie, I <u>do</u> love you. I never said that to no boy before, and you bet I never will again."

"Well, Annie, there's no shame in that. I love you too. You were a pure gift to me when I was a chubby little kid. I have loved you good and hard since you were old enough to walk around, and I will always be here for you. You can love me, and I can love you, which I do. Just, we can't make a baby, you and me, not now, nor ever. I hope you understand that."

Annie was silent, kicking through the grass of the river path; then sighed, and put her arm around Forde's waist. "I know. I guess I do understand. That whole business about wanting a helper was a kid notion I made up back in Kinnygarden to make you love me. But it don't make me any happier."

"You don't have to <u>make</u> me love you, Annie. I flat-out worship you. I never known anybody, man, boy, or woman, that's as strong and smart an' full of spirits as you."

Annie shrugged. "Well. I think you love Faye better than me."

"Nuh-uh, Annie. I do love her different, and you bet I'd be ready to ... go to bed. Have sex, dang it. With her. Trouble is, she don't seem to feel the same about me."

"Huh. Join the club. Except you're flat wrong."

"Yeah? This the Gift talkin'? You're gonna break my faith in it."

"You wait and see, all I'm gonna say to that."

*   *

Sister Rose Penitentia watched from behind the gabbro outcrop as Sheriff Al Burns got out of the County cruiser and mounted the steps to the cottage. The water was warmer at that side of the Eddy, but the current was strong, and hanging on to keep herself from being swept downstream was tiring. While Burns' back was turned, she pushed off, leaving the Ivory gleaming pure against the black of the outcrop, and swam as silently as she could toward the dock, hoping Burns would have a seat on the porch and read an Agatha Christie, to let her get to her towel and clothes undetected. When instead, he turned to descend, she took a breath and dove, setting off under water to reach concealment under the dock.

Rosie Bynum had no good feelings about this strange human who had appeared out of nowhere while she was napping. His shoes were hard on the cottage steps, and his scent of ill-will was overpowering. His gun reeked of trouble and panic - the farmer who'd raised her had one of those things, and Rosie would never forget the smell of gun oil and the ear-shattering noise. Rosie stopped barking, stood on her hind paws and began to worry at the hook that held the screen door shut. She had once seen Faye paw at it to make the door open, and she hoped it would do the same for her if she pawed at it long enough.

Stripes and tangles of refracted sunlight followed Sister Rose Penitentia across the sand at the bottom of Morgan's Eddy. She was conscious that her very pale skin was going to be spotted by anyone really looking in the right place, but she hoped that the wind-ruffled surface would make that harder. Below, she saw the puffs of sand that marked the central spring; and dancing at its center, a half-spherical object, neither sand nor stone, but a partial human skull, borne aloft by the spring, flashing tiny crystals of fool's gold as it rotated to bring its single eye socket onto Rosie Aspen doing her tank act.

Alfred Burns spotted the towel and the ladies' clothing at the end of the dock, and saw that he had happened onto a little situation. Saturday must be her bath day. He would have smart-face bitch Bynum trapped, and maybe there would be a chance to spank her smart ass without panties in the way, and with wet skin to make the spanking sting all the more. He sauntered out to the end of the dock, just missing the entrance of Sister Rose at depth into its shelter. He settled smiling on the end of the dock and surveyed the Eddy, looking for bathing beauties.

Forde and Annie, rounding the last bend on the river path above the cottage, spotted Burns as he settled on the pile of clothing.

"Well, will you look - "

"Shh. Annie, you know he's dying to find some reason to put that business with the Scotland County deputy on you. Why don't you let me handle this first thing, and you can come along later. Cover my back."

Annie snorted. " 'Cover my back' don't make no sense. I got no gun nor nothing to cover it with. But, OK, I might kill the sucker with my bare hands if I got close to him, so g'on ahead. I'll be right here."

So Forde strode around the bend and into the sunshine of the cottage yard, making noise enough to alert Burns. There were stiff-legged acknowledgements:

"Well. Look who's here. How do, Mr. Morgan."

"Al. What brings you around on a weekend?"

"Duty. You?"

"On a walk."

"Don't let me detain you."

"Matter of fact here's where I was heading."

"That right? You walked all the way out here?"

"Parked at the head of the trail."

"Huh. That's near Godfire's."

"So it is."

"Huh."

Forde decided to get the conversation off its butt with a little fiction. "You waiting for Faye, I give her an assignment, I believe was gonna take her over Bozlee way for pretty much the afternoon. You might could find her at the Bozlee Elementary site, checkin' on repairs from the tornado."

"That so?"

"Ye-es." In the rising tone that signifies confirmation of a demonstrably simple fact.

Burns did not have the Gift, but he knew a lie when he heard one. He shrugged and turned to look out over the Eddy, hoping to spot Faye, and give the lie to this pansy. No luck. Forde took a step onto the dock, his knees shaking, but feeling that he had something to prove both to Burns and to Annie, who 'had his back.'

"Al, I told you Faye isn't here. Don't you have better fish to fry than hang around like some schoolboy hopin' she'll show up? Or ... " He spotted the towel and clothing Burns was trying to conceal with his boots. "Oh, I get it. Well, whoever's clothes you got there, they sure's hell ain't yours. That Sister Penitentia, I believe, is visiting just now. You tryin' to shoot nun beaver, Al? Wait'll that gets around."

"Ain't gonna get around, you know what's good for you."

And the confrontation developed, two dogs stalking around each other, threatening and wagging at the same time, trying to figure out what to do next, while Sister Rose listened from waist-deep water under the dock, and cast about for strategies of escape. Annie got tired of lurking and watching a scene that looked hostile, but whose words were unclear. She sauntered across the grass and joined Forde at the foot of the dock, in time to meet Rosie Bynum, free at last, who dashed down the cottage stairs and down to the dock, barking at Al Burns. Burns, on one foot preparing to punt Rosie back onto the grass, stepped on the edge of the pile of clothing and turned an ankle. He didn't fall in the Eddy, but his arm-waving, leg-hoisting dance to keep from it, set off laughter from Forde and Annie, and a fresh round of clamor from Rosie.

When Al Burns had recovered his balance, he snarled at the giggling pair who had him trapped on the dock. "Ha! Here's your voodoo step-sister too. What a pair."

"She's my sister, Al, so you can take back your cheap remark. And get the hell out of here, while we're at it. Shame on you, ya peeping tom." As Faye's Chevy appeared, lurching and creaking down the lane, Forde walked onto the dock, looking like he wanted to finish the job of getting Al into the water.

Al reacted badly, out of wounded dignity. He drew his pistol. "Get back, God damn it, ever one of you. I'm an officer of the law, and I'm giving you a die-rect order." And when Forde did not get back, Al Burns fired a shot into the ground in warning. Of course, he was not standing on the ground, but on a dock. The bullet penetrated the ancient wood like paper, and entered Sister

Rose Penitentia's right shoulder. After shattering her collarbone, its path was altered enough to break two ribs on her right side, exiting her body just above the diaphragm and the critical organs below it. Bone fragments from the collarbone sprayed into her chest cavity and nicked the subclavian artery in several places, starting an internal hemorrhage, and damaged her right lung. Sister Rose cried out in pain and sorrow, and floundered into the open. After two or three steps, she fell face-down into the reedy shallows.

Faye was the first to recover from the shock, skidding the Chevy to a stop at the shoreline and jumping into the shallows to rescue Sister Rose. Ford dashed onto the dock with Rosie Bynum under his feet, tripped on her and fell against shocked and flustered Al Burns. They fell together onto the dock, heads dangling over the water. Forde was angry, but not much of a fighter; he popped Burns under the jaw with a mild uppercut and tried to butt Burns' face with his forehead. He landed one pretty good shot out of three tries that hurt enough to change Burns' mood from guilt to annoyance.

Rosie, kicked sideways by Forde's stumble, recovered and sank her teeth into Burns' leg. Burns roared and raised his revolver. He could have settled matters by pistol-whipping Forde, or shooting him for that matter; but chose instead to bring the pistol to bear on Rosie, who was now hurting him worse than Forde had. But raising the gun above the dock gave Annie, rushing from the shore, a clear target, and she place-kicked it from Burns' hand into the center of the Eddy, where it sank onto the spring and, being far heavier than water, plunged deeper into the roiling quicksand. The partial skull, spinning in the upward current, followed its disappearance with its empty socket.

That done, Annie picked up Forde in one hand and Al Burns in the other, putting Forde on his feet and Burns in a hammerlock. When Forde had himself upright, Annie snapped the fingers of her unoccupied hand. "Keys."

"What?"

"Not you. ... Burns! C'mon, keys to the cruiser."

Faye managed, in waist-deep water, to get Sister Rose turned face-up, and drag her to the edge. Sister P's eyes focused. "Thank you, Faye dear," she gasped. She pointed to her ragged and bleeding shoulder. "I seem to be wounded. You can't believe how it hurts."

"Lie still, Sister," Faye said. "We'll get you to the hospital."

Forde took Sister Rose Penitentia to Gabbro Memorial Hospital in the County cruiser, hitting seventy miles an hour on East Church, and laying on the siren. Faye and Annie followed in the Chevy, with Al Burns wired immovably into the rumble seat with two or three lengths of baling wire. When Forde got Sister P. onto a gurney and under the care of a nurse ("Gunshot, lost a lotta blood, Chrissake, hurry!") he returned to the Chevy and relieved Faye of guard duty. Faye sprinted into the hospital; Forde stayed with Burns and Annie, who pulled a pair of wire-cutters from her overalls.

"I'll hold him up, you cut the wires."

*　　　　　*

Peter Maribel had been thinking of quitting the *Intelligencer* for a couple of months. He needed the job, but how many times can you take pictures of the Jaycees kicking off their jelly sales before you turn into jelly yourself? He had groused to Forde about it - about giving Peter more freedom to come up with photo-essays on his own, really. At Forde's noncommittal encouragement, Peter had done some shots and story boards that Forde had promised to look at, but it always stopped there. The pictures of squalor and decay in the schools had been a big hit, but that was months ago. Forde had been preoccupied, and Peter was pretty sure he knew what it was that was so much more important than his own job satisfaction. Christ, it was obvious as hell that Bynum was going to take up with Forde once she got over her embarrassment about that Wayland guy who'd been screwing her, so why didn't they get on with it, and let the world get on with its business?

In this brown study, Peter wandered toward the emergency entrance of Gabbro Memorial after he'd done shots of goddamn Beachum Prothroe snipping a ribbon on the "newly refurbished" Children's Wing - changed the light bulbs, was all that Peter could see in the way of refurbs - and Beachum hugging a kid with a broken arm, the kid looking pained because Beachum didn't seem to be all that aware of what the kid's problem was. Peter had gotten what he thought was a great shot of the kid wincing while Beachum laid it on.

Now there seemed to be some kind of ruckus coming from outside the Emergency Room. Hoping for photogenic crises, Peter loped down the hall, unlimbering his new Graflex.

Faye caught up with the gurney as it turned the corner into the surgery corridor.

"Miss, doctors and patients only in here."

"But she's - I'm her friend."

"Have a seat in the waiting room."

"Oh, please, give me just a second."

"In that second, she'll lose another half a cup of blood, not sure how much she's got left. Go sit down."

Faye stood on tiptoe, cupping her hands, and hollered, *"Ave Maria gratia plena, Benedictus tecum ..."* trying to bounce it off the ceiling and onto the moving target on the gurney.

The operating room door sighed shut.

Peter Maribel followed the ruckus and burst through the emergency waiting room and out under the portico to find the Sheriff of Gabbro County, minus his stupid sheriff's hat and his six-shooter, in the grip of a kinda handsome Lumbee-looking chick who seemed to be handling him with minimal sweat, like a man made out of balloons, even though he was red-faced and kicking, and hammering his fists on her leg, which was the only part of her he could reach, pinned under her armpit as he was. Every time his fist hit her thigh, it sounded like somebody pounding on a telephone pole. She carried him to a green bench under a moss-draped turkey oak. Peter - heart fluttering, shit, a goddarn Amazon, Wonder Woman in a tee shirt and overalls - followed, taking shots as fast as he could crank film. The chick sat down on the bench and slammed Burns - Sheriff Alfred Burns, the macho lawman - across her lap, which knocked his breath out.

Alfred Burns shifted his attention from banging on Annie's leg to getting a breath. Peter got a good shot of red-face, gulp-mouth Burns while he was lying across her lap, working on breathing normally. When he managed it, Annie got in six or eight pretty solid whacks on his butt that made Burns holler ten times as loud, the Graflex clicking and cranking, before a pair of orderlies came through the door and told her for God's sake keep it down, didn't she know this was a hospital zone?

*   *

Sister Rose Penitentia was in surgery for seven hours, and wheeled from Operating to Recovery to await death or survival, the surgeon having declared her "in God's hands." Faye spent this time pestering nurses and interns for information, changing out of her wet clothing into something she improvised out of hospital gowns, and dozing on the waiting room's folding chairs until a night nurse took pity and led her to a spare gurney. She cat-napped there until she was roused at dawn with the news that God had not yet opted to welcome Sister P. to His bosom. She went home, changed, and dragged herself to St. Ann's, intending to make some intercession, and ended up lighting a candle. The rest of that Sunday passed in a blur, with visits to the hospital every hour or so, always to meet the same frustrating rebuff that Sister Rose Penitentia was in critical condition, and could on no account be visited. When she returned to the cottage at dusk, Forde and Annie were there, gathered for a post-nonmortem.

"So, what's the latest?"

Faye shook her head. "Same as the earliest. 'Holding her own, no visitors.' Whatever 'holding her own' is supposed to mean. What are we going to do about Burns?"

336

Forde shrugged. "What can we do? It's gonna be like he said about police brutality that time, 'I felt like I was in danger, the gun went off accidentally, you gonna take their word against a defender of law'n order?'"

"In danger from a half-naked nun six feet below him in a lake?" Faye sighed. "But you're right, anyhow. His word will be law." She stood with a quick intake of frightened breath at the sound of a car coming down the lane, headlights jouncing.

Annie stood, smiling, looking down the steps. "I believe our solution as to Mister Sheriff is here. This will be that cute little Peter fella, that I invited here to show us some pitchers. C'mon in, Peter."

"Call me Pete," Maribel said, opening the screen with a shy glance at Annie. "Yeah, well, so I was over't the hospital getting shots of boring Beachum Prothroe cutting a ribbon on the Children's Wing spiff-up that the Jaycees paid for. Heard the sher'f making this ruckus, and tracked it down, and here's what I found." He pulled some 8 by 10's from an envelope and passed them to Annie, who looked at the top one and smiled briefly before passing it to Forde. It showed Alfred Burns face-down across Annie's lap, registering surprise, outrage, and pain. Annie's hand was flat across his rump, and you could see a blurry shock wave spreading across his pants from the area of impact. The next four were variants on this theme: Al Burns red-faced and struggling for breath; Annie's hand raised, blurred in descent, impacting.

"Land, Pete," Faye said, admiring the shock wave. "Some high-speed action here."

"Thousandth of a secont." Pete turned to Forde. "We gonna run it above the fold?"

"Aw." The last photo on the table before Annie was a wide-format soft-focus close-up study of Annie's face and raised arm, lovingly punched up with darkroom techniques to make her look like a serene angel in the act of chastising Sodom and Gomorrah.

Annie looked up from the portrait while Forde was clearing his throat to tell Peter to forget it, the pictures were scurrilous and would never see the light of day.

"This'n's right pretty," Annie said. "You mind if I kept it, Pete?"

"Well, heck," Peter Maribel shrugged. "Who'd I make it for?"

33.

SISTER ROSE PENITENTIA WAS RELEASED from the hospital on August 10, Faye's 22nd birthday. The weeks of hospitalization were occupied with further surgery to reinforce the hasty stitch-up of her right subclavian, and to make some sense out of the fragments of her right collarbone; and otherwise with vigils, visits, and prayers by Faye, Forde, and Annie, who was sometimes accompanied by Peter Maribel. Faye prayed, talked, and read to Sister Rose; Forde practiced what Sister Rose called a "ministry of presence;" that is, sitting largely silent until Sister dozed off, and then tiptoeing out. Annie mostly conversed about spirits and spirituality until Peter dozed off.

Sister Rose was frail, not used to walking or to strong daylight. Her right arm was in a sling. Faye enfolded her carefully when the nurse appeared with her at the drive-up entrance.

"For heaven's sake, Faye, I'm not made of spun glass."

"You are as far as I'm concerned. What would your Mother Superior say, I invite you down here and get you shot, and then I pop your stitches by hugging you to death, which is what I'm inclined to do."

"I spoke to Mother Superior by telephone yesterday, and she got in a good deal of told-you-so as it is. You'd think I had been bathing with carnal intent."

"The old poop. She surely didn't think you flung yourself into that situation on a whim."

"She took no pains to disabuse me of any such thought. She also wanted to know who is going to pay for my care, which is a good question. Faye, I know I have enormous gall to ask you this, but I can pay you back over time."

"No such thing. In the first place, it was not backbreaking, and I would have been delighted to pay it myself; but in the second, the County of Gabbro Department of Law Enforcement is coughing up the money, in view of their employee's careless discharge of a firearm when not in danger of life or limb."

"Well, I … Well." Faye saw that Sister P. was on the brink of tears.

"Oh, foo. They spend more than what it cost every week, putting gas in that cruiser. Let's get you home and into bed for a nap."

The suite of five photographs of Alfred Burns squalling on Annie Godfire's lap never saw publication, except for an accidental viewing when Faye happened to drop a manila folder containing them on the floor of the Salonnette, on the way to visiting Sister Rose. The ladies noticed, as Faye had figured they would, and were greatly tickled. Descriptions of them spread across Gabbro County like the shock wave from Annie Godfire's hand. They may have been influential in Burns' announcement, a week after the shooting, that he was resigning to take a job in Indiana that he had been considering for some weeks.

*   *

Faye and Sister Rose Penitentia lay side by side in the cool, roomy bed. Spoiled Rosie jiggled on a towel at their feet, having accompanied Forde and Annie to the meadow, chaperoned the sibling-kiss they shared, herded Annie into the trailer and Forde into his DeSoto, and galloped back to home base, arriving in time to lick the supper plates. Somewhere in that round, she apparently picked up a night bug.

"Rosie! If you can't lie still, you'll have to get down."

Rosie stopped chewing at her tail and subsided, recognizing 'get down' as the worst possible outcome. The bug, seeming to see where its interests lay, subsided as well.

Faye took Sister Penitentia's hand. "I feel so wonderfully lucky. I have a Sister and a spirit sister."

"You also have a young man with a very strong spirit who worships you through thick and thin. Annie tells me that he attacked and defeated Sheriff Burns - an armed professional lawman - with no thought of danger to himself. He thought the clothing I left on the dock might be yours, and he was prepared to fight Burns over it. Did you tell him about the spanking incident?"

"No. You and Annie are the only ones who know about that. Well, other than Burns himself. I hope he roasts in Hell for shooting you."

"I thought I heard something from you about judging not, some time ago. Shooting me was accidental, and involved no real evil intent. But Forde somehow knew that Burns was no better than that other Sheriff's deputy, in his willingness to violate you. And he was prepared to act on it, whatever the danger."

"I formed a very poor first impression of Forde over two years ago, and I haven't given him a break since. I thought he was a spoiled redneck. But since I've been here, I've seen that there's more to him. Plus, after all, I believe in Annie's so-called Gift, and I believe in the Spirit Catcher, so I'm getting to be a redneck myself. Maybe we're meeting in the middle. I don't know. It is still so important to me that you are here to discuss it." She stretched, and wiggled to snuggle her nightie'd butt against Sister Penitentia's unwounded side.

Penitentia reflected that she was in bed with a very desirable and strong-spirited woman, and experienced a twinge of wistful, nostalgic lust. It was short-circuited by Rosie Bynum, chasing a squirrel in a dream sent by him whose bride Sister P. has sworn to be. She smiled with gratitude and turned toward Faye, neither seeking nor avoiding incidental contact, to sleep the sleep of the Saved.

*   *

From the Gabbro *Intelligencer* for Wednesday, August 30, 1949:

NEW SCHOOLS OPTION WINS

Gabbro County voters, expressing confidence in their ability to meet substantial future debt, voted by a solid plurality to adopt "Option III," under which new schools will be built to house students currently at Gabbro High School and West Elementary. The new schools will be erected on land freed by the demolition of Frederick Douglass High School and Benjamin Banneker Elementary.

Colored students presently attending Douglas and Banneker will find new homes in the existing Gabbro High School and West Elementary buildings, respectively, where ...

Faye folded the paper and tossed it onto the coffee table. "I wrote it, and I still don't believe it. This little - I will never call it 'hick' - this quaint town whose only sources of wealth are a towel factory, a half-broke parson's college, and a played-out quarry, is going to spend a million dollars on new schools so their little white darlings can keep on having the best of everything, and not be contaminated by the presence or sight of descendants of Africans that their Grannies and Grampas enslaved so that ..." She yawned. "Where was I going with that? My mind is in complete shock."

Forde shook his head. "Shock, is that what that stuff is? Label says Blue Nun. Know what I bet? Those new school buildings won't be half through their hundred-year lifetime before they are known as 'Gabbro Consolidated High School' and - oh, I don't know. 'Abraham Lincoln Elementary,' something like that; and you'll see all colors of kids running around in them, and we'll be glad we made 'em solid and roomy. In our lifetime, Faye. I saw that suit you talked about, down in South Carolina, is going to trial, and the Klan is worried sick about it."

"Well, listen to you, you flaming liberal. The Klan's sick to start with."

"OK, fine, but still. Mark my words."

Annie Godfire slung an arm around Forde beside her and ruffled his damp hair hard enough to rattle his teeth. "He's right. He's my brother, and he's right as rain. And sooner'n he thinks."

"Thank you, baby sister."

Faye felt a surge of affection for this pair of half-siblings, and gratitude that was almost erotic, at being the honorary sister of one, and apparently incurably loved by the other. For their part, Annie and Forde seemed to be mightily enjoying a love affair in which sex played no role. Faye supposed she should feel jealous, whether in regard to Annie or to Forde was unclear; but just watching it was so much fun that she could not work up the spitefulness.

"You told me no one can see the future."

"That was what I thought at the time. Sometimes any more, I get some feeling for it. F'r example, I can see clear as day that Forde is gonna stop calling me 'baby sister,' any day now. If he knows what's good for him."

My dear Lord. How I love these two. How I wish I deserved them. Faye teared up, and had to turn her head to hide it. "Even so, it'll never happen."

Forde grinned. "Put some money on it?"

"Not on integration. I'd never bet against Annie's gift. I just know that Gabbro County will never in this world name a school after Abraham Lincoln." She rose from the chaise, toweling her hair to hide the wetness in her eyes, and Forde was treated to the sight of her elegant back in the now faded daffodil swimsuit, overprinted in a wicker pattern. It felt to him like an elaboration of his initial vow of fidelity to the screen-door moment, as she turned at the kitchen door.

"How's barbecue sound? I got a half-chicken from the Wiggly that's looking for a new home."

They are gone, and Rosie is asleep beside her on her towel, after seeing Annie home and collecting her milk-bone reward. Faye dozes, stirs, and peers half-awake into the raftered space above and in the dusk and flicker of the dying fire in the living room, sees herself again, naked and content at Travis' bedroom window. Strange, that what should be a memory full of shame and self-loathing feels clean, harmonious, admirable. Travis is nowhere in the scene. She does not remember seeing him as he beckoned her back to compound the disaster; what she sees now in the lines and shadows is his view of her plain and smiling self, washed by morning rainlight. She lies still, hardly daring to breathe, dreading to dispel the vision; but it grows stronger as the light fades, and Faye's breath quiets. The vision is no longer above her, but opposite, across a room. She feels briefly as if she is floating again in the waters of the Eddy.

Under the benign touch of Morgan's Eddy and this cottage, she has begun to see herself as if in Annie's eyes. And in the innocence of that vision, finds that her love for Travis, and she herself, were never polluted by the hard fact that Travis never loved her as Annie and Forde love her. The entire affair, as a love affair, was of her own making; Travis was a walk-on, in it only to get laid. Her love for Travis - the gasping intensity of it, the nutty notions about enfolding and engulfing her beloved, the manifold orgasms of everyday life in Eden - never pertained to him at all. All that was her joyful creation, and hers alone.

And because of that, finally - Faye now laughing tears of release into Rosie's fur - she knows that she is and has always been a lover, and that to be a lover is infinitely better than to have one, which depends entirely on someone other than herself. She is free to love many others as comprehensively as she once loved unworthy Travis. Years ago, she enfolded Sister Penitentia to her heart, and thus achieved that grace as a lover, who yearned to love and enfold her sister Annie. And - yes, all right - Annie's brother Forde Morgan, too. Hell, she even, shockingly, loves Gabbro, North Carolina. She will live here, loving every stupid, ignorant custom, provincial denizen, every stone in her shoe and mule pie in its streets, for the rest of her life.

Maybe it will not be perfect love, because Faye is far from perfect. By the mistaken act of loving Travis and paying the price in love's sorrow, she has allowed into her soul a wariness that will alloy her love with caution: when she loves, it will be on her terms or not at all. Still, it will be love, if never again as heedless as she was with Travis; Eden being the one place to which we may never return.

34.

F ROM THE GABBRO *INTELLIGENCER* for Friday, September 15, 1949:

> **EDITORS WILL GIVE AWARDS**
> Managing Editor Forde Morgan and City Editor M. Faye Bynum will journey to Asheville this weekend to present North Carolina Press Association awards to winners of the 1948-49 prizes. This newspaper was honored with two awards in the 1947-48 competition, and it is tradition that previous winners ...

*   *

The AfterGlow party was half the reason newspaper people from all over the state bothered to come to the North Carolina Press Awards. The organizers were perfectly aware of that, and spared no modest expense to make people glad they'd come. An open bar with acceptable liquor; serving stations with ham, barbecue, and turkey; an actual seven-piece orchestra that competently faked Guy Lombardo. Given the heavy predominance of men in newspaper management, the Press Association hired a cadre of female English majors from local colleges at 50 cents an hour to mingle with the crowd and look good, fishing for internships.

So people dressed up and prepared to be catered to. Faye resuscitated the diaphanous blouse of Greensboro, backed up in chilly Asheville by a lacy slip and the last drops of Silken Rain. It had more than done the job.

She took a sip of Bristol Cream and looked around. "Funny," she remarked. "Clem's gone. You'd think, after he won a prize and all, he'd stick around for the AfterGlow. More chance to nudge my, um, behind. Dim light, an' all."

"If you're looking for me to confess, I was politely deferential of one of my elders in North Carolina publishing."

Faye suppressed a giggle. "That what you call it? He was afraid for his life. You were polite as hell about grabbing his shirt and deferentialing him up against the wall. And all the time, in the shadows by the Ladies', my heart is pounding with gratitude, I'm thinking, Golly! I got a champion who will not let me be trifled with like a tackling dummy. Forde, you come through like a champ, and I appreciate it more than I can say. Though I seem to be saying a lot."

"Now come on. I didn't do all that. Don't tease about stuff that you know it gets me upset."

Faye took his arm and walked him to a dim corner. "I'm not teasing, Forde. Or at least on most of it. I have been awfully hard on you, and I'd like to clear up something about a matter that we never, um, … resolved."

Forde felt a pang of mixed hope and apprehension. Clearing up matters with Faye had usually been the occasion of disappointments and other mature acceptances. "Yes? About the 'Thing' thing?"

"No." She felt Forde slump a bit, but his face betrayed nothing.

"No, it's about that other matter. The one Annie was promoting this spring, about me helping you helping her make a baby."

"Aw, come on, Faye …"

"I know, she's finally gotten over it. And Pete Maribel spends an awful lot of time out in that part of the county anyway. But, I have to tell you, it's rather a disappointment to me. I spent hours devising lessons and work-sheets and labs and filmstrips, all for nothing. So I thought maybe what might work just as well is a kind of a practicum."

"A what?"

Faye broke out her man-eating growl. "A prracticum, Fordie. Like an internship, but with more real-life experience. You think Annie learned to weld by reading a book? What you wont is a chance to get your hands dirty. So listen, there's a place downtown that rents camping stuff, tents and all … "

Epilogue

F AYE BYNUM AND FORDE MORGAN remained discreet occasional lovers for almost the next half-century; slowly exploring the hazards of love, without falling in. Never marrying because Faye would not allow the conflict of interest to become institutionalized. The sex was hardly ever - after the very first, now history - less than solidly satisfactory; and after a few years, their policy of 90% celibacy led to achievements in love-making that the younger Faye would have rated a solid 10 in all four categories - the days of scores above that being gone for good. Much use for that and other purposes was made of the trail between Annie's meadow and Morgan's Eddy; in time, Rosie learned not to bark at Forde when he appeared out of the dark.

For all their discretion, of course, within a month of its inception the affair was public knowledge. But once it was known to and appropriately discussed by all who mattered, it was never referred to again.

Gabbro Schools integrated by consolidation, as Forde predicted they would, in 1973, nineteen years after *Brown v. Board of Education,* and a year before a court order would have required it under pain of occupation by the National Guard. Gabbro High School remained so named, but West and Carver became Custis B. Morgan Unified Elementary. The Gabbro Chamber of Commerce always described the consolidations as "intelligent and forward-looking," never referring to the role of the *Intelligencer* in forwarding them. The Jaycees admitted Abe Cousins as their honorary first Negro member in 1975, on the occasion of his retirement after 27 years as Acting Superintendent of Schools.

Annie Godfire remained childless, though she never appeared to be much bothered by it. It seemed to Faye that Annie, if anything, twinkled when Faye confessed the sex practicum arrangement with Forde. And on a full-moon midnight in the summer of 1953, settling into bed after a ladies-only dip at Morgan's Eddy, something Annie said to Sister Penitentia, something Sister P. did not say in return, and a flick of an eye in the kerosene twilight roused a suspicion in Faye that the whole show-me-how business might have been a hoax on Annie's part to trick her into a tent with Forde, the brother for whose happiness Annie would do anything. Faye was indignant for a minute or two, and then snorted in spite of herself.

Annie was well into her eighties when in December of 2017 she completed the final weld at the very top of the Spirit Catcher, a flawless seam that held the second of a pair of steel seats from Farmall tractors that had labored on little sand farms through good harvests and bad, flush times and foreclosures, for forty years. She took off her welding mask and sat on one of the still warm Farmall seats to commune with Mary Godfire on the other, while a Carolina wind crooned through eleven stories of hard-worked steel. And laid herself on a sun-warmed steel plate from the Gabbro River bridge, for birds and spirits to carry into the sky.